HARD BY A GREAT FOREST

HARD
BY
A
GREAT
FOREST

Leo Vardiashvili

RIVERHEAD BOOKS
NEW YORK
2024

RIVERHEAD BOOKS
An imprint of Penguin Random House LLC
penguinrandomhouse.com

Simultaneously published in Great Britain by Bloomsbury Publishing,
an imprint of Bloomsbury Publishing Plc, London, 2024

Grateful acknowledgment is made for permission to reprint the following:
"My Fate" from *The Pleasures of the Damned* by Charles Bukowski. Copyright © 2007
by Linda Lee Bukowski. Used by permission of HarperCollins Publishers.

Library of Congress Cataloging-in-Publication Data
Names: Vardiashvili, Leo, author.
Title: Hard by a great forest / Leo Vardiashvili.
Description: New York : Riverhead Books, 2024. |
Identifiers: LCCN 2023010792 (print) | LCCN 2023010793 (ebook) |
ISBN 9780593545034 (hardcover) | ISBN 9780593545058 (ebook)
Subjects: LCGFT: Domestic fiction. | Novels.
Classification: LCC PR6122.A368 H37 2024 (print) |
LCC PR6122.A368 (ebook) | DDC 823/.92—dc23/eng/20230517
LC record available at https://lccn.loc.gov/2023010792
LC ebook record available at https://lccn.loc.gov/2023010793

International edition ISBN: 9780593719671

Printed in the United States of America
1st Printing

BOOK DESIGN BY MEIGHAN CAVANAUGH

To my parents—Tina, Malkhaz, and Ketino.
I could live a thousand years and
never have the courage you do.

A man without history is a tree without roots.

Anzor Sulidze

HARD BY A GREAT FOREST

1

WHERE'S EKA?

Where's Eka?" We must have asked a thousand times.

Our mother stayed so we could escape.

See, war trumps most things. You'll find that a volley of AK-47 rounds fired right down your street will override almost any other concern. We heard gunfire by night and saw brass twinkling on the pavement in the morning, as though it had rained shell casings all over Tbilisi. Sounds manageable so far.

But when a stray tank shell breaks the sound barrier by your bedroom window, screams on, and deletes the corner grocery shop and the entire family living above it, you'll begin to make plans. Our parents, Irakli and Eka, made plans to get us all out, divorce be damned.

Getting out of the country meant shady bribes, stolen travel stamps, and counterfeit certificates. What money the family scratched together was barely enough for one parent and us children. Eka didn't even have a passport. Together we couldn't leave the country.

Meanwhile, the civil war was warming up, bullet holes in familiar places and people no longer a surprise. We had to go. Eka stayed and we escaped with Irakli.

That's how we became motherless, Sandro and I. I was eight and Sandro was two years older. At that age, the difference was a whole ocean of experience. Even so, Sandro had no inkling of what motherless meant, and neither did I.

There was no fanfare upon our arrival on the capitalist shores of the UK. They put us straight in a refugee shelter in Croydon. In that cold warehouse of bunk beds, communal toilets, and food tokens, nervous faces haunted the hallways.

Eventually, somewhere deep in the guts of the Home Office machine, gears clicked, a screen flickered to life, and we were granted refugee status, with "Tottenham, N17" printed on our case file.

In those early days we floundered in a city we didn't know. Tottenham in 1992 wasn't the London we'd imagined. There were no top hats, no smog, no Holmes, no Watson, no ladies, no gents, and no afternoon tea. Not for us.

We lived in a different London. In our London, people swore and spat, drank, quarreled, and laughed in fretful bursts. They spoke strange words in accents we couldn't parse. They walked bowed by the weight of mouths-to-feed, bills-to-pay, and how-many-days-till-payday?

Our da walked among them. Our Irakli—a man out at sea without a compass, searching for a woman he'd managed to lose twice. First, he lost Eka to a divorce shrouded in mystery. Then, to a civil war that reunited and parted them in one breath.

"Where's Eka?"

"Soon, boys. We'll get her back," Irakli would say. A promise not yet a lie.

He broke his back trying to buy Eka a way out. He picked fruit, painted walls, stacked shelves in warehouses, sweated and toiled in nameless, windowless factories across North London.

Those jobs wore him down in subtle, vital ways. We watched him erode. Once, he fell asleep at the table, spoon halfway to his mouth. We laughed and laughed. Sometimes you have to laugh at a thing to strip it of its power.

It's hard to save thousands by pounds and pennies. It's harder to send what you've scratched together to a country on fire. Georgia was eating itself alive—no banks to speak of, no working postal system. Those of us who'd escaped were not exactly keen to go back to a war zone.

Somehow, Irakli found someone willing to fly back there, for a fee. He was a tall, skinny man with earnest eyes. He looked honest and said the right things. Held his cigarette just so. He ate our food and drank our drink. He took the pounds and pennies meant for Eka and left, smiling and shaking hands. For a while, we stopped asking where Eka was.

I don't remember the honest man's name, but in my dreams he's died a thousand deaths by my hand. Eka never got the money and we never saw the honest man again. Irakli drank, and one night from the bedroom we heard him break the coffee table. The next morning, we found the table glued back together and Irakli gone back to work.

His efforts to buy us a mother turned frantic. Tense telephone conversations, sometimes Georgian and sometimes broken English, muffled by a closed door and often cut short by the angry boom of Irakli's voice.

We found strange clues around the house. Phone cords ripped from sockets, strange dents in the plasterwork, red bank letters ripped up and stuffed under the sofa, and the faint shrapnel left behind by crockery smashed and hurriedly cleaned up.

"Clumsy Da" was all he'd say. "Clumsy, clumsy me."

We didn't understand it then, but we do now. Irakli was trying everything to buy Eka's freedom. And he was failing.

"Where's Eka?" We didn't want to ask, but we couldn't help it.

"I'm working on it, boys."

Almost a year after our arrival in London, we started school, and that cost money. The old washing machine broke that same winter and that cost money. Irakli dropped a cinder block on his toes and for a lean two months he couldn't work. That cost a lot of money. Some money did make it to Eka, but never enough. Things back in Georgia cost money too. And so it went.

Over the next six years, we lost Eka piecemeal. We lost her to gas bills and groceries, bus passes and pencil cases, books and school uniforms.

Irakli's promise slowly curdled until we finally got the call on a sunny January morning. Eka's dead. We breathed a guilty little sigh of relief. There was no need to ask anymore. Irakli could stop promising us lies.

As we inched our way through a clammy, snowless British winter, someone turned the volume down on him. He'd drift into the room, look around, and leave without saying anything. He'd watch TV with disconnected eyes, coffee mug grown cold in his hand. The crockery stopped disappearing.

Our da aged a decade that winter, right in front of our eyes. Relief spiked with guilt shocked all his hair gray. We never once saw him cry, but he often rushed out of the room on some sudden errand.

"Ever been struck by lightning, my friend?" he'd say if you met him back then.

Crazy Eastern European, you'd think—a fever glint in his eyes and an odd accent you couldn't place.

"There's more chance of being struck by lightning than meeting a Georgian outside of Georgia."

Maybe you'd offer a polite laugh.

"Did the calculations myself." He'd tap his temple. "You're very lucky, my friend."

His eyes would gleam.

"But you're ve-ery unlucky too."

He'd wait for you to ask why.

"Because the odds of winning the lotto are much better. You could have been a millionaire, my friend. Instead, you met me."

He'd laugh, loud and from the heart. You would too.

"Let me pour you a drink, to apologize."

AFTER THAT CALL ABOUT EKA, it was hard to find the right words about her and even harder to say them aloud. So we made an unspoken pact to never mention our mother.

That pact served us well for eleven long years. But last year, Irakli started to break the agreement. He'd talk about places he'd been with Eka, the parks and cafés where they spent time, the trails and paths they cut through Tbilisi. Day by day, he lost interest in the future and his eyes filled up with the past.

He often looked at flights to Tbilisi. A couple of times he bought tickets, but didn't use them. He didn't even pack a bag. He seemed scared.

"Those people hold grudges past the grave."

He wouldn't tell us what he meant by "those people." We assumed he meant old friends or acquaintances we'd slighted by escaping when they couldn't.

On his next doomed attempt, Irakli packed a suitcase. He even left the house. He came back a few hours later, shamed and subdued. When they announced his flight, he admitted, he just stayed in his seat and watched everyone else board. When they called him by name on the Tannoy, he walked out.

Yet with every attempt, he edged closer, until one day he left for Heathrow and didn't return. We didn't hear from him until he landed in Tbilisi. His early reports from Georgia rambled with nervous energy, as though he had no way to get his heart around it all.

"I can't believe what I'm seeing. I just can't believe it," he told us on the phone.

Exactly what he couldn't believe, he struggled to explain. Sandro and I left him to it for two months. We were both in our twenties, with our own lives, and felt no great urge for a long-lost homeland.

Meanwhile, Irakli's calls and emails began to falter, but we weren't paying attention. His last email forced us to:

> My boys,
>
> I did something I can't undo.
>   I need to get away from here before those people catch me.
> Maybe in the mountains I'll be safe.
>   I left a trail I can't erase. Do not follow it.
>   I love you, best I can.
>
> Irakli

The email made no sense. Something ill hid among those words. "Those people"? Who was chasing Irakli? What trail? As for mountains, most of Georgia is a damn mountain.

We called and emailed, over and over, and got no response. Sandro spent weeks harassing the Tbilisi police, the British embassy, and anyone else who'd listen. He even convinced a charity for the homeless to put up posters around Tbilisi. The posters had Irakli's picture on them and a message asking him to get in touch.

Missing-persons posters have that unmistakable air of crying over spilled milk, but I didn't say anything to Sandro. Looking for Irakli was taking all of his time. Maybe Irakli saw the posters, maybe he didn't.

Maybe he'd left Tbilisi by then and maybe he hadn't. There was no way to know, not all the way from London. And that's exactly where Sandro's thinking went—charge to the rescue, as usual.

He decided to go to Georgia himself. Not a soul left back there to help him—our family had gone extinct over the seventeen years we were absent. Grandmothers, grandfathers, uncles, aunts, and cousins blinked out like cheap Christmas lights. We missed all their funerals. Refugees returning to the country they've escaped raises eyebrows. By the time of Eka's death, there was no family left to gather at her grave. We're not even sure who buried her, or where exactly.

Grief without closure has a way of fucking with you. There's an ancient, bone-deep instinct we all share: when those we love die, it's important that we see *evidence*. That's what funerals are. They're for our own good.

Maybe some ancient, hateful creature put a curse on our family. Maybe not. Either way, Eka's side of the family—the Sulidzes—they died out fast. Irakli's side—the Donauris—were already decimated before we even escaped Tbilisi. Those are the two halves of me. I'm half Eka and half Irakli. Just like my name—Saba Sulidze-Donauri.

With that need for closure left hungry, I lived my life in London constantly thinking of the dead. I'd wonder what they were doing of an evening, what plans they had for the weekend. Then I'd remember they were gone—a snow-globe miniature of the first time I heard the news. Bite-size heartache.

I became obsessed with them. I caught glimpses of them in strangers' faces, heard their voices cut through the din on the Tube. In the sly gaps between my thoughts, the dead came to life. And I liked it.

I'd imagine what Lena might say in a given situation, or Eka, or Anzor, or Surik. Soon enough, their voices crept into my head. I spoke to them when I needed to and soon they spoke back:

Anzor, my superhero uncle, who taught me everything useful I know. He donated two fingers to the Socialist Cause via the painful method of a faulty hydraulic press in a Soviet car factory. His was the slow, calm voice of logic.

Lena, my spartan grandma. Two world wars, a steady diet of Stalinism, Communist Pioneer camps, and being shot at by German soldiers turned her spine to steel.

Eka, the mother who stayed behind to let her children escape. Both our hearts broke when we spoke.

Surik, our drunkard neighbor and my first friend. He was like a big brother to Eka and always managed to make me laugh, no matter what. Surik spoke to me whenever he felt like it.

Nino, the keeper of my darkest secret. My sister in all the ways that matter but blood. Her voice the hardest to quiet.

I knew it was cruel to keep these crude caricatures alive, their deaths forever pending. Eventually, one by one, I silenced them for good. It hurt me as much as it hurt them.

Anyway, the point is there would be no welcome party waiting for Sandro at the airport. But he could never leave Irakli out there alone. Nearly thirty by then, Sandro was rattling around in a hollow, dead-end department of the civil service. Nothing to his name but books and a rented apartment. So, one day, he paused his London life, packed a bag, bought a one-way ticket to Tbilisi, and left.

At first, we spoke daily. He told me about the hassle he was having trying to track Irakli. With his *Sulidze-Donauri* surname now stamped in a shiny British passport, the Tbilisi police wouldn't help him much.

Irakli was also on a British passport, and it was soon clear the police wouldn't lift a finger unless pressured by the British embassy, and the embassy wasn't keen on doing a job that the Georgian police should have handled.

"Sometimes people just disappear," the detective told Sandro and smiled. Something off about him, Sandro told me.

He started his own search where we used to live, in the dusty maze of Sololaki, adrift among its ramshackle streets and crumbling buildings. He heard someone matching Irakli's description had been seen in shady neighborhood bars. But nothing came of it.

Sandro put up more posters. Still nothing. He found a hostel owner who recognized Irakli's picture. Maybe he stayed at the hostel, months ago, or maybe not. Another dead end.

Then there was the shopkeeper who definitely remembered Irakli, but only because Irakli had burst into his tiny shop looking for camping gear.

"Man looked unhinged," the shopkeeper told Sandro. "Looking for tents and sleeping bags where I sell cigarettes and magazines."

Sandro started talking about coming back to London. He'd been out there for weeks, all alone, looking for traces Irakli might have left in Tbilisi months ago. He seemed desperate for a clue, a hint, anything to keep him going. And I guess he found it, because things took a turn.

Sandro's emails started to shrink just like Irakli's had. He wouldn't talk on the phone. He sold his laptop and would only write from internet cafés. Even then, just a few words at a time.

The last email I got from him said this:

> I found Irakli's breadcrumb trail. At his old flat in Sololaki. No time to explain.
> I'll email when I know more.
>
> Sandro

And that's it—I haven't heard from Sandro since. Weeks have sailed by. My frantic emails and calls to the Georgian police, the British embassy, and Tbilisi hospitals got me no further. The whole time, I knew what had to be done. I just didn't want to face it. . . .

· · ·

WELL, HERE I AM NOW, facing it. I'm sat in a taxi, in the middle of Tbilisi, Georgia. The driver, Nodar by name, is chain-smoking like his life depends on it. Something strange is happening in this city. I feel like I've missed some crucial piece of information—some unknown-unknown. There are a lot of people in the streets for this time of night. They huddle by streetlights, smoking, talking, and looking over their shoulders.

The deeper we go into Tbilisi, the stranger it gets. There are empty police cars parked on corners, their lights flashing silently. Nodar drives past a row of parked pickup trucks with muddy, canine shapes piled in the back.

"Are those dogs?" I ask.

Nodar ignores me as he peers through his windshield. Up ahead, another silent flashing police car blocks our way. Behind it I glimpse the swaying glimmer of water where water doesn't belong. Nodar swerves to avoid a large apron of silt that's somehow snuck onto the road. The moist mud mutes the rattle of the car's suspension. That's when I look up and see it.

There's a rhino standing in the road directly in front of us. Nodar frowns and leans on the brakes. The rhino turns its huge head away from Nodar's headlights in an oddly human gesture. Behind the rhino is a mangled shop front, all glass and chrome. "Swatch," the broken sign says. The neat little display has spilled its twinkling guts onto the pavement. Must be the rhino's handiwork.

"That a fuckin' rhino? In the road?"

A clutch of people stands a safe distance away and watches the animal. A policeman steps forward and waves at us to come through.

"That's not a rhino. That's Boris."

"What?"

"Boris the Hippopotamus."

A wry smile from Nodar.

"No, I mean, why's it here?"

Nodar turns his balding head toward me. "You don't know, do you?" He chuckles.

"Know what?"

"Big mess, brother. The flood yesterday washed the zoo downriver. All the animals escaped. Wolves running wild by the airport, ostriches roaming around, penguins in the Mtkvari, a tiger up in Sololaki."

Nodar lists these things while squinting and turning the wheel with his palm. A cigarette hangs from his lips as he tiptoes the car around Boris the Hippopotamus.

"Welcome to Georgia."

Boris's flank goes past my window. He's the size of a small van. I can smell him. I lean out and let my fingers run over his gray tree-bark skin. Boris turns his head and shows me his huge, sparse teeth and his fist-size black eyes.

"Saw these idiots on my way to the airport two hours ago. They'll be herding that poor animal all night."

Nodar grunts and changes down a gear. The car judders but keeps going.

"My place is nearby. Five minutes, brother."

Just as we turn the corner, there's a loud crack. I turn to see the hippo's neck sprout a little red flower on a white stem. A tranquilizer dart. No reaction from Boris—he doesn't even flinch. He just follows our car with his ink-black eyes, as if to say, "Beware."

Wait, I should tell you how I got to Tbilisi in the first place.

BACK IN LONDON, in my little flat-share on Holloway Road, I packed for an adventure unknown. When I finished, I sat back amid the glossy pamphlets, forms, branded pens and key chains, and all the other traveling-salesman garbage that had settled on every flat surface in my room.

My job was to travel the country and give people bad news. In corporate, air-conditioned meeting rooms, I told my audiences that someday they would die. Yes, you in the back—you too. A Doomsday Peddler, according to Sandro.

Like a good snake-oil man, though, I had miracle cures to sell. I offered pensions and life insurance, investments and savings accounts. Useless acronyms, yield rates and percentages, sold to profit my employer. But also sold to stop these people from *really* absorbing my message and walking out of their jobs.

Every evening I'd wash these things from myself in the shower, like a coal miner might scrub grime from his body. Afterward, I'd still believe that by some sneaky fairy-tale trick, I'd dodge the system.

Anyway, all that was a flimsy distraction. I was fooling no one. I was about to return to a place I'd worked so hard to forget.

Deep into the long Tube pilgrimage to Heathrow, at the arse end of the Piccadilly line, I took out the antianxiety pills my housemate gave me to help me sleep on the flight. Two innocent-blue pills wrapped in tissue paper. Among unfamiliar stations—Boston Manor, Osterley, and a procession of Hounslows—I doubled the dose and swallowed both pills. I hoped they'd stop my heart fluttering the way it was.

The effects came on slow but forceful. By the time I got to Heathrow my whole spine was soaked in magic. I wafted through the duty-free and found myself in a queue. At gate 19-A, I fell in love with the woman checking the boarding passes. She was a perfect porcelain doll—pale skin, crimson lipstick, dead eyes.

I caught her attention. Her eyes unglazed and focused on me. No wonder. I was standing there half-melted and staring at her unblinking. I saw a cute frown gather on her brow, like a tiny stormfront. All I could think about was planting a big, fat kiss on those miniature red lips and getting arrested right after.

"Are you OK, sir?" Her eyes scanned me head to toe.

"I'm a nervous flier. The sleeping pill." I pointed at my head. "I think it's kicking in."

I felt her attention go, like the sun slipping behind a cloud.

"Better get to your seat then, sir."

She gave me a disinterested smile and motioned me toward the door. I took a few steps toward it, stopped, readjusted my aim, and tried again. She didn't notice.

When I found my seat, the pills *really* got to work. As we took off, I closed my eyes and erased the whole world and everything in it.

"Excuse me, sir." Someone nudged my shoulder. "Sir?"

When I opened my eyes, all I could see was my knees. My head felt like a concrete lump and my lips were drool-dried shut.

"I'm sorry, sir. We're landing in Kyiv. Straighten and lock your seat, please."

The Kyiv airport was deserted, apart from the occasional chain-smokers keeping vigil in the smoking booths. Built in the early days of the Soviet Union, the Kyiv airport of 2010 was like time-traveling back to the USSR, minus the hammer-and-sickle flags and Lenin portraits. I was stuck in that airport for hours, waiting for my connecting flight.

That's where I first felt something wasn't right. As I wandered through the windowless coarse-concrete corridors, someone followed. It was a surly man, wearing a leather jacket and an unhappy face. He had nothing with him, no bags, no shopping, not a thing. I thought that was odd.

He sat at the other end of the food court and watched me shove lukewarm capitalist Burger King in my face. He didn't eat anything. Then he followed me to the smoking booth, where we chain-smoked three cigarettes each. He was halfway through a sentence before I realized he was talking to me.

"... go to Tbilisi?"

"I'm sorry, what?"

He gave me a mournful look, as though he felt sorry for something that hadn't happened yet. I couldn't quite tell through the cigarette smoke, but his eyes might have been different colors, one blue and one green.

"I said, do you *have* to go to Tbilisi?"

"What? Yes. Why?"

He shook his head. "Tbilisi's not the place for you. You'll find nothing but trouble there, friend. Turn back, go home."

"Who are you?"

"I'm nobody."

He stubbed out his half-smoked cigarette and walked out. I tried to follow, but I lost him. Later, I saw him from the airplane window, talking to the boarding staff as my plane taxied away. I dismissed him as a sleep-deprived airport nutjob.

Surrounded by sleepy Georgian mumblings, I sat awake the whole flight to Tbilisi and stared at the tip of the wing, blinking a lonely red out there in the huge darkness. The air hostess made her rounds, stopping and murmuring at each seat in Georgian. When she got to mine, her eyes flickered away as though she was trying to remember something she memorized as a child. Then she straightened up and composed her face like she was about to recite a poem.

"Every-sing to your liking, sir?" she said.

This drew a few glances from the other passengers. I looked down at my clothes and wondered why she picked me out to be an English speaker.

"Yes, thank you," I said in Georgian.

She looked down at the clipboard in her hands.

"Are you Mr. Sulidze-Donauri?"

I looked around as though "Mr. Sulidze-Donauri" was someone I'd seen a second ago but couldn't spot anymore.

"Uh, yes."

"Thank you, enjoy your flight," she said and left.

She didn't ask for anyone else's name. Just mine. I should have known something was wrong.

When the airplane wheels hit the Tbilisi tarmac, everyone clapped. As we taxied to the terminal, I caught a glimpse of a cluster of lights in the distance. The city of Tbilisi, my long-lost birthplace. I stared at it, dumbstruck, while my belly filled with ice. I was beginning to realize just how fucking ridiculous an expedition this was.

Outside, the night air smelled like hot tarmac and spilled gas. I'd only been to the Tbilisi airport once, when I was eight. I was leaving then, wrestling with a Stalin-era leather suitcase held together with two belts. I remember heaving it onto a trolley, proud that I was strong enough.

Everyone was there—Irakli, Eka, Sandro, even my grandma and my uncle. It was the last time we were all together.

It must have been something, that night we left. I can't imagine what was going through their heads—sending the three of us off to some vague, faraway place where "things are better." That's all they would say: "Things are better over there."

What things? Better than what? I didn't understand why I couldn't just stay home.

Georgia broke away from the Soviet Union and became a republic in 1991. Crudely formed parties fought over the throne to this newly minted "republic." It didn't take long for the guns to come out. That very winter, we plunged headlong into a bitter, disorderly civil war.

By the time we arrived at the airport that night, six months into the war, among hundreds of strained-smile families just like ours, Tbilisi was a living nightmare. No electricity, no gas, no running water. Go out for bread and you were just as likely to catch a bullet as a loaf. They say almost half the population fled the country in those days. Most, never to return.

Lit so bright by the fluorescent airport lights, my family looked shamed by the shabbiness of their clothes, the dirt in their worry lines. Those harsh lights stripped them of the superpowers I knew they had. They looked worried and hesitant. They looked fragile. I was only dimly aware that something important was happening, while around me hearts broke.

Only Irakli, Sandro, and I would board the flight we waited for. The rest of my family would never clap their eyes on us again. They just didn't know it yet. Well, Eka had Sandro in her lap when I caught a strange look on her face. Maybe she knew.

ALMOST TWO DECADES LATER I found myself back at the same airport. At border control, the guy behind the desk raised an eyebrow at my passport. He picked up the phone and said my name. A few seconds later an airport guard appeared at my side, holding an assault rifle to his chest. He escorted me away from the queue to a side office, where a stern woman in surgical gloves was already going through my suitcase.

"Random check." She barely looked up. "Take a seat, please."

I watched her grope her way through my things. Leaving my clothes piled on the table, she snapped off her gloves and threw them in the bin.

"Purpose of visit?"

"Holiday."

"Holiday," she deadpanned.

"Yes," I said.

She raised an eyebrow. "Follow me, please."

She took me next door, where I got fingerprinted by a doughy technician wearing a lab coat two sizes too small.

"You need my fingerprints?"

"Random check, sir," the woman said behind me.

The technician looked at her sleepily, then back at me and nodded.

"Yes," he concurred.

He handed me a wet-wipe for my inky fingers. I was marched back to the first room, where the stern woman questioned me. She wasn't happy that I had no address to give her. She asked why I hadn't booked anywhere to stay and what I was planning to do. Those were all great questions that I didn't have answers to.

I filled out a form while she packed my suitcase with more care than I had. Just when I started thinking this really was a Georgian-style random check, she handed me a business card.

"What's this?"

Detective Kelbakiani, Tbilisi Metropolitan Police, Sololaki District.

"Thank you for your cooperation," she said, while I stared at the business card.

"What *is* this?"

"Please visit Detective Kelbakiani as soon as possible."

Random check, my arse.

"Why?" I said.

"He'll return your passport to you."

They'd pulled me away so fast I forgot they never gave my passport back. Before I could slap together a sentence in protest, the woman handed me over to the armed guard, who marched me and my newly packed bag to the same border-control man.

"Oo-elcome," he said in English and grinned.

I could see my passport on his desk. I paused, but the armed guard nudged me forward. That nudge sent me, rattling and nervous, through the meager duty-free and to a flimsy set of automatic doors flanked by more guards with machine guns.

I took a deep breath, stepped through the doors, and almost collided with a wall of eager, waiting faces. Automatically I scanned them for a familiar one. But they wilted into anonymity, one by one, under my gaze. My bag tried to tip itself over and broke the spell. No one was waiting for me there. I wrenched my bag onto its wheels and aimed myself at the final set of doors to Georgia proper.

Outside, I found myself surrounded by an even larger crowd of people hugging, kissing, talking excitedly, and haggling with a small regiment of taxi drivers. I stood aside and tried to take it all in while fiddling with a cigarette that I just could not light.

I stood there a long time, thinking in narrowing, accelerating circles. If I could smoke, if I could just light the fucking cigarette, maybe I could slow things down. I scraped my thumb raw on my lighter and produced nothing but sparks.

I let the lighter slide through my fingers. The words *panic attack* sliced through my head. I felt my skull drain of blood. My fingers started to tingle. My pulse pounded in my jaw. My breath was uneven, shallow. That was the cruel pause at the lip of the roller coaster. It was coming.

Everything around me slowed and froze. My eyes came to rest on a dented communal ashtray, overflowing with cigarette butts. This was it—the ugly sight the panic attack would sear into my memory.

Suddenly, I heard a voice cut through the muddy hubbub like a knife. *"Saba."* It winked silver.

I recognized it. It was one I'd silenced long ago. It was Surik! Surik, my drunken accomplice, charging to my rescue. Surik ex machina, whose house smelled like old newspapers, mothballs, and secrets.

"Vai, vai, vai! Look at these balding hyenas."

"Surik?"

My eyes welled up.

"*Who'd you expect, Father fuckin' Christmas?*"

"You're back."

"*Thought you could use the help. Want me to leave?*"

"No."

"*Vai, look at this mess. More taxi drivers than passengers.*"

The crowd of taxi drivers shifted and churned, digesting a new wave of arrivals. Feeling the blood return to my brain, I watched them swallow a blithe tourist whole. Oversize backpack and all—he vanished. I was just happy to have a friend with me, even if imaginary.

"*Imaginary's better than nothing,*" Surik said.

"Help me, Surik."

"*You don't need help, Saba. Pull the dry thumb out your arse. Get moving. Don't matter which way—any way is good. The rest is momentum.*"

That's when I noticed a man eyeing me. He stalked through the crowd, downwind and watchful. He paused often, so I wouldn't spook.

"*Here he comes.*"

Finally, he surfaced beside me, lifted his hairy arm and put a hand on my shoulder in one quick movement. With his other hand he lit the cigarette still dangling from my lips. Not a word was said. He watched me try to inhale half a Mayfair Light in one drag. The corners of his eyes wrinkled as he smiled.

"Thanks."

Surprised, he took his hand off my shoulder and leaned back for a better look.

"You Georgian?" He scratched his chin with an audible rasp. "You don't look it."

"I know."

This made him chuckle.

"But you look like you need a taxi." He glanced at my bag. "Where's your people?"

"My people?"

"The usual airport welcome committee. Mother, father, auntie, uncle, cousin, dog, cat . . ."

"Oh, it's just me."

Those wrinkles at the corners of his eyes again.

"Alright, then. Let's go, brother."

He slapped me on the back and set me in motion almost against my will. We walked through the garrison of taxi drivers.

"Nodar, Nodar! Does he know he'll be pushing you down the motorway?" someone said, and there was a smattering of laughter.

When I saw the taxi, I got the joke.

"I never thought I'd see one of these shit-buckets again." Surik chuckled.

The car was a black GAZ Volga. At least half a century old, it was covered in grime you can't wash off without taking the paint with it. There were mud splatters on the wheel arches, and the rear bumper was tied in place with blue nylon rope.

The taxi driver creaked the trunk open and threw my bag in.

"I'm Nodar."

"Saba." I shook his hand.

He nodded at his dinosaur of a car. "Ugly as sin, brother. But God loves ugly." He stroked the flank of the car like it was a racehorse. "Back door's jammed; sit up front."

The Volga started up on the fourth attempt. Nodar drove away without even asking where I was going. He got us up to motorway speed by revving second gear until the whole car was shaking, and then jumped straight to fourth. The car made unholy noises.

"Where's the fun in life if you have all the gears?"

With one hand on the wheel, Nodar patted down the front of his check shirt. He found a box of L&M cigarettes in his breast pocket and got one out with his teeth.

"Here, hold this, will you?" he said and, leaving no time for a response, let go of the wheel.

I clutched desperately at the hard-plastic wheel while he lit his cigarette.

"That's better," he said, exhaling smoke.

That's how his outright assault on the box of L&Ms started. For a long time, I sat there like a bump on a log, staring out the window. Sirens and police car lights whipped past in the other direction. An ambulance shrieked by doing about twice our speed. It left behind a wake of ringing silence.

"You alright, brother?" Nodar said.

"Where are they going?"

"Nowhere good, brother."

He shrugged and flipped the radio on. An odd station. A sleepy, disinterested voice read out a never-ending list of messages sent in by listeners—anonymous love notes, cryptic meeting places, and so on.

"What is that?"

Nodar smiled at the radio. "It's like the internet for broke Georgians."

"Talk radio?"

"Not really. They call it 'If You're Listening.' Any message you've got, they'll play it for free. No questions asked."

I realized the radio dial was taped in place so it would never lose the station.

"Definitely not the kind of thing an ex-Soviet serial killer would listen to," Surik said, and I almost laughed.

I looked over at Nodar, almost expecting him to have heard Surik. But Nodar was busy ignoring the road, steering with his knee while lighting another cigarette.

"So, where to, brother?" he said eventually.

"I need a hotel."

"Which hotel?"

"Any."

Nodar raised an eyebrow. "Hotels won't take you this late. Or they'll triple the price."

He scratched his chin, thinking. "Brother, don't worry. I rent out a place of mine. It's empty, so you can have it tonight."

"Listen, Saba, when I said any way is good, I didn't mean get yourself chopped up and tucked away in a freezer by some taxi maniac."

I shut out Surik's voice. There was something about Nodar I wanted to trust.

"OK," I said. "Thanks."

"A guest is a gift from God," he replied with an old Georgian proverb.

The road into Tbilisi took us through a Soviet ghost town—Didi Digomi. Didi Digomi lingers on the outskirts of the city like a leper exile. Built in the eighties to house thousands of people, it was going to have parks, playgrounds, an Olympic-size swimming pool complex, and even a football stadium. It was going to be glorious. But the Soviet Union collapsed in 1991 and Didi Digomi ended up gloriously Communist instead—half-baked.

Fleshless ribcages of unfinished apartment blocks stood atop the hill in neat rows. The passing wind whistled through the yawning holes where people were supposed to have their cozy, warm living rooms, their standard-issue Soviet sofas, and their standard-issue Polish-made TVs.

As we drove past, I saw lights twinkling in some of the buildings.

"People live in there?" I said.

"Sure they do, brother."

"How? There's nothing there."

Nodar sighed. "Ossetia refugees. It's better than what they've left behind."

As we entered the city of Tbilisi, I began to recognize things—a crumbling street corner, or a building, or a peculiar twist of the road. At the same time, I didn't recognize a damn thing. The way your teeth feel after the dentist leaves you with unfamiliar edges to snag your tongue on.

Tbilisi's a city that was invaded, leveled, and rebuilt more than thirty times. Over the centuries, all manner of empires and their unhinged rulers had their way with the city—the Ottomans, the Byzantines, the Russians. As a result, Tbilisi architecture's schizophrenic. Stately facades and colonnades sit right alongside clusters of shabby wooden buildings leaning into each other like books on a lopsided shelf. Shiny, modern shop fronts, brand-new and gleaming, are conspicuously wedged among buildings from a different age altogether.

Away from main roads, the Tbilisi I remember showed through. Streetlights were sparse and dim. Houses watched us with an orange glow in their dusty windows. Overgrown oak trees crowded the pavement and invaded the road.

If you live in Tbilisi, you know the *texture* of the streets as well as you know the imperfections on the ceiling above your bed. Uneven, cracked pavements reward loyalty and punish newcomers with missteps and odd angles on which to trip.

Even from the safety of those shabby side streets, I caught glimpses of giant, sparkling skyscraper monoliths that didn't belong there. I rolled the window down and let the air wash over me.

"Smells like home, don't it, Bublik?"

Surik was right; it did smell like home. I forgot he used to call me Bublik. I didn't feel like saying much else after that. We drove the rest of the way in silence.

So that's how I got here—nudged along by imaginary friends, strange taxi drivers, and Boris the Hippopotamus.

By the time we get to Nodar's house, the night is losing its grip on the city. A faint warning of sunrise hangs over the horizon and thins the soothing darkness.

"Let it happen, Bublik. The sun will rise—no avoiding that."

Everyone and everything is asleep. Nothing stirs and the darkness hides the courtyard approach to Nodar's apartment. I take in my surroundings by smell alone. Sharp aroma of spilled beer and stubbed cigarettes from the seating area, wet-ash smell of a fire long gone out, and the stink of spilled garbage bags already picked clean of anything edible by stray dogs and cats.

The waiting mouth of an entrance draws near. It strikes me just then that no one actually knows where I am. If I was to vanish, like Sandro and Irakli have, no one would have a clue. My landlord would notice, sure. My cluster of friends too. At best, they'd come looking for my next of kin—Irakli and Sandro. But I doubt their concern would stretch to missing-person reports and trips to Georgia. No, I'm last in this line.

Nodar heaves open the heavy nuclear blast gate he has for a front door. We enter the humid darkness of his flat and I see a bedroom at the end of the hallway. The foot of the bed is lit blue by a murmuring TV. They're showing clips of the flooded zoo and blurry phone-cam footage of Boris the Hippopotamus wrecking the Swatch shop.

"Keti, you still watching that rubbish?"

"You're alive," a female voice says.

"I am."

"Well done."

He looks back at me standing there, gormless, in his hallway.

"Keti, listen, we have a guest. Why don't you give me a hand?"

"A guest?"

"A tenant, actually."

"What do you mean, *tenant?*"

"Come on, Keti, come give me a hand with Natia's room."

It dawns on me that what Nodar meant by "a place of mine" is a spare room in his own damn house. A middle-aged woman in a dressing gown and slippers emerges from the bedroom. Her hair's tied back with a handkerchief.

"This is my wife, Ketino. But she prefers 'Keti.'"

She gives him a look.

"Stick with Ketino for now, brother."

"Hi, Ketino. I'm Saba."

Ketino nods and motions me toward the living room.

"Alright, you better come in. Can't send you out there to the wolves, hippos, and tigers," she says.

The living room's filled with old, carefully repaired furniture. Nothing matches, but everything works as it should. Things are eternally mended here. The mechanics of living poor are the same everywhere. I recognize the signs at once.

I see napkins lifted from cafés, single-use salt, pepper, coffee, and sugar sachets. Water bottles and plastics are kept and reused. Pots and pans in the kitchen are dented and black with soot. The crockery and cutlery's chipped, scuffed, and wildly mismatched. I'm guessing "use by" dates mean nothing here and there's no such thing as leftover food. Everything has secondary and tertiary uses. Old bread re-baked into rusk. Bones kept for soup, then for pets.

Nodar shows me a small bedroom off to one side of the living room. A child's single bed by the window, pink wallpaper, and scruffy teddy bears queueing on the bed. A row of Michael Jackson posters stares at me from the wall.

"My daughter's room."

"You rent out your daughter's room?"

Nodar's cheeks redden. "Well, I'll rent it to you, brother."

"Where is she?"

"Natia's not here. Make yourself at home."

The Hotel Grand du Nodar tour is officially over. Ketino appears behind us with a large steaming mug of something fragrant.

"Here, drink this. It'll knock you out. Come on, Nodar, leave the man be. Come, I've made you a cup too. Sun's almost caught us out of bed—it's bad luck."

As Nodar leaves, it occurs to me that I haven't paid him a penny. I open my mouth to say something. But what is there to say? I don't even have any cash with me.

"Thank you," I manage.

He waves the words away like flies buzzing around his head.

"Sleep well, brother."

I know I won't. But I climb into the bed, taking the mug with me. It's some kind of spiced tea and I can tell it's laced with booze. The smell triggers an eerie sensation of recalling a memory that belongs to someone else. It makes me smile, despite myself. And then I hear a voice I haven't allowed to speak for years.

"They left me behind."

The electric jolt of it shocks me upright.

"First my brother left me. Snuck out of the hospital like a thief in the night. Then my mother followed him. She always liked him better—the heir to her throne. Then, my aunties. My cousins. All of them. They left me behind."

"Eka."

"You never called me Mum, not even when you were tiny. 'Eka,' not Mum."

"I'm sorry. . . ."

"You left me too."

"You made me go."

"I thought we'd meet again."

I don't answer.

"It's OK, Saba. Just how it goes sometimes. Anyway, let me tell you a story. This actually happened to your great-great-grandpa."

This is how Eka's bedtime stories always began. What would follow was a disorderly fabrication, a sweeping, epic fairy tale plucked from thin air. I loved it.

Eka tells me a story while I watch the sunlight pour into Tbilisi from the hills like slow syrup, illuminating street after street in a dusty golden light.

2

ONE SIP OF THE CHAILURI

I wake abruptly, confused and surrounded by teddy bears. I flail around and see the Michael Jackson posters on pink wallpaper. Things begin to fall into place:

London, innocent-blue anxiety pills, Kyiv airport, Tbilisi airport, the "random check," my passport, Nodar and his prehistoric taxi. Then Boris the Hippo, Nodar's house, Ketino's potion, and Eka's fairy tale.

"No, not a dream, Bublik. Welcome back." Surik chuckles.

Outside, the city's already awake. It gives off a hum I can hear through the closed window. I step into the empty living room, which faces Mtatsminda—an imposing, forested hill acting as a natural limit to the city. Mtatsminda translates as the Sainted Mountain—now probably home to all the escaped zoo animals.

There's a gigantic TV broadcast tower on top of Mtatsminda. It's painted in stark red and white stripes and so big that it's visible from anywhere in Tbilisi. Nodar's window frames this scene like a postcard.

"Morning."

Nodar's standing in the doorway. His gaze follows mine out the window.

"I don't like that overgrown aerial. Doesn't look man-made."

He's right. That antenna wasn't built. It traveled here from some dark corner of the galaxy and landed on Mtatsminda, where it now sits almost motionless, like a praying mantis.

My old school was at the foot of Mtatsminda. I used to cut classes and climb up there. The steep, hardy forest does not relent until the summit. The only way up, without scrabbling your way through the dense trees like I used to, is a miniature funicular railway that cuts through the forest.

"Have they fixed the funicular?"

"Very fancy nowadays. Tourist trap."

The funicular of my childhood was derelict and disheveled, with the carriages rusted to the track. One carriage was painted the mandatory Lenin-red color and the other a jaunty blue, in that Soviet legislated-cheer kind of way. But back then, they were so sun-bleached and chipped that you could barely tell.

There were crazy stories about that funicular. Apparently one fine day, the main cable snapped under the weight. Set free at last, the carriage wrenched itself off the rails and careened off into the forest. Snapping huge evergreens like matches and taking hungry bites out of the turf, it killed everyone inside before it fetched up at the bottom of the hill.

"Ever hear the story about the accident?" I ask Nodar.

"There was an accident?"

"I don't know. Maybe."

Sandro and I spent days cutting school and combing the forest for clues left by that crash. Eka had just read us *Treasure Island*, so we were also looking for skeletons and buried treasure.

We found no clues, no skeletons, and no treasure when this season of exploration ended. Older kids from our school caught us and beat the crap out of us both. My torn shirt and dusty trousers and Sandro's missing shoe secured us a far scarier beating from Grandma Lena. Soon, our prolific absenteeism was also discovered and our adventures came to an abrupt end.

"Listen, how long you been away?"

Nodar snaps me out of it. I tear my eyes away from Mtatsminda.

"Eighteen years or so."

He gives a low whistle. "You're in for a surprise, brother."

Our breakfast is a bowl of indistinct gruel hiding a submerged inch-thick slab of cheese. Nodar tells me the price for a suite in the Palais du Nodar—one hundred lari per week. This translates to twenty pounds. I stop chewing and look at him in surprise. In London, I could trip over in a shitty hipster coffee shop and accidentally spend more than that.

"And as much of Keti's cooking as you want." Nodar transitions into a hurried sales pitch. "You can cook your own, of course, in the kitchen. But you won't do better than Keti, I promise you that."

I bite into the delicious salty cheese in my gruel—Nodar's not joking.

"And I can drive you, if you need a guide or . . ."

"It's OK," I say. "Hundred lari's OK."

Seeing me struggle to finish my bowl, Nodar smiles.

"Keti will fatten you up, brother. You just watch."

He slaps his hand across his stomach in a gesture that requires a belly for full effect. But Nodar doesn't have one. He's gaunt, just like Ketino.

He pats the front of his shirt, finds his L&Ms, pulls one out with his teeth, and lights it. He does all this one-handed, as though he was keeping one hand on a steering wheel.

"So," he says, exhaling smoke. "Tell me. What brings you to Tbilisi? Sure, you have a bit of an accent, but you're no tourist, seems to me."

I want to give him a sane, measured answer. But before I can, something makes me launch headlong into the story. Nodar has a face you want to trust, and I've been holding onto this shit too long. It comes pouring out, barely controlled. I skip over things, lose track, double back. In places I stumble to a stop to shake the feeling that none of it really happened.

I tell Nodar about how we escaped Georgia when the war broke out. We sold everything we could, everything we had, but still came up short for the bribe to get Eka a visa. We escaped to the nearest European country, where our refugee status was rejected and we were given twenty-four hours to vacate the country.

I tell Nodar about our vagabond trek across Europe with our shrinking supply of money and blinkered courage. I tell him about Grandma Lena's diamond brooch, a wedding gift from her father that she'd kept for decades, carefully polished and cleaned. Irakli stowed it in his boot, just in case. That was our get-out-of-jail-free card.

By the time we reached France, we had no money for food. We were sleeping in train stations and parks. So, Irakli sold Lena's diamond brooch to a crooked vulture in Paris. That money bought us Channel Tunnel tickets to London and two McDonald's meals.

I tell Nodar about the honest man who stole what Irakli had saved to bring Eka to us, and then about the doomed plan to send her money from London—money Irakli failed to ever collect, because Sandro and I ate it all.

Nodar listens with his face poised on the verge of a smile or a frown, I don't know which. I tell him about the curse that wiped out the Sulidze family. I tell him how it crossed them off the list, one by one.

I tell him about Irakli's disappearance and then about Sandro's. Finally, I tell him about the "random check" at the airport and my passport. But I stop short of telling him about the voices.

Nodar slides the L&M pack across the table. "Take one, brother."

I light a jittering L&M and take a lungful.

"Sipped the Chailuri water, eh?"

"Sipped . . . what?"

Nodar chuckles.

"Means disappeared without a trace. Chailuri's the river between us and the Turks. If the Turkish marauders caught you and got you to their side of that river . . . well, you disappeared for good. Just a saying, brother." He shakes his head. "Never mind that. Don't *ever* give up your passport without a fistfight."

"I know."

"Well, you do now."

"I need to see this detective today."

"One slight problem, brother."

"What?"

He picks up the remote and turns on the TV. The first thing I see is a photo of a wet, miserable bear clinging to an air-conditioning unit right outside someone's first-floor window. "Misha the Bear," the caption says.

Nodar changes the channel—quivering, pixelated mobile phone footage in a forest. "Mtatsminda," the banner says. The footage is dark, until someone yelps and the camera whips up and points at a cluster of trees. One voice frantically shushes another until a huge, shaggy Bengal tiger shoulders his way through the foliage. It looks directly at the camera, pauses, and then disappears among the trees, like it was never there at all. After that, there's so much swearing that the audio is a continuous bleep.

Next channel—a helicopter searchlight slides over craggy ground, chasing four lithe gray shapes: wolves. They bound effortlessly between rocks and clumps of dry brush. The searchlight follows them until they reach a thick tree line, where they vanish from sight.

The next channel shows our old friend Boris shopping for Swatch watches. A casual swing of his arse and the shop window spills into the street like a glass avalanche.

"Your timing needs work, brother. Might be hard to speak to the police today. They're a bit busy."

"Should I still go?"

"They told you to come, didn't they?"

"Yeah."

Nodar shrugs and offers me his palms.

"They say go, you go."

WHILE I'M SHOWERING in Nodar's tiny bathroom, I finally get a front-row view of the shitshow I've bought tickets for. I'm crouched in the shallow bathtub beneath a leaking showerhead when it finally sinks in what's in store for me out there.

This city's littered with memories that await me like land mines. Just enough time has passed to make everything just foreign enough. The dearly departed voices I silenced long ago have come back without my permission. Then there's the biblical flooding, runaway zoo animals, civic disarray, confiscated passports, missing brothers and fathers. The situation calls for someone with a plan. I didn't even bring toothpaste.

After this disappointing enlightenment I remember the solitary thing on my itinerary. I need to go to Irakli's old flat in Sololaki. Sandro's last email said he found Irakli's trail there. That's the best place to start.

I dress myself in Natia's room, while the teddy bears and the Michael Jackson posters watch on. By the time I'm ready, my plan has escalated. The way I see it now is:

1. Go to Sololaki
2. Find Irakli's old flat
3. Knock on the door

4. Sandro answers the door
5. I crack the entire length of my anger and frustration across his blond dome
6. We start looking for Irakli

The more I think about it, the more it makes sense. But before I can enact this flawless plan, there's the question of my passport and the police.

I ASK NODAR to drive me to the nearest bank on the way to the police station. It takes me awhile to get money from the cash machine because I insist on not changing the language to English. I mouth the green text like a five-year-old while a small, unhappy queue builds up behind me. I count out the unfamiliar notes and hand them over to Nodar.

"For the room and for yesterday's driving and today."

"I'm sorry, brother," he says, "to take your money."

"Why?"

"I was raised better." He shakes his head.

The transaction has somehow shamed Nodar and we drive in silence. I try to keep my eyes in the car, away from the dusty sunshine out there and the roving bands of unclaimed dogs darting between cars. Strangest of all is seeing the trappings of modern life everywhere, as though they followed me here from London: franchise shops, touch screens, video billboards for online casinos, smartphones, soft drinks, and TV shows.

These things make the rest of Tbilisi seem like a giant anachronism. The world has moved on and Tbilisi's trying to keep up in a race where it doesn't belong.

"Bublik . . . did you think we'd wait for you?" Surik pipes up.

"Not now, Surik."

"Did you want to see empty shops and bread queues? Stolen manhole covers sold for scrap? People trapping pigeons for food? Families scratching each other's eyes out for a slice of Grandpa's will, for a hovel they'll never manage to sell?"

"No, Surik."

"No gas, no water, no electricity? How about people leaving their babies at church doors?"

"It's just . . . not how I remember it, Surik."

"You've been gone eighteen years, Bublik. That's long enough to polish a memory into anything you want it to be."

Familiar-looking faces on the street make me flinch because somehow I'm expecting my eyes to happen across Eka, or my uncle Anzor, or any of those people I know aren't here anymore. Maybe the last eighteen years have been nothing but a fever dream. Maybe they never happened.

Any second now we could bump into one of the revenants we left behind when we escaped. They could be anywhere, sensing my presence, searching. They could be any passerby going about their business—buying milk at a kiosk, or at a street corner waiting for the light to change.

Nodar will slow the car for some old woman crossing the road. I'll only realize it's Grandma Lena when her eyes meet mine. And then all of this, everything around us, will shatter like a kaleidoscope and I'll wake up somewhere else.

"Unclench, Bublik." Surik chuckles in my head. *"There's no coming back from where we are."*

I keep my eyes well inside the car anyway. The Tbilisi heat is really leaning in on us. Overnight, the breeze dropped out of the sky like a dead bird. There's no hiding from the sun. The car interior smells like ancient Soviet leather heat-shocked to release long-ago odors.

We're stuck in heavy traffic and haven't moved an inch in the last ten minutes. When Nodar finally speaks, I'm so glad of the distraction that I almost hug him.

"I wasn't always a taxi driver, you know."

Another taxi is angling to cut in from a side road.

"Look at this Nobel Prize laureate."

Nodar presses his palm into the horn and leaves it there. He leans his entire upper body out of his window and gestures at the other taxi with a theatrical flourish.

"After you, brother!" he yells at the car trying to merge with standstill traffic.

The other driver just stares at him. Nodar slides back into his seat and grins.

"These motherless taxi drivers . . ."

He winks at me, lights a cigarette, and wedges it into the corner of his mouth. He doesn't smoke all the cigarettes he lights. Sometimes they dangle from his mouth forgotten, snowing ash all over his chest until he realizes and replaces them.

"I was a teacher back home."

"Back home?"

"You thought I was from *this* cat factory? No, brother, I'm from Ossetia," he says, tapping his chest.

"What did you teach?"

"Math."

"Math?"

"Mathematics—two plus two and all that. Why so surprised?"

"Sorry."

"I had two hundred pupils, you know. Most of them dim as a firefly armpit but—"

I finally connect the word *Ossetia* to something useful.

"Wait, you mean South Ossetia?"

His smile fades.

"Where the war was?"

He glances at me and nods silently.

"That's why you're in Tbilisi?"

South Ossetia is a breakaway region Georgia and Russia fought over, not even two years ago. Both sides shelled the only Ossetian city to rubble, while the residents hid in their basements like rats.

"Yeah, we got away. Got lucky."

He stresses the word *lucky*, though his life shows no signs of it. I have so many questions. What happened to him and Ketino? How did they get away? Where's their daughter?

But I can't bring myself to ask and Nodar knows it. Our glances don't cross paths and the car fills up with a conspicuous silence. Thankfully the traffic inches forward. We finally approach the roundabout we've been staring at through the gritty heat haze.

There's commotion ahead. Cars swerve and horns bleat. As we draw closer, I realize there's a dog trapped on the painted circle of the roundabout. Every time it looks like there might be a gap, the traffic lights release another herd of cars into the fray.

This dog isn't quite the right shape for a dog. It's dark, almost black in the torso, with big ears and a long reddish tail. The panicked animal is dashing side to side, trying to nose its way between moving cars. A dusty white van gives a honk and narrowly misses it. The animal skitters away, limping. Any second now, the poor thing will stick its nose in too far and catch a faceful of hot metal.

"These heartless fuckers," Nodar grinds out between his teeth.

"Is that a fox?"

He doesn't answer.

"It is. Nodar, it's a fox!"

Instead of turning right like everyone else, Nodar slows the Volga, cutting off the cars around us. They slam their brakes, horns blaring. Nodar takes no notice.

"What you doing?"

He almost wrenches the handbrake out of its socket and gets out of the car. The fox doesn't notice him at first. Its eyes glitter with fear and pain. Suddenly they snap to Nodar, pin-sharp, as though among all this chaos they've finally found the real enemy.

The cars around us are howling. People are getting out and converging on the Volga. Nodar ignores them. He's focused on the hunched, tail-tucked fox. It's ready to fight to the death.

Arms out, Nodar approaches it, circles it, tries to guide it into the gap he's made with his car. The fox snaps at him, but shrinks away from his size. Suddenly, like an elastic band snapping, it bolts through the gap. It reaches the pavement and disappears up the nearest alley.

"Little bastard almost bit me," Nodar says as he gets back in the car.

"It must be from the zoo."

"These motherless bastards." He turns his head away and spits. "Take your foot off the pedal at least, brother. Only takes a second. But no, everyone's in a hurry. Hurry, hurry, hurry."

He crunches the Volga into first gear and veers back into our lane.

"God, I hate this place," he says, thumping the wheel.

Not much later we approach an odd little building sitting on a neat patch of grass. It looks like someone's left a glass Rubik's Cube on a trimmed lawn. The outer walls are all glass. We can see all the cheap office furniture and the plastic, plywood, Velcro crap that constitutes an office. People in the building mill about, walk to and fro, talk on their phones, type their emails, and gossip in full view of the outside world.

"What is that?"

Nodar looks up.

"That's it. The police station."

"That's the police station?"

He chuckles. "Our president's cod-shit crazy. His idea."

"What do you mean?"

"He demolished all the old, Soviet stations in Tbilisi and built these things. All glass."

The road takes us around the front of the station and I finally see the red-on-silver signage—"Tbilisi Metropolitan Police."

"They're all like this. Copies. I'm telling you, brother, like toy houses. They sit there in the middle of everything, proud, like a dog turd in a pigeon park."

"Why glass?"

"He's got this idea we'll trust the police more, if we can watch them scratch their arses all day."

"Does it work?"

"A snake in a glass box is still a snake."

He stares at the station with contempt.

"But they're *westernized* snakes now. All these new laws. Just new ways to take bribes, brother. Some turnip in a uniform stopped me the other day. Says I can't be on the phone driving. What if you crash, he says. If I can't talk and drive at the same time, maybe I ought to crash, I said. Would teach me a lesson."

"What happened?"

"I paid him."

"He let you go?"

"I paid him, didn't I?"

We approach the gate to the station.

"Look, I understand. Everyone needs to put shoes on their kids' feet. I wouldn't mind the bribes if they showed a little heart when *you're* desperate."

"What do you mean?"

The gatehouse guard, clutching a machine gun to his chest for comfort, opens the gate. Nodar gives him a hostile look.

"Forget it, brother. We're here."

We step into the chilly, sterile building and get told to fill out a form and wait. Nodar crumples his form into a ball and drops it on the seat beside him. Only inches away from us, on the other side of the glass, the harsh sun bakes the ground to clay and makes overnight garbage bags across the city blossom with new, exotic smells.

A fat fruit fly is beating itself to death on the glass pane. The receptionist—a thin woman constantly adjusting her oversize glasses—looks at the fly, then back at me and Nodar. Somehow, I feel a little unclean and ashamed for having brought this buzzing, suicidal nuisance in with me.

"The officers on call are busy with the flooding," she says.

By the time we get called in, the sweat on my back has dried and I'm shivering. The fruit fly has long given up. The officer that comes out surprises me. I was expecting a burly man with his head covered in steel wire stubble and a skull shaped for cracking rocks. What we get instead is a lean young man wearing a waistcoat. A careful beard and whiskers hide his unreasonably pink lips.

He scans us with slow blue eyes. We're an odd sight. Nodar's wearing the black shirt from last night, dusty black trousers, and an irate look. Then there's me—old jeans, my lucky Pink Floyd T-shirt, and sneakers. All of which I've worn for three days running. I look bewildered, eyes bloodshot with jet lag, my clothes wrinkled by sleep in unfamiliar places. We look like a punch line to a joke you missed.

"Sorry for the wait," the officer says to some middle space between me and Nodar.

He grabs the form I filled out and leads us through the door to the back corner of the office. I see that all the walls in here are glass too.

"I'm Detective Kelbakiani."

We shake hands and sit.

"If you don't mind, let's get straight to it," he says. "You were referred over by airport security after a random check."

Nodar snorts. The detective pauses and glances in Nodar's direction before turning back to me.

"Can you please tell me the reason for your visit?"

As I begin to explain the core elements of my missing persons clusterfuck, the detective keeps looking at Nodar.

"Mr. ah, Sulidze-Donauri . . ."

His mouth doesn't seem to like the taste of those words.

"Is this a relative of yours?" He gestures toward Nodar.

Nodar stiffens in his seat.

"No."

"How do you know this man?"

Nodar's holding his breath.

"He's helping me."

The detective gives Nodar a lingering look.

"OK," he says to Nodar. "Your name?"

"Nodar."

"Full name."

"Basriani."

The detective writes this down with deliberate accuracy.

"Detective." I try to flatten the quiver in my voice. "Why was my passport taken?"

"Standard procedure. It will be returned in due course."

The detective launches into questions about Sandro. He starts in full sentences at first, but soon the questions shrink until they're just handfuls of words thrown across the table. He stops taking notes.

"Recent photo?"

"No."

"Where was he staying?"

"I don't know."

"Did he have an itinerary? Places to visit? Relatives, friends?"

"No. I don't know."

"Problems at home? Family, money, work, depression, alcohol?"

"Not that I know of."

He's ticking his way through the standard missing persons checklist.

"Last contact?"

"Few weeks ago. His email says he found something in Sololaki. That's all I know."

I can feel Nodar swallowing anger next to me, like a ship taking on water. The detective's tongue darts out to smooth the wayward hairs of his mustache. He looks at his watch. This sets Nodar off—he can't help himself.

"Listen, brother, tell me something—what's the point of you?"

"Excuse me?"

"What is the point of *you*?" Nodar enunciates. "Shouldn't you pay attention? Take notes?"

Nodar flicks the notepad across the desk toward the detective. The detective sits motionless as the notepad teeters on the edge of the desk and flutters into his lap. He glances down at it. Then he pins Nodar in place with a glare.

"Please don't interrupt," he says.

"What if he paid you a nice, fat bribe? Would you help then?"

I picture glass holding cells, glass handcuffs. The detective straightens up, opens the notepad, and places it on the table. His eyes find Nodar's.

"Don't interrupt me again, sir."

His voice is calm but this is the last warning. Nodar gets the message. After a tense silence, the questions resume and I know instinctively that we were seconds from disaster.

"Sandro's been in Tbilisi for how long?"

"About two months."

"Two months and no clue where your father might be?"

"You said Sandro filed a missing persons report here. Didn't he give you all the details already? He said he would check Irakli's flat in Sololaki. That's all I know."

He ignores my question.

"Mr. Sulidze-Donauri, do you know why your father's here?"

"Like I said, just visiting."

He sighs. "A final question. Do you think Sandro is in any immediate danger?"

"Danger? Well, yes, he's missing."

The detective shrugs. "He's fallen out of contact. That doesn't mean he's missing." A malicious little smile materializes on his lips. "Maybe he just doesn't want to talk to you?"

It's over. The checklist is finished. The detective leans back in his chair and stares at me down the length of his nose. He slaps his notepad shut. This is the part where I'm told there's nothing he can do. I can feel the situation slipping from me.

"I'm going to consult my colleague. I'll be right back," he says.

This forces another snort out of Nodar. Through the glass wall, we watch the detective stroll through the room. He perches on the edge of someone's desk and talks to its occupant, who glances over at us. With a jolt, I recognize him. It's the surly man who followed me around the Kyiv airport and warned me about coming to Tbilisi. He gives me the same mournful look he gave me at the airport. I warned you, a slight shake of his head says.

"Nodar, I know that guy."

"What guy?"

"I saw him at the airport. He warned me."

"Warned you?"

"From coming here . . ."

Nodar looks at me and then at the policeman. He's about to say something but the detective is nearly on us again. He's one glass door away.

"Listen, don't leave here without your passport, brother. I don't like this greasy fuck, or his greasy fuck friend."

"Nodar, they're the police."

"Just ask for your passport back."

Nodar fiddles with his box of L&Ms. His clammy hands have already softened the edges of the cardboard.

"Without a passport you're a ghost. You don't exist. Those people can do anything."

With a chill, I remember Irakli's mention of "those people" and realize they may not be what I thought. I don't tell Nodar. He already has a strange score to settle with the police and doesn't need my encouragement. He already seems to be trying to get us shot, or worse. The detective returns to his seat.

"We have all the information we need for now, thank you."

"That's what you were *consulting* about?" Nodar says.

The detective ignores him.

"Where are you staying in Tbilisi?" he asks me.

I look over at Nodar and he recites his address to the detective.

"OK, good. Thank you for coming."

"What about his passport?" Nodar says.

The detective ignores him again.

"Your passport hasn't arrived here from the airport. I will let you know as soon—"

"How long will that be?" Nodar cuts in.

The detective stretches his lips over his teeth in a facsimile of a smile. "I'm afraid I can't say. The flooding is causing . . . issues."

The conversation's over, but the detective doesn't make a move to get up. He's waiting for something.

"What about Irakli?" I say. "Any news of him?"

Frowning, the detective pauses and seems to consider his answer.

"Actually," he says, suddenly alert, leaning forward. "We have a warrant for his arrest."

The words take a few seconds to register.

"Arrest? For what?"

"Suspicion of attempted murder."

My legs snap straight and I find myself on my feet. The cheap plastic chair skitters across the floor behind me. Both Nodar and the detective stare.

"Saba," Nodar says.

There's a note of warning in his voice. His expression's the same as when he was saving the fox, as though a sudden move, a lunge in the wrong direction, could get me killed.

The detective watches me. He's one synapse away from springing into action. I turn away to retrieve my chair, to buy myself some time. I must have done it too abruptly, because when I turn back, I notice the detective is halfway out of his seat.

"Please," he says, "stay calm."

"I'm sorry. You surprised me."

I hear Nodar exhale.

"Did you say murder? When? I mean, who . . . ?"

As the words leave my mouth, I know what the answer will be.

"I'm sorry, I can't tell you more. Ongoing investigation."

A smile sidles onto the detective's face, giving us a good view of his moist, salmon-pink lips.

"Listen to me very carefully—don't leave Tbilisi. I told your brother the same but I don't think he heard me. If you leave Tbilisi, or don't report anything you find here, I will arrest you for obstructing my investigation. Do you understand?"

I nod.

"I need to hear you say it. Now."

"I understand," I say, teeth gritted.

With that, the detective marches us out and leaves us in the reception. Back in the Volga, Nodar's very quiet. The car dips into its bucket of rusty gears and finds one. We move off. Nodar lets his Volga do the talking for him. We move through the streets at a thoughtful pace, taking our time, letting people cut in. He must be wondering what to do with me and whether what I'm paying him is worth the hassle.

"I don't understand," I say.

"Listen, hang it, brother. Usually, they can't find their own ass with both hands. But they have reason to spy on you now."

"Spy on me?"

"Look around, you're not in London anymore. Once they have an excuse, they do what they like."

It finally dawns on me why Sandro's gone radio silent. *Those people.* Is our name tainted here? Did Irakli put himself in danger simply by returning here?

"Maybe that's why Sandro broke contact. Maybe they're watching him?" I say.

"Probably. He's being smart."

Nodar starts on his second L&M box as we stop at the lights.

"Listen, tell me about Irakli."

"What do you want to know?"

"Any idea what got him in trouble?"

"I don't know. But . . . murder?"

Nodar exhales smoke and frowns.

"There's no way Irakli would try to kill someone. No. They're trying to pin it on him."

"Why?"

I confess. I tell Nodar about Irakli's cryptic mentions of "those people" and what grudges he might have left here to fester. "I think the murder is made up. They just want Irakli caught and I don't know why."

Nodar's not impressed.

"Brother, you knew all this and let me walk into that snake pit butt-crack naked?" He thumps the wheel. "Bastards! I gave him my name, my address."

"I'm sorry."

"It's not your fault. You have a crazy problem in a crazy country full of crazy people," Nodar says, but his frown remains.

"Something not right with that detective, brother. You hear how he spat your name out like an insult?"

He doesn't say another word as we make our way home through the irate rush-hour traffic. Back home, he disappears for a walk. He's gone for hours. I spend the evening staring at the TV, trying to digest the news about Irakli.

When Ketino offers me her knockout potion I accept it gladly. I gulp it down in one go and get in bed.

"Sleep on it, Saba," Eka's voice says, the way it used to after a bad day. *"It won't seem as bad tomorrow, I promise."*

THAT NIGHT *I find myself wandering the hill overlooking Sololaki, with all of Tbilisi sprawled in front of me. Barefoot in the wind-tilted grass, I watch the sun time-lapse across the sky. When it gets dark the broadcast tower lights up so bright it makes me look away.*

The grimacing moon chases the sun across the sky and within seconds it's morning again. The sun rises behind the tower. In the gnarled Mtats-minda forest the predatory shape of a tiger flits between trees like a ghost.

This is a hunt. The prey is a little boy. He's running, but fading fast. The tiger slows, almost to a stop. This is it—the boy's exhausted, cornered.

This is the last stand. Belly to the ground, throat rumbling, the tiger's about to pounce.

I look away, close my eyes, and try to wake up somewhere better. But the spell won't break. The wind brings me the last note of a dying wail.

There's someone here with me on this hill, I can feel it. An austere presence. My eyes snap open on the dark shape of a woman. Her face hidden by long black hair. The wind tugs faint threads of black smoke from the edges of her outline. She points her sword at me.

Friend or foe?

Friend.

Welcome back, boy.

Tbilisi grows dark again. Something sinister approaches us from behind. I don't know what scares me more: this woman or whatever's coming for us. I close my eyes and try to wake up somewhere better.

Not so fast.

When the woman looks at me, I feel a wave of terror and a measure of relief. Her mismatched eyes blaze blue and green in the darkness. I hear a distant snarl from the trees.

Don't turn around.

The wind picks up. It blows ice-cold, straight into Tbilisi. Suddenly, as though brought by the wind, dozens of hungry dark shapes whip past us, down the hill, and into the city. Wolves. They run with purpose, silent as crib death. Already they prowl among the sleeping Sololaki houses, hunting.

Can't you warn them?

They deserve it.

Who are you?

They left me up here to rot. Their own mother.

Please, let me wake up.

Hush, child. Or you won't hear the screams.

3

HARD BY A GREAT FOREST
DWELT A POOR WOODCUTTER

I wake in a room echoing with the last remnants of a scream. My eyes dart around, looking for the source. As it fades, the scream resolves into a distant ambulance siren.

"Fuck me." I shake my head.

I hate these dreams—the kind that hold you captive. I have dark rings of sweat under both armpits and one around the neck. My hair's soaked at my temples. I climb out of my sweat pit and get dressed while the bleak aftertaste of the dream retreats to the back of my mouth.

I can't wait anymore; I need to get on with this. I have to find Irakli and Sandro. Nodar's in the living room, still blinking the sleep out of his eyes as I tell him my plan of starting with Irakli's flat in Sololaki.

"Brother," he says, smiling. "Good for you. But do you remember your way around?"

"I guess I'll find out."

He looks at me, tilts his head to one side, and squints.

"OK," he says eventually. "Just don't get eaten by anything, OK?"

"I'll try."

"I'll drive you to Sololaki."

"No, it's fine."

"I'll get you there and leave you to your business, I promise," he says and winks.

By the time we reach Sololaki, he's changed his mind.

"Listen, I can't let you go on your own. They're saying Artyom's up in Sololaki somewhere."

"Artyom?"

"Artyom the Tiger."

"They all have fucking names?"

"Of course. Russian names, though. They were born in the glorious Soviet Union, after all."

"And you'll protect me from this Artyom?"

"You might have to protect him from me."

Nodar grins and I smile back. I don't tell him but, to be honest, I could use the company.

Sololaki is the oldest district in Tbilisi. Faded pastel-colored houses, loose-cobbled streets, blind alleys, and cul-de-sacs creep up the hill in shapes that create no discernible, logical pattern. Centuries ago, someone built a small huddle of houses at the bottom of the hill. They had no plan in mind. More people arrived and more houses were built. Still no plan emerged, and it never would. Sololaki is blissfully unplanned.

As the district grew, they added more houses, more extensions, little balconies, open-air balustrades, communal yards, creaking stairways, opportunistic roads, crooked streets, and blind alleys. The growing needs of Sololaki battled the steep contours of Mtatsminda and won.

The disorderly assortment of houses, flats, shacks, and balconies in Sololaki is interconnected by a complex network of washing lines.

From that crazy mesh a million garments of all colors flutter in chaotic unison, as though Sololaki were a colossal wishing tree.

Watching over this mess from an adjacent hill is a giant silver statue of a woman holding a sword in one hand and a cup of wine in the other. She's at least a hundred feet tall and double that if you know what she symbolizes. She's the Guardian, the Mother of Georgia. The woman from my dream. The wine is for those who come as friends. The sword is for those who come as foes.

Under her stern gaze, Sololaki scrabbles up Mtatsminda until the incline gets too steep. Even there, the occasional house stubbornly clings to the hill, half-submerged in the Mtatsminda forest.

"OK, brother. One step at a time."

Nodar's beside me, hand on my shoulder. He nudges me into taking a step, as though he knows I'm not going anywhere otherwise. I take a step. Then another and another and soon we're walking.

"First, let's get you *into* Sololaki, brother. Then we'll see about the how and the who-what-where."

As we enter the district, the streets narrow, the tarmac turns into cobblestones, and buildings begin to loom over us. Sololaki is a maze. I'm looking for a house I barely remember in a maze, guided by nothing but childhood memories.

It isn't long before I find my first land mine of a memory, eighteen years in waiting. It makes me stop walking. Nodar's a few steps ahead, babbling away about how you can only taxi around Sololaki if you don't mind denting your car a little.

". . . it's a mess, brother. You end up in some dead-end alley, being towed out because the road's too steep to reverse."

He stops.

"Saba?"

I'm looking at a sharp corner building with a large circular balcony hanging over the street. The balcony's held together by a collection of precarious devices. Support beams hold it up from below. Frayed, sun-bleached ropes nailed into the wall support it from above. The whole construction is a firm gust of wind away from disaster.

Nodar follows my gaze up to the balcony, takes a couple of wary steps out of its shadow, and crosses himself.

"Jesus. Let's go before it collapses."

I remember walking past this balcony with Eka. She was bringing us to Irakli's place, where a car was waiting to take us to the airport. Right here, under this balcony, is the last time Sandro and I were in Sololaki with Eka.

It was during that bleak winter, after the civil war left Tbilisi wall-to-wall fucked with no electricity, no gas, no water, and no food in the shops. Bewildered, hungry people wandered the streets, punch-drunk by their sudden poverty. Last week they were in the Soviet Union; this week they're watching ragtag militias fight over a republic barely born. Last week they were fine—now they're queueing for bread and fetching water from a well.

Eka guided us through the dark streets of Sololaki by the light of a small key-ring flashlight. We heard people up on that old wooden balcony—flickers of candlelight and the smell of kerosene lamps. Among the chatter, someone was absently strumming a guitar and humming something hopeful.

"The whole city's starving and these degenerates are having a party," Eka said.

"Halt! Who approaches our gates?" someone shouted from the balcony.

There was laughter.

"It's Eka. Who's that up there?"

In Sololaki everyone knew everyone. A face appeared in the uneven orange light.

"Rajiko," the voice said. "Come join us, Eka!"

"What you celebrating?"

"The last of our food." There was an explosion of laughter.

"Another time, Rajiko. Don't mind me—you let your sails fly."

"There won't be another time, Eka."

Another burst of laughter. As we walked on, I remember thinking—how silly, why would you celebrate running out of things to eat?

"Cretins. The city's dying and they're singing accompaniment."

There was a note of laughter in Eka's voice. The party on that balcony was the ill-advised, counterintuitive, and very Georgian way of coping with adversity—a big, juicy "fuck you." We've seen hardship too many times to be cowed by it. We know living is more important than surviving.

"You OK, brother? You look like you've seen a ghost." Nodar snaps me out of it.

I'm surprised to find that tears have filled my eyes. Strange thing, memory, the way it slides the knife in.

"I know where to go," I tell him.

Nodar follows me to a small alley that fetches up against a cliff at the far end. A handful of two-story wooden houses with tumbledown interlocking balconies huddle together for safety. Take one house away and the whole tenuous contraption would crumble.

"Up there."

Nodar raises an eyebrow but doesn't say anything. Halfway up the alley we find a wooden gate that leads to an internal yard. "21 Rizhinashvili Street" the sign says. The gate is ancient. I put my hand on the sun-warmed wood as though it was the holy end point of some absurd pilgrimage.

"It's here."

"You go in, I'll wait."

I turn to the gate and realize there's nothing I can do to open it. Putting my hand on it has turned me into a child. I'm terrified. I move to

face Nodar on the opposite side of a street so narrow we could shake
hands across it.

"I just need a minute to—"

What I see on the wall behind Nodar stops me short. A large graffiti
looms over us. It's in a spot you'd only see coming out of the gate and is
at odds with the surroundings. It's in English, for a start, and an odd
mustard-yellow color.

> *Hard by a great forest dwelt a poor woodcutter with*
> *his wife and two children.*
> > *The boy was called Hansel and the girl Gretel . . .*
>
> > > *—Brothers Grimm*

"Appropriate," Nodar says and laughs.

I start to laugh too, but the sound catches in my throat.

"What's the matter?"

"That's Sandro's handwriting."

"You sure?"

"Of course."

Nodar studies the graffiti. A smile sneaks onto his face.

"Well, at least you know you're on the right path, Hansel."

He feels sorry for me, wants to make me laugh.

"Doesn't that make you Gretel?" I say.

While Nodar chuckles, I light a cigarette, sit on the curb, and plant
my feet among the gaptooth cobblestones. From here, I can see movement through the holes in the gate. Someone's in that yard. I sit and wait
for my heart to pick a rhythm and stick to it.

No matter how many times Eka read that story to us, "Again!"
was the only applause she got. An exotic, mysterious air about those

names—Hansel, Gretel. Something about the story promised a different path through the forest, if only Eka would read it again.

Back then, Eka read to us constantly. Sandro would listen close, rapt, the outside world falling away. Me, I was a nuisance. I just couldn't stay as still as Sandro. My mind fired off on tangents at unruly trajectories. "Why?" I always wanted the why of everything. Sometimes why isn't the point at all, Eka would say and smile.

The books Eka read to us weren't the USSR-approved, mandated books. Most Western books were banned in the Soviet Union and being caught in possession was no joke. We weren't to tell anyone about Eka's mysterious library and her contraband stories of wizards and magic slippers, pirate adventures, and little princes wandering the stars.

Eka's books were magic, smuggled in from sunnier places than Soviet Georgia. Their sharp edges smoothed by hundreds of secret readers, covers all but faded. Some were printed, but others had been copied, longhand, by some saintly, patient soul. Those were the really good ones.

Once we were in London, Irakli barely had time to sleep between shifts, never mind read to us. Left without Eka, Sandro and I developed our own language—part Georgian, part broken English, and part Eka. Like a swallow's nest, it was knit from small artifacts of Eka's books: quotes, names, in-jokes, and characters.

In the gaps we couldn't fill, we put new words you won't find in any dictionary. Words we misheard, or invented. Words with no etymology, no genealogy—our words. It was our own bootleg, motherless language.

In those early days, before we got shunted into a Tottenham school that spoke a language we didn't, Sandro and I entertained ourselves by building elaborate scavenger hunts in our little council flat. Small scrolls of paper hidden in unlikely places, messages and clues written in our own secret language.

Sandro's hunts were always more intricate than mine. They baffled me so often. But Sandro's no cheat. His game was always fair. He knew I'd solve the riddles eventually because we shared a vocabulary. Just think, he'd say and grin. Think. But I rarely finished Sandro's games before Irakli came home, an exhausted interloper in our world.

So, this is the beginning of a Sandro scavenger hunt. The signal to tell me the game has started. This one's going to be hard. But you can do it, Saba, he would have said.

I light another cigarette using the butt of the first. I listen to the ceaseless hum of Sololaki. Distant shouts, laughter, yelps of children at play, car horns, TVs and radios left to play to no audience. The volume of it all starts to mount until I can't think right. I look to Nodar, but he can't hear what I'm hearing. Out of the rising din comes a voice, rung loud and unapologetic, like a church bell.

"If the mountain doesn't come to Mohammed, then Mohammed must go to the mountain."

I recognize the words and the voice. It's Anzor, my eight-fingered, cast-iron uncle.

"You hear me, Sabo?"

He always called me Sabo instead of Saba, and elongated the *-oh* at the end. I swear, I could hear him say my name from two streets away.

"I want to go home, Anzor."

"You are home."

"I mean London."

"That ugly swamp?"

"It's home now."

"I knew it was a bad idea. Boys will never come back, I said. And if they do, they won't be the same. But Eka didn't listen."

"You were right."

"You don't belong in London, Sabo. Look around. This place is grown through your bones. Can't you feel it?"

"Not anymore."

"You never made real effort to put down roots in that mountainless swamp. Get a good grip on that soil. You or Sandro. Be honest, God is watching—why is that?"

I don't have an answer for Anzor. But he's right, England never felt permanent to me, or to Sandro. More like a rest stop on the way to a destination not yet known.

"You were just running down the clock."

"Until what?"

"Until something called you here."

I don't answer.

"Enough, Sabo. No one will go in there for you. Stand up, take charge."

I throw my half-smoked cigarette away. If Anzor's with me, I'm bulletproof. It's always been like that. The gate opens with a creak and I find myself in a small, clammy tunnel leading to a yard dazzling with midday sunlight. An elderly woman sits on a stool in the middle of it all.

"She looks like Grandma."

"She's no Lena."

I step out of the tunnel, wincing at the brightness. The small yard's surrounded by wooden balconies that run the entire length of the walls. The small square of china-blue sky visible from the yard is crisscrossed with washing lines.

The woman sits next to a length of copper pipe protruding from the ground. The pipe's been hammered into the shape of a tap. Water gushes into an aluminum pail filled with clothes. An industrial-size slab of coarse soap rests on top of the sodden clothes. I can already smell it.

"The smell of my whole childhood. Everything on us smelled like that Soviet chemistry," Anzor says.

"I remember."

"Go on, say hello."

The woman is thin, her gestures sparse and concise. Dusty black clothes hang loose from her frame. Elbows on knees, she snatches a rag from the pail and rubs soap into it. She slaps the lathered rag back into the pail. When she sees my shadow edge closer, she looks up, shading her eyes with her hand.

"Greetings," she says.

"Hello, auntie."

She straightens up and wipes her brow with the inside of her wrist. Just like Grandma Lena used to.

"Oh," she says. "Thought you were a lost tourist."

Which would have been a shrewd appraisal.

"Let me see you."

I step forward as though I'm in a police lineup. Shielding her eyes from the light, she studies me.

"What's your father's name?"

"Donauri."

She frowns.

"Is your mother a Sulidze?"

I nod. Her eyes seem to brighten.

"Good Sololaki surname. You're Eka's boy. The naughty one. Didn't you move to America?"

"England."

She nods, looking away. "That's it. England. Country with a queen. As things should be."

Her hands snatch up another garment. She's done soaping and rinsing it when she speaks again.

"Don't just stand there, son. Sit down, splash some water on your face."

I sit down as she shoos away a cat sniffing at her pail.

"What can I do for you?"

"I'm looking for someone."

"I know. You're looking for Irakli."

She chuckles at my expression.

"Don't look so surprised, we don't get many visitors. I know who you are. Sandro's been here already."

Her hand, clutching the bar of soap, sweeps a dripping semicircle around her.

"Who else would come here? Look at this place." She sighs. "How is your brother?"

"I don't know."

She frowns and slops a rag back in the pail with a splash. "How do you mean, you don't know?"

"He's missing. That's why I'm here."

She shakes her head. "He came by not long ago. Said he was looking for Irakli."

She tilts the aluminum pail and pours the soapy water down the drain and stands up with an audible *oof*. She plugs the tap with a piece of wood, which she hammers home with the heel of her palm.

"I've had enough of this heat. Here, help me with this. Come, I'll show you what's in Irakli's old flat."

She hands me the pail and motions me toward a staircase.

"Wait till I get to the top," she says. "Then come up."

When I start up the stairs, I understand. Each crooked step yields under my weight. The wood's exhausted and begging for a little extra weight to put it out of its misery.

"Here, sit, sit," the woman says.

We're on a wooden balcony that doubles as a makeshift kitchen. A bulky Soviet-era fridge rusts serenely in the corner. It looks like it could take a solid beating. A brass plate slapped across the off-white door says "POLUS," in Russian.

"Recognize it?" Anzor chuckles in my head.

"Our fridge."

"The damn thing's carved out of a block of steel. Only two models you could buy in all of Soviet Georgia. This one and the one that worked."

The old woman opens the fridge and gets out a tomato, a cucumber, an onion, and a block of cheese wrapped in newspaper. She puts down a plate and starts slicing the cucumber and tomato in her hands. Then she chops the onion. The whole thing takes seconds.

I watch her, mesmerized by an ancient déjà vu. I've seen Grandma Lena do this exact routine. She could chop together a salad using nothing but a knife in the time it took you to say you wanted one. As I watch, something vital in my chest works itself loose and drifts, exposed and unsafe, about to snag in the machinery of my heart.

The old woman produces a hunk of rock salt from a cupboard, scrapes a few flakes into the salad, and mixes it all with her hands. She puts the salad, the cheese, and some bread on the table in front of me and sits opposite. The newspaper print has transferred itself onto the cheese so well that it's fully legible.

"It's not much. Eat, eat."

"Thank you. But you shouldn't—"

"A guest is a gift from God."

She crosses herself. Idiotically, I cross myself too. I try the salad and realize I've been eating counterfeit vegetables in London. This woman had the real stuff hidden in her fridge all along. I bite into a slice of cheese, newspaper font and all, and then the bread. She smiles at me.

"You look like Eka, you know."

For so many years, I heard that name so rarely. I've avoided direct thoughts of Eka, the way your eyes might swerve the sharp light of the low winter sun. Hearing her name come out of a stranger's mouth makes me pause.

Despite our unspoken pact in London, or maybe because of it, Eka's absence became a real presence in our flat. A thousand ways it intervened in our daily lives—tutting over Irakli's shoulder as he cooked us eggs for dinner, chiding Sandro for brushing his teeth too quickly, shaking her head at my math homework.

Maybe that's why both Sandro and I moved out first chance we got. Not because it was an ugly plywood flat, cheap and efficient, among dozens of others just like it on our road. No, we wanted to get away from the absence of Eka.

The old woman reads my mind.

"After you left, I'd see her standing at your school gate sometimes, watching the kids come out. I knew not to speak to her then."

A thought comes to her and she pauses.

"Tell me something. . . ." She puts her elbows on the table and draws closer. "Why did you never take her to England?"

I think of Irakli's awful, minimum-wage jobs, his phone calls to scrape money from anyone who'd listen, his meager bank loans, and the honest man who stole all our money. I distill years of white-knuckle effort to buy Eka's freedom into one word.

"Money."

The woman understands in full. She sighs and shakes her head. "The root of all evil."

Looking around the yard I realize there are other people camou-flaged in the surrounding clutter, all but invisible as they go about their afternoons. The sunny nooks and shaded crannies of the balconies are populated by slow-limbed cats, languid in the afternoon heat.

"Did Sandro say where he was going? Or where he was staying?"

"No. He just wanted to see the place Irakli rented from me, back be-fore the war. I say 'rented,' but Irakli never paid enough, or on time. I was more an auntie to him than landlady. Had to teach him how to boil water, bless him."

She smiles and hands me another piece of bread.

"Anyway, Sandro came to see it. So I showed him the place. I told him, like I'll tell you now. Irakli snuck in like a ghost and snuck out again on a gust of wind. I only know because I caught him leaving while it was still dark out."

"Irakli was here? When?"

She waves her hand. "I don't know, months ago. All my Mondays are Saturdays these days."

I look down into the yard as though I expect to see Irakli there.

"How gray he's gone, bless him. I barely recognized him. He recognized me just fine though, even after all these years. 'Peace to you, auntie,' he said. Just like he used to. 'Door was locked, so I slipped the rent I owe you under it. . . .'"

"Did he say anything else?"

"He was about to. I saw it in his eyes. But something stopped him. Left without another word."

Once I've gobbled up the salad, I thank the old woman.

"For what? It's nothing."

As she puts everything back in the fridge, I catch a glimpse inside. Nothing in there but a couple of tomatoes, cucumbers, and empty shelves. She notices my stare.

"I looked in here the other day and found the cockroach had hung himself."

She laughs and creaks the fridge door shut.

"So, you want to see what's in Irakli's flat?"

"Please."

The door to the old woman's flat has plastic bags taped up where the windowpanes should be. In the close darkness inside I spot a small cot, a low table, a chair, and a small cathode-ray-tube TV. That's all there is to her flat. She emerges holding a brass key on a string.

"Let's go." She winks.

Irakli's balcony is barren but for a collection of ancient glass bottles gathering dust in the corner. This is it—Irakli's bachelor pad in Tbilisi. After the divorce, nobody told Sandro and me anything useful. Ma and Da still love you very much—that sort of thing.

But we heard things around the house. Things said in hushed, rumor-mill tones. Irakli's renting a place in Sololaki, right by the botanical garden. Or, Irakli's run off to some monastery. It's not unusual in Georgia, to serve a sentence in a monastery, to get away from the things you've fucked up in your life. Plenty of people did. But no one told us why Irakli did it.

Sparing you a painful truth is a national habit. Georgians call it a "black truth"—a truth that will only do harm. When my uncle Anzor lay in hospital, his life evaporating out of an open window, they spared him the black truth. Even the doctors and nurses were in on it. Lung infection, they told him, just a bad infection. The black truth was that his lungs were riddled with tumors the size of tennis balls.

It boils my blood to think they didn't tell him. I can't imagine anything worse than lying in a hospital, waiting for a lung infection to clear up while my insides fall apart.

"I knew, Sabo," Anzor says.

"You knew?"

"They started giving me morphine. People I hadn't seen in months came by. Everyone smiling and joking around. Of course I knew."

The old woman opens the door to Irakli's flat and stands aside.

"Go on in."

I take a deep breath and step inside. There's so much dust on the floor that I'm leaving footprints. I look closer and realize I can see someone else's prints. They must be Sandro's.

The two rooms of the flat are bare. No furniture but an old writing desk in the corner of the smaller room. The only thing in the main room is a wood-burning stove with a small pile of firewood by its side. The stove has a small door, rusted shut.

A frail construction of mismatched segments makes up a pipe that comes out of the stove, runs along the ceiling and out the window. The only thing keeping it all in one piece is rust and sheer obstinacy. The smoke, escaping the ill-fitted joints of the pipe, has dyed the ceiling black with soot. I hear the woman chuckle behind me.

"Every morning, he'd go searching for firewood up in the botanical garden. He refused to harm the trees, so he only ever came back with the twigs he found lying around."

She pinches the bridge of her nose and shakes with gentle laughter.

"A tree is a tree, I told him, it'll burn just like any other. I don't care if it came from Africa or China. But he wouldn't do it. You'll never make a good woodcutter at this rate, I kept telling him. . . . But then the winter got *serious*."

Her laughter fades away.

"And then him, me, and the rest of Sololaki stripped those trees naked."

She falls silent.

"Who lived here after he left?" I say eventually.

The old woman chuckles. "No one, son. Who'd rent *this* place unless their life was coming down about their ears?"

As I stand in the middle of the room, it occurs to me that this is it. There's nothing else in the room, nothing to rest your eyes on. This is the end of me playing detective.

"That's all you've got?" Anzor says.

My eyes drift to the floor as though drawn by gravity. I look at the footprints Sandro tracked through the dust—back and forth, around the fireplace, the window, the desk. They're frantic steps, uneasy ones. He was here, worried, shaken, looking for something. I can smell his fear; he left a trace of it in the air. So unlike Sandro, to be scared.

I follow him to the little writing desk. I open the drawers, one by one—nothing in them but the smell of old pencils. The bottom drawer doesn't even open all the way. Doesn't matter, nothing in there but dust anyway. I can picture Sandro's face now, half-smiling but somehow still serious. I'm eight years old again and stuck. Failing to decode his clue. Look closer, he would have said. Think.

I wrench the last drawer open. Still nothing. I'm about to slam it shut when I register a dusty pattern of color winking at me from the back. There is something in there after all—Sandro's games are always fair.

I can feel the old woman watching me. I glance back at her and she smiles faintly. I rush to the window to see what I've found.

Manuscript pages. The first page is a hand-drawn sketch of a kaleidoscope. Cracked along the bottom, the kaleidoscope is raining shards of color on a lone gray figure of a man with his back to us. He's holding his head in his hands. There's a bottle of wine next to him and a plume of smoke rises from the ashtray.

I've seen this before. I know exactly what it is. It's the damn play Irakli took with him when he returned to Tbilisi. *"Kaleidoskupi,"* the title reads in a colorful font. *Skupi* is Georgian for a jaunty hop or a skip. *Kaleido-skupi* is a play on the word *kaleidoscope*—like skipping through a kaleidoscope.

I search the rest of the pages for a hidden message. I find none. Only the opening act of the play.

"What's this doing here?"

I show the old woman the *Kaleidoskupi* pages.

"Sandro," she says simply.

Her smile widens.

"After his first visit, I didn't think I'd see him ever again. But a few days later he came by, dead of night, like the wolves were at his heels— auntie, let me in please, hurry, it's important. So I did."

"What did he want?"

"He left those pages for you. I'm trusting you with something important, auntie, he said. I can't tell you what—safer that way. If my brother comes here, make sure he gets them. Don't breathe a word about this to anyone else, he said. He really meant it."

I shuffle the pages in my hands. What's Sandro up to?

"Some ugly lizard of a policeman came the day after and searched the place. Read the pages back to front and upside down, like a jumped-up yokel with a badge. I suppose he found no sense in them, because he balled them up, tight as can be, and threw them at the wall. Don't worry, I ironed them out and put them back. They're all there."

"I'm sorry about all this," I say, looking around.

She taps her chest twice. "Takes more than the likes of him to scare me, son."

I feel my knees fold until I'm crouching. I lean against the stove with a thump and the whole thing rattles. I try to picture Sandro's face and what he's trying to tell me. You've made the game too hard this time, Sandro.

"Ready to give up, Mohammed?"

I ignore Anzor's voice.

"Forget this misery, go back. Your finest talent—forgetting."

The words make me grit my teeth, but he goes on.

"Where were you when strangers buried Eka? My little sister. It was cold and raining. They had better things to do. They threw her in, crossed themselves, and got on with their day."

"We weren't allowed to leave England."

"More excuses. Go on then, give up."

The woman watches me as I rise to my feet and cast a final glance around the room.

"I'm going to go," I say.

She nods. It's only here that I realize that set deep in her wrinkled face, the woman's eyes are different colors. Errant shards of a spilled kaleidoscope—one blue and one green. Like the woman from my dream. Her eyes drift from mine.

"Sandro said the oddest thing . . ." she says softly. "'I'm off to the great forest, auntie, to cool my feet in the river. Wish me luck. If you see my brother, tell him that.' What do you suppose that means?"

"We used to call the botanical garden the great forest . . ." I say, almost to myself.

She smiles kindly. With a firm touch, she ushers me back to her balcony. She holds her finger to her lips and doesn't say anything else. Her blue eye winks at me.

"Never come back here," she says in parting. "For both our sakes."

She watches me leave from her balcony, as though to make sure.

I FIND NODAR in the alley where I left him, guarding the graffiti. Only now he's holding a bottle of beer and is surrounded by a sprinkling of his own cigarette butts.

"What took so long?"

I tell Nodar about the old woman and what she said. I tell him about Irakli, Sandro, the *Kaleidoskupi* pages, and what Sandro said to her in parting. He looks thoughtful.

"Great forest, eh? Well, you could say you've found the first crumb in the trail." He winks, chuckling. "Sorry, brother. My Natia's obsessed with Hansel and Gretel. Been standing here reciting it from memory."

He continues in a singsong voice.

> *"Hard by a great forest dwelt a poor woodcutter with his wife*
> *and two children,*
> *the boy Hansel and the girl Gretel.*
> *He had little to bite and to break, and once when great*
> *hunger fell on the land,*
> *he could no longer procure even daily bread. . . ."*

He claps me on my shoulder.

"I can remember all that, but not what I ate for dinner last night."

He glances back at the graffiti.

"So why all the secrecy and breadcrumbs, brother?"

Once Sandro and I found out Irakli was living by the botanical garden after the divorce, he became the poor Hansel and Gretel woodcutter to us. Which naturally led to endless bickering over which one of us was Hansel and which one Gretel.

"I don't know." I shrug. "But we used to call the botanical garden the great forest."

"Well, listen, the garden's just up there, if you want to go now."

"If the garden doesn't come to Mohammed . . ." Anzor's words coming out of my mouth. "Mohammed must go to the garden."

Nodar laughs.

"I don't think it's the garden you remember, brother. No one's looked after it in years. God only knows what's in there now," he says.

The cobblestone road to the old botanical garden starts out steep and gets steeper as we go. Soon the houses thin out, the view opens before us, and I feel like I can breathe unimpeded again. All of Tbilisi is visible behind us, and windowpanes across the city wink reflections of the setting sun as we go.

Nodar mumbles part-remembered Hansel and Gretel bits to himself as we walk.

"Nibble, nibble, munch, munch; who's nibbling my little house?"

He smiles at his feet.

Eventually, the road dips around the shoulder of the hill. Now no matter where I look, all I can see is a crowd of dense, forested hills. Here, Tbilisi doesn't exist. It may have never existed.

The road ends at a large army-green gate with a small ticket booth by its side.

"One lari, friend," the man in the booth says in monotone.

He sports an impressive set of eyebrows, merged into one unruly caterpillar across his brow. He has a plastic cup of wine and a hunk of bread on the counter in front of him. While the radio in his booth tells tall tales of escaped tigers spotted in Sololaki, he looks me up and down.

"You hear that?" He thumbs toward the radio. "And it'll be dark sooner than you think. Look."

He points at the sun barely clearing the horizon.

Nodar looks at me and shakes his head. "He has a point, brother," he says.

"Why?"

"Well, if you're a zoo wolf, or hyena, or a damn *tiger*, where would you hide? The city? Or in there?"

"Wait, hyenas now too?"

"The zoo had a pack of them. No one's seen them since the flood." He looks at the garden and frowns. "If I get eaten by something in there, Keti will track me down and kill me again."

In the fragrant sprawl of treetops beyond the gate, the gaps between branches are already filling with a liquid gloom. Sandro's next clue is in there somewhere. I know he wants me to go in.

But he doesn't know this forest belongs to Nino. *She* is in there somewhere too—the keeper of my secret. Bloodless-pale, she stalks among the trees like a furious little ghost, waiting for me. I pray she hasn't sensed my presence.

The wind shifts and the forest exhales a cold gust of pine tree aroma. The smell of our childhood. The smell of *her.* Nino's was the hardest voice to silence. . . .

It's too late, she knows I'm here.

"Come on in, what are you afraid of?"

A chill runs down my spine. I don't dare reply.

"Fine, mummy's boy. I'll come find you where you sleep."

Nodar nudges me. I stare at him blankly.

"Let's come back in the day."

He pauses.

"Brother, you look like a ghost. You OK?"

I nod. "Just tired."

"OK. Now, listen, please—it's killing me."

"What is?"

He points at the pages in my hand. "You gonna read them or what?"

He's like a damn child. We sit on the little wooden bench by the garden gate and read the *Kaleidoskupi* pages together. They're written in different shades of pencil. The yellowing pages are not all the same size and the writing's fading. Doodles and odd words have crept onto the margins, like someone kept the pages for scrap paper by the phone.

Irakli wrote *Kaleidoskupi* in the monastery where he took himself after he and Eka divorced. He even brought the dog-eared handwritten manuscript with him to London. Kept it hidden away in a box, like it was cursed.

"I'll go back there, to all those places I didn't say goodbye to," he'd tell us, before each abortive attempt to fly to Tbilisi.

"I'll leave the pages, here and there, like breadcrumbs. Right pages for the right place. My farewell. When I'm done, the breadcrumbs will bring me back here. Back to you."

We heard this plan so many times that it really did start to sound like a fairy tale. We no longer took notice. But when Irakli disappeared off to Georgia, the play went with him.

Sandro and I did read *Kaleidoskupi* when we were kids, in London. Of course we did—things hidden away in boxes are irresistible. I only read it in passing, like I read most things, and didn't retain much of it. Sandro held on to it for days.

He told me the play was about a man by the name of Valiko, drinking himself into a stupor in a café in Tbilisi. Valiko is visited, one by one, by people he knows: his mother, an old friend, his ex-wife, and so on.

By the end, Sandro told me, it turns out no one's actually visited Valiko at all. Those people were just hallucinations, as he drank himself into the grave. I don't know if either of us understood what that meant back then, not really. But I do know that *Kaleidoskupi* gave birth to the myth of Valiko.

London life had Irakli out working all the time, frantic, trying to gather pennies into pounds—tiny little coins that would one day buy us a mother. In those endless hours when he was at work, as we crafted our scavenger hunts, Valiko shaped his own mythology.

Valiko became the author of many a cryptic note. He was our convenient hero, our master of clues, and an occasional scapegoat. Especially that time someone spilled an entire glass of soda into the crevices of our sofa. That was Valiko's doing. That poor sofa was sugar-tacky for months after.

I open the *Kaleidoskupi* pages and say hello to Valiko once more.

ACT 1—SCENE 2

*Decrepit Soviet-era café. The room is dim and the **WAITRESS** can be seen going about her business, wiping down tables and cleaning out ashtrays. **VALIKO** sits at a table in the corner, alone, with a drink in hand. He looks haggard. His clothes are well looked after but obviously very old. His table is lit by a candle melted to an old wine bottle.*

WAITRESS: How many times have I told you to stop coming round here?

*(**VALIKO** takes a sip and nods)*

WAITRESS: Valiko, you listening to me?

VALIKO: Who else would?

WAITRESS: Funny. Where are your folks, your people? Why aren't they setting you straight? Moping around like this all day. Drunk, aimless.

VALIKO: Drunk? Please, you water down your wine so much it sobers me up as I drink it.

WAITRESS: Don't make me cut you off.

VALIKO: You'd go bankrupt.

WAITRESS: Good point.

(They share a smile)

WAITRESS: When I finally get rid of this place, I'll take the money back home. Maybe buy my granddad's vineyard back. Leave here for good, live a cleaner life.

VALIKO: You're stuck, like the rest of us.

WAITRESS: Not me. You'll see.

(Enter MARINA—an elderly, frumpy, plump woman wearing a handkerchief around her head. She's out of breath and walks with a slight limp. The WAITRESS retreats into the darkness behind the counter.)

MARINA: Valiko? That you?

VALIKO: Yes, Ma, you found me.

MARINA: I looked all over. Where have you been?

VALIKO: Just here.

MARINA: Haven't seen you for days, Valiko. Why didn't you call?

(MARINA rushes to VALIKO's table and takes a hasty seat)

MARINA: Listen, Sasha managed to get me some good bread. I bought some chicken bone from the market. For soup, see. I hope it hasn't gone off. I hung it out the window last night, God knows it's cold enough out there.

VALIKO: Alright, Ma, don't fuss. Here, have a sip of wine. It'll do you good.

MARINA: *(Suddenly angry)* Has it done *you* any good?

VALIKO: No. It's too watered down.

MARINA: Look at your shirt, Valiko, you've ripped your collar.

VALIKO: It's just worn out. Tired and worn out, like everything else.

MARINA: Don't start that nonsense again. Leave that bottle and let's go home.

VALIKO: Come on, Ma. Sit, rest a minute. How are the headaches?

MARINA: Oh, they're a bloody curse, you know that. Rusiko told me to tie this thing round my head. Really tight, she said. I don't think it's doing anything.

(MARINA takes off the handkerchief and throws it on the table)

MARINA: Did you hear they arrested Miron? Dead of night, pulled him out of bed in his underpants. Woke the whole street, shouting, waving those flashlights everywhere. I bet it was those music tapes he's always copying. That Western rubbish is banned and you know that. If someone found out . . . Valiko, did you buy any from him? You have to get rid of them.

VALIKO: Where's Miron now?

MARINA: You can't have them around the house. What if someone reports you?

VALIKO: I know, Ma, I know. I threw them away.

MARINA: I couldn't stand losing you to those jumped-up hooligans with guns. To do such cruel things to their own folk, their neighbors, people they grew up with. Can you imagine?

VALIKO: Don't fuss, Ma. I threw them away, I promise.

MARINA: I'll have a good look when I get home. Just in case.

(Long silence. VALIKO takes a drink, pinches the bridge of his nose, and sighs. MARINA watches disapprovingly.)

VALIKO: *(Absently)* Ma, remember when Dad would play those old records of his? The two of you would dance in the kitchen. I'd get jealous and cry until you danced with me instead.

MARINA: You remember that?

VALIKO: Been on my mind lately. Listen, I'm sorry I did that.

MARINA: What nonsense you talk when you're drunk.

VALIKO: Well, maybe. But still, I wanted to say sorry.

MARINA: I don't even—

VALIKO: *(Rising from his seat. Suddenly frantic.)* Listen, Ma, will you dance with me one last time?

MARINA: Here? Now?

VALIKO: Yeah, why not?

MARINA: There's no music.

VALIKO: Who needs music? We'll pretend. Dance with me, Ma.

MARINA: You've lost your marbles, Valiko.

(VALIKO pulls MARINA out of her seat. She follows him reluctantly and returns to her seat almost immediately.)

MARINA: Valiko, you stink of wine.

VALIKO: I'll never drink again, Ma. I promise.

MARINA: Really?

VALIKO: *(Sinking back into his seat)* This is my last night. I mean, look at this place.

MARINA: Let's go home, Valiko, I beg you.

VALIKO: OK, Ma, let's.

MARINA: I can get that chicken cooking right away. Bread's still fresh, I hope. Everything will be ready before you know it. You'll see.

VALIKO: We have any butter?

MARINA: I'll pop across to Ina's and get some. She owes me for all that sugar—God knows what she does with it all. Will you really come, Valiko? You know I can always tell when you lie.

VALIKO: Why don't you set off before it gets too dark, Ma? I need to finish up here with my friend and I'll be right behind you. Probably catch up to you before you get home.

(MARINA hugs him across the table)

MARINA: Don't dawdle like you do.

VALIKO: OK, Ma, I won't.

(As MARINA reaches the exit)

VALIKO: Wait, before you go, Ma . . .

MARINA: Yes?

VALIKO: When you came in, I was trying to remember something and for the life of me I still can't.

MARINA: What is it, Valiko?

VALIKO: *(Approaching **MARINA**)* You used to read me that fairy tale—the one with the breadcrumb trail. It really scared me, but you read it to me anyways. It has a happy ending, you'd say.

MARINA: Hansel and Gretel?

VALIKO: How does it start?

MARINA: Hard by a great forest dwelt a poor woodcutter with his wife and two children. . . .

VALIKO: Keep going.

MARINA: The boy was called Hansel and the girl Gretel—

(Interrupting MARINA)

VALIKO: Horrible thing to read to a child, don't you think?

MARINA: It's a fairy tale, Valiko. It's got a happy ending.

VALIKO: What if you never hear the happy ending—is it still a fairy tale, Ma?

MARINA: What are you saying?

VALIKO: Think about it. Without the ending, it's just a nasty little tale about poverty, kidnapping, abuse, cannibalism, murder—

MARINA: *(Flustered)* Stop it, Valiko, you're drunk.

VALIKO: You never read me the ending, Ma.

MARINA: *(Angrily)* Enough, Valiko!

(MARINA exits the stage. VALIKO watches her go. He returns to his seat. His head hangs over his drink.)

WAITRESS: You're not going, are you?

VALIKO: Too late for that.

WAITRESS: Drink?

VALIKO: Another glass.

(The WAITRESS reemerges from the darkness)

WAITRESS: Do you want another bottle instead?

(Lights dim and go out as the WAITRESS brings VALIKO a bottle of wine)

4

NINO, SAY SOMETHING

Back at the Palais du Grand Nodar, Ketino heaves the front door open with a grunt.

"The borscht is ready" is all she says.

With Nodar gone to the shop and Ketino in the kitchen, I retreat to Natia's room to think. Obviously Sandro wants me to go to the botanical garden—our "great forest." But something else nags at me. The link between the *Kaleidoskupi* pages and the Hansel and Gretel graffiti is obvious. But I'm still missing some deeper meaning that unlocks this puzzle.

Why is Sandro being so secretive anyway? Why the scavenger hunt and the elaborate clues?

Anzor's voice calms me, sits me down and unclenches my jaw.

"Think it through, Sabo. He's looking for Irakli, but so are the police."

"So?"

"Well, he has to somehow lead you, without leading them. This game, it's yours—you two invented it. The police can never follow this trail."

"Why leave a trail at all? Why not just one message?"

"What if the police find it? This search took Sandro weeks. This trail, he put it together for you as he went along."

"Yes, but why?"

"A fail-safe."

"Fail-safe?"

"He's scared, Sabo, just like you are. What if something stops him? At least he's left you something to start with."

The thought of Sandro scared makes my insides clench and brace for impact.

"You'll find what you need in the garden. You'll see."

As soon as I hear Nodar return, I head to the living room, where I find him at the center of a flurry of activity.

"Father Christmas has brought gifts for everyone."

He's unloading a large plastic bag on the living room table. Ketino ferries the groceries to the kitchen, trying to keep up. The table's a miniature metropolitan skyline of groceries—bottles of milk, canned food, eggs, oil, butter, bread, and blocks of L&M cigarettes.

Nodar looks at me and I force a smile in response. I know shopping sprees like this aren't common. The money I tossed him so casually will feed him and Ketino for weeks.

"Fuck your mother." Nodar claps a hand to his forehead. "I forgot hummingbird milk."

He winks at me—it's an old Georgian saying about being so rich that even the impossibility of hummingbird milk is affordable.

"Shut up, Nodar. There's no room left in the fridge," Ketino says, inoculated against the worst of his jokes.

"That's a good problem to have, Keti."

"I'll ask next door if we can keep some things in theirs."

Nodar saves the best for last. Like a magician pulling a rabbit out of a hat, he produces a large bottle of vodka with a flourish. He thumps it on the table just as Ketino walks by. She stops and stares. Then she grabs an armful of groceries and leaves. The front door slams behind her with a deep boom that makes the walls shudder.

"She doesn't like it when I drink."

The tall, narrow bottle of vodka has the word *Dubroff* plastered down the entire length of it in electric blue font.

"Couldn't you find a louder one?"

I watch his fingers struggle with the elaborate lid.

"It's the loudest one they had. Will you drink with me?"

As he finally conquers the lid, my heart's already singing the song of vodka.

"God, yes."

He pours us two solemn glasses.

"To vodka," he says.

His sharp Adam's apple bobs up and down four times and the glass is empty. He wipes his mouth with the back of his wrist and exhales pure ethanol fumes. I only get through half of my glass.

"Jesus, how many shots is that?" I say to him.

"Shots?"

"Shots. You know, measurements."

He taps his glass. "About this many."

His mouth works around a newly lit cigarette, making it bob and weave in front of his face as he speaks. "Listen, brother, we don't really gel with the concept of measuring our drink."

Ketino returns and sets the table around the lurid centerpiece of lukewarm Dubroff. We sit and eat the bloodred borscht in strained silence. Grandma Lena made the best borscht. Sometimes, if she'd been lucky at the market, there would be oddly shaped lumps of beef in the borscht. That's when I struggled with it—I couldn't stomach the gristle in that cut-price meat.

I remember one winter evening, she caught me at the open window, about to fling my bowl of borscht into the garden. I heard the unmistakable sound of Lena clearing her throat, the way she always did. I froze.

"Do you have any idea what it takes to make—" she started and stopped.

Sandro soldiered on with his bowl, speeding up at Lena's surprise appearance. Frozen in place, with borscht dripping off my fingers, I wondered if it was too late to sit back down and eat the damn stuff. You didn't mess around with food in Lena's domain. Even the adults didn't. Nothing went to waste.

"Two wars," Lena used to say. "Two world wars! I starved and scraped and starved and scraped. And you're leaving meat, good meat, on your plate?"

She'd been a child in the first war and a Red Army nurse in the second. Of all the things those wars took from her, food was something she could reclaim. Eka and Anzor poked fun at her sometimes.

"Two wars!" they'd say and wag two fingers at each other. But only after they were doubly sure Lena had left the room. Even so, at the end of a meal there was nothing on the table but plates wiped so clean you couldn't tell they'd been used.

So, there I was, facing all of Lena with the mortal sin of wasting food already committed and witnessed. I knew I'd really fucked up when, without a word, she turned and left the room.

She didn't speak to me for days. Eventually, my uncle Anzor brokered a peace deal. He told me to wait until she was cooking dinner that evening and apologize properly. Lena accepted my apology with a curt nod. She didn't crack a smile while I helped her cook and watched me real close while I ate. I finished everything and scrubbed my plate clean with a crust of bread.

"Careful, now. You'll take the enamel off," she said.

Anzor burst out laughing. I only just caught Lena's expression reset from a smile. That's how I knew everything would be alright again. But those few days Lena ignored me were worse than any beating I ever caught. I can see Nodar's getting a similar punishment now. Ketino finishes her thimbleful of stew and leaves the table.

"Keti, you've barely eaten."

There's a neat row of old plastic yogurt tubs lined up on the windowsill in the living room. Each tub's filled with soil and there are green shoots growing in each one—Ketino's herb garden.

"Keti."

She ignores Nodar, takes a plastic water bottle with a pierced lid, and starts to water the plants with her back to him.

"Keti, answer me."

"What, Nodar? What is it?"

Nodar pauses.

"Nothing, never mind."

Ketino gives Nodar and his Dubroff bottle a sidelong glance and goes into the kitchen. He follows her and I only hear snatches of an argument, murmured low for my benefit.

". . . you're drinking like a heathen. Unblessed. Like an alcoholic. Say a damn toast at least. Pretend."

Nodar mumbles something unconvincing.

"I'm tired, Nodar. Do what you like. But I'm not fixing you tomorrow."

She goes to the bedroom and I hear the TV come on. Nodar returns to the table.

"You should see how much *she* can drink."

He brings the tiny TV from the kitchen and puts it on the table with us. We sit, watch, and drink mostly in silence. Nodar takes gulps of vodka and follows them down with clumsy slices of sausage and ripped lumps of bread. I keep up with him the best I can.

"She doesn't understand. Sometimes you just need to switch this off, you know?" He taps his forehead.

The news channel cycles through stories of the flood and the escaped zoo animals. The police shot and killed six wolves near the airport after the vets failed to tranquilize them. Boris the Hippo was eventually knocked out by over a dozen darts to the neck. They show a picture of him slumped in the scoop of a JCB backhoe.

There have been no further sightings of Artyom, the Bengal tiger. Authorities suspect he's hiding in the Mtatsminda forest and advise Sololaki residents to avoid the forest and stay home after dark. Nodar stares at the TV screen with a blank face.

"How much is a hundred lari?" he says after a long silence, his voice slurred by vodka.

"What?"

"In pounds."

"Twenty or so, I think. Why?"

Nodar shakes his head. "Is that a lot? How much do you make a month in London?"

"I don't know what you mean."

"Yes, you do. Tell me." For a second, the vodka haze clears from Nodar's face.

"Things are more expensive there; my rent's—"

"Just tell me."

"About a thousand pounds."

Nodar looks up at me from his drink. His eyes are bloodshot and wet.

"How many lari does that make . . . ?" He pauses.

He smacks the table with his open palm. But there's no anger in the gesture, just sadness. With a weak clatter, everything on the table hops over by an inch. Nothing breaks or even topples over. Nodar slumps in his seat like hitting the table took the last of his energy.

"It's not fair," he murmurs.

It takes some truly horrific footage on TV to bring Nodar back. In all the panic over the escaped animals, the emergency services forgot about the Tbilisi Dogs' Home. The building was just downriver from the zoo. It filled up with muddy water and drowned over two hundred dogs right in their cages. They drained the building in the day and now we're watching footage of rows upon rows of muddy dogs, lying very still.

Nodar needs a couple of seconds to register what he's seeing. The camera pans through the disaster, past the cages and their silent occupants, and decides to focus in on a cage with several smaller shapes in it. Puppies.

"Your mother's ass!" he exclaims.

He changes the channel and in one angry movement pours and throws back another glass of vodka.

"They've no shame, showing that."

The next channel isn't any better but at least it's footage we've already seen. Misha the Bear clinging to the air conditioner. Misha being shot full of tranquilizer. The camera zooms in as he loses grip, slides off, and lands in a shallow puddle on the pavement.

"They say it's bad luck," Nodar says out of nowhere, after another long silence.

"What is?"

"What your da wrote in his play. Fairy tales."

"What do you mean?"

"You have to read them the whole way through. Even if your kid's asleep."

Nodar sags in his seat as though someone's letting air out of him. My head's swimming. My limbs are a second behind where I expect them to be.

"Have you switched it off?" I ask him and tap my forehead.

I meet Nodar's bloodshot eyes. His face is wreathed in L&M smoke.

Between us, we've created our own little ecosystem over the table. Un-stirred, the cigarette smoke has settled like a miniature layer of clouds above our heads. Any minute now, the tiny storm fronts, lit blue by the TV, will turn sour and rain droplets of tar and nicotine.

He holds the Dubroff bottle up to the light from the TV.

"Nearly there," he says.

It's gone past two a.m. by the time we run out of vodka. Nodar drains his glass and looks at it. There's about a sip left. He shudders and pours it onto his plate. He struggles to his feet and points at me.

"Don't think the past holds no sway over the future. Tomorrow's hangover is proof of today's sins."

With that slurred philosophy, he's gone. There's an irate exchange of words as he stumbles into his bedroom and wakes Ketino, then silence descends on the house.

It's just me and the TV now. I fumble for the off switch—I press every button but the one I want. In the end I just pull the plug out of the wall and stagger to my little bedroom. Barely taking my shoes off, I roll into bed, safe in the knowledge that I'm drunk enough to sleep a dreamless sleep.

But no, I get no rest.

"WAKE UP," a haunted little voice says.

Nino—my sister by all measures but blood. She drags me out of bed.

"I told you I'd come find you where you sleep. This way, mummy's boy."

"What about Sandro?"

"This is between you and me."

I follow her voice through a cold, candlelit Tbilisi. Time flows un-evenly, poured by an unsteady hand. It surges forward, barely controlled, then freezes.

We're standing at the yawning mouth of a tunnel carved right into the

Sololaki hillside. The dark entrance is breathing in slow, fetid breaths. Fragrant Tbilisi air is inhaled and corrupted by whatever the Soviets buried here. Cold, wronged air is exhaled like the breath of the drowned dead.

On the other side of the tunnel, the botanical garden waits for us like a predator. Nino speaks in a voice paused in childhood.

"Heads, we go in. Tails, we don't."

I look over my shoulder. "Let's wait for Eka."

"You're such a mummy's boy."

"No I'm not."

"It's heads. We go."

The tunnel entrance inhales us into a clammy darkness—no sound but the dripping of foul water from a ceiling we can't see.

"This way, mummy's boy."

Nino's voice leads me through this darkness too. The brave, impish sound of it echoes around this deathly place. It promises to lead me through many more darknesses. I know the promise to be a lie. But a debt is owed. So, I'll follow. Always and into any darkness.

Time rushes forward again. We're in the deserted, unkempt forest of the botanical garden. Off the beaten path and willingly lost, we walk among the trees, ankle-deep in autumn leaves.

Always just me and her in this place. Me forever chasing her elfin frame. That ratty hand-me-down dress she always wears. Charred hole on the back matching the hole on the front.

"Hey, wait." I'm always struggling to keep up.

Faint, worried voices call our names, maybe Eka's, maybe Sandro's—so distant that I can't tell. Nino pulls me in deeper. She's in charge now.

"Don't worry, they'll never find us," she says.

"Don't we want them to?"

"No."

The forest is dense. So easy to get lost here. The undulations of the ground beneath your feet tempt you from your path. A sly degree or two here, a few steps astray there and soon the only thing you'll find is Baba Yaga's hut. All the sinuous paths of this forest lead to her. I hear twigs snap somewhere out of sight and the low vibration of a growl. Wolves.

"We have to go back," I say.

The forest snuffs out my words inches from my mouth.

"Too late, mummy's boy. Baba Yaga knows we're here."

"I want to wake up."

"Not yet," she says. "First, I'll teach you."

"Teach me what?"

She turns and glares, her eyes mismatched, green and blue. Stops me in my tracks.

"Flip the coin."

"Why?"

"You know why."

"No, I won't do it."

"Heads you die. Tails I die."

"I won't do it."

"Flip the coin, Saba. Or I'll come find you when you wake."

"Jesus, fuck."

My eyes snap open. For an awful moment, I'm convinced I'm about to feel Nino's breath on the nape of my neck. The momentum of that fear makes me get up and take a few steps away from the bed. Nino's was the last voice I silenced, and she put up a fight.

The inevitable physical realities begin to kick in. My head's pounding from all the vodka last night. My mouth tastes like badger shit. I've sweated through my T-shirt. The hangover's really taking hold. Nino was a dream, but still, I get away from the bedroom as soon as I can.

I find Nodar slouched in his usual spot in the living room. He gives a racking cough as I enter and raises his hand.

"You look terrible, Nodar."

With disgust, he nudges away the cigarette box he was contemplating. He smiles a little.

"You look like warmed-up shit, brother."

Ketino comes into the room with a steaming bowl in one hand. She runs her fingers through Nodar's thinning hair and gives him a swift upside-the-head tap. He groans. She puts the bowl in front of him. Then she looks at me.

"You want one too?" she says.

Seeing my shipwrecked, hopeful face, she turns away before her frown can crumble into a smile.

"I'll get you a bowl. Fix two idiots in one."

The bowl is the same gruel from the day before. But some secret ingredient has made it more fragrant—it smells like salvation. Nodar starts to spoon it into his mouth. I swear, with each mouthful his back straightens and color returns to his face. By the time my bowl arrives, he's leaning back in his chair, tapping an unlit cigarette on the table.

"You look like a sheet of paper. Here, eat," Ketino says.

I start shoveling. Nodar watches me go through the same transformation I just witnessed.

"I warned you about her cooking."

I manage a smile.

"What is this stuff?"

Nodar shrugs. "If we knew, it wouldn't work," he says and finally lights his cigarette.

It's already well past midday, but we sit and ponder this disaster narrowly avoided until Nodar goes to work. He can't babysit me today. I leave the house shortly after he does. On the way out, I stop in the kitchen, where Ketino's making tea.

"Thank you," I say.

Honestly, it's the most heartfelt thing I've ever said.

. . .

ON THE STREET, the heat envelops me. I can feel it press against my skin. I follow the distant car horn squawks until I find the main road and flag down a small navy Fiat with the word *Taxi* written on the door in whitewash paint.

"Sololaki, please. Botanical garden."

"Sure, friend" comes the reply.

During the drive, I try to talk myself out of going into the botanical garden. Abandoned for years, it has probably grown into the great forest we wished it to be when we were kids. There's nothing in there for me but heartache. But how can I not check? Sandro left something there for me. A key to this puzzle.

"This is it," the taxi driver says, far too soon. "I can't go up this janky road. Nowhere to turn around up there and I don't got reverse."

I pay him, get out, and find myself looking right at Sandro's graffiti.

"Hard by a great forest dwelt a poor woodcutter—"

Hi, Sandro.

I take the disheveled road toward the botanical garden. The heat shimmer rising from the baked cobblestones makes Tbilisi waver and tremble like a mirage. By the time I get to the garden gate, I'm sweating pure, triple-distilled Dubroff. Mr. Monobrow sits in the booth by the gate as though he never left. He fans himself with a folded newspaper.

"One lari, friend."

I pay and he unhooks the gate for me. Before he lets me in, he pauses.

"Hope you know your way, pal," he says. "I'm not coming looking for you."

I face the chaotic forest this place has become. I brace myself. OK, Mohammed, one foot in front of the other. I crunch my way up the dry, rocky path, kicking up dust with each step. This is the main path through the garden that runs south to north.

On a hot summer day, this walk is a sweaty pilgrimage to a cool waterfall at the other end of the garden. Daydreaming of this place all the way from London, Sandro used to say that waterfall was the first place he'd go if he ever came back—to cool his feet, just like he told the old woman. The waterfall's the likeliest place to look for clues.

Nino, Sandro, and I used to come in through the only other entrance, at the north end of the garden. That was the unofficial entrance for those willing to brave a walk through the abandoned Soviet bomb shelter, which is nestled deep in the guts of the hill beneath the Mother of Georgia.

Two tunnels connecting the shelter to the outside world served as a creepy subterranean shortcut from Sololaki into the garden. The shelter and its tunnels were poured from coarse, watered-down concrete. All the lights had long blown out in some forgotten cold-war crisis. The ceiling had sprung a million leaks. Sometimes a fat rusty droplet would land on you in the dark and make you hop forward a few panicked steps.

No matter how hot it was outside, the bomb shelter was always cold. Every time I went in and the daylight behind me disappeared, I got this urge to aim myself toward the light at the other end and *run*. Even if I didn't run, my steps always sped up, unprompted.

Along the sides of the main tunnel, dark mouths of adjoining rooms were just visible. No one I knew was brave enough to explore these. No one but Nino. She would stroll right up to those nightmare doorways and vanish into the inky darkness so suddenly that it would make my throat catch. I'd hold my breath until I could see her again.

Nino was fearless. She occasionally suffered from fits of reason and calm. I loved her. Nino and I were born two days apart. She was Lali's daughter, and Lali was Eka's closest friend. Like our mothers before us, we grew up together in this garden.

Somewhere in the tunnel we'd cross an invisible line that erased the outside world. No more books, no more pencils, no more manners and please and thank you, no more Sololaki. We would charge into the garden—two yelping, dusty-foot savages—minds on fire with a hundred games to play.

Sandro was ever our chaperone, our supervisor; always so proud of being two whole years older than us kids. For Sandro, the garden was just somewhere pleasant to sit, read, and dive into worlds built by other people. But Nino and I built our own unhinged world with every visit. This garden belonged to us both then. Now it belongs to her alone. . . .

Nino's the reason we left Georgia. If you trace everything back to its bitter little beginning, you'll find Nino sitting there at the epicenter—barefoot, cross-legged, and looking like she knows something you don't. After last night's dream, I put her out of my mind and hope she stays out. Her unruly ickle voice was the hardest to silence for a reason.

It's at least an hour walk to the waterfall. About halfway, the trees crowd in over me and dim the daylight to twilight. The path under my feet fades and then disappears completely. I walk a long time hoping for it to reappear. Surik's voice pipes up.

"*Stop, Gretel, stop. The captain of your brain ship is asleep at the wheel.*"

"*What?*"

"*Look around. You've lost the path. This is how people get lost in forests. Go back.*"

I retrace my steps, but the path behind me has vanished too.

"*Surik, help me.*"

There's a long pause. Too long. Something's not right. Surik's voice is gone. Someone else says his words—the exact words he said to me at the airport.

"*You don't need help, Saba. Pull the dry thumb out your arse, get moving. Don't matter which way. Any way is good. The rest is momentum.*"

It's Nino. Last night was just a dream, but now there's no buffer between my skin and her razor-blade voice. It makes me freeze. My feet stop of their own accord. She laughs and imitates Surik's low, booming tone. The hairs on my arms and neck stand on end.

"It's you."

"Who'd you expect, Father fuckin' Christmas?"

Surik's words again.

"Where's Surik?"

"It's my turn now."

"I've got to find the path," I say and try to walk away from the voice in my head.

"Have a little faith. This way."

Through the clamor of alarm bells, I hear myself say—

"OK, Nino, I'll follow."

Soon the path melts into view.

"You should trust me a little more."

The ground begins to climb at an odd angle.

"Where are we going?"

"Just trust me."

The path opens onto a bright clearing, gritty in the dusty afternoon sun. I recognize it now. This used to be the exotic flower exhibit—a neat, paved area centered around a miniature lily pad pond. No exotic flowers grow here anymore. Weeds have cracked clean through the paving. The infamous pond itself has dried out. Its insides are filthy with dry algae, rotting in the heat.

"You knew this is where the path led," I say.

"How did you not?"

This is where Nino took a surprise swim the year we were seven. She thought she was light enough to walk on the lily pads. She fell in and flailed like a madman, drowning and screaming, until she realized the pond was only waist-deep. She walked out of the water like a pint-size swamp monster, sodden and covered in stringy green algae. She couldn't get it off no matter what she did and I popped a hernia laughing.

"*I smelled like frog for days.*"

"*I know, it was great.*"

I walk a wary curve around the pond and rejoin the main garden path to the bomb shelter.

"*Wrong way, silly.*"

"*I need to get to the waterfall.*"

"*You never want to play.*"

"*Play? How many times have you tried to kill me?*"

That shuts her up. I'm nearly at the waterfall now. A sharp hill covered in cracked, overgrown tarmac leads down to the bomb shelter entrance. This is where I took a tumble down the hill on my roller skates. Back then, the tarmac was nasty and coarse like sandpaper. It ripped gigantic portions of skin off my palms, knees, and elbows.

By the time Nino found me, I'd managed to stand up. I dripped blood all over myself and her little Soviet sandals. She looked so grown-up in that moment, like my big sister, coming to my rescue. That was the real Nino.

She made me take off my skates and put an arm around my shoulder. The whole way home, she wouldn't let me cry.

I reach the tunnel entrance sweating and bowed by the sun. The waterfall's nearby, but first I want to spend a few minutes in the deep darkness of the tunnel—the chill in there would be amazing. But when I get to the entrance, there's nothing. It's been bricked up and slathered in concrete. Like the tunnel never existed. I stand and gape at the wall like an idiot.

"*But how will I get home?*" Nino says.

For a confusing second it feels like someone's bricked up my only way out.

"*You don't live there anymore, Nino.*"

I shake my head clear. This is a good thing. After what happened at Nino's house, I never want to see that place again. I guess I'll tell you about that night. Nino won't interrupt this story. It's her favorite.

LIFE IN TBILISI was already on shaky ground when Georgia broke away from the Soviet Union in 1991. Decapitated, the government staggered on for a few months on momentum alone. It was a losing game. A question of when, not if.

When the old Soviet resources inevitably ran dry, Tbilisi streets filled with confused, hungry people. Furious, they converged on the parliament building, demanding luxuries like food, gas, water, and electricity. The government had nothing left to give. When that became apparent, the people tried to storm the parliament to oust the president.

"Oust" would have meant an "accidental" death for the president. Either that or a "suicide." So, he called in those parts of the army still loyal to him. In response, the protesters armed themselves and a scruffy, ill-equipped civil war kicked off right on our doorstep—our house was a ten-minute walk from the parliament building.

Nino and Lali's flat was nestled in a cluster of houses that had sprouted, sunless and mushroomlike, in the shadow of the Soviet bomb shelter. It was as remote as you could get in Sololaki.

When the distant gunfire started, Eka dragged Sandro and me over to Nino and Lali's thinking we'd be a little safer there. The sun had only just dipped behind the hill when the geniuses cut the power and the phone lines. The whole of Sololaki plunged into darkness.

Out came the old kerosene lamp. Nino, Lali, Eka, and I played cards in the grubby orange light. Sandro was tucked away in the little back bedroom, reading by candlelight. Eka had given him some great tome of a book—something about magic rings, dwarves, dark lords, and wizards. He wouldn't let it out of his sight. Sandro was easy to manage that way. Give him a book, any book, and watch him go. Nino and I were a different story. Supervision was required.

The gunfire coming from the parliament square didn't seem real. It sounded harmless, like gunfire on TV in a nearby room. Every now and then, stray tracer rounds would light up the sky like sparks from a campfire.

"Get away from that window!" Lali and Eka shouted in chorus.

But Nino and I wanted to see the show. We even snuck out onto the balcony to watch. When we got caught, we received an alarming dressing-down. After that, we were confined to the living room sofa.

As the night went on, the fighting spread and the sound of gunfire no longer came from just one direction. It was like midnight on New Year's Eve—firecrackers, rockets, and cherry bombs going off in streets and yards we couldn't see, set off by people we didn't know. Only this was no celebration. Every so often, the gunfire would cannonade right down our street, rattle the windowpanes, and make us freeze mid-sentence.

I knew something bad was about to happen when I saw the kerosene lamp sputter. Nino and I stood by the sofa. The lamp flickered and went out. With no lights outside, the whole room went so dark that I thought I'd been blinded. In that instant, something made me shove Nino onto the sofa. I still don't know why I did it—I just know that I did.

A disjointed volley of nearby gunfire rattled my teeth and squeezed a whimper out of my throat. Singed, muzzle-flash-orange light strobed across the ceiling. I heard a low, angry whine of a bullet and the weak tinkle of glass breaking. A tiny gasp cut short.

"Saba, you OK?"

Eka grabbed hold of me. I squirmed to get away from her frantic grip, as her hands searched me for signs of injury.

"Nino, say something," Lali said in the dark.

Nino didn't reply. Eka scrambled through the room, knocking things over and cursing, until she found a candle she could light.

"Nino, say something."

Nino still wouldn't reply. She was quiet because a bullet had gone right through her chest and ribs to where she hid her heart from the world. She was quiet because she couldn't breathe, as she drenched the sofa in her blood. The bullet had gone through her like through butter. It even went through the sofa and bit an angry lump out of the wall.

"Nino, say something."

The commotion jolted Sandro out of Middle-earth and we heard him stumbling toward us down the dark, cluttered corridor. Lali's voice rose. Nino wasn't going to say a thing. But Lali couldn't stop.

"Nino, say something."

No updates from Nino. Lali hugged her, shook her by the shoulders. Nino's head flopped back and forth, lifeless. Seeing her own hands slick with blood made Lali let go. Nino slumped back into her seat.

"Nino, say something!"

Lali's voice climbed in pitch. Like an incantation gone wrong, the words spiraled and concatenated until they were nothing but a repulsive, repeating wail I can never scrub from memory.

So, what do you do if someone you love gets shot through the chest in a city mid–civil war? The streets are full of armed men—safety off, palms clammy, and nerves jangling. They're jumpy and likely to flail round and shoot anything that might shoot them first. There's no ambulances to call, not even a dial tone in the phone—just a crackling silence. So, what do you do?

Nothing. Nothing is what you do. What does it matter anyway? Even I could tell that what happened to Nino couldn't be fixed. I stood there a long time and stared at the charred hole on the front of her ratty dress. I saw her eyes, wide open and connected to nothing. I wanted to know what the lamp going out had to do with the bullet. I wanted to know if I'd shoved Nino into its path. Those things seemed so clearly related.

It's OK, that was a long time ago. I've dealt with it. Digested it. I know that there's an explanation, a reason it happened. Maybe it happened because a balding, rotund, middle-aged man wanted to be "in charge of things" for a few days longer. Or maybe it happened because I pushed her. But reasons are cold things that give no *meaning*. For years, I tried to pin *meaning* to Nino's death. Now I know better.

But if I'm really honest, I'm angry because I can't picture her face anymore. She's gone. All that's left is this ugly counterfeit voice in my head. The little push I gave her that night is forever our secret.

THAT WAS IT. That was the epicenter. Ground Nino. After that night, Eka watched the controlled demolition of her best friend—the meager wake, the half-size pine coffin, the hasty funeral, the flowers pilfered from Tbilisi parks, the empty platitudes. I guess that's when Eka and Irakli decided we had to get out.

"You don't remember my face?"

"I'm sorry."

"I'm never talking to you again."

I walk away from the bricked-up tunnel. I know every little detail between here and the waterfall. First, cross the narrow concrete bridge without handrails. No matter what's chasing you, cross it dead center, slow and steady. Then turn off the path by the lanky, bedraggled fir tree. At first, you'll think you picked the wrong tree, but walk on and you'll find a dusty crooked trail. Follow that trail along the burbling river you can hear but not yet see.

You will soon find yourself at the Sololaki Bowl. Over centuries, the brackish green waterfall chipped an amphitheater out of the hard, dark granite. That's where the trail ends. Take a moment. Feel the cool, fragrant water spray on your skin. Now find the ugly steps someone gnashed into the smooth rock. Ignore the steps, everyone does—they're too slippery. Find a dry path down to the water. Watch your feet.

I retrace the journey Sandro, Nino, and I took countless times, only to find that nothing's changed. For once, everything's where it should be. Though the waterfall's deserted. On a hot day like today, it should be packed with neighborhood folk desperate to cool down. But with the whole cast of the Communist Jungle Book on the loose, no one wants to be here but me.

It doesn't take long to spot Sandro's clue. Scrawled on a flat section of granite, there's a large yellow graffiti.

> *The hurt can't be much, but it's enough*
> *Ask for me tomorrow . . .*
>
> —*Valiko Shakespeare*

Valiko, that familiar name. The myth of Valiko in the flesh. The name Sandro and I stole from Irakli's play.

Our motherless dialect wasn't sophisticated. It didn't brag or have a large vocabulary. It operated on a level lower, deeper than mere words from a dictionary. It held up where language failed.

Here's Sandro's clue scrawled across a piece of rock. It's not hard, brother, you'll get it—that's what Sandro would have said. Smiling against my will, I curse his name. I can feel his careful, meticulous touch. But this isn't just a game to pass the time until Irakli's home.

The *Kaleidoskupi* pages and this graffiti are two halves of the first clue. Sandro knew Irakli's flat would be my first stop—his final email made sure of that. The Hansel and Gretel graffiti and the pages he left with the old woman made damn sure this would be my next stop.

What's he trying to tell me with this Shakespeare clue?

I worry for Sandro—why is he being so cautious? I worry about what disaster has made him talk to me in a language we haven't used since we were kids. I sit down by the stream, take my shoes off, and dip my feet, just like Sandro would have. The cold water makes me shudder.

During our summers in Tbilisi, before the civil war wrecked that old life, this was our routine: run through the tunnel, run along the river, already barefoot, over baking-hot rocks, get to the water, dip our feet, and sigh in relief. We'd watch tiny people scurry across the old wooden bridge at the top of the waterfall. Nino and I would wave at them. Sandro disapproved. Even back then, the bridge creaked warnings when you stepped on it. By some unintended engineering miracle, it's still there.

Once, a neighborhood kid fell from the rocks by the bridge. He spotted a cactus flower—those were the rarest find. So, he leaned out to pluck it, to show off for his girl. He leaned out a touch too far, the shale rock crumbled under him, and he fell. He narrowly missed the deep pool that would have saved his life and landed in an inch of water.

I was horrified. Not because of the brutal, spiny rocks down here that mangled the boy. Not because they never quite cleaned up all the blood and gristly jam gobbets he left behind. No, what was scarier was that someone could just die like that. No heroics. No meaning. Just shit luck. He didn't even get the flower.

Our world at the time was Eka's books, Brothers Grimm stories, and the odd Disney cartoon that slipped through the Soviet net. In that world, no one died without some heroic purpose. Some *fanfare*. This poor kid splattered on the rocks. His death had no meaning and I found that terrifying. I still do.

I try to wrestle my mind back to the Valiko Shakespeare graffiti and how it ties to the *Kaleidoskupi* pages. I try to think like Sandro—logic fed on Scooby-Doo, odd fairy tales, William fucking Shakespeare, and a thousand other books he digested and I didn't. But it's no good. Every time I try, my mind finds Nino.

When I silenced Nino's voice all those years ago, I banished that scene at Lali's house too. But Nino's back and so is that memory. I have no choice but to relive it. Without me, the scene doesn't work—Nino doesn't die. So, you see, I have to be there.

I let the memory play. I watch the mad scramble to resurrect a dead girl with kitchen towel bandages and expired aspirin from Lali's ancient first aid kit. Eka and I run up and down the building stairwells by candlelight. We knock on all the doors hoping for bandages, medicine, a doctor, a nurse, a vet, anything. Terrified faces tell us to go away from behind doors opened only as far as the chain allows.

No matter where we go, Lali's hysterical wail follows us.

"Nino, say something!"

It echoes through the whole building, amphoric and indelible.

When the scene's over, I find myself still sitting by the waterfall. The low sun throws a leaf camouflage of shade on the ground around me. The cold stream tugs at my feet. In this familiar place, my eyes fill up with tears. I wipe them away, but they keep coming. Finally, I give up and let this play out too. I cry for Nino's sake and mine.

I DON'T KNOW HOW LONG I've sat here blubbering, but when I look up the sun's gone. It's getting dark. I pull my feet out of the water and shove them, still wet, into my shoes. The way back to the bricked-up tunnel entrance is not so familiar anymore. The gaps among the trees have filled up with murk and I can't tell the leaves from their shadows.

I stumble and trip my way back. I give the bricked-up tunnel a last look.

"Saba, don't go."

Nino's voice has a sinister edge.

"Stay here, talk to me."

"I have to go, Nino. It's dangerous here."

As I hurry down the path toward the exit, I snap my head to any little noise I hear in the gathering dark. Nino isn't helping.

"What was that?" she shrills at every sound.

Even the smell of this place has shifted. The sun-warmed scent of fir tree bark, moss, and shed pine needles cools to a tangy edge of imminent danger. Every breath brings me closer to the tipping point where I'll give up the pretense and bolt. That unnerving urge to run I'd get in the bomb shelter tunnel tugs at my sleeve.

But the option to run disappears within minutes. Shielded from the city lights, this place gets dark like the flick of a switch. The path beneath my feet is more imaginary than anything I can actually see. Pretty soon I'm walking like a blind man robbed of his cane—arms out, outstretched fingers flinching from sharp encounters with invisible branches and tree trunks.

The whole time, as I shuffle my way to the distant exit, I'm waiting for it. I'm waiting for that thing that will turn my insides liquid. I know it's near. I can't stand the wait. When it finally happens, it's almost a relief—behind and off to my left, I hear a twig snap and the unmistakable sound of something moving in the darkness. I jerk my head toward the sound and see the sum total of fuck-all.

"It's nothing. Don't worry," Nino whispers.

"Someone's there."

"Not someone . . ."

I stop to look around—the dumbest thing you could do.

"Only joking, silly."

My insides seize up just like they did in front of Nino that night. I can't move.

"It's just the forest, muttering itself to sleep."

"Nino, let me go."

There's more rustling over to my right. There's two of them, whatever they are.

"If you don't let me go, I'll die here."

"You pushed me."

"I was trying to keep you safe."

"How'd that turn out?"

I beg for the spell to break. I beg to be released. Jesus, fuck, please. Nino, let me go. I manage a small step forward.

"Don't you want to talk to me anymore?"

I force myself to take a few more steps. That's when I hear a low, rumbling growl in the darkness behind me. I turn to see an outline one shade lighter than the night materialize a few feet from me. It's the shape of a large dog. With the idling growl still vibrating the air, the shape lowers itself to the ground.

"Nice doggie. What's your name?"

That's no dog and that growl was a warning—move again and we have a problem. But that's it for me. That's what breaks Nino's spell. I take a ragged breath and run headlong into the dark, along where I think the path should be.

"Wrong way, silly! You'll never get out that way!" Nino screams as I run.

Between the sound of my breath, the sound of my feet, and Nino's shrill voice, I can't hear anything behind me. Low branches slap me in the face and tear at my clothes as I crash through the forest, blind. I finally run out of breath and slow to a walk in a small clearing. It can't be far now.

"Saba, if you go, you'll kill me again." Nino says this so quietly that I almost stop.

I want to tell her I can't undo the things that happened. No one can. But as my breath slows I hear something behind me. I turn to face the sound. Two shapes emerge into the clearing. They've tracked my idiotic run through the forest effortlessly, silently. No more warning growls— this is a new game. They split up, trying to encircle me.

I take off at a sprint across the clearing and don't stop for anything. Over the next few minutes, I swear off anything I've ever had to do with Georgia.

Fuck this place.

Fuck Sandro.

Fuck Valiko too.

Fuck the cryptic clues and the gloomy graffiti.

Fuck Irakli and his shitty breadcrumb play.

Fuck Nodar and his shabby, balding life.

Fuck Ketino, fuck her cooking, and fuck her potted yogurt plants.

Run.

I'll keep going until I get the fuck out of here, get the fuck out of Tbilisi, and get the fuck out of this country.

I run a long time, while my heart pumps pure, cold fear through my veins. When the trees thin out, I catch sight of the gate. I see the faint glow of the city halo the hilltop. I look behind me and see nothing. I know I've made it, but I can't stop. I clamber over the gate and keep running until I reach the first of the Sololaki houses.

5

LOOK FOR ME TOMORROW . . .

Y ou fall off a moving train, brother?"

Nodar's in his usual spot at the head of the table. Ketino hovers by my elbow.

"It was probably just stray dogs," Nodar continues.

"In the botanical garden?" Ketino says.

"They're everywhere, Keti."

"They don't attack people."

I catch the tangy stink of Soviet-grade antiseptic and I know Ketino is coming at me with the zelyonka again.

"Stay still. Let me see your arm."

In addition to the dozens of scratches all over me, I gouged four angry gashes into my arm clambering over the garden gate during my great escape. Ketino has already been at the cuts with the green zelyonka, leaving my arm stinging in an odd polka dot pattern.

"It's fine, honestly."

She's frowning and holding a dripping ball of cotton, looking for a spot to dab.

"Keti, stop fussing," Nodar says.

She's not listening.

"Keti."

"OK, OK, fine," she says. "But if it gets infected . . ."

"It's fine, honestly, I'm OK."

Honestly, I'm not OK. But I've been parroting those words since I got back. I shouldn't have told them anything about what happened in the botanical garden. Instead, I told them everything—Sandro's clue, the waterfall graffiti, my idiotic escape.

They must think I'm a prize idiot. I'm dying to get away. I just want to be in that little bedroom. I want to be alone.

"Well, it definitely wasn't wolves or hyenas," Nodar says.

Ketino sighs. "Fine, Nodar, why are you so sure?"

She turns on Nodar as though she's about to slather him with zelyonka too.

"You'd need a lot more zelyonka."

Ketino shakes her head and walks away. I can tell by the shape of her shoulders that Nodar's finally cracked her and made her laugh.

"So, Mowgli, does it hurt?"

He's on a roll.

"Doesn't that make you Baloo?"

He laughs.

"Nodar, it's late." Ketino's voice carries from the bedroom.

"OK, OK. Coming."

He slaps his hands on his thighs and gets up with a groan.

"Nodar, leave the man be. It's late."

"OK, alright, Nurse Keti. I'm coming."

He rolls his eyes and winks.

"Stay in the human village from now on, understand?"

At last, I collapse onto Natia's bed and close my eyes. All I want is sleep. The kind you remember nothing of. I want to switch it all off. But that switch isn't wired to anything. I lie awake, orbited by the things that happened since my glorious repatriation. I can't make any sense of them. They whip by so fast that I can't get hold of them.

Irakli told us about his planned pilgrimage, seeding Tbilisi with pages from his play. His strange breadcrumbs. Where else has he planted those pages?

I can't connect one thing to the next. I think about the blue-green, glaucoma-stained eyes of the old woman and the way she sliced the tomato in her hands. Just like Grandma Lena.

I think about Nino in my dream and how she turned to glare at me. Again, I try and fail to remember her real face. All I can picture is mismatched blue and green eyes.

I think about that first stutter of the kerosene lamp. Nino's tiny gasp in the dark. Lali's runaway mantra.

Then I come to the surprise wall where there should have been a tunnel entrance.

I try parsing Sandro's clue—"The hurt can't be much, but it's enough. Ask for me tomorrow . . ."

Nothing about it points to the next step in the scavenger hunt. There's no link to the *Kaleidoskupi* pages. They're all about Irakli's mother, Marina. But she was long dead before Irakli even met Eka. All I remember about Marina is our visits to her faded little grave.

My stomach sinks. When I failed to understand Sandro's hunts in childhood, I'd just give up and cheat. I'd search all the obvious places.

I've been to the police. I've been to Irakli's flat. Where else? What is it they say about missing persons?

My phone's no help. I glare at a list of possibilities some jackass posted on the embassy website.

What could cause a person to go missing? Top-ranked
possibilities:
Fell into a well.
Fell into quicksand.
Fell into the crater of an active volcano.
Buried by an avalanche.
Swept into the ocean by a tsunami.
Eaten by a tiger.
Caught by Baba Yaga.
Or! Over 50% of missing persons are found
incapacitated in hospitals . . .

Cold, cold, cold. Colder by the minute, Sandro would say when he caught me cheating like this.

I can't focus.

My mind's running headlong down the vanishing path through the botanical garden. Running from a darkness that has grown teeth. Running from the new cruelty in Nino's voice. Parting words frosted with malice.

"Saba, if you go, you'll kill me again."

I give up on sleep and decide to wait for the morning to come. I cling to the 50 percent idea—by that theory, tomorrow I'll find either Irakli or Sandro incapacitated in a hospital.

"Check your math, Bublik," Surik warns, but I ignore him.

When the sky brightens above the broadcast tower, it feels like I've weathered a crisis. I feel better for not sweating through an alcoholic coma like the night before. The day ahead doesn't seem so bad. I think I'm going to be OK. I think I'll be fine.

I'M WOKEN BY VOICES in the yard and a car horn blaring somewhere out of sight. My body betrayed me. Once again, it's well past midday. I'm more tired than I was before I fell asleep. Outside, another barely supervised bedlam of a Tbilisi day is already in full swing.

I force my creaking, groaning body out of bed. Mohammed must go to the mountain. I find Nodar in the living room, watching TV with a mug of coffee in hand.

"Morning."

"I don't know how you do things in the jungle, Mowgli, but after midday it's afternoon."

He's watching footage of a trio of panic-stricken Somali ostriches on the Tbilisi orbital motorway. Fueled by sheer terror, they gallop right through the heavy midday traffic. They're so fast they're overtaking cars, weaving between them at reckless speeds.

When the ostriches stray into oncoming traffic a new level of chaos breaks out. In the face of the suicidal flock of giant birds, the cars lose their minds. They slam on their brakes and swerve across lanes. The ostriches launch headlong into this new pandemonium without hesitation.

The leading ostrich gets clipped by a van. The impact rag-dolls the bird instantly. It tumbles on the hard tarmac, boneless, leaving a trail of feathers. The other two don't even look back.

"Fuckin' overgrown turkeys. Two brain cells. One says 'eat,' the other says 'run.'"

Nodar pretends the miserable, twitching lump of feathers on-screen doesn't bother him. The helicopter camera zooms in for a trembling close-up. The bird tries to stand. A couple of disjointed steps on broken legs overwhelm the animal. It collapses and doesn't try to stand again. It lies there, neck craned, spasmodically stirring up dust with its wing. Nodar clicks off the TV.

"I oughta burn down that TV station and piss on the mess."

The remote clatters onto the table from a height.

"Nodar, I was thinking about hospitals. . . ."

"I thought you said they were just scratches, Mowgli?"

I glance at my green-polka-dot arm and almost smile.

"No, I mean we should check for any record of Irakli or Sandro."

Nodar's eyebrows come up.

"Look at you, Dr. Watson." Nodar assigns me a new nickname.

"So, you're Sherlock?"

Nodar spreads his arms wide as if to say—of course, can't you tell?

"They say it's one of the first things you should check when looking for a missing person."

"Who's 'they'?"

"Google."

He glances at me sidelong. "OK, maybe not quite Dr. Watson. But it'll do."

THE SOLOLAKI HOSPITAL overlooks the Mtkvari river. It's a coarse concrete block that looks unsteady on its feet, a hallmark of the corner-cut Soviet architecture. It gives the impression that it's leaning over the water. A strong gust of wind might topple it into the silty, cardboard-colored Mtkvari.

The grandiose hospital entrance is like a theater stage set. It's all glass and polished chrome coruscating in the sun, uneasy with its ancient surroundings. The adjacent buildings are typical Sololaki. Everything's old, exhausted, chipped, and cracked. Sharp corners rubbed smooth by centuries of touch. Grooves worn into hard stone by a billion footsteps.

The hospital entrance sits there like a fake diamond in the honest rough of Sololaki. All the signage is written out twice—in English and in Georgian.

"Why's everything in English?"

"We're pretending we're American, brother."

"Why?"

Nodar shrugs. "All I know is sticking feathers in your arse does *not* make you a chicken."

The hospital reception couldn't be more different from the entrance. Bare light bulbs hang under a lumpy ceiling covered in overlapping water stains. There's a bucket in the corner of the room, standing guard under the slow drip of some incurable leak. Nodar asks for the records department at the reception desk.

"Vai, vai, look at this place, Bublik. What a shitshow. The only thing they cure here is breathing."

I'm so glad to hear from Surik instead of Nino that I smile to myself.

"Seriously, Bublik. They try to put you in here, you run. We brought my mother in here, bless her ugly soul. Three weeks later, we planted her in Kukia. Anzor too. Went from here to Kukia in a month."

"You're back."

"Like a stubborn rash."

I almost laugh and draw an odd glance from Nodar.

"Everything where it should be, Dr. Watson?"

"Everything's OK," I say and I mean it. Surik's back.

"Did you know Uncle Surik built this place?"

"Don't lie."

"I'm not. We did the plumbing. Probably why it holds water like a colander."

The dull-eyed receptionist waves a spindly arm in a vague direction down the hall.

"Records. Down the hall, lift, fourth floor. Don't go wandering about."

Nodar leads us down a long corridor running the length of the hospital. The signs in this corridor are the crustacean-shaped Cyrillic leftovers from the Soviet days.

"You should have seen this place new, Bublik. A sparkling, polished Soviet turd—quietly rotting from the inside."

A cat hugs the wall as it slides past and eyes us intruders. Along the corridor, someone's growing herbs in large plastic containers.

"Lovely. Sluice tubs," Surik's voice says.

"Sluice tubs?"

"From the sluice room. You know, the room where they flush all the leftovers into the river."

"Leftovers?"

"The usual, Bublik. Medical waste, bedpans, blood, old organs, surgery fuckups, plasma, placentas . . ."

"Enough, Surik."

He chuckles.

"No stomach, you Westerners."

In the care units along this corridor, people have moved in wholesale. Entire families and their messy paraphernalia pack the rooms. Two, three families to a unit. The rooms are so crammed with TVs, kettles, makeshift beds, fridges, and domestic debris that you can't see the medical equipment. Relatives, kids, acquaintances, and family pets roam the corridors. As we walk past doorways, heads pop up from rusting steel-frame beds like sickly meerkats. They know we're strangers by the sound of our footsteps.

Up ahead, a skinny kid on a seatless bicycle oversteers around the corner wildly, doing some serious speed. The linoleum floor shrieks under the back wheel. The kid, he can't be more than ten, regains his balance and pedals straight toward us. Two smaller children, barefoot, chase him around the corner, yelping. The whole giggling, echoing ball of noise cannonades down the corridor. First Nodar and then the cat hop out of their way.

"Easy, boys," Nodar says, barely raising his voice.

I put my back to the wall too and watch them go. A woman in a faded kimono-style nightgown comes to her doorway and watches the kids disappear around another corner. She gives me a mournful look and shuts the door. Nodar nudges me.

"What's the matter, Dr. Watson—never been to a hospital?"

I have. I've been to this very hospital, in fact. I remember very clearly how I ended up here. But I don't exactly want to tell Nodar.

"Tell him. It can't hurt." Surik chuckles. *"He already thinks you're a motorized, four-wheel-drive moron."*

It happened when we were out in the country for the Christmas holidays. Lali had a small cottage in a village just outside Tbilisi. That's where we usually spent Christmas.

Grandma Lena took me out there a few days earlier. Eka, Lali, Nino, and Sandro were to follow the coming weekend. But then it snowed. It snowed in that Georgian, all-or-nothing way. The blizzard didn't relent until the village was an expanse of unblemished white, dirtied only by the occasional glimpse of a doorway someone had burrowed out.

Lena and I were stranded. The others (and the presents they were to bring) couldn't get to us, not until the roads got cleared. We couldn't leave the house and we couldn't go back to Tbilisi. I was bored to the point of lunacy.

Lali's cottage was three floors, if you included the attic. The blizzard completely blotted out the downstairs windows and made a basement of the ground floor. So, I went up to the first floor, then up into the attic, and found a window I could pry open.

I shouldn't have jumped. I knew that as I climbed onto the windowsill. But I was seven years old and invincible. The very next year, Nino taught me there's no such thing as invincible. But that Christmas, I didn't know yet. Plus, the snow was soft as a pillow—what could go wrong?

The problem was the snow was fresh and uncompressed—basically, mostly air. I went right through it and landed on the frozen mud underneath. The brutal impact of it articulated up my leg. First it scrambled the fine bone network in my foot, then my ankle. My right knee locked as I landed and snapped my shin like a toothpick. I remember the sound of it. A solitary wet snap, muffled by flesh, like popping a grape with your back teeth.

A new voice clears its throat, the way Grandma Lena always did. It was the soft sound that preceded many a time she caught me doing stupid shit I shouldn't have.

"Does it still hurt, Saba?"

A voice I haven't heard from in a decade. Grandma Lena. Lena, my army. Lena, who remembered all my victories and forgot all my mistakes. Lena, always on my side, no matter the details. Lena, who would lay her life down for mine. I always knew this, but not because she told me. It was implied in every gesture and every word. No one says my name like she does.

She always spoke to me like I was an adult. Not once did she call me by an affectionate name. That was just her way. Even when she found me buried in the snow with a shattered leg. No longer supported by tendons, my foot pointed off to the side at a sick angle. I almost threw up at the sight. Even then, especially then, I was just "Saba." All her worry confined to those two syllables.

"Lena?"

"I've had enough of that lout and his sluice talk."

I stop walking completely.

"You know how Surik is. I'm sorry."

"Don't be. Surik had a harder life than most will ever know."

Lena's was the first voice to quiet. Unlike Nino, she went willingly.

"So, does it still hurt?"

I was in this hospital for weeks, with a dozen stainless-steel spikes holding my shattered bones in place. To this day, if something startles me, those terrorized nerve endings in my leg set off a small firework of pain, like a tribute to a forgotten tragedy.

"Sometimes."

"Good," Lena says. *"Think twice next time."*

Lena didn't leave the hospital the entire time I was there. The nurses were nervous around her. She scolded them like wayward children. Despite her back bothering her as it did, she slept in a chair by my bed for three weeks.

"You never left the hospital the whole time. How did you do it?"

She sighs.

"The only way to find out if you can do something in life is to try. And hope you haven't taken on something bigger than you."

"What if I have?"

"Try. And you'll soon find out."

Her voice fades.

"Don't go yet."

"This is no place for me, Saba. I'm already gone."

Nodar waits for me at the end of the corridor. He looks back, tilts his head to one side.

"All good, brother?"

Lena's voice made me stop walking.

"Yeah. All good." I sound vague, like a woken sleepwalker.

Nodar smiles his rusty, wrinkled smile and his usual tone resumes. "Look at this death trap."

He points at the lift. No politely sliding doors here—the wall just opens onto the dark lift shaft, which reeks of machine oil and untreated steel. Nodar pokes his head in.

"Anybody up there?"

After a short silence the steel cables creak into motion, so taut they hum under the weight. Nodar puts a hand across my chest and we both step back.

"These fuckin' things make me nervous."

"Why?"

"I know who built them."

Surik chuckles in my head.

The lift arrives bearing a rotund woman on a stool, sat under a naked light bulb. She gives us a smile and a flourish, as though the lift was her personal magic trick.

"Where to?"

"Fourth floor, auntie," Nodar says.

She thumps the side of the lift so hard it makes me jump. The metallic sound echoes up the lift shaft. Someone from way up there yells down a "yeah."

"Four!" the woman bellows back.

The lift jolts into motion.

"The electrics don't work so good," she confides.

Three floors, all with doors missing, glide by serenely. At the fourth, the lift stops with a grinding clunk. I promise myself to take the stairs on the way back. After a haphazard search of the fourth floor, we finally find an unmarked door with a plain piece of paper pasted to it.

"Hospital Records"—the sign is handwritten.

"What's the matter?" Nodar says.

His eyes follow mine. On the adjacent wall someone has scratched words into the dirty green paint:

Getting colder by the minute.

—Valiko

Cold, cold, cold. I'm caught cheating.

I heard these words so often on Sandro's hunts in London. Impatient with his clues, I'd ransack our flat in all the obvious places. Debasing his game into a dumb Easter egg hunt, with the prize already guaranteed.

Cold, cold, cold—you're getting colder by the minute, Sandro would say, staying in character, while his eyes shone with disappointment.

Here I am, Sandro, a disappointment staring at a wall.

Nodar gives a low whistle. "Watson? Ideas?"

"This is the wrong place."

"Wrong place?"

"Sandro's been here. There's nothing to find. This isn't a clue—he's telling me I'm in the wrong place."

Nodar pauses and taps his temple.

"Yeah, but things might have changed since then, Watson."

He's already opened the door halfway before he knocks on it. The room's occupied by a sluggish man wearing thick glasses. He looks up from the book in his hands, eyebrows raised. Somewhere out of sight a radio gossips, tuned to Nodar's favorite station—"If You're Listening."

The man's desk has grown several paperwork towers, each crowned with an unfinished plate of food. He snaps off a grape from the bunch on his plate, pops it in his mouth, and stands up.

"I told them not to send you up," he says, still chewing. "Lazy bastards could have checked from down there."

Slightly bowlegged, he waddles out from behind his desk. He tries to usher us back out of the room, arms outstretched. Nodar ducks him like a boxer in a ring.

"I know, brother, I know. But since we're here, do us a kindness. Me and my slow nephew here are looking for someone."

Nodar takes out his wallet. Mollified by the sight, the man stops chasing him around the room. He retreats behind his rampart of paperwork and plates of unfinished food. On a modern, flat-screen monitor attached to a great clacking keyboard from the eighties, he starts to type.

"So, who's in trouble?"

"What?"

"I need a name to search, don't I?"

"Irakli Donauri."

He's far too fast—fat practiced fingers type as I say the words. He almost finishes before I do, before I can brace myself. I open my mouth to ask him to wait, just one second, please, let me gather myself. But he looks right at me and hits "enter."

Then he leans back and scans the screen. Now he takes his time, a sadist stretching a pause to the limit. He turns the monitor away from us.

"You understand I can't give this information to just anyone off the street." He glances at Nodar's wallet.

Nodar hands over a folded note.

"How about now, comrade?"

The man's expression trips over the word *comrade*, which Nodar says in Russian. But he swallows the small insult.

"No recent visits. Not a thing."

I exhale for the first time since we walked into this room. Nodar glances at me with concern. Then he turns to the fat man.

"You're a marvel of customer service. Try 'Sulidze-Donauri,' brother. First name, Sandro."

Things speed up again. This time, somehow, the man finishes typing before Nodar finishes talking. He thumbs "enter" from a height and everything slows to a syrup. I can't exhale until he lets things speed up again. But he's in no hurry, a smug expression on his face. He lets the silence hang suspended until Nodar shatters it like glass. Nodar moves at normal speed; he's not under the man's spell.

"You need better glasses, brother. What's it say?"

Reluctantly, the man relents.

"No recent visits to Sololaki hospital . . ."

I can breathe again.

"Like I said, they could have done this downstairs without—"

"What about other hospitals, not just Sololaki," I blurt out. Irakli's last words—"Maybe in the mountains I'll be safe"—come to me.

"Please, if you could, try those names in the other hospitals, comrade," Nodar says.

The records man is suddenly on his feet. "A national search needs police orders. What did you say your name was?"

He starts toward Nodar.

"Those folks, they've gone missing. Have a little heart, brother. Where are you from? You don't sound from Tbilisi."

This is Nodar's sales pitch.

"I'm from Gori."

"You work the land in Gori? You seem a winemaker to me."

"A little grape for my wine, you know, like everyone else."

He's falling under Nodar's dusty charm.

"Let's talk then, farmhand to farmhand. . . ."

Nodar turns to me. "Watson, listen, why don't you check on the car?" He winks and motions toward the door. "Go, Watson. Someone might steal my expensive car," he says.

Sandro's right, nothing to see here. At least he and Irakli are alive, and I can get away from that man's spell. I step into the hallway and hear Nodar take up his sales pitch again.

"Brother, forgive me for the 'comrade' stuff. Bad habit of mine. Listen, what's your name?"

I smoke cigarettes in the hospital parking lot and guard Nodar's shitbucket Volga. I try to recapture the calm Grandma Lena's voice brought me earlier. But Sandro's hurried graffiti itches away at me until there's nothing left of Lena's visit. Sandro was here and he found nothing. Which is what Nodar's now finding, no matter what sweet-talking he's doing.

I hear you, Sandro. Colder by the minute. I need to follow your trail, not just search the whole damn place in all the obvious spots.

NODAR EMERGES A solid half an hour later. He hurries toward me, and glances over his shoulder.

"Come on, Watson. Let's go."

We get in the car and make as hasty an exit as the Volga can stomach.

"What happened?"

"I got him to do the search."

"How?"

Nodar taps his nose with his forefinger. "Never mind that. Irakli and Sandro weren't admitted to any hospital in Georgia. I guess that's what you'd call the good-news section of the—"

"What's the bad news, Nodar?"

"Well, Sandro was here, asking for the same search."

"We knew that already."

"Alright, Dr. Watson. But did you know that your favorite detective also came by with a warrant?"

"A warrant for who?"

"Sandro."

Nodar glances at me. "I'm sorry, brother, Sandro's on the run now too."

"For what?"

Best he can offer is a shrug. Silence descends as I absorb the news. Nodar fills that silence with scattershot chat about the state of the roads in Tbilisi and the mental health of the Georgian president. The sun has set. In the gathering darkness, Tbilisi fades to a gray blur in my window.

"Keti, please make us something. I beg you. We're starving," Nodar says to Ketino as soon as we walk in. Forced cheer for my benefit. They exchange a few muttered words behind me.

"Saba," Ketino says after me. "Will you eat with us?"

"I'm not hungry."

"Saba," she says as I reach the bedroom door.

"Let him be, Keti."

I shut the door on them and sit on the bed a long time, thinking about Sandro.

What kind of trouble is he in? What did he do to piss off the police?

He's all alone and I'm still a disappointment, three steps behind, sulking in a pink room. When I decide to have a few cigarettes to distract myself, Anzor steps in.

"Focus, Sabo. Now's not the time for distractions."

He stops my lighter from working. Once again, it produces nothing but sparks.

"Cheap piece of shit."

I fling the lighter along with the cigarette and the whole cigarette box into the corner of the room.

"Sandro's on the run, Anzor. I can't focus."

"Think it through, Sabo. What could he possibly be in trouble for?"

"I don't know! Maybe he tried to kill someone too."

"You're smarter than that, Sabo. He comes to Tbilisi, searches Sololaki, the hospital records, the police—all the obvious places. He finds nothing, right?"

"Right."

"Then all of a sudden he goes quiet, stops emailing, and starts building you this trail out of Irakli's crumbs. Why?"

I finally make the connection. *"He's found Irakli!"* The thought makes me stand up and pace Natia's room. *"He wants to lead me to him, without the police following right along."*

"Slow and steady, Sabo—we got there in the end. Like we usually do. So, why would the police possibly want Sandro?"

"They want to know what he knows."

"Exactly. Forget the hospital records, forget Irakli's mountains, and all the obvious places any other half-wit would search too. Sandro's built you a trail for a reason—follow it."

"The play pages with Marina. The trail is something to do with her. Irakli's mother. Maybe something about mothers."

"Whatever you do, Sabo, watch for someone following you on this trail."

Here, at last, only a full day of stumbling later, the Shakespeare quote clicks into place. Sandro's a genius—I should have known.

A couple of years ahead of me at school, Sandro had *Romeo and Juliet* memorized by the time I got to read it. I didn't like it. Each sly line had to be read once, twice, three times, just to unpack what Shakespeare had packed in because he was feeling clever. It seemed a chore. Why read the same stupid love story three times over? Everything goes to shit and everyone still dies at the end.

It drove Sandro insane that I barely skimmed my school copy of *Romeo and Juliet*. He wouldn't stop hounding me about it. Maybe he thought it was an easy enough example for his dim brother to decode. Or maybe it was just dark enough to be his favorite quote. In any case, the Shakespeare for Idiots course by Sandro started with that quote from Mercutio:

"Ask for me tomorrow . . . and you shall find me a grave man." The words Sandro left out of his graffiti.

I remember how he walked me through it, step by step, all those years ago. Mercutio's fatal wound. His fury at an unfair, inevitable death. The word *grave* was the hinge to it all. It blew my mind, how much *feeling* could be crammed into one sentence.

I know where Sandro's trail goes now. The *Kaleidoskupi* pages point to Marina. The Shakespeare reference to the "grave" is the key that unlocks it all. I hear you, Sandro, I see you smile. I've cracked this one—next stop is the cemetery where Marina's buried.

I should feel better, now that I know where I'm headed. But I don't.

You're hunted for what you've found, Sandro. What if they catch you, brother? What then?

For the rest of the night, Anzor tries to calm me with more logic. But sometimes logic's no help at all.

6

ARTYOM

Next morning, it's too early to wake Nodar and demand that he take me to some long-forgotten church cemetery to find Irakli's mother's grave because that's where I think Sandro's oddball Shakespeare graffiti and the *Kaleidoskupi* pages point. I'd have to get him to stop laughing first.

I pace Natia's bedroom and vibrate with unspent excitement until I hear someone turn on the TV in the living room.

"Nodar, I've cracked it."

He moves slowly, limbs still sluggish with sleep. My outburst makes him wince. He rubs his eye with the heel of his palm.

"Brother, have you slept any?"

"No. A bit. Listen, Nodar, I figured it out."

"Alright, alright, give me a second, Dr. Watson."

Eventually, with a coffee and a cigarette in hand, Nodar listens as I try to explain the link between the *Kaleidoskupi* pages, the weird graffiti at the waterfall, and the church I need to find.

"The play pages tell me *who* to look for—Marina. She's in those pages, see? The graffiti, well, that's Sandro telling me *where* to find her. That's where the next clue is and—"

Nodar laughs.

"What?"

"Nothing, brother." He shakes his head. "No one else could ever figure that out. You and Sandro, you must be like this . . ."

He twines his index and middle fingers together. We were that close once, but that time is long gone. A distance neither of us will acknowledge keeps us apart now.

"You know where this church is, brother? There's hundreds in Tbilisi."

"It's in Vake. Irakli used to take us there—I'll know it when I see it," I say and will this to somehow be true.

Irakli lost Marina when he was a teenager. A chronic heart condition took her long before she could see him married with kids. Maybe he would take us to her grave to show her that he'd got his life in order—look at these boys, Ma, they're mine. Or maybe he just missed being near her.

I only faintly remember the first time we came. We entered the tiny graveyard through the meager church. I was perched on Irakli's shoulders, probably so that I didn't run off after some distraction. Meanwhile, Sandro strode alongside Irakli like an equal, asking pertinent questions:

"Why's there no names on the stones?"

Irakli looked down at him.

"The rain, Sandro. It washed the names off."

"The rain can't do that!"

"It can . . . if enough years go by."

"How many?"

"Many, many years."

Sandro nodded sagely, but then another thought occurred to him.

"Then how do you know which one's your ma?"

"I used to come here long before her name vanished."

That church, if it still stands, and that graveyard wait for me some-where in Vake. Nodar's excited, like a child promised sweets.

"We waiting for a sign from God? Let's go, Watson. We've got churches to search!"

He claps me on the back.

"OK, OK, just drop me off in Vake."

"Oh no, I'm coming with you this time. I let you go to the botanical garden alone and look at you now."

He points at my arm, still a fading green from Ketino's zelyonka. I see him grin and I realize just how lost I'd be without the dubious miracle that is Nodar. Without him I'd still be milling around at the airport, smoking unlit cigarettes, dodging panic attacks, and bracing myself for Tbilisi.

"Anyway, Keti says she feels something."

"Feels something?"

"She gets these premonitions."

"Premonitions."

"Laugh all you want, brother. She's right more often than not."

"What do you mean?"

"Once, for no reason that I understand, she woke Natia in the mid-dle of the night and pulled her out of bed. Had her sleep in ours in-stead."

"Why?"

"That's what I said. Sleeping next to them's like sleeping in a bed full of hot-water bottles."

His eyes grow distant and he smiles at the floor.

"Anyway, that night the ceiling in Natia's room collapsed. I swear to

God, lump of plaster *this* big landed right on her bed. Would have killed her dead."

He searches my face for a reaction.

"OK."

"OK? Brother, trust me, when Keti says *premonition*, you listen."

On our way out, we run into Mystic Keti in the kitchen.

"Keti, have the zelyonka ready."

Mystic Keti's not amused. She just stares Nodar down. But I can tell she's smiling, on the inside.

"Don't stand in the doorway," she says. "It's bad luck. Either come or go."

Nodar drives us into the heart of Vake—the affluent part of Tbilisi. The streets and houses clamber up Mtatsminda's incline, just like in Sololaki. But in Vake they do so with a dignified air. If you wanted to, you could walk from Sololaki into Vake. But it's a perilous journey. Sololaki wants to keep you lost in its maze and Vake isn't sure you're worthy.

They say there are ancient portals hidden along the ever-shifting border between the two districts, somewhere among the labyrinthine streets and alleys of Sololaki. These portals are the only way to cross from the lunacy of Sololaki to the quiet grace of Vake. They're well hidden, disguised as cul-de-sacs, blind alleys, and dead ends. If you find one, take a deep breath, step through, and hope for the best.

It could be a false portal, or a rigged one. There's a few of those around. Those will spit you back out still in Sololaki somewhere, baffled but unharmed. But step through a real portal and you'll feel Sololaki lose its grip on you. The streets will open up and the buildings will straighten their backs.

Nodar triggers a small chorus of irritated car horns as he parks on a main road.

"Can you park here?"

He looks from me to the Volga, blinking.

"I did, didn't I?"

"It's a main road. Won't you get a ticket?"

"Ticket?"

I don't trouble him any further with the concept of parking tickets.

"Never mind. Don't worry." I smile.

"You been gone too long, brother."

I like Vake better than Sololaki. I don't feel like I'm in a crumbling maze anymore. Mtatsminda isn't as punishing here. The houses are bigger and, for the most part, structurally sound. The streets are wide and straight and show promising signs of forethought and town planning. You can smell fresh sap on the evergreens that punctuate the streets.

As we walk up the hill, I'm waiting for that eerie homing instinct that found Irakli's house in Sololaki. But the instinct fails. I recognize nothing. I've no clue where I'm going. Nodar's conspicuously quiet.

Maybe I like Vake because I don't remember anything about it. Walking around Sololaki and the botanical garden, something in my chest was wound so tight it was ready to snap. Vake feels so different it's a relief. It could be another country entirely.

When Nodar has to replenish his dwindling stock of L&Ms, we walk into a small grocery shop. The shopkeeper's a thin woman with quick eyes and small, birdlike features. Her shop's a sauna. I count three fans pointed at the woman's chair.

The "If You're Listening" station chatters faintly from above, from some hidden speaker. I ask the woman for directions to a church with a graveyard, expecting a blank stare in return. Instead, her sharp eyes focus on me.

"Which one? There's a couple around here."

Realizing I won't have an answer for her anytime soon, she continues.

"There's the big ugly one they built. Gold roof and all." She shakes her head. "Then there's the tiny, ancient one that—"

"That one," I interrupt.

She raises an eyebrow at me. "That one burned down last year. Probably closed now, if it's still standing."

"Can you give us directions, auntie?" Nodar asks.

"Sure, it's not far. Second, no, third left up the hill. The church with scaffolding and . . . well, you'll see it." She winks.

When we find the building, the wink makes sense. The church is the last building on the street. It has its back to Mtatsminda. It's slumped forward, leaning alarmingly over the pavement beneath, and surrounded by a web of scaffolding on which it leans heavily for support. The older layers of scaffold have rusted and barely hold themselves together. The newer, more urgent layers groan and suffer visibly under the weight.

The Mtatsminda forest wants to reclaim the moribund church. The walls are thick with creeper plants. Tree branches inch into windows, into places people used to pray. Sly forest fingertips curl themselves into cracks and crevices, trying to get a good grip on their prey.

"That thing could let go any second," I say.

Nodar shrugs and glances up at the church.

"Good for at least ten years, Mowgli." Just like that, we're back in the Jungle Book.

The car by the church entrance is missing both front tires and is held high in the air by two car jacks. One of the jacks is shorter than the other. Someone wedged in a plank of wood to level the car. Rusty paint buckets sit beneath the engine block. Signs of good intentions lapsed.

Judging by the sun-leached paint job, the car's been here for years. Two cats, slowed to a loll by the heat, hide in the rusty shade under the car. This serene little scene's poised on the brink of disaster. Like so many things in Tbilisi.

When it happens, it'll happen in the night. The jacks will give out and the car will crush the cats. Either that or the church will finally defeat the scaffolding and throw itself giggling down the hill, taking the car and the cats with it.

Nodar sticks his head so far under the car that it makes me wince. The cats shoot him a hostile glance and disband. He studies the underside of the car. Pulling his head out, he tuts.

"What a waste."

Taking a hefty swing, Nodar thumps the side panel of the car and makes the whole tenuous construction shudder.

"Volga. A king among cars."

The gap-toothed marble flooring of the foyer leads to a single small door. In there is the church, and out the back is the cozy cemetery and Marina's grave. I put my hand on the door and stop. What if I'm wrong? What if this is just a dead end? Sandro and I have drifted apart since our childhood.

"What if Sandro and I have lost our language? Then what?" I ask.

I'm hoping for Anzor's voice and he doesn't disappoint. He never does.

"Don't be stupid, Sabo."

I can almost feel his hand on my back.

"If the mountain doesn't come to Mohammed . . ."

With those words, Anzor pushes the church door open with my hand.

The door gives, but the bottom grates across the uneven floor. The doorway exhales a huge whiff of stale, wet ash. I squeeze through the gap and find myself in a church hall that's been burned to cinders. Everything in sight is charred. Floorboards creak and snap under my feet. The smell's so strong that I have to put a hand to my face.

"Fuck your mother's sister's—" Nodar stops the swear short, looks up, and crosses himself.

"I'm sorry," he mumbles.

Who knows how long this place stood unstirred, digesting the same stale, singed air? That air slides into my lungs and makes me shudder.

The dead spider shape of a fallen chandelier lies on its back in the middle of the room. Some glass beads still cling to it and glint like uncut diamonds. The wooden beams of the ceiling have bellied toward the floor. The sunlight filtered through part-melted windows gives everything a charcoal sheen.

My eyes are drawn to the back of the church. A charred, warped door left ajar shows me a glimpse into the church cemetery. If Sandro left a clue here, that's where it will be.

The door creaks and closes behind me. The cemetery I remember from our visits with Irakli is now a riot of grass and stubborn weeds grown knee-high. The advancing Mtatsminda forest has flattened the back fence. There's maybe fifty graves in here, most of them crooked or toppled. They're gathered into family groups for comfort. I recognize the meager Donauri collection near the collapsed fence.

My eyes are drawn to a stone at the back of the group—that's Marina. I rush to search the ground around it. A toppled headstone of an unknown Donauri fails to completely hide the twinkle of a plastic folder. Excited, I pull it out. It's more *Kaleidoskupi* pages.

Our language holds, Sandro. Even now, years after we set it aside in favor of inattentive emails and belated birthday text messages. It still holds, brother.

I'm about to start reading when Nino's voice cuts the air. I freeze.

"Don't you want to see what's out there?" Nino's voice is oddly calm and careful not to betray something she knows and I don't.

With the *Kaleidoskupi* pages clutched to my chest like a shield, I stand up and look past the flattened fence into the forest. The underbrush grows darker the farther I look. Thick, vine-swaddled trees and their foliage merge into an impenetrable, murky-green darkness. Something in that darkness shifts as though I startled it. I peer into the trees, but you could hide Boris the Hippo in there and I wouldn't see him.

"Saba, go back." Anzor speaks in a strained voice. He tries to make me step back, but Nino's stronger. She holds me still.

I stare into the forest as though I'm trying to decipher one of those 3D pictures they used to print in TV guides.

"Bublik, step back. Right now." It's Surik. He speaks slow and even, like he's talking me down from a ledge.

I hear a low growl vibrate through the thick bushes.

"Saba, if you love me, step back." Even Eka speaks up.

At last, I see it. A pair of inhuman eyes, gold-leaf flecks trapped in amber, stare at me from the mass of green. An image materializes out of the puzzle. The shape of a Bengal tiger, standing stone-still among the trees. Hungry, sapient eyes stare unblinking from a huge, shaggy head. The fur on its snout is notched and pocked by years of abuse, from humans just like me. Only there's no fence between us now.

"Go on, 'Bublik.' He won't bite," Nino whispers and nudges me.

I hold out my hand and take a step toward the monster among the trees. Ears folded back, his yellow canines glinting wet, the tiger lowers himself closer to the ground. Poised to pounce.

"Say hello to Artyom, mummy's boy." Nino urges me forward.

I'll follow her, always and into any darkness. But Nodar disturbs this intimate little tableau. He shatters Nino's spell. I hear him step into the garden behind me.

"Mowgli, what are you—"

Artyom's eyes dart in Nodar's direction. He produces a bass growl that vibrates in my breastbone. I don't dare turn to look at Nodar. I can hear him edge toward me. Artyom widens his stance, weighs his options.

"Saba, step back. Slowly."

We're only a few steps from the church door, but those steps may as well be a full country mile. If we escape now, it's because Artyom lets us.

"Easy, easy," Nodar whispers as we back away.

Artyom's burnished eyes follow us until we slide back into the church. Nodar slams the door shut, leans his back on it, and exhales swear words I can't understand.

"Have you lost your last two marbles?"

"I froze."

He studies my face close.

"Were you walking *toward* him?"

"No," I lie.

He hands me a jittering cigarette after lighting his own.

"Keti and her fucking premonitions . . ."

"Do we call the police?"

A smile creeps onto Nodar's face. "What, so they can arrest Shere Khan back there?"

He appraises the door and gives it a shove.

"It'll hold. I need a minute."

He squats with his back to the door and wipes sweat from his brow.

"Let's give Artyom a chance to fuck off."

After a few minutes, something makes him smile again. "I think maybe Mowgli's a bad nickname for you, brother."

We smoke another cigarette by the rusting Volga out front. As far as Nodar's concerned, a good cigarette is the solution to any calamity.

"At least you found more pages."

Another semi-successful expedition. I have new *Kaleidoskupi* pages. Another crumb along Sandro's trail.

Are we nearly there, Sandro? Am I getting warmer, brother? Not sure how much more I can stomach.

We set off toward Nodar's own rusting Volga. A small crowd of people has congregated a little way down the hill, forming a chaotic circle around something at their feet. More people watch from their balconies, as though this is a pivotal moment in a play. Two men with rifles rush past us.

"Went up there, into the trees," the older of the two men says as they hurry past.

"What's going on, lads?" Nodar asks, and they ignore him.

Before we even get to the crowd, I know it can't be anything good. There's a pool of blood on the ground. Amazing how vivid a color it is, like someone knocked over a can of paint. Two cherry-red tendrils of blood spill down the hill in an unhurried race.

"Fuck your mother," Nodar mutters and rushes toward the crowd.

I don't remember which type of blood is bright like this, arterial or venous. Arterial, I think. Cut a big enough artery and you'll bleed dry in minutes. Your loyal heart will pump blindly no matter what leaks you've sprung.

The man on the ground is convulsing weakly, sloshing around in his own blood and urine. You only need one look at him to know he won't see this day turn to night. This is it for him. His eyes roll side to side, seeing some adjacent world no one else can. His feet scuffle spastically, looking for a foothold in that strange land.

A furious woman kneels by his side, her bare knees dipped in blood. Her arms are slathered red up to her elbows. She's two knuckles deep in the wound on the side of the man's throat. She flails her head around at the tentative crowd, which has already doubled in number.

"Don't just gawp! More bandages, you hear me? More bandages!"

Someone hands the woman a towel. While readjusting her grip, she loses hold of something inside the wound. Several juicy pulses of fresh blood escape. The man's skyward eyes widen at the sensation. Nodar looks away.

You can't tourniquet a throat wound. It's a death sentence. If you had it happen to you while you were disinfected, scrubbed, plugged in, and on an operating table—then maybe you'd have a fighting chance.

Amid all this blood and yelling, we stand and watch this man drain. His throat and jaw have been slashed open. Even though his mouth is closed, I can see the porcelain gleam of his back teeth through the missing flesh of his cheek.

"Saba." There's new wonder in Nodar's voice.

He grabs my shoulder and tugs. I force my eyes away from the bleeding man.

"Brother, tell me you see this."

He points to a ragged brick wall that looms over the crowd. We didn't see it on our way up to the church, but now you can't miss it.

On the wall, coolly observing the blood-spattered scene, is a large graffiti:

They work just the same,
but why are the slippers red?

—Tottenham proverb

While the graffiti is the same mustard yellow as the others, the word *red* is the same cherry-red color as the blood creeping down the hill. I can't take my eyes off it. Nodar crosses himself beside me.

Hi, Sandro. This one I get. This one's easy.

I remember it so clearly, the first time we watched *The Wizard of Oz* together, immobilized on the sofa by a heavy London heat, staring at the TV. We were in school by then, our talents and likely trajectories already showing. Sandro, the smart one, the one going places. Saba . . . well, maybe he'd learn a good trade.

Yet none of that mattered when *The Wizard of Oz* came on TV that afternoon. Sandro and I were swallowed whole by that film. Especially when we realized the story was familiar because it was one from Eka's bootleg magic library.

We made a bemused Irakli buy us *The Wizard of Oz* on VHS and watched it over and over until the tape snapped and had to be glued back together. It was Eka's story come to shiny, colorful life. Only some of the details were off. The slippers were red, not silver. The world in the film turned out to be a silly dream, while Eka's world was real—a place that might just be found if properly searched for.

Back then, it didn't seem too much of a stretch that some specific combination of magic and willpower might transport us back home. Back to Eka.

It never did work. But that phrase became our private, bittersweet in-joke—*But why are the slippers red?* Our security blanket against this strange new life in London. Whenever we were confused, unsure, and maybe just a little terrified—but-why-are-the-slippers-red? made us smile. We said it so often that eventually even Irakli was in on it too.

I hear you, Sandro—the slippers are red, but they do the same job. They send you home. That's where you went and that's where you want me to follow. Yet it's the last place I want to see. Funny how the thing you once loved so much can become what you fear the most. . . .

THE AMBULANCE ARRIVES FIRST. They lift the man's limp, disarticulated body onto a stretcher. He's stopped spasming. His feet no longer search for a toehold in that adjacent dimension. The police arrive next—two vans full of them. The ones in full tactical gear, armed with assault rifles, head into the forest. The rest begin to question people from the crowd.

"We should go, brother. Before your detective turns up here too."

We edge away from the scene.

"Poor bastard just popped out to the shop." Nodar shakes his head. "The neighbor saw it. His car scared off the tiger. It was dragging the guy off into the forest. To feed."

He crosses himself for what must be the hundredth time.

"Brother, that could have been us."

"Watch your step, Nodar."

Two tendrils of blood still creep down the hill, slowing and darkening as they begin to clot. We step over them, carefully, knees up, and carry on down the hill.

By the time we get home, it's almost dark. The sounds of children in the yard are gone. The city's cooling as it murmurs to itself in the thickening twilight.

"I told you. Didn't I tell you?" Ketino's agitated.

Nodar confessed everything immediately, even though he swore he wouldn't. We eat dinner in silence, under Ketino's disapproving gaze. When we finish, I trudge off to Natia's bedroom like I've been grounded.

In the yard, concrete that's been baked all day gives off a fusty smell. The wind carries it to me in great, warm breaths. Cats begin to prowl, edging along fences and dipping in and out of the darkness beneath parked cars.

There are three men sitting in the yard, drinking from plastic liter bottles of wine. Later, I see Nodar join them. He talks animatedly and gestures wildly. He must be telling them about Artyom.

As for me, I turn away from the window and pick up the *Kaleidoskupi* pages that Sandro left at Marina's grave.

ACT 2—SCENE 1

The Soviet café is illuminated by a kerosene lamp on the café counter.
VALIKO sits at his table by the window. He appears to be asleep.
The WAITRESS is behind the counter, wiping down the surfaces
and tidying.

WAITRESS: Another drink?

(VALIKO doesn't respond)

WAITRESS: Valiko.

(WAITRESS comes out from behind the counter)

WAITRESS: Valiko, are you breathing? Hoy, Valiko!

(VALIKO wakes)

VALIKO: What? The Germans coming?

WAITRESS: You were asleep.

VALIKO: And your reaction's to yell? Something's not right with you, you know.

WAITRESS: You can't sleep here. You know that.

VALIKO: I closed my eyes for a moment, my dear, that's all. Felt like I was going somewhere better.

WAITRESS: Oh, yeah? Where's that?

VALIKO: Somewhere that isn't this place.

WAITRESS: Oh, thanks.

VALIKO: Nice as you are, this isn't exactly the Ritz.

*(The **WAITRESS** retreats behind the counter abruptly. She blows out the lamp, making herself barely visible. Enter **EKA**—a stern, dark-haired woman, wrapped up against the cold. She enters the café, goes straight to VALIKO's table, and sits opposite him.)*

(After a long pause)

VALIKO: Hello.

EKA: Hello, Valiko.

VALIKO: How's Saba? How's Sandro?

EKA: We're doing OK.

VALIKO: You want a glass of this?

EKA: Thought you stopped.

VALIKO: I did. I will.

EKA: *(Abruptly)* Listen, Valiko, when will you sign the papers?

VALIKO: I don't know. I don't really understand them.

EKA: We talked about this.

VALIKO: I'm not ready.

EKA: Ready for what? The lawyer says to force you. I don't want to do that, but it's been a year. More than a year.

VALIKO: I'll sign them, I promise. It's just that . . .

EKA: *(Softly)* OK, Valiko, I'll wait.

(Long pause)

VALIKO: I think about it all the time. I break it down, take it apart, look at all the parts. But I still don't get it—how we got here. Do you?

EKA: A lot of things happened.

VALIKO: That's no reason. Things are always happening.

EKA: Let's not, OK?

VALIKO: Sorry. Can't get it out of my head, that's all. For so many things to go so wrong. Everything, really. At just the worst time. How does that even happen? How's that possible? Don't you ever think about it?

(Pause)

EKA: Sometimes.

(After a long pause)

Maybe it was all just shit luck?

(Another long pause, during which EKA and VALIKO lock eyes. Eventually, they smile.)

VALIKO: *(Chuckling)* That's a lot of shit luck.

EKA: Give me that bottle.

VALIKO: It's bathtub wine. I'll get you something else.

EKA: I don't care. Give.

(They both take a drink and lapse into silence)

EKA: Listen, Valiko, you need to leave this place. Stop drinking. Go home. Get on with living.

VALIKO: Not you too.

EKA: Look at this place. It's falling apart around you.

VALIKO: Some things have a momentum of their own. You have to see them to the end.

EKA: I don't know what that means. But, I hate to see you like this.

VALIKO: I know, I know. I promise, you'll never see me like this again.

EKA: Promise?

VALIKO: Promise.

EKA: I'm glad I came.

VALIKO: It wouldn't have worked without you. None of this.

EKA: Come back, Valiko. Saba misses you. So does Sandro. If you lose us, you won't find us again. Come back.

VALIKO: Maybe I will.

EKA: Promise.

VALIKO: *(Smiling)* On my mother's grave.

EKA: Good. I have to run.

VALIKO: OK, you go on.

EKA: Be good, Valiko. See you soon.

VALIKO: Goodbye, Eka.

*(Exit **EKA**. The **WAITRESS** reemerges from behind the counter into the light. She comes to **VALIKO**'s table with a bottle of wine and leaves it by his side.)*

VALIKO: What would I do without you?

WAITRESS: Sober up, probably.

7

NOT OVER YET

M y uncle Anzor comes to me in the night, hushed like a sickbed visitor. No boom to his voice anymore, not since the cancer stole it from him. He puts his arm around my shoulders like he used to. Somehow, I'm half his size again. This is just a dream. But since when does that matter?

We're on the hill with the Mother of Georgia. She stands behind us, sword in hand, still, mute, and forgotten. No blaze of color in her inert eyes.

We face south, watching the verdant flatland stretch out until it meets the horizon. In places, the sun has burned patches of ocher into the green land.

A crawling, insectoid mass swarms on the horizon. Thousands upon thousands of men. Curved swords and shields glint in the last of the daylight.

"They're coming for us, Sabo."

"What do they want?"

"Nothing."

"Then why are they coming?"

"The worst kind of enemy is one that doesn't want anything from you."

The army spills across the flatlands toward Tbilisi like a flood. Waves of cavalry edge out ahead as the men and their mounts smell blood. Behind us, people flee Tbilisi.

"They're going to the mountains, aren't they?"

"Half the men are staying."

"Why?"

"To fight."

"They don't stand a chance."

"No."

"Then why are they staying?"

"It's the cost we bear."

The army draws closer. I can hear the clatter of their swords and shields. Voices shout orders in a harsh foreign tongue. The first waves of the army lap the Tbilisi walls. The Mother watches on, motionless.

"You should look away, Sabo."

I watch men scuttle over the walls and through the fallen gates. Too many to count, too many to stop. I see them form a wedge and face the gaunt line of defenders. The wedge charges, the defenders dig their heels in. The two masses collide. Screams are cut short as steel bites flesh.I should have looked away.

I WAKE UP in Natia's bedroom, queasy with the sound of meat hacked by dull steel.

"Jesus, Anzor, did we have to see that?" I say, hoping to hear his voice again.

He was forever teaching me Georgian history. He taught me about the Mother of Georgia statue and why she looks over Tbilisi, sword in hand.

"It's our history, Sabo. A man without history is a tree without roots."

Tbilisi happens to sit right on top of the most direct route from Asia into Europe. A key strategic location for many a psychopath emperor. The Ottoman Empire, the Byzantine Empire, the Russian Empire—they all sliced their way through Georgia.

Tbilisi was invaded so often that the Georgian people developed a standing strategy. Each time the city was threatened, the people escaped into the mountains. Each miserable exodus was a Noah's Ark of what it meant to be Georgian. Comforts, provisions, and lives were sacrificed to rescue that which can't be replaced—things to be preserved no matter the price. Our history.

"Do you remember the cost we bear?"

"I do, Anzor."

"Tell me the cost a Georgian must bear."

"Every family is to leave an able-bodied man behind," I recite.

Every escaping family left a man behind. Their job was simple—trade their lives for time.

That time, purchased in blood, let the refugees escape into dead-end, last-stand villages in the mountains. In a way, the refugees bore the heavier burden. It was their job to hide and preserve things that couldn't be replaced.

"What happens if the enemy finds us in the mountains?"

"When last stands fail and all else falters, the fearless of heart will do their last sworn duty," I recite.

"What is their last sworn duty?"

"Set the food stores on fire. Scatter the village into the mountains. Those who can't run are to be killed by their kin, unsullied by the enemy."

"And why do we do this?"

"The enemy will find no solace here. No relief from the cold and not a morsel of food. We make Georgia their hell."

Each generation of refugees raised an army and sent it into stubborn, bloody rebellion. No matter the cost, no matter how many revolts were decimated, the invaders were always banished in the end. The refugees would reclaim and rebuild Tbilisi and live happily ever after. Until the next invasion.

Through this miracle of spilled blood and intimacy with death, Tbilisi still stands today. The Mother watches on from her hill, forever awaiting a new foe.

"Good. Some things I taught you stuck."

Anzor was a giant. I was terrified and awed by him in equal measure. His booming voice would cannonade around the house and blow cobwebs out of corners.

When he got home from work, he'd find me and swoop down with one of his huge hands. He'd grab my ankle, or my wrist, or my whole damn leg, and up, up I'd go! The thrill of it would squeeze uncontrollable giggles out of me. He'd set me back down, wild-haired, heart thudding, and begging to go again.

Once, mid-routine, we heard Lena softly clear her throat and we knew that one or both of us were in for it. She paused long enough to register what she was seeing and then Anzor got a scolding like he was my age.

"How tall were you, uncle?" I ask him.

"As tall as you want me to be."

"You scared me a little."

"Did I?"

Anzor cured my fear of swimming one fine summer day by taking me fishing. We rowed to the middle of the lake, where he handed me a sandwich as a distraction. Then he shoved me and the sandwich overboard into the murky water and started rowing away.

"Remember the lake?" He chuckles.

I paddled after that boat like a maniac. I think it ended up being a floundering, doggy-paddle-front-crawl-butterfly-style swim.

"Whatever it was, it worked," Anzor says.

Somehow, I kept my head above water and caught up with the boat. I'm not sure why it worked. It shouldn't have—but I was never afraid of water again.

"You knew how to swim, Sabo. You just didn't know that you knew."

Anzor was too strong for the curse that wiped out the Sulidzes. He was the Sulidze foundation, entirely unafraid of trivial things like sickness or death. The neighbors called him the Soviet Superman. Sandro was convinced he could fly.

So, the curse bypassed Anzor and went after his wife instead. She went to the Sololaki hospital for a knee operation. There was a fuckup with the general anesthetic and she came back from the operation with brain swelling. Every time she reached into her mind for words, she came back with the wrong ones.

"Don't snuff burn, candle angry—she kept saying," Anzor says.

She had a message for Anzor, but her scrambled mind kept encrypting it. She tried to make him understand through sheer, unrelenting repetition. But he couldn't. He tried to have her write what she meant. All she could manage were odd insect-leg shapes—lines that held no reason.

"Residual complications, they said. Temporary."

"What was she trying to say?"

"Sometimes the order changed. But the same words came. Snuff the candle. Don't burn angry. Like that. Over and over."

If Anzor couldn't decipher it, no one had a chance. For weeks, he sat and listened to her desperate koan. Meanwhile, the doctors prepared her for another operation. A second operation to fix the first one—they decided to go straight to brain surgery. This time, they fucked up so hard that they put her in a coma.

"They brought her back bruised, like she'd been in a fistfight. Shaved half her head. She lay and stared at the ceiling all day. We taped her eyes shut. Nothing in them anyway."

The doctors said she could wake up tomorrow, next week, or in a few months—but she would wake up. By then Anzor knew not to listen. He knew she was long gone. He waited, uncomplaining. Two years later, she gave up the fight and exhaled her last.

"These things happen in life. Can't mourn the dead forever. It's not fair on the living."

Anzor moved to a smaller place, got himself a cat (he loved cats). According to Eka, he was doing OK. But there was a crack in the Sulidze foundation. The curse pounced.

That winter, Anzor picked up a cough he just couldn't shake. He never went to the doctors, in case they put him in a coma. He just soldiered on. Eventually, Eka forced him to see a nurse, who sent him to the hospital for tests. Anzor was cornered.

You already know the rest of his story. He never left that hospital. Died in the room he was admitted to. Slipped away on a gust of wind, while Eka was buying a paper in the cafeteria. I guess these things happen.

I LOVE TO WATCH Nodar and Ketino go about their morning routine. They're in sync. Some watchful part of them always aware of the other.

Yesterday, Ketino was making tea when she spilled a little boiling water on her hand. Nodar had his back to her. Ketino didn't make any noise; she just put the kettle down and went to run cold water over her hand. Almost instantly, Nodar's chaotic peruse through the newspaper stopped. His head came up and he half turned toward her.

"Just a little burn," she said over her shoulder, responding to a question he didn't ask.

He turned to look at her fully.

"I'm OK. Really."

"Sure?"

She nodded and went back to making tea. That was it, simple as that—a perfect, self-contained moment.

This morning, though, things are different at Nodar's. Something's cut their telepathic ties. They move about the house irate and disconnected.

For the first time since I've met him, Nodar's wearing a different outfit. Black trousers, battered shoes buffed to a matte sheen, and a short-sleeved black shirt, without the chest pocket bulge where he keeps his pack of L&Ms.

"What's the plan today, Mowgli?"

"Another expedition."

"Where?"

Nodar's more curious than usual this morning. Something's made him nervous. Some invisible patience has worn thin.

"Sololaki again."

I don't want to admit it aloud yet. But I know Sandro wants me to go to our childhood home—a place neither of us thought we'd ever see again.

"Look at me, look at me!" Words I might have said to Eka, had she been there, only annoyed Sandro when we were growing up in London. But I always wanted him to look at me, to be impressed.

Well, look at me now, Sandro—am I doing alright? You left me clues as you hunted for Irakli. Your fail-safe. Now I hunt your clues.

They've led me by the nose to painful places I didn't want to see. Places that felt impossible. Places I know hurt you just as much as they hurt me. Even with police breathing down your neck, you've built a trail only I can follow:

Hard by a great forest . . . Well, you did always like to open your scavenger hunts with a bit of drama, brother.

So how am I doing now? Do you see me yet?

The first crumb was the hardest—the Marina pages from *Kaleidoskupi* you left for me at Irakli's made no sense on their own. But you knew that, Sandro. So you made sure to send me to our great forest. I almost died in that forest, brother. But that's not your fault. I never told you the secret I share with Nino. I never will.

The Valiko Shakespeare graffiti at our waterfall was what finally unlocked it. You sent me off to another place I never thought I'd see again—Marina's grave. I almost died there too, Sandro. Maybe the third time's the charm, isn't that what they say? But what choice is there? I have to follow your trail.

This last clue's easier. I've read Eka's pages from the play, hard as that was. That *Wizard of Oz* clue almost made me smile, until I knew where it led. I'm scared to follow, Sandro. There's a reason they say you can never go home again. . . .

Thankfully, Nodar derails my thoughts and nudges me back into the room.

"Sololaki's a big place, Mowgli," he says, prodding for detail. "Did you figure out the clues? Where are we going?"

Something stops me from telling him that Sandro's last clue is calling me to our childhood home.

"It's a long story," I say instead.

Nodar's eyes shy away from mine. "Tell me on the way. But, listen, I have to run an errand first."

He gives me a smile that retreats into a frown.

"Errand?"

He glances over his shoulder at Ketino.

"Taking Keti to the cemetery."

Ketino disappears into the bedroom and slams the door behind her. The flat falls silent. We sit like this for a while until Nodar grinds his cigarette into the ashtray with his thumb. He stands in the bedroom doorway as terse words are exchanged.

"OK, alright. We'll go," he says to the door she closes on him.

He sweeps his keys from the table.

"Come on, Mowgli, let's wait by the car. Keti needs to get ready."

"You're looking smart," I say once we're outside.

"This? Blame Keti."

He nods in the direction of the flat and sighs. "We take our dead very seriously. Sometimes more seriously than the living."

There's no sign of Ketino for what feels like a solid hour.

"Is she OK?"

Nodar sighs again. "She will be."

He pats his chest for cigarettes. Finally finding them in his trouser pocket, he lights one.

"The war scared her. When we first got here, it was bad. She's better now. But the thing is, she gets nervous leaving the house. Takes her a while. She has these . . . these tics."

Nodar wipes his forehead with the inside of his wrist.

"Everything needs to be just right before she'll set foot outside. If it isn't, she won't budge. Some kind of superstition."

"How bad is it?"

He smiles. "I waited four hours last year."

"Last year?"

He nods.

"Has she left the house since then?"

"Of course. A couple of times. Maybe."

149

He frowns over the cigarette in his mouth, bringing the cherry almost to the tip of his nose.

"Think she has OCD?"

"OC what?"

Nodar looks at me, eyes sharp.

"It's an illness. A mental illness."

"Mental . . . what?" His face darkens into a frown.

"More like a mental block."

"Listen, brother, are you saying she's crazy?" He twirls his finger by his temple to illustrate.

He pushes himself away from his Volga and faces me, eyes backlit by ire.

"She's not cuckoo, if that's what you're asking. She was fine back home and she'll be fine here too."

He flicks his cigarette away and glares at me.

"I didn't mean it that way."

"What way *did* you mean it?"

"I don't know, Nodar. Sorry."

"Not a good day for bad jokes, brother."

He backs away and pats his chest for cigarettes again. Not finding them there, he murmurs a few swear words and retrieves the pack from his trousers. This cigarette is the beginning of another spirited assault on the box of L&Ms. He's three cigarettes in when I hear him shift.

"I'm sorry, Mowgli."

He pats my back once.

"Not a good day today, that's all."

"What's going on?"

Nodar gives a big sigh. But before he can tell me, Ketino emerges from the building wearing a black headscarf, clutching her handbag to her chest and looking deathly pale.

"Anniversary. We lost Natia today," Nodar mutters under his breath.

"Lost?"

"Not now."

He steps toward Ketino, raising his voice.

"Keti, listen—"

"Stop looking at me like that. I'm fine. Start the car, let's go."

With Ketino and Nodar in the front seats, we camouflage into the noisy, dusty Tbilisi traffic. Nobody says a word. Nodar glances at Ketino every time he changes gear. I can see a miniature reflection of her face in the wing mirror—sickly, chlorotic skin overlaid with a fine network of veins. Her face shows no emotion, but her eyes are frantic. She rolls down the window and inhales deep, uneven breaths.

I know where she is. I know that place well. Inches away from a panic attack. When you're in that limbo, it's a matter of blind luck. Any small detail, a careless thought, could trigger the awful downhill rush to that black hole where reason and logic lapse. But equally, an unexpected distraction could be your salvation.

"Ketino, try one of these." I offer her my pack of Mayfair Lights.

The words register on her face one by one. Her attention edges back from the brink. She wipes a bead of sweat from her temple.

"Yeah—" She clears her throat. "Yes, please."

"They're my favorite. I want to see what you think."

Ketino takes a Mayfair, lights it, and takes a drag. She holds the cigarette out in front of her and looks at it.

"They're from London?"

"Yeah."

"They're terrible."

She manages a smile.

"I told him," Nodar says. "If you're gonna die, at least die in better taste."

Ketino turns in her seat to look at me, with her eyebrows raised.

"You want this back?"

I shake my head and back away from the Mayfair. She laughs and throws the cigarette out the window. The pressure eases off a little. Some color returns to her face and her eyes lose that telltale unseeing sheen. Nodar's movements at the wheel loosen up too. That familiar bob and weave he does with his head, as he scouts for other cars, comes back. The spell's broken—we're OK for now.

Tbilisi hides Kukia cemetery among a complex, undulating crowd of buildings. Everyone knows it's here, but nobody knows where exactly. There's no way to approach Kukia intentionally. You only ever see it when you turn that last corner. Intending to find the side entrance, Nodar surprises himself by taking a sharp uphill road that ends squarely at the main entrance.

"Ah, fuck your mother-father-sister-brother. Now we have to walk through the whole fuckin' place."

"Nodar," Ketino warns.

"Sorry."

Kukia is the oldest cemetery in Tbilisi. A rust-infected Soviet SU-85 tank guards the entrance. Its turret points up and over us as we approach, as though it means to shell the other side of Tbilisi.

"What's this?"

"First Red Army tank into Berlin. Every Soviet city has one just like it."

Forget what you think cemeteries are supposed to look like. In Kukia there are no neat, polite rows of well-tended graves. It's a chaotic, gorgeous mess. The land's divided into small burial plots that fit together like a jigsaw puzzle. The plots are different sizes and odd shapes, sectioned off by waist-high fences. Some are carefully kept while others are so overgrown you can't see the gravestones.

Pines, evergreens, and cherry blossoms grow wherever they can scrounge a toehold. Their branches spill into the plots and onto the narrow paths that crisscross the cemetery like capillaries. This barely contained chaos stretches out as far as you can see. The patchwork of burial plots undulates with the contours of the land. A pretty scene, if you ignore the thousands of silent occupants in the ground.

As we walk along a main vein into the heart of the cemetery, Nodar puts a hand on my shoulder and stops. His hand's clammy and unsteady. Ketino looks back and stops.

"What's the matter?" she says.

Nodar leans on my shoulder but doesn't answer. He glances at the sun, for something to blame.

"It's hot."

"Are you coming?" Ketino says.

They've traded places since we left the car. Certainty has returned to Ketino's gestures. It's Nodar who now looks like he's been drained of all his blood. Ketino looks him up and down.

"Nodar?"

"You go ahead."

"OK."

We head back toward the entrance as Ketino watches us go. At the Kukia gates, Nodar buys homemade wine in a plastic lemonade bottle from the kiosk by the rusting tank.

"You're charging me for plastic cups?"

The shopkeeper mumbles something.

"You've lost your way, brother."

Nodar drops a handful of coins on the counter from a height. They wink silver midair, bounce on the counter, and scatter. Glancing around and seeing no one but us, the shopkeeper goes to collect them.

"Keep the change."

We set up at the concrete platform in the shade of the alleged first tank into Berlin. It reeks of old, untreated steel, left to rust in the open.

Nodar sloshes the wine into our cups and we lean against the tank, facing into Kukia.

"Your people in there? Your mum—Eka, was it?" he says after a while.

I nod.

"All of Sololaki's buried in there. Everyone. Stalin's own wife, they say, maybe."

Nodar pauses.

"Listen, brother, you ever see Eka again after you left?"

"No."

He gives a low whistle. I stare into the mess of Kukia and brace myself for the question I know is coming.

"You wanna go see her, Mowgli? I don't mind. I'll wait." He wags the bottle of wine at me and winks.

I struggle to find the right words. In the end, I just say it.

"I don't know where she's buried, Nodar."

Without a word he glances at me and then stares into Kukia. He opens his mouth and closes it. He can finally sense the Eka pact. Maybe he's a signatory to a pact just like it.

"To Eka," he says after a long silence.

Nodar lifts his cup and we toast. He takes a healthy gulp of the wine and his solemn, graveside manner crumbles.

"F-fuck me."

He blurts this out with such force that it makes me laugh. He peers into his cup and then at the bottle.

"This is fucking gulag wine. Grape juice and engine degreaser."

Nodar strides over to the kiosk. After a loud exchange of swear words, he makes the shopkeeper taste the wine. I hear him ask the man his surname and tell him, shame on you, you've forgotten your father's face. I take a sip of the wine. It's like any other cheap red wine I've tasted. Nodar comes back with a small loaf of bread.

"Nodar, this is OK."

He raises his eyebrows. "This is ditchwater."

I shrug and take another sip.

"Brother, listen. When the Turks came, or whoever's turn it was to fuck us, people ran away and hid in the mountains. They left everything behind, but they took grapevine cuttings from their vineyards. They kept those alive at all costs so they'd have someplace to start if they ever returned home. Sometimes, brother, cuttings passed between generations. Kept alive in the mountains for decades. Wine isn't in our blood. It *is* our blood."

He taps his chest.

"All that burning the Turks did only made the soil richer in the end."

He looks at his shoes and pauses a long time.

"My da grew white grapes. Looked like bunches of pearls in the sun."

"You had a vineyard?"

"Anyone with a scrap of land does. But we had our own kvevri— that's a big deal."

"Kvevri?"

"Brother, you really have been away. I oughta call your school and lodge a complaint. Kvevri's the huge clay pot in the ground. To ferment the wine in."

Nodar tuts and takes a generous swig of gulag wine. He makes a face and refills his cup.

"Ours was big enough to fit a grown man inside. But the neck's narrow, see. When I was little, I'd climb in there to rub wax into the walls."

"Wax?"

"Keep germs out."

He chuckles.

"Once, I fucked it up. Rushed it. Next year, the wine came up bad— like vinegar. My da was furious. I got a beating to last me till the year after."

Nodar's eyes grow distant.

"The next year I spent the whole day in the kvevri. Waxed it to death. The wine came out perfect."

His words flow without effort.

"It's the most amazing thing, Saba. Listen. In September, we dig up the kvevri. See, when it's buried, you can only see the lid. It's sealed with beeswax this thick. My da would work the seal like he was carving a sculpture. The lid's heavy, so I'd help him shift it."

Nodar doesn't notice but as he talks, his hands go through the motions of it all.

"The smallest crack and the room fills up with the most amazing smell."

I nod like I know what he's talking about.

"I swear on my father's soul, bless him, that first sip is the best wine you'll ever taste."

He picks up his plastic cup as though he's expecting his father's wine in it. He disappears the contents in two gulps and sucks back the saliva with a hiss.

"This is pisswater."

He flings the remaining droplets of wine to the floor, wipes his mouth with the back of his hand, and takes a bite of the bread.

"At least the bread's edible."

We drink and smoke as Nodar tells me more stories of his home in Ossetia. The wine warms my belly. It's working on Nodar too—he's not gray in the face anymore.

"Nodar, what happened to you in Ossetia?"

It's my turn to watch Nodar struggle to put the right words together.

"Just . . . war. I don't care who started it, or why. Russians, Georgians. I just don't care. All I know is they bombed Tskhinvali in the middle of the night."

"You were there?"

"No." He shakes his head. "No, we lived a few kilometers away, by the forest. But we heard the shells come screaming in. We had no idea what they were until we heard them land in the city. Ground rumbled like an earthquake. Brother, the sky over Tskhinvali was bloodred. Then we knew for sure."

Nodar falls silent and lights a cigarette for comfort. He knows my next question will be about Natia. This is his unspoken pact. In the end, I don't have to ask.

"Natia was staying with Keti's sister and her kids. In Tskhinvali."

This story is Nodar's poison. He needs to get it out.

"We ran all the way to the city. It looked like hell. Actual, real hell on earth. People running around, digging through rubble while the shells were still coming in."

He takes a quick swig of his wine.

"Natia's building collapsed on the front side. People crawling out of the rubble like gassed rats. Begging me for help—"

Nodar takes a deep breath and rubs his frown smooth with his palm. Each sentence costs him something. He crosses himself.

"God forgive me, I ignored them. I searched the rubble for Natia. The parts I could reach, anyway. Nothing."

"I'm sorry."

"Keti's sister probably hid in the basement with the kids, we thought. But the basement entrance was blocked. Not a sound inside, brother."

He takes another sip and wipes his mouth.

"They shelled the city again that evening. The block of flats next door collapsed onto Natia's. That was that. We couldn't get to it anymore. Anyway, the army was already evacuating folk. Almost shot me for resisting."

Nodar exhales.

"We went home, brother. . . . We just went home without our daughter. Sat in the house like flies on a cowpat."

He stays silent a long time while his gaze roams among the burial plots of Kukia. When he speaks again, it's barely audible.

"Few days later, the Russian army arrived."

"Wait, I thought the Russians shelled the city?"

"Russians, Georgians. What's the difference? Shell's a shell—it still kills."

He shakes his head.

"I tried to get into Tskhinvali, but the Russians had it locked down. No one in, no one out—almost killed me trying to sneak past. Then the *real* fighting started and we got evacuated all the way out to Tbilisi."

He looks over at me and back at the empty plastic cup in his hands.

"Whatever we weren't wearing, we sold. For a pittance. And then we started from scratch. Keti wasn't well for a long time. Stayed in bed for days. I couldn't get her to say a word. She watched everything there was to watch about the war, over and over and over. . . ."

A new thought makes him pinch the bridge of his nose.

"Brother, she would sit still and cry without her expression changing. I mean, tears just rolling down her face, like she was paralyzed. I didn't know what to do. How to shake her out of it.

"Eventually, slowly, things got better. I bought the Volga to make a little money. And here we are, almost two years later."

"Any news of Natia?"

Nodar shakes his head. "Not a word."

"So, she's not actually . . ." I nod at the cemetery.

"No, she's not in there. But Keti's convinced she's dead. We spent our last money on that plot in there. I mean, you can barely fit a chair in it."

"You think she's still in Tskhinvali?"

"Maybe she is, maybe she isn't. Maybe she's in a village nearby. It doesn't matter. What I know is that she's alive."

He taps his chest twice. "Her heart's still beating. Almost nine years old."

He looks toward where Ketino disappeared up the winding path.

"But when Keti gets on her mule, there's no sense arguing. She comes here, leaves flowers, lights candles, prays. Talks to Natia for hours. It's hard to watch, brother."

Nodar looks at his feet.

"Thing is, I can't prove her wrong. I've tried. Ossetia's locked down. There's patrols both sides of the border. No way in. They shoot first and if they don't kill you, maybe they'll ask questions after."

"That bad?"

"Listen, brother, it's gone dark in there. No information in or out. No calls, no mail. If you try, police turn up at your door asking questions. It's crazy. They caught me both times I tried to cross. Another time and it's twenty years in prison. Treason, they say."

He chuckles, but there's no mirth in it.

"One day it'll end, brother. The border will open. Until then, I'm waiting. Waiting and losing my mind."

The poison's out. Nothing I can think of to comfort him. I look at the floor, sprinkled with pine needles.

"Don't look so sad, Mowgli. It's not over yet."

I wonder which of these opposing fantasies, Ketino's or Nodar's, is more fragile. I smile at him but if I'm honest, I think he's wrong. Chances of an eight-year-old surviving in the middle of a war zone? On her own? No, Nodar. It is over.

"You're right," I lie.

He knows Natia's dead. Of course he does. But he lies to himself, tortures himself with the prospect of finding her. He can't stop. Because if he stops, Natia really is gone.

Meanwhile, Ketino's facing the mirror image of the same problem. It isn't grief that's got her to the point where she can't leave the house. It's hope. Real, honest hope that Natia's alive.

If Ketino doesn't go to the cemetery, she must admit that Natia's alive. Alive and alone. A child in a war zone. Worse, Ketino can't do anything to find her. So she pretends her daughter's dead and somehow feels better for it.

They're working the same problem from opposite ends, heading for some painful middle ground. That painful middle ground is where we left Eka. Her two boys, alive but inaccessible. Six years she paced that awful middle ground.

What kind of damage does such a thing do to a person? What does it cost? Ketino is only two years a prisoner there, and already the toll's visible.

I look out across the chaos of Kukia. One of these plots must be Eka's.

"*When this is all over, I'll come back. I'll come back and find you,*" I say, hoping for Eka's voice.

But she doesn't reply.

BY THE TIME Ketino comes back to us, the sun has dipped past the horizon. She looks like someone who just weathered a crisis—her frown's smoothed away and her eyes glint with hard-won relief. She's the Ketino from the morning she cured us both, me and Nodar. She even has a cup of wine with us.

"My God, Nodar. Shame on you. What *is* this?"

Nodar shrugs. He looks tired. All the nervous energy that animated him long drowned in bad wine.

"Where did you get this? Throw it away—but don't pour it on the ground. Nothing will grow there again."

Ketino reaches for the bottle but Nodar tucks it under his arm, shielding it from her. He walks toward his Volga.

"Let's go," he says over his shoulder.

In the car, he flips on his usual radio station. The endless litany of messages resumes and makes me wonder if the station is ever off air. Ketino turns it down.

"This garbage again."

Nodar turns the radio back up. They exchange a sidelong glance.

"Fine. Let's go," Ketino says.

As we drive through the darkening streets of Tbilisi, Ketino's reflection in the wing mirror is porcelain still. We're almost home when it happens. The radio station's been going through a dense patch of love messages, as it sometimes does. Nodar's maneuvering the Volga into a parking space only a couple of feet longer than the car itself. Just then, clear as a bell, the message plays:

> *"To Natia Basriani of Tskhinvali. Natia, if you are listening, we love you. Stay safe, we'll find you. Love, your da and Keti."*

Ketino inhales with a hiss.

"Again, Nodar?"

He's silent.

"She's gone. Get that through your peasant skull," Ketino grinds out through her teeth.

Nodar exhales a low moan of frustration that forms into words— "Shut up."

"She's gone, Nodar. Please. Stop."

They turn on each other and lock eyes. When that stare breaks, all bets are off. Ketino flings the door open and steps out of the car, which is still moving. This makes Nodar hit the brakes. The Volga stalls and judders into silence. Ketino stumbles and almost falls.

"Keti, you alright?"

Without looking back, she storms off toward the flat.

"Fine then, go."

She's almost out of earshot. Nodar's voice rises to a shout.

"Go and hide. All you're good for anyway!"

Ketino's steps stutter at the words, but she doesn't stop. Nodar almost rips the handbrake out of the socket, gets out, and takes a few steps after her. Then he changes his mind and stops. He turns to me instead. Tears shimmer in his eyes.

"You see this?"

He paces the pavement by the semi-parked Volga. He looks up and down the street, as though someone called his name from afar.

"Fuck it. Listen, Saba, you go up. I'm going for a little walk."

Over his shoulder I see Ketino emerge from the dark mouth of the doorway. Nodar doesn't see her bearing down on him as though she means to kill him.

"Nodar," I try to warn him.

She's on him before he can brace himself. She has a fistful of lari notes in her hand. As Nodar turns to face her, the hand holding the money comes down on his face. Nodar staggers back, holding his cheek. Crisp, new banknotes confetti to the ground.

"I won't have this sin in my house," Ketino says.

The wind catches the notes and they start to flutter away.

"You lost your mind?"

Nodar scrambles after the banknotes, but Ketino freezes him in place with two words.

"Tell him."

Nodar stops dead. He looks at me and then at Ketino.

"Tell him, Nodar. Or I will."

Nodar stands locked in place while the money escapes from him up the road, under cars, and into storm drains.

"Tell him where you got it."

"Keti, don't."

His eyes shy away from mine. He shakes his head.

"Tell him," Ketino repeats in a cold voice.

"It's not that simple."

Nodar looks at the banknotes he's rescued in his hand. He stuffs them into his pocket, losing a couple in the process. He watches them fall to the ground and makes no move to pick them up. Without a word, he turns and walks away.

"Fine, run along, get drunk. All *you're* good for anyway. I'll tell him myself."

Ketino turns to me.

"I'm so sorry, Saba. This place has changed him."

"Tell me what?"

Her features soften a shade. She sighs.

"He sold you, son. Sold you to that detective. For a few lari." Ketino gestures at the money strewn about us.

"Sold me?"

"They know everything—the pages you found, the graffiti, the burned church . . ."

I turn to look at Nodar. He pauses before rounding the corner as though he means to return to us, but then he walks on.

"He did it for me—money runs dry here like water in a desert. His taxi, it's not enough."

Ketino doesn't ask questions or press me to say anything. There's nothing to be said. We return to the flat in silence; she retreats to her room and leaves me be. She knows what I have to do next and she gives me the space to do it. I can't trust Nodar anymore, no matter how much I wish I could. If I want to find Irakli, I have to leave Nodar behind.

The apologetic silence from Ketino's bedroom seems to acknowledge my decision.

While the TV in the living room tells more fairy tales about zoo animals, I pack my bag. Artyom the Tiger continues to elude his captors. Two stray dogs found eviscerated and partly eaten in upper Sololaki. Their owners are traumatized. Police special forces units now patrol the forest.

A waddle of gentoo penguins escaped their pursuers and disappeared into the Mtkvari storm drains. Boris the Hippo has died despite the best efforts of the vets. Police reprimanded for their enthusiasm with tranquilizer darts. These stories slide past, barely making contact.

I decide to wait and see Nodar one last time before I go. I want his explanation. He comes home late, looking like a poor forgery of himself. His words come in a stunted cadence. His eyes swim about the room, disengaged from what they're seeing. He's drunk.

"I need to sit."

As soon as he's on the sofa, he starts listing to one side with his eyes half-shut.

"You OK?"

After a delay, his eyes flutter open. He scratches his nose and straightens up.

"Pass me a smoke, will you?"

I hand him a lit L&M. He takes a couple of eager drags. But then his hand tires and wilts into his lap. He starts leaning to one side again. I watch his cigarette burn down to the filter.

"Nodar."

He jumps, spilling ash all over himself.

"Present, sir!"

"What did you tell the detective? How much do they know?"

Nodar takes a final drag on the dead L&M, winces at the taste, and lets the butt fall to the floor.

"I'm not sorry, Mowgli." He shakes his head. "It's not the money. I don't care about that."

"What then?"

"He offered something I couldn't turn down."

A bitter laugh escapes him.

"He promised to get me into Ossetia, for Natia."

He shakes his head. Nudged loose by the movement, two tears roll down his face. He wipes them with his wrist.

"He tricked me. He never meant to keep his end of the deal. I kept asking about the border, until last night he told me if I even set foot near Ossetia, he'll vanish me in prison for good."

He puts his head in his hands.

"That's the brown end of the shit stick, Bublik," Surik says.

"Not now, Surik."

"He sold you to the wolves. They know everything you know."

"He's in pain, Surik, can't you see that?"

"Fuck him and his crocodile tears. Get out of here. Never look back."

I watch Nodar's face lose elasticity. It drains of color and reveals a sickly blue network of veins at each temple.

"Nodar, I'm leaving."

His eyes focus on my packed bag. He tries to sit up.

"Don't leave, Mowgli. Stay."

His words come out sluggish, each one a struggle.

"Please don't leave, brother. I can fix this." He lowers his voice. "You'd do the same in my place. You would."

He tries to stand up and fails.

"Stay tonight, please. I can fix this."

"OK, Nodar, OK. I'll stay. Here, just lie down."

I get him a glass of water, turn the radio on, and find the "If You're Listening" station.

"Mowgli," he mumbles. "It's not over yet."

I throw a blanket over him. I need a saner voice than Surik's to help me think this through. I try speaking to Anzor.

"All of Sandro's clues, the graffiti, the sneaking around Tbilisi, dodging police—all of it—he just flushed down the toilet."

Listing these things out makes me slam Natia's bedroom door shut behind me. Nodar mumbles something but I can't tell what.

"Easy, Sabo. Calm down. Sit down. You're right, he sold you. But, put Eka in his place, or Irakli. Would they have done anything different? Would you?"

"I need to get out of here."

Anzor sits me back down.

"There's no rush. The damage is done. You need to think this through. What do the police know?"

"He told them everything, Anzor!"

"Slow and steady, Sabo, think."

"They know I went to Irakli's, then to the botanical garden, and then to Marina's grave. They know what I found—the pages, the graffiti."

"They do, sure. But think about it—you never told Nodar how you connected the clues. That's your and Sandro's language. Nodar doesn't speak that language and neither do the police."

"So what?"

"All they know is that you're following a trail, but not how—"

"Jesus, Anzor, they know where I'll go next!"

"Do they?" I feel him smile. *"Think about it—all you told Nodar is you were going somewhere in Sololaki. No more."*

I shake my head at my own stupidity.

"You're right. I can still go home."

"Not quite, Sabo. One thing you're forgetting . . ."

"What?"

"If you were the police, what would you do?"

"I've no idea, Anzor. What would you do if you were the police?"

I hear him tut.

"Always in a tizzy, Sabo. Think. Me, if I was the police—I'd be waiting out there to follow you. Or, I'd be waiting for you somewhere I know you'd come."

The words make me stand up.

"I need to go right now."

"Get a couple of hours of sleep, Sabo—you'll need it. Leave in the dead of night."

With his calm touch, he sits me down, shuts me up, and somehow puts me to sleep.

8

WHY THEY SAY YOU CAN'T
GO HOME AGAIN

*M*ost nights, I came here as a dreamer, my body shed and left behind. *Before the smell of this place was washed from me for good. I came all the way from London to visit with them:*

Anzor, forever imprisoned in the yard, elbow-deep in the unfixable engine of his car, frowning and wiping his fingers on the rag hanging over his shoulder. I'd sit and watch him, but he wouldn't look at me.

Lena, always in the kitchen, flakes of chopped parsley dotting her hands. Her stern touch. Fingers dipped in countless wounds, across godless, nameless muddy fields of the German front. A witness to a thousand deaths; her face the last one you saw. She'd look right through me, like I was never really there.

Eka, filling the lounge with cigarette smoke and fleecing an unfortunate cousin at backgammon. She never looked up from the game to notice me.

I used to wander through this house and smell the faint stink of mothballs in the bedrooms, run my fingers along the whispering curtains, and watch the oak leaf shadows dance on my bedroom wall.

But memories shed detail. This place, my home, soon faded to a forgery of what it really was. Once it was bleached of the finer detail, it lost its power over me. I only came back to make sure it didn't vanish entirely. I came to hold up the walls so they wouldn't cave in, to check the rooms were at least in the right place:

Anzor's, first on the left from the front door.

Next the dripping bathroom, then the threadbare lounge.

Eka's room, Sandro's, and mine, side by side.

Our oddly shaped kitchen overlooking Lena's herb garden in the backyard.

Lena's little nook right by the back door.

How dark this place has grown now. Ceilings lost in shadows. Windows blind with dust. All the doors shut. There's no smell left to this place, no flavor. Bleak noise of ambient sounds I no longer remember. Walls bleached of all texture. They're bone white now, though they never were.

I put my ear to Anzor's door. Feigned silence.

Anzor?

Racked coughing muffled by cloth. I leave him to his black truth.

Faint, choked sobbing coming from Eka's room. Groceries falling to the floor through disobedient fingers. The door won't budge, no matter how much I wish it would.

Eka?

There's no answer.

Lena's room lies empty, like no one ever lived in it at all.

Part of the kitchen mutates into my London kitchen. I stare at the obscenity of a gleaming electric stove where Lena's cast-iron, old-dependable Atlas oven stood.

I can't fix this place. It's too far gone.

I need to get out.

. . .

IT'S STILL DARK when my alarm wakes me. There's an iodine taste of dread at the back of my throat. I decide to leave at this ungodly time of day to avoid the police, in case they try to follow me. All thanks to Nodar.

Since the day I got here, I felt my family home tugging me like an ocean current and I resisted it. I know Sandro must have felt it too. In the early days in London, we fantasized about returning home all the time. Because that's where Eka would be, fleecing a doomed cousin at backgammon. That's where Anzor would be, fixing his car in the yard. Lena in the kitchen, cooking something from nothing.

But things have moved on. Nothing in that place now but ghosts, stale air, and dusty furniture.

Sandro knew it too. I feel his hesitation. Why else did his trail lead everywhere but to this place that we crave and fear the most?

How much shit have we landed in, Sandro? You went to our home out of necessity, brother, with all the less painful options exhausted. Whatever predator hunts you has my scent now too. Your clues make me worry—they're accelerating toward some bad end.

Standing in Natia's dark room, I feel that tug of our home once again. But I know it to be a riptide now, pulling me out to a place I can't swim back from. This time I don't resist. I let the riptide take me. Wish me luck, Sandro.

I pick up my bag and slide into Nodar's living room like a burglar. He's asleep on the sofa, face mushed into the seat. The sleep of the dead.

"Peaceful sleep of a traitor caught," Surik chimes in, but I don't answer.

The radio hisses faint static into the room. The door to Ketino's bedroom is shut. I take one last look around. My heart hardened overnight, the way hearts do. I click the front door shut behind me and turn my back on Grand Hotel du Nodar and its sad occupants.

The sky's dark and the streetlights are still on. This early in the morning Tbilisi's like an abandoned film set. No cars out here and no people. No one follows me as I leave Nodar's street.

Left unstirred, the fine dust that flavors the air has settled like faint snowfall. Tbilisi guides my feet downhill, toward the Mtkvari. The water's only a shade lighter than the muddy-black sky. I cross the river by the crumbling monolith of the Sololaki hospital. I pause on the bridge and wait for any sign of someone following me.

Away from the river, I join the central road through Tbilisi. Indistinct shapes of strangers creep this road with me. They stay in the shadows and skirt around the lurid pools of fluorescence from shop windows and city lights. We're all the same—head down, teeth gritted, walking unwilling in a direction not chosen. We exchange glances of a discomfort shared. These people are no predators or police tails. They're my kindred spirits.

Walking around a city this time of day means something in your life has slipped its groove. These people are running from an imminent hangover, walking off an argument, failing to sleep yet another night for reasons known and unknown. Me, I'm headed for Tabidze Street. I'm headed home.

Like a dim forest trail reaching a clearing at last, the road opens onto a huge square.

This is Lenin Square: a cobblestone monstrosity of Soviet proportions. It seems to have grown with time. Lenin's long gone. Only his pedestal remains. No other monument will take root here. Not until decades of rain have washed the soil clean of the old poison.

I was here when they toppled Lenin from his perch. Back then, the whole Sulidze family was glued to our black-and-white TV—footage of tanks in foreign streets, crowds charging armed soldiers, tear gas canis-ters skittering among feet like stray fireworks. The Soviet Union was crumbling. It was ruining my *Tom and Jerry* time.

"Sabo, there's a revolution out there and you want to watch car-toons?" Anzor said.

He was right. A spasm of revolutions shuddered through the entire Eastern Bloc. The Berlin Wall fell. The Soviet Union started shed-ding entire countries—Bulgaria, Czechoslovakia, Romania. Georgia too shook off seventy years of slumber. The exiles returned from the moun-tains, bearing seventy years' worth of distilled ire.

The Soviet rule in Georgia vanished before the people could get their hands on it. Government officials fled, or simply took off their uniforms and slipped into the crowd. Finding the parliament build-ing deserted, the crowd ended up in Lenin Square, brimming with unspent anger. Oblivious, Lenin stood as he always had—manifesto in hand, gesturing pompously. Anzor and Eka took me and Sandro to the square that day.

"You boys will live ten lifetimes and never see anything like this," Anzor promised.

He hoisted me up onto his shoulders and waded into the crowd. The whole of Lenin Square was a murky sea of weary, sullen faces. Men and women dressed in clothes endlessly passed down, mended, washed, and faded to the dreary, uniform color of Soviet life.

They tied steel cables around Lenin's legs. Two trucks were burning their engines and ripping up the cobblestones to pull the statue to the ground. With a sound like a rifle crack, one cable snapped. But Lenin was already on his way. He tipped into the scattering crowd like a felled tree and shattered as he hit the ground.

Thousands of faces turned in the same direction and produced a sound I'll never forget. A deafening, unprompted "Oooooh" heaved through the crowd, blowing hats off heads and clearing the dust

Lenin's demise had kicked up. It reverberated around the square and made the hair on my neck stand on end. I felt the same sound go through Anzor beneath me, like air through a bellows. There was no joy in that cry, no triumph. Just rage without recourse. I looked down at Sandro from my perch. He was leaning into Eka and crying. So unlike him to cry like that.

The crowd surged forward in grim silence. Finally finding some token release, they tore the statue to pieces. Eka came away with a chunk of the statue she claimed was Lenin's fingertip. Later, we stashed it in the corner of our garden under a rosebush, where it looked like a casual rock. People from the neighborhood would come by to look at it and Eka never tired of telling its history.

In the end, Georgia's new independence wasn't all it was cracked up to be. Good times lasted as long as the Soviet supplies did. Then the civil war *really* kicked into gear and Tbilisi saw no daylight for a decade.

Food was scarce. No running water, no gas, no electricity. We lived with the smell of candle wax on our fingers. The kerosene lamps tanned our walls so slowly that you didn't notice until you ran your finger through the grime. Then Nino caught her bullet and, well, I guess you know the rest already.

I look across Lenin Square now, searching. I spot Tabidze Street on the other side and commit to it the way deer commit to headlights.

"*Bublik, listen.*" Surik's voice startles me. "*You sure about this?*"

"*No choice, Surik.*"

"*This might be dangerous.*"

"*Dangerous?*"

"*He might be there.*"

"*Who might?*"

"*Him.*"

"*What are you talking about?*" But Surik gives no answer.

The Mother of Georgia statue looms over this part of Sololaki.

Under her auspices I enter the long row of pastel-colored town houses that is Tabidze Street. Wider than most streets in Sololaki, it lures you in under a false pretense.

The town house facades are a marvel. Recessed, arched windows and elegant Juliet balconies everywhere you look. Carved faces of grinning cherubs, lions, gargoyles, and miniature devils adorn the walls.

But time's been unkind. Entire sections of the elaborate facades have crumbled away to reveal the ugly symmetry of brickwork. Corners and sharp edges have been melted blunt by decades of rain. Lines that should run straight don't. Some houses recline or lean into the road, while others simply sink into their rotting foundations.

Sickly, varicose-vein cracks infect the walls. The delicate balconies have bled aprons of rust down the walls beneath them.

"Seen enough yet?" Surik says.

"You're back."

"Leave this place, Bublik. Let's go home."

"Where is that, Surik, if not here?"

I know he has no answer to that. All around me dozens of childhood memories beg me to witness their bittersweet dilapidation. Details I don't remember forgetting tug at my sleeve. I grit my teeth, lock eyes with the Mother, and walk on.

Farther up Tabidze, I come across a heavyset woman surrounded by a gaggle of kids. She's the calm center of the yelping sticky-fingered chaos around her. Her face bears the stern serenity of a decorated veteran of motherhood.

She stops at a ground-floor window kiosk. A hand passes her a bottle of milk and a box of cigarettes. She pays and leans up to chat with the shopkeeper. As I approach, her eyes dart in my direction.

"Holy Jesus, Mary, and horny Joseph," Surik exclaims. *"It's her!"*

Recognition dawns slowly. This can't be her. Kristina—the (unreciprocated) love of my childhood.

"That's Kristina, your faithless wife."

While Surik chortles at his own joke, I take another look at the woman. Surik's right. It is her.

Eka was reading us Pippi Longstocking the summer Kristina conjured herself into our lives. Some mischievous magic stitched and crafted her from the essence of that book. When I saw her standing in the yard, I knew why all the words in Eka's book had vanished—they'd been used up in bringing Kristina to life.

She had the freckles, the pigtails, the ratty dress, the whole lot. She was never still, her bare feet always dirty in her hand-me-down-again sandals. She was always climbing things, perched up in tree branches, flashing her huge pants to the world.

She was a little older than the rest of us in that yard and that made her our boss. She broke our hearts like she was pulling wings off flies. Apple-green eyes and dark skin—we never stood a chance.

Some summer nights, the grown-ups would let us build a little firepit in the yard. That's the only time Kristina was still. The fire hypnotized her, and the miniature flames dancing in her eyes hypnotized me. What I felt for Kristina is what "falling in love" wants to be someday, when it gets its act together.

She's only a few feet from me now and I'm about to open my mouth with no idea what words will fall out. Our eyes meet and I almost stop walking. I watch her slack face for a glimmer of recognition. It doesn't come.

"Say something, Bublik."

"It's been eighteen years, Surik. What's there to say?"

"How about 'hello'?"

I jam my hands into my pockets and walk by. She gives me a curious passing glance but doesn't speak. I keep going until I find myself staring right down the barrel of No. 22 Tabidze Street.

"You don't have to do this," Surik says.

"I do."

"On your head be it."

I approach No. 22 with a cold mind, as an observer, a witness. I step into the passage that leads to the internal yard. Water pipes run the length of the walls, sporadically wrapped in moldy insulation. The passage smells just as I remember it. Rust, oil, and damp. On hot summer days these walls would perspire like a cold glass of water left in the sun. I take the corner onto the yard. There's a wooden chair part-nailed, part-tied to the corner wall—our makeshift basketball hoop.

"You made that for us, remember?"

Not a sound from Surik. He made the hoop for us the summer he lost his job as an engineer. That's when the drink really got a grip on him. I'd hear people talk about Surik: there's no reason for him to drink, mind like a razor blade. He could make something of himself, but he's just wired wrong. He can't help it. Runs in that family, they'd say and shrug.

I didn't like hearing it. Surik wasn't defective—he never did anything without a reason. Rumor was, the KGB wanted him in the Soviet space program. But the boozing ruined everything. He rolled up to the interview drunk, slurring his physics equations.

"No rumor, Bublik. All true."

"We called you 'Miracle Hands.'"

We called him that because he could fix anything.

"Valuable skill to have in Soviet Georgia."

Without a job to keep him sane, Surik leaned into the drinking and became no more than the local handyman. He was always in the yard, a slight tremor making his hands dance. He made toys for us when he could.

The kids from across the road, our sworn enemies, had armed themselves with catapults, made from crude twigs and underwear elastic stolen from their grandmothers' wardrobes.

"Caveman catapults. What I made for you lot were the peak of Soviet engineering. Those things could whip a wing off a bee."

Surik's catapults were metal, with a wrist rest and a rubber grip. It was with one of those catapults that Kristina put an end to our bitter feud with the cavemen across the road. She shot one of their mothers in her fat ass "by mistake" and got us grounded for the rest of that summer.

I step out of the passage and into the yard. Lena's little herb garden, just under our windows, has dried up. There's nothing growing here anymore and all our windows are boarded up. I sit in the little seating area by the garden, across from where Kristina would perch and stare into the fire. I light a cigarette and try to let all these details glide through my mind like water.

With Lena's garden so naked, I can see Lenin's fingertip where we hid it under the rosebush. I can already tell there's something stashed behind it.

"How much you want to bet it's Kaleidoskupi *pages?"* I say to Surik.

"Take them and let's go."

"Calm down, Surik."

I move Lenin's fingertip aside and find a solitary, damp page. It's been folded hastily and left open to the elements. I unfold the paper, fingers trembling. The first and last lines have been washed away by the rain. The rest is barely legible. This is a page unannounced by an act or scene number, shed of any context. It's a hurried clue—something important left in a rush.

TAMAZ: *(Drinks a shot of vodka)* Oof, that's nasty.

VALIKO: Paint stripper.

TAMAZ: Oven cleaner.

VALIKO: Even Red Moskva tastes better.

(They both laugh)

WAITRESS: Feel free to take your business elsewhere. Pair of you. Can't you see I'm closing up?

VALIKO: I won't be long, I promise.

WAITRESS: Get on with it, already.

(WAITRESS tuts and returns to her task)

VALIKO: You were telling me about your job. Something about a promotion?

TAMAZ: Don't make me laugh. Cutbacks, they're saying. Reorganization. They're letting me go.

VALIKO: Why?

TAMAZ: You tell me. I've done nothing.

VALIKO: That might be the problem, Tamaz.

TAMAZ: Pour up, before the paint stripper evaporates.

(VALIKO pours two measures of vodka. They drink.)

TAMAZ: Listen, Valo, I don't get it. What did they do to you up in Ushguli?

VALIKO: What do you mean?

TAMAZ: I mean that crazy monastery up there. You weren't the same when you came back.

VALIKO: Nothing ever stays the same.

TAMAZ: See? You say shit like that now. What did you do up there?

VALIKO: Well, mostly prayer.

TAMAZ: I'd go nuts.

VALIKO: You get used to it. It helps you stop thinking things you don't want in your head.

TAMAZ: I don't think that's the point, brother.

VALIKO: Probably not.

(They take another shot chased with beer and a gherkin)

VALIKO: Did I tell you they almost kicked me out?

TAMAZ: For what?

VALIKO: Well, I couldn't sleep on those rock-hard cots. So, day three, I went and built myself a nice bed. I stuffed it with rags and hay and whatever I could get my hands on. You should've seen it, Tamaz, it was like a sultan's bed. You just had to look at it and you felt drowsy.

TAMAZ: And that's not allowed, I take it?

VALIKO: It's an indulgence. Sin. Father Serafim told me I was missing the point. Told me to think hard about why I was even there.

TAMAZ: Why *were* you there, Valo?

VALIKO: I couldn't stay here and stay sane. And after Eka . . . Well, after that, I didn't even *want* to stay here.

*(During a long pause all that can be heard is the **WAITRESS** counting coins. Both men take a drink in silence while staring awkwardly out the window.)*

IT TAKES ME a near-endless minute to remember a "Tamaz" from that life we lived decades ago. He was Irakli's close friend. An absentee godfather to Sandro and me. I picture Tamaz opening his front door on

179

Irakli—a man he hasn't seen in twenty years. That strange fever glint in Irakli's eyes, making him look like he just cried or is about to.

Awkward silence followed by awkward words. I picture Irakli handing over the strange play pages, asking Tamaz to keep them. A memento. A crumb.

"Why?" Tamaz would want to say, but one look at Irakli and he'd know there's no point asking.

I barely remember what he looks like. Nicotine-stained fingertips and the smell of unfiltered cigarettes, rock-solid beer gut—that's all. Yet somehow Sandro tracked him down, found him, retrieved that *Kaleidoskupi* page from him, and brought it here for me to find.

I'm sorry, brother, I'm too slow. What are you telling me with this page? Your trail's fading. Birds peck at the crumbs you leave. There's barely anything left.

I feel exposed, standing in the yard like this for everyone to see. I cram the page into my pocket and retreat into the stairwell, where we used to hide from the rain. Who knows what I'm hiding from now? I try to read the *Kaleidoskupi* page again but a familiar childhood fear shivers through me when I spot the slack, dark mouth of the communal basement.

I used to go down there with Lena. The odd angle of the entrance and the steep steps made it look like she was descending into her own clammy tomb. I'd refuse to follow her until she hit the light switch. Unable to resist, I dip into that same darkness now.

The Soviet-era clacking plastic light switch still works. Probably Surik's handiwork. I descend into the chill, moist air of the basement. A feeble glowworm trapped in a light bulb illuminates a large exposed-brick room. The walls are damp and the air's choked with the smell of rotting cardboard. Other people's junk piled into corners and against the walls.

"Bublik, look."

Surik guides me to a pile of boxes labeled "Sulidze," the dust on them undisturbed for years. The tape, grown glue-less, comes away without protest and the box falls open.

I pull obsolete possessions into the light against their will—old lamp shades, bundles of cutlery rusted solid, moldy cushions, magazines and newspapers faded of all color and meaning.

The faint odor of our home is the only useful thing in these boxes. I know I'll smell it on my skin later.

"Wait, Bublik, wait. Look again." Surik stops me.

Tucked under a grimy oilcloth I find a bundle of unopened letters tied together with twine. They're addressed to me and Sandro, in Eka's handwriting. Under the letters, past a layer of *Communist Health* magazines, something winks bright green. I throw the magazines clear and find a Christmas card staring at me:

> *My boys,*
>
> *Merry Christmas! I hope you like your presents. I can't send them to you just now. So I'll keep them with me for when I see you next.*
> *Be good now, look after Irakli.*
>
> *Love, Eka*

The whole damn box is filled with old birthday and Christmas presents from Eka. They're still wrapped, completely untouched. These are the presents she never managed to get to us. Sending them in the post back then would have been a roundabout way of handing them to the corrupt postal workers to put under their own Christmas trees.

But Eka continued to be our mother, despite the miles and miles between us. The proof is here, in this box. I can't think of a single word to say to her now. I stand still and fight back the tears while my guts fill up with fruitless anger.

The pressure builds. Water drips from the ceiling. There are distant footsteps outside, in the stairwell. Tired feet returning from some irrelevant errand.

"Hey you!" A voice from the basement entrance makes me jump.

I drop Eka's letters. The fall snaps the twine and spills the letters across the floor. I turn around and lock eyes with Surik. He's right there, in the flesh, squinting down at me.

"Get away from there!"

He's not the Surik I remember. Stark against the light in the stairwell, he's thin and weather-beaten, with dark hollows in his cheeks.

"Who the fuck are you?" he says.

"Surik . . ."

"No, *I'm* Surik, you little shitbag. What you creeping around here like a fart for?"

I wipe away the tears and stand under the light bulb to let him see me. I swear, if he doesn't recognize me I might punch him. His eyebrows come up in slow surprise.

"No," he says. "No."

I nod.

"Saba?"

"Hi, Surik," I mutter.

"Holy Jesus, Mary, and fuckin' Saba! Is that really you, Bublik?"

"Yeah, it's me."

"Don't just sit there like a cowpat. Come up!" He motions me up with a gesture I've seen a thousand times.

I bound up the stairs, two at a time. Surik slaps my handshake away and hugs me. I feel the sharp angles of his bones through his shabby, oversize clothes. There's no padding to him at all. He wears a bandage around his throat like a scarf. The gauze is frayed and dotted with bloodstains yellowed by washing.

"Come in, come in." He drags me into his flat by my shoulder, glances down the staircase, and closes the door.

Surik's flat looks like he hasn't thrown anything out since the last time I was in here. He's plastered all the windows with newspaper. Daylight filtered through old newsprint casts a sepia hue over everything. Jumbled piles of junk cover most of the floor. Books, newspapers, and old magazines are stacked on every flat surface. Cockroaches roam the ruined kitchen with impunity and there's an overpowering smell of mold.

Surik's daily movements have worn a path through the junk, like tracks through deep snow. The path goes from his prolapsed army cot in the living room to a small clearing around the armchair and TV. Then the trail heads to the kitchen, with a discreet detour to the bathroom along the way.

"Sit, sit," Surik says. "Want coffee? A guest is a gift from God. Especially when it's our own fuckin' Saba. I don't believe it." He shakes his head. "How are you, Bublik?"

Whenever not occupied, Surik's hands remain at the idling tremble of a lifetime alcoholic. He makes two cups of instant coffee. Then he studiously fills half of his cup with vodka and tops it off with four heaped spoons of sugar.

"Decades ago, Lena came up here in the middle of the night. She wanted the zipper fixed on her shitty Soviet suitcase. I couldn't fix it and then the zipper broke off completely. Out of nowhere, she burst into tears right where you're sat. Can you imagine? Lena crying?"

I shake my head.

"I thought she was carved out of steel, that woman. Anyway, we strapped a couple of belts around the suitcase in the end. . . . I guess that was the day you left."

"I guess it was."

Surik scratches absently under the bandage at his throat.

"What is that?" I ask.

He looks up.

"Cut myself shaving." He smiles. "It's nothing."

"What happened?"

He waves the question away with a trembling hand.

"Doctors, operations. It ain't pretty, getting old."

He picks up his coffee, then puts it down without taking a sip.

"I half thought I might see you here, you know."

"You did?"

"Well, first Irakli dropped out of the sky like a Tsar Bomba. Then Sandro came through here. In and out in five minutes. Couldn't even sit and chat."

"When, Surik? When were they here?"

He takes a wobbly sip from his cup and tops it up with a splash of vodka.

"Irakli? I don't know." He shrugs. "A few months now."

"And Sandro?"

"Days, maybe a week or two."

"Which is it, Surik? Days or weeks?"

Surik's expression cuts my anger short. He spreads his arms.

"One day spills into the next in this place. I'm sorry."

"What did Sandro want?" I ask, a little softer.

"Nothing, really. Said he wanted to find Tamaz. Your godfather, remember him?"

I nod.

"Well, I thought it was odd. But what do I know? I told him, I said, Tamaz is long gone to Kukia. Only his wife still rattles around that big house, all alone, bless her."

"Then what?" I keep my voice from rising.

"I gave him the address and he left. Barely a goodbye. Not like Sandro, to be rude." Surik shrugs. "I guess he had his reasons."

"What reasons?"

"I don't know, Saba. All I know is I saw him a few days later in the yard, pottering around in Lena's garden. Ran off before I could even get the window open. . . ."

That was Sandro leaving me the page I've crumpled into my pocket. The police must have been right on him, for him to rush like that. I take a breath and try to bend my thoughts back into some kind of useful orbit. I ask Anzor to slow my heart a little.

"What about Irakli? What did he want?"

Surik's expression darkens and he fails to hide it.

"Nothing. He came by, we talked. Old times and that. We were classmates—me, Eka, and Irakli. But you know that. He gave me those pages from his play. What for, I said to him—why? Said I was a character in them. Humor me, he says, you don't have to read them. It's a crumb to prove I existed here. Once upon a time."

Surik taps his temple.

"Always a little funny, your da. I still have them somewhere. But gun to my head, I couldn't find them for Sandro. I still can't."

He shrugs, looking around the room.

"Then we drank, Irakli and me. Then we drank some more. Then I drank a lot more and then it was done."

Giving a short, sharp exhale, Surik drains the rest of his coffee and continues.

"He said to me, Surik, he says, once I'm done with these pages, there's nothing left for me here—like that. I'm flying back to my boys."

Surik pauses and glances at me.

"Well, I guess that's all down the toilet now," he mumbles.

"What?"

He ignores the question. Instead, he jumps up to make another coffee, even though I've barely put a dent in mine. He tops up my cup until it's brimming. Then he makes himself another Nescafé cocktail. No wonder he's emaciated. His breakfast is tepid coffee, sugar, vodka, and whatever dust accumulated in the mug overnight. He scratches under the gauze at his throat again and his fingers come away daubed with blood.

"Surik, you OK?"

"I drink too much. Thins the blood. It's OK."

A thin trickle of blood appears from under the bandage.

"You're bleeding."

He waves my words away, wiping a trail of blood up his trouser leg.

"Listen, we argued, Irakli and me. Said some hard things . . ."

"What things?"

"Well, he wouldn't shut up about how he was hurting. All the things he did to send Eka money, how hard he worked in London. Poor me, poor Irakli. Boo-hoo."

Surik waves his hand dismissively.

"He just wouldn't shut up. Sort of lost control of it, he did. I'm done with this place, he kept saying, no one and nothing for me here. Just like that, over and over."

Surik glances at the collection of part-empty bottles of vodka huddled together on the table. His hands are really shaking now.

"I was ready to slap him. Irakli—the center of his own Irakli-universe. Always has been. I set him straight. You've no idea what you did to Eka, I told him."

Surik shakes his head to calm himself, but it doesn't work.

"I know, Surik, I know, he says—it's all my fault. Cried like a damn child, right where you're sitting."

He stops to take several gulps from his mug. Suddenly he looks at me, eyes no longer flitting around the room.

"Saba, listen to me. I told him about Eka."

"What about her?"

"The truth."

"What truth?"

"Eka and me. We grew up together, right in this building. Our flats shared a kitchen back then. They say the kitchen is the heart of a household. Our families shared a heart. Your Lena, and my ma—like sisters. Fought all the time. Somehow, one didn't strangle the other."

"Surik, what's this got to do—"

"I've loved Eka as far back as I can remember. My first memory is of her in that yard down there. An angel. And then . . . and then Irakli comes swanning in here."

Anger kindles in Surik's eyes.

"Suddenly, Eka has no time for Surik. Surik the drunk. Surik the fucking handyman. Always good for a laugh, Surik. But only if Irakli's not around."

He sloshes more vodka into his mug.

"When Irakli took you and Sandro and left, I got my Eka back. My angel. She came back to me at last."

Surik puts his head in his hands.

"But she wasn't Eka anymore. Not really. Without you and Sandro, she was only part-Eka. She would take you boys to school in the mornings, did you know that? Right up to the gates, as usual. Every morning. Only you weren't fucking here anymore. . . ."

His fingers scratch under the bandage and come away bloody again.

"Four o'clock, sharp, she'd be there, watching the kids come out. It's crazy, Eka, I told her, it's abnormal. They're not in there. They're in London! I know, Surik, but it makes me feel better, she'd say."

He looks away and shakes his head. There are tears in his eyes.

"She told me the cat thing. Broke my ugly heart."

"What cat thing?" I manage, but I already know the answer.

"Eka's cat. The way that poor cat searched for her kittens. All over the house, for days and days—"

"Surik," I interrupt.

But he didn't sign the pact about Eka. He's not tied by those restrictions.

"Eka wandered Sololaki for hours. At first I thought, running errands. But then she widened the search, went all over Tbilisi. Gone all day. So, I pressed her. Pushed her to tell me, and I wish I hadn't.

"I'm like that cat, she said. I know they're gone, Surik. But I can't stop looking—do you think I'm crazy?"

He knocks his coffee over and ignores the murky brown liquid as it spreads across the table and drips to the floor. He takes a deep breath to steady himself.

"I kept a secret, Saba, I'm sorry."

They say you can smell the lightning before it strikes. I smell it now.

"What secret?"

"Things like that, they take a toll. You can't keep a secret like that forever."

He holds up his shaking hands, to show me the proof. The evidence of damage.

"I lost count how many years I kept that secret. Then Irakli drops on me out the sky. I broke—I couldn't hold it anymore. I told him everything. I stuck the knife in first, Saba. I did. I don't blame him one bit for—"

"What secret, Surik?" I try to guide him back before he veers off again.

"The money, Saba, the money!" he blurts out. "I had the money to send Eka to you. My dad's flat sold to some rich Armenian. God knows how. A miracle—I had the money. Not much, but enough to bribe someone, pay someone off, get her out. Send her to London to you. But I didn't. I didn't do any of that. Because I needed her. Without her I'm . . ."

He shows me his shaking hands again. He goes on, but I can't hear him anymore. They say losing a limb is completely painless at first.

Shocked, your body dumps your entire supply of adrenaline, endorphins, and whatever else is lying around directly into your veins. It's an instant reaction wired right into your spine. It doesn't need your permission. With all those chemicals sloshing around in your veins, there's no pain.

That's how this feels. I sit and absorb the words, note the new information down like you might note the color of someone's eyes. Surik stands up and moves toward me. Seeing my face, he stops short and goes back to his seat.

"You OK?" he asks.

I shake my head.

"It's the drink, Saba, I'm so sorry. . . ."

He starts to rock back and forth in his seat.

"I heard this thing on TV, maybe radio, I don't know, it's hard to remember these things. They said the memories you make when you're drunk—they're not real memories. Because when you're drunk you're not really you, you see? So, the memories aren't yours. They're not *real* memories. Whatever decisions you make, they're not yours either—"

His hands jitter along the tabletop looking for something they'll never find. He takes a breath as though there isn't enough air in the room.

"By that theory, I have no memories at all. Someone else lived my life for me. Stole it from me. I made no decisions—I didn't trap Eka here. I could never do that to her."

There's sweat on his brow.

"Question is, who did? Where is *that* Surik? Where is *he*?"

"Surik." I raise my voice to cut through his rising panic.

He takes another drowning gulp of air and seems unsatisfied. His voice rises to a hoarse shout.

"Who was it—was it him? Was it *me*?"

His head swings side to side as though he's surrounded by dangers only he can see. His hands go to his throat to help get words out. But no more words come. He tugs the bandage down and with a soft tearing sound it comes away, uncovering the sight beneath. A barely healed, jagged scar, running ear to ear. Stitched and stapled together by an indifferent hand, it seeps milky pus and blood in places where the stitches have popped.

Surik sweeps his hand toward the bottle of vodka, knocking it off the table. He rises and reaches for me instead.

"Bublik, help."

But it's too late. His eyes roll toward the ceiling and his face loses tension, like worn-out elastic. He slumps forward and falls. Before I can catch him, he clatters his head off the hard edge of the table and lands facedown at my feet. I jump up and my coffee spills across the table. I turn Surik's limp body over onto his back, shake him by the shoulders.

"Surik!"

His breathing's very shallow. Every few seconds he rattles down a deep lungful, like he's about to dive underwater. I slap his face, like I've seen people do on TV. Nothing. Somebody's home, but the lights aren't on.

A bright ray of inspiration shines through the shit. I stagger to the kitchen, knocking junk out of my way as I go. I come back with a dirty aluminum bowl, water sloshing off the sides, and dump it all on his face. It does nothing but wet him. I'm all out of ideas. I stand over Surik and wonder if I should do anything at all to save him.

He spares me that crime. He wakes up in stages, like a computer booting up. First his eyes flutter and stop. Then his limbs twitch. His ramshackle system tests for damage sustained, burned-out synapses and large gaps in memory. He stops gasping and his eyes open.

"Surik, you OK?"

He groans and leans up on one elbow. "I think so."

He climbs back into his chair like a toddler.

"That last sip of vodka's always poisoned," he says.

What starts out as a chuckle turns into a hacking cough. He wipes his mouth with his palm.

"Just a little mal-fuck-tion."

He wipes the wet hair away from his eyes. He looks at his hands and then at his crotch.

"Not where I expected to be wet."

"I didn't know what to do."

"Ah."

He looks around, spots the vodka bottle on the floor, and picks it up.

"Just so you know. The way to bring an alcoholic back to life is alcohol."

He shakes the vodka side to side and takes a swig straight from the concussed bottle.

"Surik, your hands . . ." I say, pointing.

He holds them out. They've stopped trembling.

"Funny, isn't it? They'll behave for a few days now."

He takes another swig of neat vodka. His hands reach for his throat. Finding no bandage there, they flinch away. He looks at the blood and pus on his fingers. Suddenly, he spreads his arms wide and offers me his throat.

"No one will know, Saba. Do what Irakli fucked up."

I back away from him until I stumble back into my seat.

"Irakli did that?"

Surik smiles and looks away.

"He strolled to the kitchen, came back with my bread knife, and—" He runs his thumb across his throat and clicks his tongue. "Ear to fuckin' ear. Did a shit job. Shame, that."

I try to rest my eyes anywhere but his throat.

"The neighbors called the police, the ambulance. Irakli ran away. The hospital did this Frankenstein job."

He points at his throat.

"I should have kept my mouth shut. But he nearly cut my head off. I was on their useless drugs, instead of what I *really* needed. Not a drop of alcohol in me by the time they questioned me. So, I told them everything. Now the police want Irakli and he's run off to fuck-knows-where."

Surik sighs. Silence descends while I try and fail to find words to say. He shambles about the room and cleans the mess we've made. After a while, he stops.

"Saba, you OK?"

There's a hand on my shoulder and I recoil like it burned me. I regret it when I see Surik's face. That gesture hurt him more than Irakli ever did with the damn bread knife. I watch him reset his expression with effort. He tries to smile. I still can't get words to join up. This is too much. I need to think.

"I should go," I manage.

"Wait," Surik says. "Do you want to see the old place downstairs? It's been empty all this time. I heard someone bought it not long ago. You could still look around. Might cheer you up."

There it is. I can't say no to it now. Maybe I'll take a walk through the old house. Maybe I'll run my fingers along the whispering curtains and watch the shadows of oak leaves dance on my bedroom wall. Maybe just for a minute. Maybe it will help me make sense of all this.

I could check the rooms are still in the right place:

Anzor's, first on the left.

The dripping bathroom, then the threadbare living room.

Eka's room, Sandro's room, and mine, side by side.

Our oddly shaped kitchen overlooking the yard.

Lena's little room right by the back door.

Surik breaks the spell.

"I still have Eka's key somewhere. Hold on."

From a shoebox under his cot, he produces a large brass key and points it at me like a gun.

"OK," I hear myself say.

Surik gives me the key. In a trance, I head downstairs. I come to our door and that's when I see the marks Sandro left for me. They're scratched right into the door itself. The scratches are shallow, hurried. A good scrub would vanish them forever:

Like the fox, I run with the hunted

And if I'm not the happiest man on earth

I'm surely the

Luckiest man alive

I smile. There you are, Sandro. This clue isn't signed by our "Valiko," but I know it's your doing—your favorite Charles Bukowski quote. Surik didn't tell you his secret, I know that now. Because if he had, Surik would be dead. I know you well, brother—slow to anger, but deadly when pushed to your limit.

This graffiti, your steps here, they're my distractions. I love you for them. OK, Sandro, let's do this—you and me. I face the door to our expired childhood and push.

As soon as it opens, I know something's wrong. A strong smell of wet plasterboard and sanded wood wafts out. This is not the place I haunted in my dreams. There are no rooms, no whispering curtains to caress, no piano to sit under, and no walls for shadows to dance on. In fact, every wall in the damn place has been knocked down.

I can see all the way to the other end of the flat, where three dusty workmen are preparing to knock through the outside wall onto the street. Ugly piles of crushed brick, plaster, and broken wooden slats dot the ripped-up flooring. Naked pipes and wiring are obscenely visible along the ceiling.

The workmen look in my direction in unison, as though I've interrupted some clandestine meeting. The one standing by the wall unshoulders his sledgehammer and rests it on the floor. He lifts his hard-hat brim to get a better look.

"Who are you?"

I consider my options. I can answer the question. I also want to run headlong at them and tear them limb from limb. But the problem isn't the workmen. The problem is where it always is—higher up in the food chain than you can ever reach. I decide to answer, but nothing intelligible comes out.

"I'm . . . this is . . . Surik gave . . ."

They stare at me blankly.

"You can't be in here," the nearest workman says. "How did you get in?"

Idiotically, I show him the brass key and he snatches it from my hand.

"Can't be in here, brother."

"I used to live here."

"Well, this is a shoe shop now."

The workman by the wall picks up the sledgehammer and rests it on his shoulder.

"Please. Wait, just wait."

"What for?"

If they knock through this wall, this place will never be my home again. If the wall stands, I can still fix this. I'll make myself remember the details that have faded. I could put it back to how it was, if only they let me. There must be something I can do to stop them. I look at the man with the sledgehammer and all I see is slate-blue indifference staring back.

"Get rid of him," he says and lifts the sledgehammer over his head.

Grunting, he heaves the sledgehammer through my bedroom wall. An uneven, beach-ball-size hole crumbles open. Daylight pours in. I can see Tabidze Street and a row of parked cars. A handful of passersby glance toward the noise.

It feels like my heart's stopped beating. Yet somehow, I'm still standing. At last, my heart picks up a beat. I feel it thudding through the veins in my neck. The workman wrenches the sledgehammer out of the hole he's ripped in my wall. There's a heavy hand on my shoulder.

"Just go, man."

The workman shoulders the sledgehammer again, then lifts it overhead. I can't watch this. I turn and bolt. I'm out of there, almost at a sprint.

I run through the yard, out of the tunnel, and onto the street, where I run into Kristina. We collide with a grunt and step back from each other.

"Where's the fire, idiot?" she says.

The children are gone. We're alone, just me and her. I look into her Pippi Longstocking eyes and see them widen.

"Saba? Is that you, Saba?"

Her face tiptoes into a smile.

"No, I'm sorry," I mumble.

"My God, Saba, is that really you?"

"I'm sorry. I have to go."

"Saba, wait. Where are you going?"

I'm already past her. She says my name one last time, but I can't stop. I'm gone.

9

DOUBLE, DOUBLE TOIL
AND TROUBLE

W hile I was at Surik's, Tbilisi stirred, woke, and filled the streets with strangers. I look up and I'm already among them. It would take so many words to make even one of them understand.

I try to outrun Surik's secret. How he kept Eka from us. How Irakli's answer to this news was to run a knife across Surik's throat. I'm scared of what my answer might be.

"Surik, talk to me."

There's no response. There won't be one. The imaginary Surik didn't survive the real Surik and his secret. Where his voice used to be there's a numb silence, like the aftermath of a migraine.

A nearby car radio reads out fairy tales:

"... airport baggage handler last recorded on CCTV exiting the building for a cigarette break, found this morning on the

disused emergency runway. Lower legs amputated due to severity of wounds. Not unusual, veterinary expert says, wolves are opportunists. If the prey's still alive after they immobilize it, so be it—I've seen them eat a cow elk alive. Hospital confirms the man's in critical but stable condition. . . ."

I try to get away from the sound of the radio, but it follows me:

". . . severed hand discovered some distance from the body. No attempt made to reattach the hand due to its part-masticated condition.

Three of the six gentoo penguins from Tbilisi Zoo washed up on the Mtkvari shore, near Sololaki hospital. Bravely, hospital A&E staff attempted a rescue. Efforts were in vain. Dead penguins returned to the zoo vets. It's expected the remaining penguins won't last long in the Mtkvari waters.

Local man claims to have shot the Mtatsminda tiger, Artyom, in his garden in Sololaki. No body found . . ."

Again, my mind tries to make contact with what Surik did to Eka, to Irakli, to us. But I force it onto a more manageable hurt. My home's becoming a shoe shop. My memories in that place are no longer mine to visit. They flash by like trees past a train window. I can't tie one to the next. I can't pin them to a time or a place. Some ridiculous cosmic oversight has erased me from my own childhood.

A nameless, faceless imitation of me lives out my memories. I search for this un-Saba who stole my childhood from me but I'm always a step behind him:

I crawl under the piano in the living room to find the un-Saba already wrote out "Kristina" in the dust on the underside, while the grown-ups strategized getting through the winter. He's gone, I missed him. Nothing but a handprint in the dust to mark his passing.

Or that summer day the dusty muslin curtains stopped sighing and hung still. A sudden darkness like a solar eclipse dimmed the day. The un-Saba watched from the window as walnut-size hailstones fell from a flaxen sky. I've missed him again. Nothing to see but the destruction in the yard—Lena's battered garden and shredded leaves, nasty dents the hailstones hammered into the cars. The un-Saba just left here. His strange exhalations are still fading from the windowpane.

I try another memory, but it's no good. The un-Saba's been here too. He stole the best one.

He knew the bathroom door didn't creak if you opened it slow. That's how he caught Lena flushing newborn kittens down the toilet. One by one they went, furslick and blind. Unstruggling, sinking like stones. Slop, flush.

Meanwhile, locked out of this massacre, Eka's cat scratched at the kitchen door with rising panic. The kittens are very poorly, Lena lied.

The cat searched for her kittens for weeks. In every room, every closet, under every bed, in every corner of the flat. Her search always ended in the bathroom, sniffing the air and meowling weakly.

This is how Eka felt when she lost us. Now I know the practicalities—her widening, one-woman search party for sons she knew to be gone. Waiting at school gates . . .

No, that's no good.

Coming out of this trance, I find myself wandering around the Lenin-less square. The car radio and the fairy tales are gone. My mind finally makes contact with Surik's secret and what it means for Irakli—he's on the run from the police, heading for some ending he can't yet picture.

Then there's Sandro, ever loyal. He'll follow Irakli to any ending.

Somehow, Sandro's search and the trail he built for me has made him hunted too.

The last clue he left was the single page of *Kaleidoskupi* and the Bukowski quote about running "with the hunted." I try to force a connection between the two, but my anger builds. Irakli and Sandro have disappeared because of Surik.

"What am I supposed to do? Swan-dive off the cliff after them?" I ask the question, unsure which voice will answer.

"They need you, Saba. Chin up. Kittens or no kittens." It's Eka.

I shake my head clear. Pick a direction, get moving. I need to get out of this fucking heat, get somewhere safe, somewhere I can think. Nodar's is out of the question; I can't go back there. But where?

I start walking. Cross the road—get away from this square first. Silent for days, my phone picks up a signal and suddenly delivers a whole Morse code sentence of chirps and vibrations. The notification sounds stutter and trip over themselves. Absurd, irrelevant missives from my life in the UK.

"Saba, parcel for you, needs your signature."

"Left it by your door."

"You're welcome!"

"Camden London Borough Council Tax:
Direct Debit payment failed. Please contact us
at www.camden . . ."

"4 missed calls and 3 voicemail messages from:
Work
Work
Work
Work"

"Argos Summer Sale—30% off all garden furniture
and barbecue sets!"

I stare at my phone as it delivers a pent-up fury of backdated garbage that means nothing anymore. The electric current of Surik's secret is still live in my head and these messages from another world pour water on the whole mess. My synapses and neurons short and bring my body to a stop.

There's a distant horn of a car. Someone shouts something behind me. The horn grows louder, closer. I turn just in time for my whole view to be filled with the dusty blue hood and grille of a Toyota. It's going too fast to stop before it hits me. The meaningless, animal bleat of the horn finally resolves into what it always was—Nino's voice.

"Got yaa!"

The Toyota bites my legs first and flings my torso onto its hood. There's a glass crunch of my head meeting the windshield and then I'm flying. All I see is sky, ground, sky, ground, while Nino and the awful car horn shrill *"Weeeeeeeee!"* right in my ear.

I land on my back. My lungs empty themselves on impact. That's it. That's the last auto-recovery file on my hard drive.

WHEN I REBOOT and come back online, I'm draped boneless across a hospital bed. My wrists are tied in place and the sun is burning a hole in the wall above me. I lift my head to look around. The movement sets off overlapping peals of Sunday Eucharist bells inside my skull. I lie back down and close my eyes. I hear Nodar's voice somewhere in the room.

"Why's he tied up?"

A female voice answers.

"As I explained, physically he is fine. Some bruising, minor concussion, no serious brain trauma. He's lucky. But he was agitated and violent when he was brought in and had to be restrained for us to treat him."

"Violent?"

"Verbally and physically. He—"

"He's had a bad day," Nodar's voice interrupts. "Who hit him?"

"Some waste of a taxi driver."

I hear Nodar snort.

"What did you give him? He can barely move."

"He's been sedated. He'll be fine to be released in an hour or two."

"Listen, can I be *sedated* too? I've a hangover you wouldn't believe," Nodar says, chuckling.

To the sound of the nurse laughing along with Nodar, my bed starts to rotate and accelerate, until it spins me off into darkness.

When I come back online, I find myself slumped in the back of Nodar's Volga, bounding over potholes.

"Nodar?"

"Our hero stirs!"

"How did you find me?"

"You called me, remember?"

I raise my head and clap eyes on Nodar. He's back in his taxi driver uniform, an L&M hanging from his mouth. He grins back at me.

"Feel better?"

"No."

He laughs, making the cherry on his cigarette bob in the gloom.

"I don't know about London, but here you look both ways, *twice*, before you cross the road."

I start to remember the ambulance ride. My lucky Pink Floyd T-shirt cut from me with surgical scissors to check for broken ribs. My now-scratched and dented phone held to my ear by the paramedic, while I spilled my guts to someone on the other end of the line. I thought I was talking to Sandro, Irakli, maybe even Eka.

"What did I say on the phone?"

I remember crying.

"Nothing. Heartache cut with a concussion. Something about cats. Hang it." Nodar spares me the embarrassment.

Back in the flat, I see that Nodar and Ketino have reached a tentative cease-fire. At least they're talking to each other again. Nodar guides me to the sofa and sits at the other end. I know what he's about to say.

"Listen, brother, about yesterday."

I watch him search for the words and realize I've already forgiven him.

"It's OK, Nodar."

"Look, I had no choice. He offered me a way into Ossetia. And like a twenty-carat moron, I believed him."

"I know."

"That whoreson detective . . ." Nodar shakes his head. "Someone oughta go shit in his oven. But, anyway, doesn't matter—I can't believe I stabbed you in the back. I was raised better than that."

More than his awkward words, I believe his eyes.

"I'm not telling that detective anything else, brother, believe me."

He watches me for a reaction.

"Mowgli?"

He says the word the way he did the first time, unsure if I'll take offense. I stretch my face into a wan smile.

"Mowgli, listen, you're killing me. What did you find? Tell me what happened."

And I do. I confess everything. How I connected Eka's *Kaleidoskupi* pages to *The Wizard of Oz* clue and how that led me home. Nodar knows just to smile this time, instead of calling me Dr. Watson. I even tell him about the Bukowski quote scratched into our door and the single page of *Kaleidoskupi* Sandro left for me.

"I've no idea what it all means," I say.

"Probably because you tried to headbutt a moving vehicle, brother." Nodar taps his temple.

But then I get to Surik and his secret, how he could have sent Eka to us. Once I start talking about that, the words get away from me. I can't stop even if I wanted to. I recognize these things to be true as I'm saying them. If I swallow them, they will burn their way out.

"If he'd helped, she would have been with us in London. Maybe Irakli wouldn't have lost his fucking mind working every shit job he could find. Maybe we could have built something there. A new home, a new life. Isn't that the point, Nodar? Isn't that the fucking point of moving to another country?"

Nodar raises his hand slightly. The whole block of flats can hear you, brother, he wants to say, but he doesn't. I ramble on about Surik's shipwreck of a life, how Irakli cut his throat open, Kristina, the workmen in my ruined home, and finally, I land on the last truth.

"Irakli wouldn't have come back to Tbilisi, looking for ghosts. None of this mess, the clues, the play pages, the fucking graffiti, the police—none of this had to happen. It's all him, Nodar. All Surik's fault."

Nodar lights a cigarette and hands it over. Then he lights one for himself. His eyes twinkle with the beginnings of a smile.

"It also means you wouldn't have met me, brother. And your life is so much richer with me in it."

And then Nodar gifts me a new truth that I would have never found by myself.

"Surik loved her, Mowgli. Plain and simple. Without her, he was ruined. People say 'my life for yours' all the time here, brother. But no one really means it."

Nodar's right. But I'm exhausted.

"Don't look so glum, Dr. Watson. There's good news your dented skull hasn't processed yet."

"What?"

"Sandro's trail—it's working. The police have no idea."

"Only if you stop telling them everything I find."

Nodar smiles at his own feet. "I guess you've earned a few free shots, brother. I deserve it."

While I was telling him of my adventures, my whole body began to ache. Now that I've stopped, the pain makes me squirm.

"Nodar."

"Yeah?"

"I feel like I've been hit by a car."

"You probably dented the car more than it dented you. Better lucky than smart, they say."

He fishes around in his pocket and produces two large white pills, carefully cut from a sheet and stapled to a prescription note.

"They said to give you this, you know, if you started to feel like you got hit by a car."

Nodar disappears into the kitchen. Left unsupervised, my mind drifts back to Tabidze Street and Surik's cockroach-speckled life. I picture how he looked on the dirty floor—a man drowning on dry land. Nodar comes back with a small, chipped glass of water and the pills.

"They said take one now and one later," he tells me, after I've already swallowed both.

"Fuck, Mowgli, OK," he says. "I guess I'll keep an eye on you."

He sets me up on the sofa and covers me with a blanket. We sit and smoke while I wait for the pills to kick in.

When I was seven, Eka took Sandro and me to the seaside. Sandro sulked behind his book because it was my turn with Anzor's swimming goggles. He thought I squandered my turn by splashing in the shallow water, looking for seashells. But sometimes, I would dive under and stare out to sea, where I could almost make out the shapes of monsters in the shifting darkness. The prospect of spotting something in that murk scared me as much as turning my back on it. Paralyzed between the two fears, I'd freeze and wait for the monster to come for me.

That's how this feels at first—like a sinister presence just beyond the reach of my senses. The feeling doesn't last long. Five minutes later the pills hit and they hit hard. . . .

"Don't worry, Mowgli, I'm here. I'll call them if things go south."

I can barely hear Nodar. Words some Shakespeare sadist made me memorize once upon a time bubble to the surface. I grin like a fool and follow the spell as it casts itself in my head.

Double, double toil and trouble

The moment I stepped off the plane that first night in Tbilisi, I felt a timer start. It's been ticking ever since. What's it counting down to?

Fire burn and caldron bubble

"What's that?" Nodar says somewhere behind me.

I have to roll my eyes back into position and lick my lips before I can reply.

"Did I say that out loud?"

"You all there, Mowgli?"

"Yeah, I'm fine."

Nodar chuckles.

"So, what is it? A song?"

"I don't remember."

He flicks a switch and somewhere a voice starts reading out love messages from all four corners of the ceiling. Another wave washes over me and melts me into the sofa. I go back to the incantation.

Eye of newt and toe of frog,
"Something" of bat and tongue of dog.

"What part of bat goes in the potion?"

"What potion?"

Nodar's head sails past like a balding frigate.

"I'm OK," I say to it.

"Goo-ood, Saba, gooo-oood," it foghorns back.

They say two witches live in the forest north of Tbilisi. Twin sisters, they say. Killed their mother coming into this world. But that's nothing compared to what they did to their father. So it is said.

If there's ever trouble in your village, this is what you do:

Step one: Pick one of your kids—your least favorite.

Step two: Bring the child to the edge of the forest. Search the trees until you find sweets hanging from their branches. This is the first step of a trail that leads deep into the dark, lovely forest. Set your child off along the trail. Do *not* follow.

Step three: Go home and lock your door for the night. The trouble in your village will resolve as if by magic. Don't worry, your child won't suffer or want for anything. But you'll never see them again.

"But what happens to that kid?" I mumble.

While I was looking for the trail of sweets, fog has filled Nodar's living room. The air's so milky thick I can barely see him. He leans his face right up to mine and shows me the toll a hard life takes on a man.

"What kid?" he booms through cotton wool.

I turn my face away.

"Eka's that kid. We gave Eka to the witches. It's Eka."

"Shh, brother—I'm right here, I can hear you."

I try more of the spell.

> *For a charm of powerful trouble,*
> *Like a hell-broth boil and bubble.*

What was that thing that snuck up on me when I was playing with Kristina? It was raining, so we sat cross-legged on the cool stone floor of the stairwell, playing cards. I found myself looking at her underpants, which were on display, as usual. But something didn't feel right. Something about it was sinister. I couldn't look away from her crotch. I wanted to, but I couldn't.

"No, that's a lie. I didn't want to."

"What's that, brother?"

Like a drop of poison, that moment curdled everything with Kristina. I was ashamed, like I'd stolen some innocent part of her and she didn't even know it. The incantation turns dark.

Finger of birth-strangled babe,
Ditch-deliver'd by a drab,
Make the gruel thick and slab . . .

Something in my head is on the hunt for my off switch. It stalks room to room, calm and methodical. No way will it fail. There's nowhere to run.

"Is there anything worse than knowing how your story ends?"

Someone's shaking me, pulling me up from underwater. It's Nodar. He calls my name over and over. I try to warn him.

"I'm sinking like a stone, Nodar. Let go, or I'll take you with me."

"Saba, Saba, quiet, listen! They're about to say it again."

"We gave Eka to the witches. We gave Eka—"

"Shut up, listen."

He puts a hand over my mouth. The voice on the radio comes into focus.

"Saba and Sandro, if you're listening—"

I fight to move Nodar's hand.

"Shh, listen!"

"—don't follow my trail. It was never meant for you—it will get you killed. Your da."

"Hear that?"

Nodar takes his hand away. I take a deep breath to say something, but everything dims and no words come out.

10

RUN WITH THE HUNTED

I wake up pressed, stone-heavy, into the bed where I slept unmoving. I don't know what year it is, never mind what time. If you asked me my name, I'd have to think about it. I feel rested, through to the bone. My legs and back are bruised, but it's bearable.

I need to unlock Sandro's clue. With the single, damp page of *Kaleidoskupi* in my hands, I pace Natia's room with my new limp—four steps up, four steps back.

I need to hurry . . . and then I remember the Charles Bukowski words Sandro scraped into the door of our home:

> *Like the fox, I run with the hunted*
> *And if I'm not the happiest man on earth*
> *I'm surely the*
> *Luckiest man alive*

Sandro and I discovered Bukowski the year Eka died. His books were in a similar language to mine and Sandro's. Only this time, Sandro wasn't leading the charge. In Chuck's books, I read deeper, baser things than words. Guts and innards poured onto the page. Things that taught me that sometimes life will try to break you. But that's OK, Chuck told me, it happens all the time. You can let life break pieces of you. Don't worry, they will heal. If they don't and you're still standing, you never needed those pieces anyway. Smile right in life's ugly face and keep going. But whatever you do, never let it break your *spine*.

Hooked, I let the Bukowski books build a small tower on my desk. One by one, I pressed them into Sandro's hands. Your turn, brother. Read this. Promise me. I hoped Chuck would help him sleep better.

Sandro was calm and unflappable by day, but sleep betrayed him. In the middle of the night, he would stir and call out Eka's name. Sometimes so softly that I barely woke. Sometimes, so loud that he'd startle himself from his own dreamings. I never told him I knew. I hoped Chuck would help him the way he'd helped me.

Sandro digested Chuck's inebriated wisdoms in a few days. The magic needed a few weeks to really take hold, but soon he stopped calling out for Eka as he slept.

Afterward, he told me that "Run with the Hunted" was his favorite poem. He said it sounded just like Irakli. As though for a moment, maybe, Chuck had stolen Irakli's thoughts. It reminded him of how Irakli vanished off to a monastery after the divorce.

Truth is, neither of us knew what caused the divorce. Or what drove Irakli to hide away at that monastery. We still don't—

My feet stop walking. I think I know where Irakli is.

He spent a full year hiding in that monastery, adrift in a mislaid corner of Georgia, where the real world couldn't reach him. Anytime Sandro and I asked about it, he would default to the same anecdote about the sultan's bed he'd built and how it almost got him kicked out. The same sultan's bed on the *Kaleidoskupi* page in my hand.

The page, the Bukowski quote, they both click into place. Hands shaking, I unfold the *Kaleidoskupi* page and my eyes find the words I need:

TAMAZ: Listen, Valo, I don't get it. What did they do to you up in Ushguli?

VALIKO: What do you mean?

TAMAZ: I mean that crazy monastery up there. . . .

I realize Tamaz doesn't matter here. He's just a bystander. What matters is the word *Ushguli*. That's where Irakli is now, a second time. Hunted again and hiding at the monastery in Ushguli.

Look at me, Sandro. I'm getting warmer, right? Are you there right now, brother? I'm coming.

USHGULI IS A PLACE CAREFULLY nestled into the impassable Caucasus mountains. It's halfway across the country from Tbilisi and about as far north as you can back yourself away from the rest of Georgia. The Ushguli people live with clouds for neighbors. That high in the mountains, the air's so thin that visitors promptly faint on arrival. At least that's what Irakli used to say. If you want to hide from the world, there aren't many places better than Ushguli.

As I cram things into my bag for the trip to this lost place in a lost country, Nino's voice interrupts. It always spells trouble when she's calm like this.

"All tied up with a neat little bow, eh, mummy's boy?"

"Not now, Nino."

"What if the police follow you up there? What then?"

"I'll make sure they don't."

"OK . . ."

Nino goes quiet and I continue to pack. But her silence builds until I feel it pressing against my temples. She finally breaks it.

"You're forgetting something, mummy's boy."

The tone of her voice makes me stop. She giggles.

"Eka's letters. You left them in that basement to rot."

The words make me sit down. When Surik startled me, I dropped the letters on the floor and never went back for them.

"Scattered them like they were trash. Your mummy's letters, mummy's boy. You just going to leave them behind?"

If I go back there, I risk the police following me.

"Oh, the police don't matter. We both know you'll go back for the letters, Saba."

She doesn't often call me by name. The way she says it this time sends a shiver through me. I feel other voices clamor to speak. Anzor almost does. I know what he'd say. Don't risk everything, Sabo, not now. But Nino doesn't let the others speak. She knows she's won. A debt is owed—I have to follow her into this darkness too.

I can't leave Eka's letters in that basement. Those workmen will be in there soon too, scavenging through the boxes and sending what they don't keep to the skip. I need to get those letters back right now.

I jump up to look for Nodar, but he's long gone. Instead, I find Ketino watering her yogurt plants in the living room. Her presence calms me. She appraises me over glasses perched on the tip of her nose.

"Sit, I'll get you something to eat."

She comes back from the kitchen with a chipped bowl full to the brim with okroshka. Ice-cold okroshka on a hot summer day is the culinary equivalent of putting your head on the cold side of the pillow.

"It's so good," I say as I spoon up mouthfuls of it.

"Don't talk with your mouth full."

She sits and watches me eat, catches herself, clears her throat, and looks away. I realize something about Ketino. Nodar may bring in some money, stomp around, shout at the TV, and drink when he wants. But he's in charge of nothing. He's just the muscle. Sat opposite me, sharp-eyed and alert, is the brains of the operation.

She waits for me to finish the okroshka. In the yard, children yelp and a dog starts barking. She turns toward the noise, about to scold some poor kid, but stops herself and sighs. When she turns back, a vague sadness softens her face.

"Don't let the day beat you, whatever it brings. It did yesterday. Don't let it today." She pats my hand, gets up, and takes my empty bowl with her to the kitchen.

I TAKE A LONG, circuitous route back to Sololaki. Every now and then, I betray Nodar and take a taxi to random landmarks, just in case someone's watching. Painfully slow, I close in on Sololaki and go down every quiet side street I can. Whenever I find myself alone, I stop and wait. I rest my bruised legs, smoke and wait for any sign of someone following my idiotic path around Tbilisi.

"You worry too much, mummy's boy."

I ignore Nino. She's already won and she doesn't interfere much. Her silence and this limping trek give me plenty of time to think. My mind keeps coming to rest with Eka.

Irakli's plan that she would rejoin us in London was both a promise and a lie. I think she knew it. I could feel the strain in her voice.

Phone calls back and forth between Tbilisi and London cost a fortune back then—we couldn't afford them. Letters were the alternative.

Instead of writing long letters, we'd record cassettes and then send them in the post. With the Georgian postal system still broken and corrupt, only a few of Eka's words made it out.

Back in London, I still have the last tape from her, bundled and hidden away like it's radioactive. I can't make myself listen to it again.

"Everyone has bad days, Saba." Eka's hesitant voice tries to preempt me.

"I'll never forget that tape."

Waiting for Irakli's myth of a reunion to materialize took a harsh toll. Eventually she couldn't keep her feelings hidden anymore. They escaped her and are now magnetized onto that tape forever. That's why I can't listen to it again.

On the tape, Eka listed all the dead Sulidzes and spared no detail. She spoke about Anzor's cancer. The urge to strangle him where he lay, when the nurses weren't watching. She confessed to unplugging his life support one night. All it did was set off alarms and bring the nurses running. She watched them drag Anzor back to this world.

"That wheezing thing in the hospital bed wasn't my brother. I wish he'd died by my hand."

A few days later he snuck out of this life while Eka was in the cafeteria.

At least Lena didn't linger—she wasn't that kind of woman. She did everything properly and promptly, even death. Lena passed in the company of masked strangers, during a potholed ambulance ride through Sololaki, while Eka followed in Surik's car, wondering why the sirens had gone silent.

"There is a logic to it," Eka says.

"What do you mean?"

"That I'd be the last Sulidze left."

"I don't see it."

"It had to end that way because that's how it was always going to end. Like a fairy tale—you finish it and realize you knew the ending all along."

"Fairy tales have happy endings."

Eka goes silent and I know she won't speak to me for a while. So I'll tell you how it did end for Eka, out here in the real world. She was walking back to her apartment from the market when her heart stuttered. She fainted. The doctors call this a "silent" heart attack. If you can get to a hospital, it's not fatal.

When she came to, she would have found herself in the stairwell of her building. By then, the silent heart attack had bloomed into the loud kind. She tried to reach the nearest door. But the nearest door was three flights up. She didn't make it. A trail of spilled groceries led the neighbor kid up a flight of steps to her body, grown colder than the stone steps she lay on.

I didn't go to her funeral. I didn't say my goodbye.

The simple truth is that I miss her. But I get by with just the grace notes of her—the way her hair smelled in the summer, or the way she called my name when it was time to go in for dinner. *March to the bathroom, wash your hands, Saba.* For a moment, she'd watch me eat in that disconcerting way mothers sometimes do. Always more food on my plate than hers.

Even without Nino urging me on, I'd still go back for her letters. They cost too much to abandon.

I arrive back at Tabidze Street winded and sweat-patched. This is the second time I'm here in two days, even though I swore never to return. I look over my shoulder at unpredictable intervals, still expecting to see someone following me. The workmen have made progress—the private insides of my childhood home are visible from the street.

A BMW with tinted windows is parked rudely across the middle of the yard. Only strangers parked like this here. I get the distinct feeling that someone's on the other side of the mirrored glass. Furtive eyes follow me from the darkness in the open windows facing the yard. Something has spooked the neighbors.

I rush down to the basement, stumbling over the steps.

"What's the rush?" Nino says. She knows something I don't. Always.

I collect Eka's letters and take the first step back into the sunny yard when the front doors of the BMW open in unison. A uniformed police officer appears first. Then I hear a familiar nasal voice from the passenger seat.

"Mr. Sulidze-Donauri." A man slides out of the car and nudges the door shut.

It's Detective Kelbakiani. New shirt, new waistcoat, same slimy mustache.

"What have you got there?" He gestures at Eka's letters.

Fuck. In my head, Nino giggles. I finally realize what she knew and I didn't. Eka's letters don't matter right now—there's nothing in them for the detective. More important is the *Kaleidoskupi* page in my pocket. The only flaw in Sandro's trail, the only thing that could lead the police to Irakli, is me.

Like a good little moron, I even circled the words *Ushguli* and *monastery* in my excitement. If they search me, they've caught Irakli and Sandro too.

"That's it—game over, mummy's boy." Nino cackles.

The detective's smile widens into a grin. Uneven nicotine-stained teeth, rarely brushed. Anzor's voice cuts through the panic.

"Get rid of the page, Sabo. Right now."

"How?"

I step back from the detective, to buy myself time. Anzor hands me the answer, perfectly formed. I take another step back and pull out the *Kaleidoskupi* page, in full view of the detective. I look right in his ugly face and fold the page into my mouth like it's a pancake. His eyebrows come up. He steps forward but it's too late. Two hasty chews and the page scratches its way down my gullet.

"What was that?" the uniformed officer says.

The detective doesn't wait for me to answer. He walks over and rips Eka's letters from my hands. Then he handcuffs me and shoves me into the back of the car. We drive to the glass police station in total silence.

I FOLLOW THE DETECTIVE into the depths of the station, like a blind man walking into a scalpel factory. We're heading down into the guts of the building, where the glass walls give way to a grubby, gray interior. Down here, they haven't bothered to wash the Soviet stench off the walls. Down here, it smells of lives ruined on a whim.

We walk past a packed communal holding cell. Hungry, sallow eyes follow us.

"The zoo animals caused a problem," the detective says over his shoulder. "And *these* zoo animals thought now's a good time to steal and loot."

Our walk through the station ends in an empty interrogation room. Lit by a naked light bulb, the room reeks of damp concrete and stale cigarette smoke. A small table with metal hoops for handcuffs occupies the middle of the room, along with two mismatched chairs.

We sit down opposite each other like we're about to play chess. My handcuffs clang on the metal skin of the table. I hold up my wrists.

"Am I under arrest?"

"Let's keep them on for now, shall we?"

He opens his notepad without looking at it. The meager stack of Eka's letters he confiscated is right there.

"Mr. Sulidze-Donauri." The detective's lip curls at my name. "You know why you're here."

He holds up his hand to silence any protest from me.

"I want to do you a favor and give you a chance."

He tries to sound kind, reasonable. But something about doing me a favor doesn't sit right with him. He can't quite hide it.

"Answer carefully. Do you know where Irakli Donauri is?"

"No."

The detective sighs, leans back, and glances down at Eka's letters. Quick as a snake.

"Fine then. What about your brother? Know where he is?"

"No."

"Why did you eat that piece of paper? What's on it?"

"What piece of paper?"

"You might actually get yourself killed in here, mummy's boy."

Despite Nino, I realize I feel calm. Now that I'm caught, all other options, possibilities, clues, and worries just fall from me. I have no control in here and I feel better for it. It's very simple—he will ask me questions and I'll refuse to answer. I'll never lead this snake to Irakli or Sandro. Whatever may come of it.

"Bravo, mummy's boy."

The detective leans closer.

"You Donauris are not doing well here, are you?"

He's dropped the Sulidze half of my name and doesn't even try to hide the distaste on his face.

"Daddy Donauri gets here and tries to cut someone's head off. Then Sonny Donauri comes here looking for his da—doesn't cooperate, doesn't tell us a thing, and then tries to run from us. Now we have to chase him down too."

His eyes narrow.

"And now you. Asshat Donauri—the bright spark of the family. You turn up, sniffing after his farts. Mysterious clues and fucking graffiti. Why were you at Tabidze Street? What did you find?"

"I just wanted to see my childhood home."

"You think this is a game? This is a murder investigation." He shakes his head.

"Go on, poke him," Nino urges.

"Attempted murder," she makes me say aloud.

"What?"

"Attempted murder," I say, louder this time.

He doesn't react the way I expect him to. Anger flits across his face and dissipates before he can even frown. He's come to a decision. He slaps his notepad shut.

"Perfect." He smiles.

Grabbing me by the handcuffs, the detective guides me out of the room. He leads me deeper into the police station.

"Where are we going?"

"They built the new station upstairs right on top of the old Soviet one. We're in the old station now, in the solitary cells."

We walk along shabby concrete hallways painted a sickly pea-soup green. We turn the corner onto a long corridor lined on both sides with heavy steel doors. Naked light bulbs hang from the ceiling at sparse intervals. A guard sits on a stool, reading a newspaper, at the other end of the corridor. He looks up and raises his hand in silent greeting. The detective does the same.

"They called these the Magic Cells."

"Magic?"

"They could make you disappear. Like magic."

He stops to lean against a cell door.

"Do you know why we call you people fair-weather Georgians?"

He runs the back of his hand down the coarse, unpainted steel of the cell door.

"Ran away at the first sign of trouble. Now you creep back here and think you're above the law."

He knocks on the cell door with a single knuckle. A muffled voice says something plaintive and indistinct from inside. With a clang that echoes like a gunshot, the detective pulls back the viewing hatch on the door.

"We caught this *specimen* at Tabidze Street." He grins. "Scratching graffiti into someone else's property, can you imagine? He thought he lost us."

I peer through the hatch into the dank cell. A shit-stained steel toilet in the corner and a grimy cot with one miserable occupant. Sandro.

He's sat cross-legged and slumped forward, with his head in his hands. He looks like he hasn't washed or eaten in days. There are bruises on his bare arms. He looks at the door and I see purple semicircles under his eyes.

"Sandro?" My voice rises.

He struggles to his feet. Eyes brimming with tears, he staggers toward the door. As he approaches, I realize his nose has been broken and left to heal untreated.

"Sandro, what happened?"

"Step back," the detective says behind me.

Sandro grips his side of the door, eyes widening. He opens his mouth to speak—words he's prepared and thought over. Sandro, always spinning the possibilities out to their logical ends. He's ready with exactly what he has to say. But the words get away from him. They build from a stutter into a bellow.

"It's just you now. Follow the trail. Follow the trail. Follow the fucking trail!"

I've never seen Sandro in such a state. I didn't think it possible. Before I can say anything to calm him, the hatch slams shut an inch from my nose. I turn on the detective and shove him in the chest. Eyes wide, he stumbles backward and thuds into the corridor wall opposite. I pull the viewing hatch open again.

"Sandro! What happened?"

The detective's bony hands grip me from behind. With surprising force, he heaves me away from the hatch and slams it shut again. I wrench myself around to face him. With Sandro's muffled yelling in the background, we lock eyes and all pretense drops away.

I know, bone-deep, this man is *"those people"* Irakli worried about. This is him. He wants more from our family than mere blood and broken bones. He wanted us before Irakli even came back here. And we keep giving him excuses to take his toll.

"This is your chance, mummy's boy. Punch him!" Nino says, and I manage to ignore her.

The guard bounds up the corridor toward us. He stops short, unclips his holster, and puts a hand on his gun. Along with the detective, he marches me back to the interrogation room.

"What, nothing comes to mind?" the detective says after a long silence.

"Why is Sandro here?"

"Obstructing an investigation."

"You tortured him."

"Torture?" He glances over his shoulder. "Did you say torture?"

A smile creeps onto his face.

"Where do you think you are, Mr. Do-na-uri?" He enunciates the name, lip curled. "We don't *torture* here."

He pauses as though those words just gave him an idea. He opens his notepad and takes out Eka's letters. He rips open the first envelope and pulls out the contents crudely. Eka's gentle words, written to Sandro and me, on pages pilfered from the school notebooks we left behind.

"December 1992. My boys, since you've been gone . . . et cetera, et cetera. Nothing useful."

He crumples up the letter and lets it fall into the bin by the table. It makes Nino angry.

"Come on, mummy's boy. Be a man. Do something."

"Next." The detective rips open another envelope, tearing the letter in half. "Oops."

He holds the two halves together and squints.

"February 1993. My boys, my dear English gentlemen, I miss you and I . . . et cetera, et cetera. Nothing useful."

"Do something, Saba!" Nino snarls.

One by one, the detective goes through every letter and destroys any trace of Eka I might have found within them. Nino's anger mounts with each one.

When the letters run out, the detective takes a lighter from his jacket pocket and winks at me. By this point, Nino isn't speaking words anymore. Words have no use here. She's just screaming, an inch from my ear. I can't hold her back much longer.

The last letter, lit aflame, drops into the bin. There's a faint crackle as the letters catch fire. It's not the sound, but the smell of it that sets Nino free. She launches me at the detective and swings both my arms, still handcuffed, for his smarmy face. The blow connects with his cheek-bone. He staggers out of his seat, lock-kneed and unstable, holding his face. Another hit and he'll fold up.

Before I can swing again, a heavy, crunching blow lands across my back. The guard is in the room with us. His truncheon swings again, connects with my ribs, and doubles me over as all the air in my lungs escapes in one heave. The guard raises the truncheon over his head for a final blow. That'll be the spine-breaker.

"Stop! I want him alive." The detective's voice booms—the unvarnished sound of *those people.*

The truncheon stops mid-swing.

"Cuff him to the fucking table."

I'LL BE ARRESTED for assaulting a police officer. I'll be in a cell alongside Sandro while Irakli loses himself out there, never to be seen again. The detective wanted a reaction and I gave him one. He's won. His eye swells visibly and makes all of this almost worth it.

"You people really think you're special, don't you?"

I don't answer. With that punch, he's shed all his facade. I'm finally talking to *those people* for real, while Eka's letters still smolder in the bin.

"Do you think we follow every fair-weather, un-Georgian cunt that comes back here? Follow you around airports, roll out the carpet, welcome home, sir?"

He moves closer. I can smell his breath.

"Irakli Donauri." He doesn't hide his disgust. "I know Irakli. I remember him well."

"What?"

"My father's *friend*." His voice is bitter, cut with stale cigarette stink. "His classmate from year fucking one. I'd see him around the house when I was little . . ."

Something makes him pause.

"How do you think you escaped? Who do you think forged you that visa and let you flounce around Europe while we starved here?"

I look the detective in his eyes. There are tears in them.

"My father. The idiot with a golden heart. He saved you and a hundred others like you. Because he could. Because he was a *true* Georgian. They caught him for it. Beat him to death in his bed while we watched."

His voice doesn't rise like it should but quiets to a whisper.

"Did you know that? We *watched*. His skull was porridge. We had to bury him in a closed casket. Wrecked our family. *My* family."

I avert my eyes, but he grabs me.

"No, look at my face. I want you to remember it. I'm *not* a true Georgian like my father. If I could get my hands on those people he saved, I'd strangle every single one. Only I don't know their names."

He lets me go with a shove.

"But I know yours. . . ."

He gets up and his chair topples over at the sudden movement. He opens the steel door.

"I need to make a call. Watch him. He's a slippery fuck," the detective says to someone in the hall.

The door slams shut and the locking mechanism crunches home. Game over.

A few long minutes later a more careful hand is turning the key. I can hear the springs, pins, bolts, and latches tick over. Whoever's opening the door doesn't want to be heard. I brace myself. Is this it—the Magic Cells disappearing act?

The door creaks open and my executioner backs into the room. Without showing me his face, he pulls the door to, but doesn't close it. He pauses and listens, then opens the door and glances down the hall one more time, before turning to look at me. It's the man from the Kyiv airport—the man who warned me off ever coming to Tbilisi.

"Who are you?"

He leans over, picks up the fallen chair, and sets it straight. He sits down.

"I warned you, didn't I? You didn't listen and now look at you."

"Who are you?"

"I'm nobody. Don't worry about me—worry about him."

He gestures over his shoulder.

"He's obsessed with your case. Everyone knows it, but no one can stop him. He's too high up, connected. I don't know the why-what-who and I don't *want* to know—I want nothing to do with this. We've been chasing your Irakli for weeks, and if we ever find him—"

There's a distant voice down the hall, footsteps coming toward us.

"Now listen to me close. There's only so far he can go. Your brother's being deported tomorrow. The embassy papers came through today. He'll be fine."

He glances at the door.

"But you—you're not safe. Irakli's a lost cause—we will find him. I'm trying to save *you*. Do what he says and you'll go home in one piece."

Quickly he gets up and opens the door. Then he pauses and comes back.

"Fuck," he whispers through his teeth.

Grimacing, he takes the chair and lays it out on the floor where he found it. He peers through the gap in the door and slides out.

Gear by gear, the lock ticks shut seconds before I hear the detective's voice outside. The lock ratchets open. The door swings into the room and thuds against the wall. The detective's face is composed and smug, just like the first time I met him. His eyes pause on the knocked-over chair, but only for a moment. Dumbfounded, I watch him unlock my handcuffs.

"You're free to go, Mr. Do-na-uri."

I SLEEPWALK OUT of the station into a darkening Tbilisi. I only really wake up when I get back to Nodar's and try to tell him and Ketino what just happened.

I keep stumbling over my own words. I can't hear myself speak over the echo of Sandro's voice, bellowing through the cell hatch: It's just you now. Follow the trail, follow the trail, follow the fucking trail!

I'm trying, brother, but my insides are shaking and I can't breathe right.

Somehow, his words merge with Lali's mantra. *Nino, say something. Follow the trail. Nino, say something.* The words echo and overlap inside my skull, and I'm on the cusp of panic. Nodar guides me to a chair. He lights a cigarette for me and shoves it halfway into my mouth. I feel the downhill rush of a panic attack draw closer. My hands are numb.

"Nodar, talk to me."

He understands without missing a beat.

"I've never seen you like this, brother. Not even when you were about to wrestle a tiger. Now, that was something. This is nothing."

He keeps talking, making jokes, telling Ketino about my run-in with Artyom, until somehow I'm not on the lip of a roller coaster without a seat belt anymore.

"A lot has happened, Mowgli, but you're not seeing the bigger picture."

"What?"

"Sandro's safe, you said—they're sending him home, right?"

I nod.

"OK, so that's one problem solved. I mean, he won't be prettier than when he came here. But he's safe."

I nod again.

"OK, so problem two—Irakli. You know where he is. The detective doesn't."

"No."

"OK. So, problem three—we've run out of problems."

"Not so fast, Sherlock." Ketino tuts and shakes her head. "That detective made a mistake arresting Sandro, instead of following him to Irakli. He's no Sherlock either. But he's not making the same mistake twice.

"Listen, Saba, he only let you go so he can follow you to Irakli."

Nodar waves his hand. "I can lose anyone he sends after us, no problem."

Ketino shakes her head. "You need to make *sure*, Nodar. Don't do anything stupid."

"I know, Keti, I know."

"Whenever you do decide to go, they'll be right there following you. Don't step one foot in your dad's direction until you're sure, Saba."

I nod—Ketino's right. They're probably permanently camped out on the street right now.

"Speaking of when. We go tonight?" Nodar says.

He's already assumed the burden of taking me to Ushguli. Not only that, he aims to somehow lose a police tail in the process. Ushguli is a solid eight-hour drive into the heart of Georgia and then straight north toward the Russian border, until all roads run out and you're staring the Caucasus range in its bleak face.

"Thank you, Nodar" is all I can think to say.

Once again I have to admit to myself how fucked I would be without him. He waves my words away like he did on my first night at Hotel Grand du Nodar.

"Leave tomorrow. You need a good night's sleep," Ketino cuts in. "It'll be easier to lose the detective in the morning rush."

That evening Ketino puts on a feast. We sit at the table, eat and drink, while Nodar entertains us with his toasts. An odd, uneasy feeling permeates the affair. So many ways tomorrow could go wrong, but nobody's talking about them. Even the wine doesn't seem to have an effect.

We tiptoe around the subject until it's late enough to go to bed. What's to say anyway? There's no way I won't make the attempt on Ushguli, and they both know that.

I lie awake in bed a long time. Irakli's message on the radio station last night won't let me sleep.

". . . don't follow my trail. It was never meant for you—it will get you killed. Your da."

"*He blames himself.*" Eka speaks to me softly.

"*For what?*"

"*For everything, Saba. Everything in London and everything here. If only he'd left Surik alone, he wouldn't have dragged you and Sandro into this hell. He's running from worse things than the police.*"

"*It's Surik's fault, not Irakli's. All of this.*"

"*Maybe. But tell me, what does that matter now?*"

I have no answer to give.

"*Straighten your back, Saba. Find him. It's later than you think.*"

Somewhere behind Mtatsminda, the rising sun ignites the thread-bare clouds as though the mountain's my only shield between Tbilisi and some awful calamity at this end of this breadcrumb trail.

11

WHEN LAST STANDS FAIL

In the morning, Ketino says goodbye to us by the door. I get a kiss on the cheek and a whispered "Be careful." Nodar gets a hug and a "Make *sure*, Nodar." He kisses her on the forehead. Then Ketino crosses herself and closes the door on us.

When we get in the Volga a blue car parked a few spaces behind us starts up but doesn't move off. Nodar and I exchange a glance. When we pull away, so does the blue car.

"OK, let's lose these asshats." Nodar forces a grin.

We leave Tbilisi in the most convoluted, meandering way possible. Nodar drives us in illogical, unintelligible circuits across Tbilisi, out to Didi Digomi, and to the airport and back.

We take the tangled, dripping tunnels beneath the Mtkvari river across to Sololaki, then Vake, then back past Nodar's house. Wherever we find a quiet road, Nodar parks and we watch for anyone following.

The blue car follows us until around the second circuit to the airport and back. After that, we can't see it anymore.

It takes two more hours for Nodar to work his way over to Mtatsminda. The Volga stutters up the steep winding back roads, through suburbs, until we end up in a huge empty parking lot on Mtatsminda. We're right beneath the giant broadcast tower, which somehow gives you vertigo even when seen from the ground up. We wait a long time for someone to turn up, but no one does.

"I guess this is it," Nodar says.

"I guess so," I say.

At last, we turn our backs on Tbilisi. Grinning, Nodar manages to get a small but enthusiastic wheelspin out of the Volga as we leave the parking lot.

The back roads out of Tbilisi are narrow, dusty tributaries that trickle through villages and farm fields toward the messy, muddy stream of the central motorway. No one follows us on these winding roads and Nodar grows calmer. The Volga calms too—the nervy accelerations and decelerations that brought us this far smooth out.

We reach the motorway and merge into the honking, lane-hopping, over- and under-taking stampede. If anyone's following us here, we won't know it and neither will they. My thoughts focus on the blue and silver mountains visible like a mirage through the dust that envelops the motorway. Somewhere up there Irakli's trapped, losing his grip on this world.

As though hearing my thoughts, Nodar finds a tenuous gap in the traffic, stomps the gas pedal, and the Volga launches us toward the mountains faster than ever. A few hours later, he takes us off the motorway and we start climbing the Caucasus foothills.

Small shacks and food stands line the road in both directions, hoping for the occasional tourist. They all seem to sell identical factory-made forgeries of things that take hard-won mastery to make by hand.

Georgian culture, industrialized, mechanized, and hungry, has pumped out too much product—it litters our way to the mountains for miles.

"Look at this junk."

Nodar's face is stiff with disdain. He refuses to stop the car until the roadside shops have disappeared. In the meantime, the mountains have snuck up on us. Their vague contours have sharpened into impossibly high peaks, razor-blade cliffs, and steep slopes silver-plated with snow. Nodar pulls over at a forlorn collection of shacks gathered around a gas pump.

While he's filling the car, a blind woman of at least a hundred years, dressed in dusty rags, shuffles toward us. I watch her find us by smell alone. She stops right in front of me and shows me her cloudy, unblinking eyes of blue and green, like grim testimony of things past.

She holds her hand out, palm up, until I've emptied my pockets of all change. Without a word, she shuffles toward Nodar.

"Not now, Ina," he says and she leaves.

"You know her?"

"Ina? Yeah. I've been through here a couple of times. Used to be the only place for petrol in these parts."

"Poor woman."

Nodar laughs.

"What's funny?"

"She's not blind. Strong as an ox, Ina. Has a little farm over that hill."

"I gave her all the money I had."

"Trust me, Mowgli, she needs it more than you do."

Nodar takes us on a huge cross-country zigzag, to make sure we approach Ushguli from an unexpected direction.

"To make *sure* the police stay lost. Anyone coming from Tbilisi would arrive by the road from the south. Not us." He winks.

Later that day, we find ourselves in the Georgia I imagined all the way from London. We're doubling back on ourselves now, heading due east, straight for an obscure mountain pass that will put us right in Ushguli, Nodar tells me.

But for now, the road beneath the Volga traverses a brief plateau. This is the fantasy land I thought Irakli had gone to. Dusty farms and homesteads, vineyards perched on steep hills, forests, and rivers glide by my window like a slideshow of scruffy beauty. London seems a fading, crowded fever dream.

Nodar sighs. "This is proper Georgia."

His Volga slows as he rolls his window down. I feel it too. Being among mountains like this is nourishment. It feeds some part of me I didn't know was starving. If I could, I'd stop here, get lost in this country, and forget everything and everyone.

Just before we reach the mountain pass, we come across a lone man ambling along the road, hunched under the sun's weight on his back. He's hailing passing cars with an air of disdain and being ignored by everyone. Everyone but Nodar.

Of course, he can't resist adopting another stray. I don't think he can help himself. He's Georgian the way Georgians are described in travel guides. Big, glowing, unstoppable heart. The poorer his own circumstance, the more generous he grows.

"Where's the road taking you, brother?" Nodar says as the Volga squeals to a halt.

"Ushguli."

"Well, get in. We're headed for Ushguli."

"You are? Why?" The man hesitates, squinting in the sun.

"We just are, brother. You want a written invite? Or you wanna walk?"

The man slides into the back seat and throws his backpack in the footwell.

"I'm Dimitri."

"I'm Nodar. This one's Saba—but you can call him Mowgli."

For a blissful, silent half an hour Dimitri appraises Nodar and me. Judging us worthy, he finally starts telling stories. . . .

FOR THREE STRAIGHT HOURS since we picked Dimitri up, he hasn't stopped talking. The countryside slides past my window. The roads are potholed and uneven. Lane markings stray off center, sometimes fading completely out of sight. Nodar takes no notice. He rams the Volga's blown suspension right over the potholes, barely lifting his foot off the gas.

It's incredible—Dimitri doesn't shut up. He's wiry, hairy, and his unassuming frame disguises an unnatural strength honed by years of working the land. If Nodar hadn't picked him up, Dimitri would have merrily walked to Ushguli.

"Words should be weighed, not counted. Have you heard that saying?" Nodar's subtle suggestions don't bother Dimitri.

The smorgasbord of odd tales we've been listening to resumes. The countryside in my window wilts from green to ocher to cold, snow gray by imperceptible degrees. I drift in and out of Dimitri's litany and try to think of nothing. Every now and then he wrenches my attention back into focus.

"I always knew there was something wrong with Gogi. Me and Ramaz, we found him in the snow, just off the road. Shaking like a shitting dog, drenched in his own blood. The crazy whoreson lost his marbles and chewed his fingertips off. To stop the frostbite, he said. We tried to help but—"

Nodar turns to Dimitri.

"The fuck are you talking about now?"

"The pass, boys. The Chuberi Pass. The worst five days of my life."

The Chuberi Pass is an infamous mountain pass that crosses from the region of Abkhazia into Ushguli. It's too steep for most cars,

Dimitri tells us. If it rains, the road turns to orange muck and then you're walking—no car can drive through that mess.

After the Soviet Union shit the bed, Abkhazia became the first region to break away from the newly minted Republic of Georgia, around 1992. Abkhazia was a mixture of Russian and Georgian bloodlines, but the majority wanted to stick with Russia. Rusty-shotgun scuffles and squabbles broke out over scraps of land. Decades-old grudges were settled in the new chaos.

Georgia sent in the army to calm things down. It worked as well as throwing gas on a house fire. Then the Russian army lumbered into the conflict and things turned nasty, especially for the Abkhazians of Georgian descent. Thousands of people were made homeless and thousands more killed in the crossfire. Those who were known to be Georgian had to escape.

There were only two ways from Abkhazia into Georgia. One was through a dense, contested woodland buzzing with bullets, past machine gun nests and forest murder holes. Many tried this route and none survived. It was an outright slaughter. Blood drenched the forest floor to human gravy. Only ghosts wander that forest now, leaving no trace of their passing.

The other way out was the Chuberi Pass. Thousands attempted that desperate frozen pilgrimage.

"I started off with a backpack. Musta weighed twenty, thirty kilo. Before I was even halfway up the pass, I gave it all to the mountain. Just threw it down a ravine. But it wasn't enough—the mountain took these too."

From the back seat Dimitri holds up his hand. It's missing the thumb and ring fingers at the first knuckle, and all of the pinky. The scars have healed to a glossy salmon pink color.

"Pretty, ain't it?"

"Put it away, Dimitri."

"They went gray and numb at first. Then corpse blue. Then black, like I dipped them in ink. Zurab, the man who took me in in Ushguli, lopped them off with his garden shears. Like chicken feet. Didn't feel a thing.

"Zurab is a saint. He's no blood or kin of mine, but he saw me and took me in without a word. Fed me, watered me . . . chopped off my fingers."

Dimitri chuckles to himself.

"He's grown gray and cranky now, so I look after him. To repay that kindness. He's more my father than my own damn father. You'll meet him soon enough, don't worry."

Dimitri smiles at the thought. Then, he resumes his story of the Chuberi Pass.

"Boys, I swear, I saw things you wouldn't believe. I saw a man stop in his tracks and put down his rucksack, all careful and gentle, like it was full of fine china. Then slowly, calmly, he crossed himself and dropped dead on the spot, right in front of my eyes. Can you believe that? He was so tired he could *choose* when to drop dead."

I see Nodar shake his head.

"I saw people bury their gold and silver, like they'd be back for it. But when it got really cold, no one bothered. People just left their things along the road. Bags, suitcases, rucksacks, dead relatives."

Dimitri crosses himself.

"God forgive me. I saw so many, I stopped caring. Frozen bodies left where they fell by the road, in ditches, under trees."

He takes a minute to recompose himself.

"One night me and Ramaz, we had enough. We stopped. The locals were yelling—'Don't stop moving! You'll freeze.' But we didn't care anymore. We built a little fire. Got nice and cozy.

"I remember these people next to us, a whole family, I think. I couldn't see their faces. Just dark shapes around a gone-out campfire.

"'Their fire's gone out,' I go to Ramaz. 'Invite them to ours.'

"'They're dead, Dima,' he goes. 'Can't you see?'"

"The poor bastards fell asleep warm. The fire went out and they never woke up."

Dimitri's story falters at this memory and the car grows silent. Nodar glances at him. Dimitri shrugs but I hear him strain to bring the cheer back to his tone.

"We drank his auntie's Red Moscow. The whole fuckin' bottle, if you can believe it."

"The perfume?"

"Correct. It's not as bad as you think, you know."

Another memory sags Dimitri's grin, but only for a moment.

"Ramaz wasn't a big drinker. It made him sleepy, so he stopped to rest. Said he'd catch me up. Well. He never troubled my eyeballs again, the ugly bastard."

Another silence fills the car as Dimitri eyes the beginning of the Chuberi Pass. With a visible effort, he resumes his tale.

"You believe in miracles, boys?"

No one answers. Dimitri laughs in this faithless pause.

"Well, let me tell you a story. The whole time climbing the pass, I had this nasty taste in my mouth. Like sucking on salt rock. I don't know why, but all I could think about was raspberry jam. I couldn't shift it from my head. Honest to God."

He crosses himself.

"The whole way up—raspberry jam, raspberry jam, raspberry jam. The kind Nana Guli used to make. Anyway, after the Chuberi crest, things eased up. The trees up there kept the wind off us. It got warmer.

"I found a campfire, to warm up and chat a little. I knew some of them from home. Anyway, this gangly giant from the next campfire, he comes over."

Dimitri nudges Nodar with his elbow, and peers at me.

"OK, so, remember, I haven't eaten a thing for four days. And suddenly there's this guy. Got something in his hands.

"'Do you want some?' he goes.

"I go, 'What is it?'

"'Jam,' he goes, like it was the most normal thing. 'Raspberry jam.'

"I looked at him with my mouth open.

"'Don't worry, brother, you keep it. I have more.'

"He left me the whole jar and went back to his campfire. Now you tell me that's not a miracle!"

Dimitri slaps his thigh and laughs.

"I don't know his name, or why this crazy whoreson threw everything he owned down a ravine but saved the jam."

Nodar laughs along with Dimitri and I can't help it either.

"I wept and laughed at the same time, eating that jam. I knew I'd be OK then. I knew I'd made it."

Grumbling, the Volga begins to climb the narrow road into the mountains. Twilight finds us partway up the pass. We sleep in the Volga that night, surrounded by the static hiss of a steady wind blowing through pine trees.

GROGGY AND ILL-TEMPERED, we set off at daybreak. The Volga takes a long time to warm up and stop creaking as we climb. The road begins to shrink beneath our wheels until it becomes a rocky dirt track barely wider than the Volga's stately arse. The pines thin out and disappear. The wind rattles our windows, whines and whistles through the gaps. This is it. This is where the pass would have done most of the killing. Dimitri's quiet the whole way up.

Over the Chuberi crest, the road enters a thick evergreen forest. Dimitri still hasn't said a word. From time to time he rolls down his window and lets the car fill with the lush smell of fresh sap, tree bark, and pine needles. Silently, he directs Nodar through the capillary maze of dirt roads that climb the mountains.

Meanwhile, my mind turns to Irakli. What will I see in his eyes? What will I say to him?

"Hi, Da" would be ridiculous. I haven't called him Da since I was in school. "Hi, Irakli"—no, too cold. A hug? A handshake?

I play out all scenarios and combinations as a form of mental chewing gum, until the daylight fades to gray. Our road falters and disappears in a thicket of holly and bramble bushes.

"What now?" Nodar says.

"Wait, what was your plan if I *wasn't* here?" Dimitri says, eyebrows raised.

"We'd have figured it out," Nodar grumbles.

"Good thing you found me then, eh? No need to *figure* it out."

Dimitri gets out of the car, chuckling.

"Well, there's no more road to ride—we're walking from here."

"How far?"

"Across the river down there and then up to Ushguli. An hour or two."

"You OK to walk, Mowgli?" Nodar says.

"I'll live."

We scrape through the thick undergrowth and find ourselves on the lip of a sharp hill that leads down to a fast, ragged river. On the other side, an equally steep incline climbs toward a meager collection of faint lights, nestled between the shoulders of two dark mountains.

"That's Ushguli," Dimitri says. "The last stand."

Past Ushguli there's nothing but desolate stretches of harsh Caucasus mountainsides gleaming with ghostly patches of snow. The steep approach dead-ends in a wall of mountains so final and forbidding that they seem unreal. The world beyond them could be coming to some violent end and we'd see no sign of its demise.

"Dimitri, do you know your way?" Nodar says.

Dimitri tuts.

"You could poke both my eyes out and I'd still walk you straight to Zurab's front door."

"OK, OK. You can keep your eyes."

Under darkening skies, we set off in silence. By the time we can hear the river chattering ahead of us, it's completely dark. That's when it happens. . . .

They say our world orbits a mysterious counterpart—a kinder world than ours. Only the dying ever glimpse that other world, on their way out of this one. They say that sometimes our orbits intersect and this world rubs shoulders with that other place. For a time, our realities share a border. The border wears thin in places and strange things from that other world spill into ours. So it is said. Who knows what horror spills from ours into theirs?

As we approach the river, phosphor-green points of light begin to appear along the riverbank. Someone's piercing needlepoint holes in the border that keeps us from that kinder world. The closer we get, the more lights appear, and the black wavelets of the river begin to glow a feeble green.

The lights float low to the ground, almost motionless yet never completely still. They form a luminescent rising tide of spilled magic, lapping up the shore toward us. I try to focus on a single point of light—it's impossible. They drift and shy from my gaze.

"I've never seen so many." Nodar's voice is a voice you might hear in church, or at a funeral.

"What are they?"

"Fireflies."

Walking in among them makes me hold my breath. I worry that by some malicious fairy-tale trick, touching one will make all of them go out in an instant. They drift out of my way with no effort. I hear Nodar inhale as he wades in with me.

Already ahead of us, Dimitri stalks along the bank of the noisy river, dipping his hands into the water every few steps and swearing. Eventually, he finds what he's looking for. He pulls a thick rope from the water, tied to a cinder block. He looks back at the mesmerized pair of us.

"Come on."

The other end of the rope is tied to a tree on the far side of the river.

"This is glacier water from the mountains."

Dimitri points in the direction of the cold darkness crouched over Ushguli.

"Very cold."

He pulls the dripping rope taut and wedges the cinderblock behind a tree.

"That'll hold. Time to pay the price."

"What price?"

"Take a deep breath before you step in. Don't breathe out until you reach the other side. No matter what, don't stop moving. Let go of the rope, you die. You hear me?"

We nod in agreement.

"I'll go first to make sure the rope holds. When I'm across, you follow. Don't make me wait."

He takes a deep breath and plunges into the water past his waist.

"Vai, vai," he exclaims, followed by a burst of muddled swearing.

The crossing is only the length of a swimming pool. The water's fast and eager to snuff you out. It takes Dimitri awhile to get across. Reaching the opposite bank, he jumps out of the water and starts stomping his feet and rubbing his hands together. The fireflies edge away from his wild dance. He looks toward us.

"What you waiting for?"

I take a deep breath and step into the water. Within two strides, I'm up to my hips. My nerve endings don't register the cold at first, but when they do, they fire off all at once. I've stepped into liquid nitrogen and it's stripping flesh from my legs in slivers.

Holding your breath all the way across is horseshit. When the water reaches my chest, all my breath leaves in one pressured heave. I try to refill my lungs but can only manage to breathe in shortening gasps. This is a losing game, with a very finite end. Only two options and no uncertainties. I reach the bank or the air runs out and the river takes me.

My numb hands can't feel the rope anymore. Fear sets in. I haul on the rope and splash through the water, jaws clenched. It feels like an eternity, getting across. A second after I step onto the riverbank my skin catches fire. I do the same lunatic dance Dimitri did. I stomp my feet and try to rub some feeling back into my limbs.

"Good man," Dimitri says. "Let's see what this Ossetian's made of. You're next, Nodar!"

Nodar lights the little flashlight Ketino made him bring, puts it between his teeth, and steps into the river. It's no good—the shock of the water knocks the flashlight out of his mouth. It lights a slice of dull-green water before the river snuffs it out. Nodar almost goes under trying to catch it.

"Your mother!" I hear him yell.

"Get moving, Ossetia, don't let go!"

Nodar inches forward. He's too slow. It takes him the longest to get across. I watch him and list out the things he's put himself through for me, price unpaid. Dodging the police, followed by two days of hard driving. Sleeping in the car, slumped across the steering wheel, shattering the idyllic dawn silence and our eardrums by elbowing the horn in his sleep. And now, at last, this cherry on top—risking his life floundering through glacier meltwater.

An ugly thought occurs to me, I can't help it. Maybe it's guilt that drives Nodar. Maybe that's his fuel. Guilt for selling me to the detective. What happens when that fuel runs dry?

Lena surprises me by interrupting this thought. She clears her throat and I know she's here to set me straight.

"I never knew you to be so cruel, Saba."

Shamed, I have no response.

"Maybe he does feel guilt. But he would have done this for you regardless. That's just who he is. He'll follow you to the end. And you didn't even have to ask."

I watch Nodar huff and puff, hauling himself through the river, and I know Lena's right.

"I'm sorry," I say, but she's already gone.

I take a few steps back into the river and drag Nodar out of the freezing water.

"My hands," he says, spraying water all around him. "My hands are on fire."

"Fastest way to warm up is to get walking," Dimitri tells us.

So that's what we do. It takes awhile for my teeth to stop chattering so I can speak.

"Those fireflies. I've never seen anything like it."

"What fireflies?" Dimitri says.

Nodar and I fall behind a few steps before we realize that Dimitri's shaking as he walks. He looks back at us and bursts out laughing.

"I wish I could see your faces. But Nodar donated his flashlight to the river."

"Keep walking, Dima. Don't let me catch up to you," Nodar says.

I think he's laughing too, on the inside.

"Bad news, those fireflies. They lure things into the river. Usually just stupid dogs, or sheep, or cows. That's bad enough, but every now and then a tourist ends up in there."

On the last leg of our journey to Ushguli, we're escorted by dark hungry-looking shapes. Calculating eyes flit among the trees on our path.

"Are those dogs?"

"Wolves," Dimitri says. "They get feisty when they're hungry."

"What do we do?"

He shrugs. "Walk."

He looks around trying to spot them.

"If they come closer, whatever you do, don't run. If you run, you're food. Don't worry, we're too close to the village for them to try anything."

Nodar looks at me and shakes his head. "Why is it wherever you go, there's wolves?"

The wolves follow us to the outskirts of Ushguli. A mournful howl hangs in the air as we enter the village. Ushguli is the beating heart of the whole Svaneti region. This high up in the mountains, Svaneti's the perfect last stand. This is where refugees would flock to in times of war, Dimitri explains, bearing treasures from all over the country.

"Not gold, not money—that means nothing here. They brought things that can't be replaced. Books, poetry, paintings, relics, grapevine cuttings—everything that makes a Georgian a Georgian. Many times, the enemy reached us even here."

"When last stands fail and all else falters, then there's us, . . ." Nodar recites.

"Exactly. That's Ushguli—nowhere to retreat here. Each home has a watchtower you can defend. A lot of them still stand all over this valley. I live in one with Zurab. You'll see."

Somewhere in the darkness among houses, a dog senses our approach and barks.

"The last building in Ushguli is that crazy monastery you want. Can't see it now, but it's got the biggest tower."

Dimitri points up into the darkness.

"They say an angel's trapped in that tower. Not the winged, glowing kind that floats on a cloud, farting rainbows. No, this one's the old Orthodox Christian kind. A terrible, vengeful angel. That tower can't be taken by any enemy. Ottomans, Persians, Mongols, and all shades of Arabs tried. Only the Mongols ever got close. The angel sent down a thick fog. When it cleared, the Mongols were found torn limb from limb, scattered all around the watchtower, with only their livers eaten, as though by a wolf hunt."

Dimitri pauses and stops walking. "Do you know what Ushguli means?"

"Ushishari guli," Nodar says.

"Good man," Dimitri says and taps his chest twice. "Ush-guli. Fearless heart."

My mind returns to Irakli and what state he might be in. Maybe the monastery has calmed him and soothed the fever from his eyes. Maybe we can start thinking about how to get him out of the mess he's made. The British embassy might help. Maybe Sandro and I can think of some way out of this.

Dimitri stops at a small cottage. Attached to the low building is a large medieval stone tower so tall that the top of it disappears into the night sky.

"This is Zurab's place and mine," Dimitri says. "I'll take you to the monastery tomorrow."

"Tomorrow?" I jump in.

"It's late, everyone's asleep. We're soaking wet. . . ."

"Listen—" I start and feel Nodar's hand on my shoulder.

"We've been going two days, Mowgli. What's another few hours? We won't make any friends waking folk, dead of night."

"Nodar, Irakli's there."

"I hear you, brother. He'll still be there tomorrow. And you'll feel better having slept some." He gives my shoulder a squeeze. "We go first thing, I promise. Before the sun's awake."

I look around at the dark, unlit windows in the houses nearby and nod. Nodar pats me on the back.

Dimitri's cottage has a neat vegetable garden out front and a large log for chopping firewood, scarred by wayward axe blows. The decorative headboard of a metal-frame bed has been fashioned into a gate to this cottage. It produces a rusty squeal as Dimitri pushes it open. At the sound, the distant dog starts barking again. We start up the path toward the house.

"Stop," a stern voice says behind us. "Don't move."

We stop dead.

"Who are you?"

Dimitri turns toward the voice. We hear a metallic click—safety's off.

"You move again, I shoot."

Dimitri laughs. "Zurab, it's me. Dimitri. Put that rusty thing away."

The bushes by the fence rustle.

"I almost blew a hole through your empty head," the voice says.

The man who steps out of the darkness, holding a shotgun to his chest, doesn't match the voice we heard. He's short, sinewy, and dried out by old age. His face is like a root vegetable, creased and folded just so, to its own unknowable purpose.

"What you got loaded in there anyway?"

"Salt."

"And what would that do?"

"Teach you not to sneak around in the dark like a thief."

Dimitri laughs and embraces the old man.

"Alright, alright, let me go," Zurab grumbles, muffled in the hug.

"I got your meds. Not all. The blue unpronounceable ones were too expensive again—I'll pick them up next trip, probably next week. You OK without till then? Nothing will fall off?"

"You worry about your health, not mine," Zurab says and glances at Nodar and me.

"These are my friends, Zurab. Nodar and Saba. They drove me all the way here, up the pass."

Zurab steps closer and I have to change my impression of him a second time. His eyes are shrewd and inquisitive—he's no doddering old man. We seem to pass his valuation.

"A guest is a gift from God," he says. "Let's go mark your arrival."

The inside of Zurab's house is a bizarre sight. It consists of a cavernous central room, sectioned off by thick, coarse wool blankets hanging from ceiling beams. Half of the room has no floorboards—the floor is naked Ushguli ground, packed harder than marble by countless footsteps. There's a faint livestock undertone to the smell of the place.

An oven the size of a van, a pechka, dominates a quarter of the cottage and almost reaches the ceiling. The pechka is the beating heart of the house. It has alcoves for firewood, all sorts of hidden nooks, crannies, and cupboards. It has cabinets for drying herbs and smoking meats, and stoves for cooking. A small ladder attached to the back leads to a tousled cot right on top of the pechka—Zurab's bed.

The other end of the room sits under the watchtower we saw from outside. I look up into the innards of the tower and see no ceiling—the walls vanish into the darkness. I can hear the wind whistling through an opening somewhere up there. A rope ladder hangs in the center of the tower, emerging from the darkness as though it's levitating.

It seems a time traveler spent a night at Zurab's medieval home and left his gadgets behind. There's a small flat-screen TV by the pechka, a large digital camera hanging from a nail in the wooden crossbeam, and a laptop on the table.

Between them, Zurab and Dimitri quickly lay out a meal. Homemade chacha, great hunks of bread, smoked cheese, sliced meat, and soured cucumbers.

"Come sit," Zurab says. "Let's bless your journey."

Dimitri pours us a glass of chacha each.

"Thank you for this day of peace," Zurab says toward the ceiling.

He crosses himself and takes a sip. The chacha is pure, liquid fire going down. We assault the food and hardly look up until only morsels have survived.

"Now, let's bless your arrival," Zurab says.

As the host, Zurab is the "tamada" of the table. It's his job to oversee the meal, control the drinking to levels fitting for the occasion. This is the centuries-old tradition of Georgian hospitality. Zurab halts the conversation at regular intervals, with toasts like ancient poetry, and we sip the chacha when he does.

Each pause gives me time to think I should have gone up to the monastery tonight. Each time I'm almost decided on up and going *right now*, I see Nodar watching me. His eyes wrinkle up at the corners and it calms me.

"Relax, brother. Irakli's here. I feel it and you do too—a little of Keti's premonition," he says and winks.

Eventually, sated and blushed by chacha, we all light up. The heat in my belly finally lets me relax. We smoke in a silence punctuated by the crackle of firewood somewhere in the unseen depths of the pechka.

"Whose camera is that?" Nodar says, when the food stupor wears off.

"Zurab Leibovitz over there." Dimitri grins.

Zurab shrugs.

"I sold a kidney for it and all he does is take pictures of every useless cowpat in Ushguli. Every day. He's filled up the laptop already."

Zurab gives a big sigh. "I'm keeping a record of this place," he says.

"Why?" Nodar asks.

"Because no one else is. Beautiful things don't last. Even Ushguli will fall someday. Someone has to keep account."

Zurab offers to show us his photos, and we sit by the pechka and look through the albums. They're not photos taken by a visitor. They linger on everyday details of Ushguli with the intimate familiarity you might have with the imperfections in your own home—the uneven part of the banister you've touched a million times, or the loose floorboard you step on daily.

"These things count. They're important," Zurab tells us.

Soon, he climbs into his bed on top of the pechka. Nodar and Dimitri are motionless in their cots. Meanwhile, I sit in the sleepy silence, mesmerized by Zurab's photos. I'm ready to go pass out in my own cot when I come across a photo that runs my blood cold.

It's a picture of a lone Ushguli tower. The narrow doorway into the tower is dark, like the entrance to a cave. Standing in this doorway, looking like a ghost caught on film, is Irakli. About to vanish into the darkness, he's looking over his shoulder toward the camera.

"Fu-uck," I whisper. "I knew it!"

It's hard to keep my voice down. Finally—cold, hard proof that I haven't lost my mind and gone chasing made-up clues to nowhere.

Irakli looks careworn and haggard. His beard grown unruly and hair grayer than I remember. New wrinkles set his face in an expression of worry. He looks a man on the run from no common predator. I stare at him a long time before I can go to bed. It takes even longer to get to sleep. I still haven't decided on how or what to say to him tomorrow. . . .

USHGULI BY DAY is a strange, beautiful sight. The village is a sparse collection of medieval watchtowers just like Zurab's. Homesteads have flourished among their deep stone roots. Dogs, cats, chickens, and livestock roam small fenced-off patches of rusty grass.

Time and weather have been eating at the watchtowers. Large, untended holes gape in their walls. Wiry tufts of weeds sprout from gaps in the stonework, dozens of feet above the ground where they belong.

The watchtowers are vulnerable. No last stand will hold here. Relics can't defend Ushguli from what's coming.

Implausible, austere mountains loom in the background and dwarf the village and everything in it. My eyes reject the view. It can't possibly be real. The sky's too blue, the snow on the mountains too white. Views like this don't exist in this world.

The biggest tower in Ushguli belongs to the monastery. At least triple in size, it can be seen from anywhere in the village. That's where Dimitri is taking us. Ushguli's covered in snow nine months out of twelve, he tells us as he leads us through a labyrinth of mud tracks.

"Fuck your mother's goat. You produce anything but fuckin' muck up here?"

The mud sucks the shoe off Nodar's foot a second time. Dimitri laughs.

"It's easier in the winter. Mud's frozen."

"I wish it was winter."

"Wish for better shoes, my friend."

The monastery itself is a collection of buildings—outhouses, barns, and a patchwork of grazing land, huddled around the intimidating watchtower.

Somber men, dressed in somber brown robes, go about their day among the buildings, tending the land, feeding the animals, chopping wood. Most of them must be monks, devoted to their Bibles. But one might be Irakli—my eyes scan every new face frantically.

We come to a small patch of sand surrounded by a chest-high wooden fence. A tall priest, fully bearded, dressed in black robes with a dirty rope for a belt, stands in the sand. He's leaning on a huge wooden mallet that almost reaches up to his shoulder. Large, wraparound sunglasses hide his eyes from every possible angle.

He picks up the mallet, hefting its weight. It has a heavy, cruel head covered in indistinct bloodlike stains. The handle's wrapped in rags for grip. He looks out toward the mountains where another priest leads a cow toward us across the muddy field. I can tell by the shape of him, it's not Irakli.

"Sand," our priest says, kicking some toward us with his boot. "Soaks up the blood. Keeps the wolves from smelling it."

The other priest brings the cow into the sand enclosure. The animal senses danger and tries to back out. It turns its head toward the gate it just walked through. But the gate's already shut—no escape.

As the cow turns its head back toward our priest, the mallet swings a tall arc through the air and comes down, dead-center, right on the cow's skull. There's a horrific wet cracking sound. It's not a sound you'd expect, like knocking two rocks together underwater. It makes my jaw clench.

The blow paralyzes the cow's legs and they fold up as though boneless. Bulging eyes glare in the direction the blow came from, as though expecting another. The cow lands on its underbelly, displacing a wave of sand. Miserably it topples to one side. Hooves begin to skitter fruitlessly, spasming, clopping into each other, walking on thin air. True to the priest's promise, the blood pulsing out of the cow's nostrils disappears into the sand without trace.

"Once, at the Soviet farm," the priest says, turning to face us, "I fucked up. Glanced the mallet off the skull."

He spits and wipes his forehead.

"The poor thing started thrashing around the pen. Nearly crushed me to death. Had to hit it another ten times. Beat it to death. It howled the whole time—sound like a gut-shot man. That kind of meat's no good. Can't eat it."

The cow's movements have slowed to a weak, spasmodic judder, fading in rhythm with its failing heart.

"I sobbed like a child after."

He looks down at the cow.

"This one didn't feel a thing."

He crosses himself and leans the mallet against the fence.

"When she stops moving, bleed her. But be careful," he says to the younger priest.

"Father Serafim." He offers me his hand.

His expression gives no clue. All I can see is two tiny fish-eye reflections of myself in his sunglasses.

"You're either Sandro or Saba."

He must know of our search. Irakli's here somewhere. Relief floods through my veins and I try to keep it from spreading my entire face into a grin. Father Serafim frowns at my effort.

"Saba," I say.

"Ah," he says and nods.

A bell rings out from the direction of the tower, faint and tinny against the imposing background. Father Serafim turns his head in the direction of the sound.

"Time for prayer," he says. "Come up with Dimitri tonight. Bring Zurab too, I—"

"I need to talk to you now," I interrupt.

He turns back to me and pauses.

"No, you don't. There's no rush. Not anymore."

"What does that mean? Where's Irakli?"

Father Serafim turns away and glances down at the young priest kneeling by the cow. The priest wedges a pockmarked aluminum pail under the cow's head.

"Lean into it like a man, you hear? Cut deep and cut ear to ear."

The priest nods in return and Father Serafim walks away.

"Father Serafim," I call after him, but he doesn't even turn around.

"Come up this evening," he says over his shoulder.

We watch the young priest put a soothing hand on the cow's throat as though he's petting it. He waits until he's sure and then reaches for the knife on his belt. The steel winks silver in the sunlight. It slides along the cow's hide at first, leaving no mark, but when I see it *grip*, I have to look away.

I've waited too long already. I clench my jaw and start after Father Serafim. I'll *make* him hear me, somehow. I can't stand another delay. But Nodar holds me back. I turn to see him frowning.

"Listen, brother." His eyes follow Father Serafim warily. "These priests . . . they don't play around. We go at their pace, or we go no-where. Trust me, we better wait."

THAT EVENING DIMITRI guides us through the muddle of Ushguli paths to Father Serafim.

"There's no rush. Not anymore, he said. What does that mean?"

"You keep asking, Mowgli, but I still don't know."

When we arrive at the monastery, we're shown to our seats around a large wooden table in the austere mess hall. None of the faces around the table are Irakli's and there's too many people here for me to just charge in with questions.

Father Serafim sits beside me. He turns to me and with a slow, delib-erate movement takes off his sunglasses. His right eye is a mess of slack, melted scar tissue huddled around an eye the color of watered-down milk. With no pupil or iris, the rheumy orb swivels blindly. The eyelids are melted away and the bad eye can't blink. It produces a steady seep of a clear, salivary liquid. With a flourish, Father Serafim produces a Mickey Mouse–print handkerchief from his robes and mops up the liquid. He catches me staring and winks with the good eye.

"Never stick your face in a tractor engine if you don't know what you're doing."

"Father Serafim, I need to talk—" I try to ask, but he cuts me off.

"These men worked a hard day. First we eat."

He puts his calloused hand on my shoulder. The unyielding weight of it tells me Nodar was right. We go at his pace, or we go nowhere. Father Serafim seems to hear my thoughts.

"Not long now, son. Go on and eat."

The food laid out before us is simple—fresh bread, cheese, skewers of beef grilled on an open flame. The centerpiece of the table is an old, dented samovar filled with icy chacha.

The meal starts with a toast from Father Serafim. He's the tamada and we drink whenever he raises a toast. The whole time he steals glances in my direction. When the modest food is gone and the others begin to clear the table, Father Serafim pounces. He turns on me and talks in a low, harsh voice. It takes me a second to parse the aggressive sound into words.

"Are you with the dogs?"

"What?"

"The police—are you helping them?"

"What? No."

Father Serafim's good eye glares at me. He looks like he's trying to divine something from my face. Silence descends and I feel the rest of the table watching us.

"Saba, all OK?" Nodar says.

"Fine," I say through my teeth and stare right back at Father Serafim.

"I'm a man of God, boy. Now you tell me you're not sent here by the police. Say the words."

His stare doesn't break until I speak.

"I'm not sent by the police."

He dabs his eye with the ridiculous handkerchief and comes to a decision.

"Irakli's not here," he says. "He left."

The tension breaks. Father Serafim nods almost imperceptibly and leaves me no time to react to the news.

"I'm sorry, son," he says. "Irakli's a brother to me. I'm not letting those people put him in a cage."

He scratches himself in the depths of his beard.

"Tell me something—in your search, did you meet a man by the name of Surik?" he says.

I nod.

"So you know about—"

He drags a huge thumb across his throat and clicks his tongue. Again, I nod. Father Serafim's expression grows softer. He shakes his head, dabs his eye, and produces a rumbling sigh.

"Irakli's not well, son. This trip has done something to him that I can't fix. He's running from more than just the police."

"What else is there?"

"The truth of things."

Father Serafim's face sags to a defeated expression.

"Irakli blames himself for everything. He said he made you and Sandro motherless. Without home or homeland. And now this sin with Surik . . . Look, son, he's afraid he's put you in danger."

"This is all Surik's fault, not Irakli's." I parrot the words I said to Eka. They've grown falser with repetition.

"Maybe Irakli's wrong. If he is, it's not by much. That is the truth of it."

Serafim shakes his head. He refills my glass with chacha.

"How did you find your way here, son?"

"I didn't, Sandro did. They caught him before he could get here. But he left me a clue I could follow."

"The police don't know?"

"No. But they know that I know. They let me go so they could follow me. We made sure we lost them in Tbilisi."

I glance in Nodar's direction and so does Father Serafim.

"They didn't follow us here, Father. I made sure of it."

"Thank you," Father Serafim says.

"It was a pleasure." Nodar grins.

For the second time, I try to ask Father Serafim the big question. This time he doesn't cut me short.

"Father, where is Irakli?"

The answer comes so fast I have no time to brace myself.

"He's in Ossetia."

"Fuck your mother," Nodar mutters.

"He can't see past that truth, Saba. Maybe if he stayed here, like I begged him to, I could help. But he's crossed into Ossetia now. That place is a dead end. The police can't get him there, but he can't come back either."

Father Serafim nudges the glass of chacha toward me.

"I've more bad news for you. He was sending us messages on the radio. It's the only way we talk to Ossetia these days. He was silent a long time, and then, the other day—"

"Don't follow my trail. It will get you killed," I interrupt.

"So, you heard that too."

"He signed off as 'Valiko,' not 'Irakli.'"

"He's not well, son. He's hurting."

He glances around the room and leans in.

"Right now, Irakli's running from you and Sandro more than he's running from the police. You're ambassadors—flesh and blood—of the truth he's running from. He doesn't want to be found, son. The farther you are from him, the farther you are from danger. I'm not saying don't go after him. But if you corner him, well, I don't know . . ."

Father Serafim doesn't seem like a man often uncertain, but he sounds unsure now. Eventually, he puts a hand on my shoulder.

"I'm sorry all you've seen here is sorrow."

The rest of the night, I sit quietly and absorb the news. I'm not sure what to feel yet, but the fireplace burns dimmer, the voices around me quiet, and the cobwebbed ceiling draws in closer.

On our way back to Zurab's, Nodar is oddly quiet. He drops back from Dimitri and nudges me.

"Mowgli," he says. "What are you going to do?"

"I don't know. But I can't leave him stuck in Ossetia."

Saying it aloud makes me realize I made the decision to go after Irakli the moment Father Serafim said the word *Ossetia*. That word, like an artifact of a magic spell, has done something to Nodar too. He speaks in a faraway voice, his mind already occupied elsewhere. He looks at me with an odd expression of excitement and dread.

"Need a lift?" He smiles vaguely.

"I can't ask you to do that, Nodar."

"You don't have to, brother." He puts a heavy hand on my shoulder. "Natia's in there. . . ."

"What about Ketino?"

He pauses to consider, shakes his head. "She'll understand. Eventually. Especially when we find Natia." Nodar tells himself lies and I don't correct him. He knows what he's doing.

"How far is the border from here?"

"A day, I reckon."

"How do we get across?"

Dimitri stops and looks back at us.

"What are you two Spice Girls gossiping about?"

"Let's talk tomorrow," Nodar says under his breath. "Keep walking, Dimitri. Your jokes need work—what the fuck is a 'spice girl' anyway?"

12

BABA YAGA'S TOLL

The enemy has our scent. They're coming.

Two nights ago, we killed everyone in the village. People too old, too ill, or just too worn out to flee into the mountains. This was our last service to them. Father and son, we stalked house to house in silence and we cut their throats. We're the fearless of heart, backed into a corner. We're the Ushguli bearing the heaviest burden.

They opened their doors willingly, though our eyes never meet.

"Stand behind me, boy. Put the knife here." I put the blade to the innocent skin under her chin, this old woman I've known all my life.

"Not there. Here."

She guided my nervous knife to the spongy flesh under her ear.

"That's it. Now lean into it like a man. Ear to ear."

That's where the expression comes from. You must cut from under one ear, down and across the throat to the other ear. It's a kinder death. She sensed my hesitation.

"They'll do far worse things, boy."

She grabbed me and sliced her own throat with my hand. An uneven cut, sliding through veins and catching on gristle. Me, just a mute accomplice to this suicide. Her hands didn't waver as hot blood poured down my fingers and filled the room with its animal stink. She made no sound as she fell to the floor. Hers was the last house.

The enemy's coming. They have our scent.

They smeared Tbilisi in our blood. They slaughtered their way across our lands in search of spoils. Now they've found our village. That's why we're here. When last stands fail and all else falters, then there's us—the fearless of heart.

We're the fail-safe. We make sure the enemy finds no solace here. No relief from the cold, no sustenance. No one to kill or rape or torture. Their ugly words will echo through a place purged of life.

With no one living to witness it, we set fire to the food stores and left our village behind.

At daybreak, we see them on the mountainside below. They see us too. We stop covering our tracks in the young snow. They know what we carry on our backs in place of food and firewood. They won't stop until they get it. It's their greed that'll end them.

"Breathe slow. Breathe steady," you say to me.

"Air's so cold it'll freeze your lungs. Shred you inside out. Drown in your own blood, if you breathe greedy like they do."

They struggle after us through the snowdrifts and turn their faces from the biting wind. They still hope to return home. Out here hope's louder than a church bell. It draws attention.

"Slow your heart, son. Breathe slow."

We stop for the night and they don't. We burrow into a snowdrift and sit in silence. We watch their torches crawl toward us. We urge our hearts to slow. Breathe slow. Be still.

"The mountains will take them."

"What if they don't?"

"They will."

Pale blue dawn finds them scattered in the snow, facedown, still and cold. Coughed-up blood marks their final steps. Air so cold it'll shred you inside out.

Our job is done. Our time almost up. We bury the bags for our kin to find when spring thaws this land. We're too far gone to return alive. So, we walk on. Away from home. These mountains feed on hope. We give them none of ours.

I WAKE IN MY COT, with the cold touch of the mountains aching on my skin like a fresh burn. The sun's not up yet. I lie still and wait for Irakli's face to surface in the darkness pressed to the window. But the rising sun burns away any comfort that darkness might have held.

So often I've felt your arm across my chest, Sandro, shielding me from harm. I wish I could feel it now. You'd go to Ossetia in my stead. But not this time, brother. Somewhere in Ossetia, Irakli needs me. Look at me, Sandro, charging to the rescue instead of you, for once. There's no more of your trail to follow, no pages to find, no graffiti to decode. It's just me now.

I'm waiting for everyone to wake up when my phone rings. It makes me jump. I've barely looked at it in days. I forgot I even had it with me. And now it's ringing, obscenely loud and unnerving in these surroundings. Unknown number. I answer it before it wakes the whole damn village.

"Hello?"

"Sulidze-Donauri, please."

I recognize the nasal voice of the detective.

"Speaking."

Nodar raises his sleep-disheveled head from the pillow.

"This is Detective Kelbakiani."

"Hello, detective."

Nodar sits up at my words. Dimitri stirs in his cot and Zurab's face appears from the top of the pechka.

"Do you remember what I asked you to do, Saba?"

"You asked me to tell you if I found something."

Nodar's waving at me, hands going side to side, head shaking.

"So, have you found something?"

"No. Nothing."

Nodar points to my phone. I put the detective on speakerphone.

"You're a bad liar."

Steel jaws of a trap on my skin. Maybe I can still wriggle free, maybe buy some time.

"Where are you right now?" The trap springs shut.

Nodar and I freeze. The detective stays silent. I stare at Nodar. He stares back mutely.

"At home, why?"

Nodar slaps a hand to his forehead. We hear papers shuffling.

"Just so we're clear, you're at forty-one Asatiani Street with your taxi driver chum? Nodar Basriani?"

Nodar mouths an almost-silent "fuck." I search his face for a bright idea, a way out of this mess. I find nothing but pale dread looking back at me.

"That's right," I say.

"So, if I was to ring the doorbell right now, you'd answer the door?"

All color drains from Nodar's face. He closes his eyes. They're at the door. Ketino's alone.

"Yes." I put as much conviction into the word as I can.

The detective lets the silence ring out until it's unbearable. Nodar puts a finger to his lips. Don't say a fucking word, his face says. I nod.

"Alright, Saba. When can you come in to the station?"

Nodar exhales audibly and then slaps a hand over his mouth.

"Why do you need me? I'm happy to talk now."

I can hear him grin. Nodar shakes his head and mouths "Fuck me."

The detective gives a hollow laugh. "Don't you want your passport? You seemed very concerned about it."

"You have my passport?"

"Arrived this morning. When can you come in?"

Nodar's already mouthing "tomorrow."

"Tomorrow," I say.

"Why not today?"

I look at Nodar. He shrugs and shows me his palms.

"I'm visiting some relatives."

"You said you didn't have any."

My mouth opens, but no words come out.

"I'm sorry, the line is bad," the detective says. "Seems like you're far away. . . . Bad signal?"

He keeps me hanging a long time. I can't think of a single useful thing to say. Eventually he sighs.

"Come in tomorrow morning, as early as you can."

I picture the detective on the floor, under my foot. I press the heel of my boot to the delicate bones around his eye socket and temple. Any second, I could put my whole weight through the heel of my boot. The thought makes me smile.

Nodar hangs up the phone for me. I've never seen him this angry.

"You brought your damn shiny phone with you?"

He snatches it out of my hand.

"They can track it, brother. That snake knows exactly where we are now!"

"I'm sorry, I didn't think . . ."

Dimitri and Zurab, now fully woken, both stare. Nodar softens. He puts a hand to his forehead and exhales.

"I didn't think either. I brought my lump of brick with me too."

He shows me his battered 1990s Nokia.

"I knew we lost him too easily. He let us go, Mowgli. . . ."

"What now?"

"Well, we can't stay here. I don't know, I need a minute to think."

He sinks back onto his cot and stares at the floor. He shoves his feet into his shoes. "I think better with my shoes on."

"He wants us back in Tbilisi, Nodar. Back at the station."

"He doesn't care what you do right now, Mowgli. He thinks Irakli's here, and he's coming. Fast as he can. We need to get away from here. Listen, brother, were you serious about Ossetia last night?"

"I was."

"Well, this is the last chance to back down."

"I'm sure, Nodar."

"OK, OK, let me think."

He paces up and down the room and formulates a hasty plan.

"We ditch our phones first. I'll take the plates off the car. Just in case. Then we can drive to the border, find a way across. The only way they can know where we've gone is . . ."

He glances in the direction of Zurab and Dimitri. Zurab is busy tinkering in the depths of the pechka. Dimitri watches us from the table, tapping an unlit cigarette on his knuckle.

"Oh no, brother. Don't even look in this direction. If you think we'll sell you downriver, then we're about to have a fistfight."

Nodar smiles a knowing smile.

"Of course. Ushguli," he says.

"But you might want to warn Father Serafim that the Mongols are coming."

After a hurried goodbye with Zurab, Dimitri walks with us to the monastery. I keep glancing around, expecting to see the detective slide out from every corner. Seeing the stride of our approach and our faces,

Father Serafim ushers us straight into the nearest room—the kitchen. Behind him, the monks are busy preparing breakfast.

"Father Serafim, the police are coming," I blurt as soon as the door closes.

He doesn't even take a moment.

"Perfect day for it." His face sets in an expression of a man longing for a good fight.

"We're heading out to Ossetia."

"I thought you might."

"But we need to make sure . . ." My words run out.

Father Serafim raises his eyebrows past the rim of his sunglasses.

"They'll have a lot of questions for you, Father," Nodar says.

The eyebrows stay up.

"Watch your step now, friend," Father Serafim says evenly.

Nodar gets the message and so do I. Defiance is weaved through this man's DNA. He's an Ushguli too. No siege he can't withstand.

"We just wanted to warn you," I say quickly.

"Irakli's a brother to me. You'll squeeze blood out of a stone before you get an Ushguli to give up a brother. You wasted a trip coming here to warn us."

"We should go, before they catch us here," Dimitri says behind us.

Father Serafim puts a hand on my shoulder and crosses himself.

"May He watch over your path, my son. Don't worry about us. We're familiar with invaders here." He smiles.

With Father Serafim's blessing, we rush back to Nodar's car. Just before we leave its labyrinth of paths and mud tracks, Ushguli has a final surprise for us. Huge white clouds, luminous in the sunlight, have wandered into the village like the wayward sheep of a giant. The rear of a homestead is buried in a cloud so thick that half the watchtower can't be seen. Another cloud has swallowed the path out of the village and part of the adjacent field.

"Just a little airborne water, my fragile friends. Don't be alarmed." Dimitri walks right into the cloud and vanishes from sight.

Nodar and I follow, glancing at each other. As I step into the cloud, Ushguli disappears. All sound is dampened. I can barely see Nodar, even though he's right beside me. It's hard to breathe. My clothes suck up the moisture and droplets form on my face.

I follow the only thing I can see clearly—the mud track beneath my feet. I walk like this long enough to doubt if I'll ever see daylight again. The village pops back into existence without warning. I blink in the sunlight. The cloud gives birth to a grumpy Nodar beside me.

"It's bad luck," he says, trying to squeeze water from his sleeves.

"Everything's a drama for you city nancies." Dimitri chuckles.

Away from the village we grow a little calmer. We cross the river at the top of Ushguli, over a small stone bridge.

"Why didn't we cross here the other day, Dimitri?"

"Tradition." Dimitri grins.

"Which tradition's that, Dima?"

Dimitri steps out to put me between himself and Nodar.

"A price is due before you enter Ushguli."

"Fuck your mother, I ought to brain you like a lame donkey."

"You know, your insults are predictable. Very mother-based."

"Fuck your father, brother, and uncle too."

When we get back to Nodar's car, Dimitri opens the passenger side door and gets in. Nodar knocks on the glass. Dimitri rolls the window down and looks up at him, squinting.

"Yes?"

"What are you doing?"

"Well, I'm no Nostradamus, but I see the Ossetia border in your near future."

At the mention of Ossetia, I see a twinkle in Nodar's eyes. He's already there, in that cornered land, searching for his dead daughter.

"And why are you tagging along, Dimitri? You can't be that bored."

"Well, the pair of you don't know a way into Ossetia," Dimitri says.

"What, you do?"

"I've been back and forth three times. I know how to get in. Without me, you'll get shot and I've grown fond of you. Well, fond of Saba."

"And why are you border-hopping so often, Dima?"

Dimitri sighs. His eyes are drawn to the floor.

"Spill it, Dimitri, or I'll drown you in that river. My tradition." There's an edge in Nodar's voice.

"My mother's there, OK? Refuses to leave."

Nodar's face softens. He whistles.

"You're telling me you're half-Abkhazian *and* half-Ossetian, you poor bastard?"

Dimitri nods solemnly. Nodar breaks into a smile.

"One foot in each war, eh?" Nodar gets in the car. "OK, Dima, but no more weird stories in the car. Understood?"

"Understood, sergeant. No more weird stories."

It takes Nodar a few minutes of cajoling to get the Volga warmed to the idea of starting. The engine finally coughs itself to life.

"She doesn't like the cold, that's all."

We set off and begin to tiptoe our way down the thawing dirt tracks. At the first ravine we come to, Nodar stops.

"Your phone still have reception?" he asks.

"Just."

"Hand it over, Dr. Watson. Both of you, stay in the car," he says, getting out.

He walks a little distance away and looks at us. Then he dials a number, puts the phone to his ear, and turns away.

"It's me, Keti."

The ravine betrays Nodar. His voice ricochets around the rocks and cliffs and we can hear him clear as day.

"No, no, everything's fine. We got here just fine and—"

He pauses.

"It's a long story, Keti, and I'm short on time—"

Ketino's asking him something. He shakes his head and looks at the sky. I catch a glimpse of his grimace.

"I'll tell you all about it very soon, OK? I can't right now, I'm losing signal."

More words from Ketino that I can only guess at.

"I just wanted to hear your voice, Keti."

Nodar takes a couple of steps forward with his head down.

"Listen, maybe soon we can sell that plot in Kukia . . . if we don't need it anymore."

More words from Ketino. Nodar pulls the phone away from his ear and speaks into it like it was a microphone.

"Keti, I love you, but I have to go now. I'll see you soon, OK?"

His hand drops to his side.

"I'm sorry," he says and hangs up.

He stands in the middle of the dirt track with his back to us for a long time. Then he wipes his sleeve across his face and pulls out his own phone.

"Track this," he says, and both phones go flying down the ravine.

I hear their plastic skitter as they shatter on the rocks below. The sound puts a full stop to any chance of letting Sandro know what's happening.

He must be back in London by now, his cuts and bruises beginning to knit. I picture him restless and frantic, like a cat on a leash. He paces, orbiting his phone. He needs to know. But now there's nothing but a dial tone on the other end of that call.

First thing I do, Sandro, first chance I get—I'll let you know. I promise.

Neither Dimitri nor I ask any questions as Nodar gets back in the car.

"Let's go to fuckin' Ossetia then," Nodar says, and we jolt forward down the steep road.

WHERE HE CAN, Nodar slips off the main road.

"Safer this way," he keeps saying to himself. "Never want to see that detective again in my life."

A couple of hours into the drive, we discover that Dimitri lied. We should have known. The weird stories begin and do not ease up.

He tells us of his route across the border, tried and tested. There's a forest that straddles the border between Georgia and Ossetia. It's called the Baba Yaga forest, not far from where Nodar and Ketino lived. It's the only place to cross unseen. The actual border runs along a small river in the middle of this forest, but it's too awkward to patrol. The soldiers stay out of the forest and watch the tree line instead.

"It's not very big, but it's dense. Very easy to get lost."

"I know, Dima, I lived right by it," Nodar grumbles.

"Well, did you know that place is cursed?"

"Don't start with those fairy tales. They don't even scare the kids anymore."

"What fairy tales?" I ask.

"They say Baba Yaga lives in that forest, in a shack built from elk bones and roofed with cured human skin," Dimitri says.

"She only eats naughty children, Mowgli, don't worry."

"Hush, Nodar. She leaves a trail of sweets, hanging from the branches to lure children to her shack."

Dimitri's poker face is unassailable.

"Nodar, I'm deadly serious. If you idiots see any sweets in that forest, for God's sake, don't eat them."

"Wait, isn't that the same story they tell about the forest by Tbilisi?" I say.

Dimitri and Nodar exchange a glance and laugh. It's good to see the wrinkled smile on Nodar's face again. It's been awhile.

"Brother, every forest in Georgia has witches in it, sweets hanging from branches, and Baba Yaga huts hopping around on chicken legs. Right, Dimitri?"

"There were *two* near my village. Once, the final-year schoolkids made me follow the sweets into the forest and left me there for the night."

Nodar laughs again.

"Yeah, you laugh. I've been in two wars since, but that forest was scarier. Anyway, a few years later, we were doing the same thing to the younger kids."

"A proud tradition," Nodar says.

Our departure from Ushguli meant we turned our back on the Caucasus for a while. Hours later, when the road plateaus again, we finally see the mountains unobstructed. We're heading directly for them again. No one speaks; we just stare.

At the end of this plateau is South Ossetia. This is the last respite before the Caucasus impose their authority. We're close enough now. The mountains know we're coming.

THE CLOSER WE GET to Ossetia, the more military presence mars the landscape. Groups of armed soldiers scuttle about by crossroads. Occasionally, we see tanks in the adjacent fields with soldiers gathered around them.

We come across a huge, armored personnel carrier guarding a vineyard.

"What is that?" I ask.

"Well, we used to call them BTRs back in the old days. Troop carriers. Bulletproof," Nodar explains.

"I've never seen one this big," Dimitri says.

The behemoth BTR revs its engine just as we're driving past. The sound rattles the entire Volga and everything in it. The noise almost jolts Nodar into driving us off the road.

"Your mother's crotch yogurt," he mumbles, looking in the mirror. "The size of that thing."

"There he goes again with mothers," Dimitri says.

Not long after, another BTR rumbles past. Nodar has to swerve and take us completely off the road to get around it. The soldiers perched on the BTR's shell follow us with curious eyes. It keeps happening— suspicious looks follow the Volga and soldiers point us out to one another.

"We need to get off this road," Nodar says.

He swivels his head, looking for a way off the main road. But before he can find one, we round a sharp, banked corner and come face-to-face with a tank blocking the whole road ahead. It's the size of a small house. There's no way past.

"Fuck," Nodar mutters.

The brakes squeal as Nodar slows the Volga almost to a stop. There's an idle group of soldiers leaning on the tank, talking and smoking. Seeing our Volga, they straighten up. One of them swings his assault rifle off his shoulder and into his hands. He spits on the ground and starts toward us.

"Not good, Nodar, not good," Dimitri says.

"I know, brother."

The soldier holds up his hand. Nodar stops the car and rolls down his window. The soldier approaches us, focused on Nodar. He can't be more than eighteen—barely a hint of stubble, and greasy hair cowlicked by sleep. He leans over and looks at Nodar.

"What you doing here, old man?"

Nodar's jaw clenches. "Driving to Ditsi. What are *you* doing here, boy?"

The cold look in the soldier's eyes falters.

"Can't go to Ditsi this way."

"Don't tell me where I can go. I know every dirt road, fence, and cowpat around here. Get that thing off the road so we can get through."

The soldier glances back at his group.

"Don't look at them. Look at me. What's your name, boy? You've forgotten what your father taught you."

Nodar sounds like he may well be the boy's father, scolding him for some passing indiscipline. Dimitri's eyes widen as he glances at the boy's rifle, his hand on the grip, thumb on the safety. Dimitri's face turns a shade of off-white. I sit and wait to be dragged out of the car. The soldier looks like he's been slapped. Nodar senses his hesitation.

"You Ossetian, boy?"

The soldier nods mutely.

"Aren't you ashamed of yourself?"

Childlike guilt flits across the soldier's face and he looks down. His eyes are drawn to the group by the tank again.

"Don't look at them. Answer me."

"I'm sorry, uncle," he says in a hushed voice. "Can't let you through. Orders."

Someone calls out from the tank, something I don't quite catch.

"Ditsi!" the soldier shouts back.

More shouts from the group by the tank. One of the older soldiers gets up.

"You better go, uncle, before you cause yourself a hurt. Roads north of here are closed. We're to shoot anyone who tries to get by. Go. Before he gets here."

Nodar's eyes snap to the soldier coming toward us—an officer. Swearing, Nodar puts the Volga in reverse with a grinding clunk from the gearbox. The officer pauses as Nodar wrestles the Volga through a creaking, jangling three-point turn.

"Hey! What do you want here?"

Nodar ignores him.

"God loves ugly, God loves ugly," he mutters under his breath, lining the Volga up for escape.

At the last moment, just before the officer reaches us, our tires give a gravelly bark as the wheels spin and we're away. I watch the two soldiers talking to each other, gesticulating. But they make no move to come after us.

"You lost your mind? Why did you argue?" Dimitri's voice has a quake to it.

"What Georgian doesn't argue? They'd have shot us if we just turned and left." Nodar wipes sweat off his brow as color flows back into his knuckles.

"Fair point," Dimitri says.

"How do we get to the Baba Yaga forest now?"

"Don't you worry. We'll find a way," Dimitri answers me.

Once we're well out of sight of the tank, Nodar's nervous foot lightens up on the gas and we slow to a sensible speed. Dimitri squints out the windshield.

"Here, Nodar, slow down."

He thumps the dashboard with an open palm.

"Stop, brother, stop!"

Nodar slams the brakes and we slide and judder to a stop. When the cloud of dust dissipates, we see that Dimitri's stopped us right by a narrow dirt track leading into the wild countryside.

"Sorry, boys, I'm a little rusty," he says. "I almost missed it. This track will take us to the forest. Eventually."

"Eventually?"

THE DIRT TRACK is rough going. Every few minutes we stop and I get out to scrape open old wooden cattle gates overgrown with thorny weeds, thick grass, and stinging nettle. Either that or I scrabble around moving logs, fallen tree branches, and boulders that the Volga can't conquer. It's tough, sweaty work. Nodar takes pity.

"Dima, give him a hand. Queen Elizabeth's melting."

"Why don't you let me drive and *you* give Elizabeth a hand?"

Nodar doesn't answer. Dimitri and I alternate clearing the road and by the time it's over we're covered in sweat and stinging-nettle burns.

"Can't see it from here, but it's there," Dimitri says, pointing. "Up and over that hill is the forest."

"You sure there's a gap there?"

"For the millionth time, yes, Nodar. I'm sure. When I go, this is the way I go, OK?"

Nodar stops the Volga and we share a cigarette to celebrate our victory over this pilgrimage.

"Your place around here, you said?" Dimitri asks.

"Other side of the forest."

Nodar lapses back into silence and stares at the hill we're about to tackle.

"Right place, wrong time," Dimitri tuts. "Let's wait awhile. I'd rather cross when it's a little darker."

We wait in nervous silence for the sun to set. Twilight descends, fragrant with wild grass and cooling soil. When our patience runs out, Nodar takes the license plates off the car and tosses them into a nettle thicket. We get back in.

"Let's get it over with," he says and accelerates toward the Baba Yaga forest.

At the lip of the hill, the dirt track crests so sharply that for a second our front wheels are in the air and our windshield's filled by the obsidian sky, already punctured by stars. The Volga's wheels crash back down and we finally see the forest. A long, flat field of grass is the only thing between us and Baba Yaga.

Nodar brings the Volga to a halt and kills the engine. We watch the forest for movement but see none. Dimitri steps out to look around.

"No one here," he says. "Why don't we walk?"

"More time for someone to see us."

"OK, so we drive across. Then what?"

"Hide the car and vanish into the forest. Then we're safe."

"Let's wait till dark."

Nodar doesn't answer. He looks around and bites his lip.

"I don't know," he mutters. "What if there's a patrol by then?"

While they're distracted, I get in Nodar's seat and start the car. They both whip around to look at me in surprise.

"What are you doing, Elizabeth?"

"Get in."

I inch the car forward.

"Get in."

They scramble into the car. I put my hand on the gearshift.

"Saba, wait."

I rip the gearshift forward and slam the gas pedal down. For a second the Volga spins its wheels, kicking up grassy clods of soil. But when the tires bite down we launch into the field, bouncing in our seats. We're more than halfway across when my face relaxes a touch. I open my mouth to say something and quickly close it again.

Among the first trees, I see three small flashes of light. A heartbeat later we hear three echoing snaps—like someone taking a hammer to a wooden plank. Three bullet holes crunch into existence in the right corner of the windshield, right by my head.

"Stop, Saba, stop!" Dimitri barks from the passenger seat and puts his arm across my chest. "Go back!"

The car squirms under us as I hit the brakes. We slide to a standstill. The engine stalls. I try to chug it back to life. An ominous silence descends on the field. I'm wrestling the gearshift and kicking the pedals. The engine coughs, sputters, and starts.

"Go, go, reverse."

It's too late. We see more flashes of light, dozens of them this time. The knocking sound echoes down the field. Someone is dumping a whole ammo clip in our direction.

My fight-or-flight instinct malfunctions. I can't do either properly. At first, I fold myself behind the wheel and hide. The only thing I can hear is the metallic thudding of bullets hitting the car. They tear the Volga apart alive. The windows explode, showering my head in broken glass gemstones. The engine stutters and stops. The tires pop and hiss. Metal shrapnel clatters and ricochets through the car, ripping up the upholstery.

To blot out the sound, I rasp a sore hole in my throat shouting incoherent half-Georgian, half-English words. When that's not enough, my shouts turn to screams as I try to cram myself farther into the footwell.

The gunfire stops as suddenly as it came down on us. The echoes dissipate and all that can be heard is the sharp hiss from the engine block. Wisps of blue smoke slither from the bullet holes on the hood. The Volga's dead. The windshield's torn to shreds and there are jagged fist-size holes in the roof.

"Saba, say something."

I've never heard Nodar's voice like this.

"I'm OK."

"Fuck are they shooting at?" Dimitri says.

"Dimitri, you're bleeding."

"It's a scratch, some glass."

"Dimitri, stop moving," Nodar hisses.

Dimitri sticks his head out of the passenger seat window.

"Even the Nazis didn't shoot without warning!" he screams across the field.

Nodar grabs him and pulls him back in.

"Dimitri, they have us zeroed. Stop. Stay still."

But Dimitri's not listening. He tugs his T-shirt off and goes to wave it out the window.

There's a short burst of gunfire. A couple of bullets bite into the hood. The third bullet hits Dimitri in the chest. The back of his seat explodes in a cloud of upholstery foam and atomized blood. Something warm sprays the side of my face.

Dimitri collapses onto the dashboard. His spine knuckles under the pale skin of his back, where there's an exit wound the size of a fist. It's a glistening maw of flesh and exposed bone. Nodar reaches from the back seat and pulls Dimitri upright, hiding the awful sight.

Dimitri's breathing in short, gasping heaves. Sharp inhales and long gurgling exhales. The corners of his mouth fill with tar-black blood.

"Dimitri, don't move, stay still."

Dimitri squeezes out two syllables.

"No-dar."

"Stop fucking moving, Dimitri. You'll be fine."

Dimitri looks down at the singed hole in his bare chest and nudges his index finger into it. His eyes widen.

"No, no, no, don't look at it. Look at me—we'll get you help. Keep your eyes on me now, understand?"

Nodar kicks his door open and gets out. He puts his hands over his head and starts shouting in the direction of the forest at the top of his lungs.

"We're unarmed, unarmed!"

Dimitri's fading. His breathing shallows. He closes his eyes as he exhales and doesn't inhale again. I grab his shoulder and shake him.

"Dimitri!"

He gasps down some air and looks at me with the eyes of a man falling off a cliff.

"Nodar, we need help!"

Nodar picks up Dimitri's T-shirt and waves it about wildly. In the gaps between his shouts he's swearing.

"Unarmed, unarmed!

"Sons of motherless bastards.

"We're unarmed!

"Donkey-bred, dimwit yokels.

"We need a medic!"

Soldiers make themselves visible at the tree line. They watch, motionless. As soon as I get out of the car, they shoulder their weapons. But they don't shoot any more—I guess there's no need. They cross the field slowly, methodically. By the time they get to us, Dimitri's long stopped breathing and Nodar's stopped swearing. We stand by the ruined Volga, silent, like men come to the end of something.

13

FUCK THE HUMAN VILLAGE

I know what'll happen if I don't do something.

"Nodar, listen."

No response. He's unnaturally still, like a gas canister that's rolled into the campfire.

"Nodar, don't argue with them."

The soldiers are almost on us.

"Nodar, say something."

His fists clench and unclench. As soon as the first soldier is within earshot, he speaks.

"What are you mongoloids shooting at?"

The nearest soldier doesn't pause his stride. He heads straight for Nodar, assault rifle in hand.

"Look what you did!"

The soldier stops two paces short of Nodar.

"Answer me. We look like the fucking enemy to you? Who is the enemy, by the way?"

The soldier's face darkens. He puts his index finger to his lips. "Shhh, uncle, be quiet." He shrugs off his rifle strap.

"Nodar, don't."

But Nodar doesn't hear me. Before I can move to stop him, he takes a step toward the soldier.

"Boy, what's your name—"

With an easy, practiced movement, the rifle butt comes up and swings into Nodar's face. There's a sound like a mallet hitting raw meat. Nodar's nose opens like a tap and covers the front of his shirt in blood. He claps both hands over it and falls to his knees. Blood streams between his fingers. He's mumbling something. The soldier leans closer.

"Pardon me, good uncle?"

Nodar takes his hands away. His nose is broken and cut at the bridge, his lower lip is split wide open, and both are streaming blood.

"F-fuck you," he says.

Taking a deep breath, he spits blood and saliva all over the soldier's feet. The soldier steps back. Nodar opens his mouth to speak again.

"Fuck your donkey-bred moth-*uh*—"

The kick lands in the middle of Nodar's chest. He collapses backward.

The soldier smiles. He leans in to look at Nodar, as though he's happened upon some trinket in the grass. He puts his finger to his lips again. "Shhhh, be still, uncle."

I take a step toward Nodar. He's gulping, unable to take in air.

"Stay where you are." The soldier aims his gun at me lazily from the hip.

He turns toward the dead Volga and its silent occupant. He takes a canister from his hip and unscrews the lid. The smell of gas cuts through the air. He pours the gas into the Volga through the shattered windows, pouring most of it on Dimitri.

Carefully putting his back to the breeze, the soldier lights a box of matches and tosses it into the car. The Volga bursts into flames, crackling like firewood. The flames stain Dimitri's face black. His hair catches fire and burns up in a wisp of black smoke. The skin on his face starts to bubble like a pancake in a frying pan. I look away. But I feel something cold press into my neck.

"No, no," the soldier says by my ear. "You watch."

I watch Dimitri roast in the Volga until the smoke from the burning plastic obscures the view. Another soldier drags Nodar to his feet. They tie our hands and march us away with Nodar dripping a trail of coagulate blood and saliva as we go. We walk a long time, skirting the forest, until we reach an old bombed-out Soviet Pioneers camp.

The wide, three-story building has its back to Baba Yaga. Pockmarked murals cover the walls. A portrait of Stalin's great unsmiling face sits right over the entrance, flanked by Lenin's great unsmiling face. Something's blown a hole through Stalin's cheek and the building interior is visible through it.

Thousands of eager kids would have spent their summers here. Hammer-and-sickle, red-neckerchief Pioneers—the Soviet take on the Scouts. Up at dawn, taking cold showers, marching twice daily, standing watch, and eating in shifts, like miniature soldiers—already inured to hardship and fear, itching to fight in would-be wars.

Inside the building, the walls are covered in Communist slogans, stenciled in a faded Lenin red:

"For the glory of the working class—prepare!"

"Pioneers—ready to fight for the Communist cause!"

"Study, train, and be ready!"

Perpetual readiness is the theme. The soldiers prod Nodar and me down a long corridor, toward a floor-to-ceiling mural of a stern Slavic woman wearing a red headscarf, holding her index finger to her lips. Huge lettering beneath her spells out:

"Don't tattle!"

I glance at Nodar. The blood dripping from his nose has stopped. I catch a glint in his eyes that tells me the rational Nodar isn't in charge anymore. The lunatics run that asylum now.

The corridor ends in an old sports hall. Dusty glass, blown into the hall by some forgotten explosion, has been swept into the corners. The hardwood floor undulates wildly; in places entire sections are missing altogether, revealing the concrete beneath, already cracked open by stubborn weeds.

There are cots and sleeping bags rolled out by the walls. A group of soldiers stops playing cards and stares at us as we walk in. Soon, every face in the hall watches as we're shoved toward a collection of school desks under the rusting basketball hoop. Radio equipment and wooden boxes of ammo are stacked on the desks. An older man, gray at the temples, is sitting behind a desk, scribbling in a notebook.

Without looking up, he motions for the soldiers to bring us to him. They shove us forward.

"Did you search them?" the man says without a change in his expression.

"Yes, sergeant."

"And?"

"Nothing. No IDs. No plates."

"Of course not. Leave them here. Back to your patrol."

I look at Nodar, hoping to catch his eye. But he's glaring at the sergeant.

"Trying to sneak into Ossetia, lads?" The sergeant sighs and glances up at us.

"Just trying to get to Ditsi." I try to preempt whatever Nodar will do to get us shot.

"Ditsi's this side of the border. Anyway, Ditsi's gone. Ditsi's rubble."

The radio equipment produces a sharp squawk, followed by indistinct chatter. The sergeant holds up his hand. He writes something down in his notebook and turns back to us.

"Do you know how many of you morons we've had to kill?"

He sighs and goes back to his notebook.

"So, what is it? What did you leave behind in Ossetia? Grandma's jewelry? Your favorite donkey?"

Nodar's face turns red but he says nothing.

"When will you people get it through your skull? The border's closed. You can't go back. You come, we shoot. Want me to draw you a picture?"

Nodar's jaw clenches as he tries to keep still. When he inevitably fails, he fails spectacularly.

"Fuck you and your border," he says, spitting a vile mixture of blood and saliva on the sergeant's desk.

The sergeant freezes. He looks down at the phlegmy mess oozing down the page of his notebook. He regains his composure quickly.

"You better let your pal with the accent do the talking, or you might have a tragic accident."

He wipes the page with his sleeve and shuts the notebook. His black shark eyes snap to me.

"Where's the accent from, pal?"

"England."

"O-ho, England! You meet the queen in England?"

I don't answer.

"OK, Mr. English. You're telling me you're going to Ditsi. But you're headed north. Maybe your compass is broken?"

LEO VARDIASHVILI

He smiles amicably and lowers his voice. "You can tell me, pal. I won't tattle." He winks.

"We got lost and—"

He holds up his hand. This isn't what he wants.

"You know what? I don't care."

He turns to Nodar. "What happened to the number plates, friend?"

"Maybe they fell off," Nodar says.

The whole room's watching us and this draws a few chuckles from nearby soldiers.

The sergeant sighs. "Well, the police will be here tomorrow. They'll make you sing and dance without my help."

He points at me with his pen. "What's your name?"

"Giorgi . . ." I say.

"Just Giorgi?"

More chuckles from the soldiers around us.

"Giorgi Gulava."

"Sounds plausible. What about you, Mike Tyson? You have a name, pal?"

"Donald," Nodar says, louder than necessary.

The sergeant sighs. "Donald what?"

I close my eyes and brace myself.

"Donald Duck."

The words echo around the hall. There's laughter from the soldiers behind us. The sergeant gives a hollow, humorless laugh.

"Fine, Donald, fine," he says. "I'll tell the police they're dealing with a celebrity. Make sure they treat you right."

He smiles at Nodar. There's a promise in that smile, of things worse than a bloodied nose.

"Davit, take our guests upstairs and tie them to something heavy."

A nearby soldier groans to his feet. He's a tall, thin man, older than most in the room. Older than the sergeant, even. Familiar fatigue visible in the way he carries himself. He looks us up and down with pity in his earnest eyes.

He walks over to us, pulling up his sleeves to reveal forearms covered in a network of scars. His face and scalp are covered in rough, wiry stubble of uniform length.

"Watch them for the night, Davit. They run, you shoot."

"Understood."

I try to catch Nodar's eye, but his head is down. Dimitri's dead. The Volga's dead. Tomorrow the police will take us back to Tbilisi—or worse. We've failed.

DAVIT SETS US up in a large room upstairs. There's no windows and the floor's covered in sawdust. The swaying leaves of the forest are visible through a head-size hole in the brickwork in one corner of the room.

Davit cable-ties Nodar to a cast-iron radiator bolted to the wall but no longer connected to anything. He ties me to a set of exposed plumbing pipes at the other end of the room.

He looks at us from the doorway and his gaze drops to the floor.

"Sorry," he says quietly. "Orders."

When he comes back, he drags along with him a prehistoric office chair. Cracked leather clings to the frame loosely and half the wheels are missing. Davit wrenches the remaining wheels off and sets the chair down by the door. A muted volley of laughter downstairs and the sound of glass shattering draw his attention. I watch him closely as he lights a crooked cigarette with a match. Something odd in that gesture, something familiar.

"Hello, 'Bublik.'"

Nino's acetone voice makes me shiver.

"What was it you said, you know, right in the beginning?"

"Not now, Nino."

"*. . . a tall, skinny man with earnest eyes.*" My words, spoken by Nino's voice.

"*Stop.*"

"*OK, fine, but tell me this guy doesn't look familiar.*"

I watch Davit sit forward, elbows on knees, holding his cigarette at an odd angle between his thumb and forefinger.

"*. . . he looked honest and said the right things. Held his cigarette just so. You see it yet, Bublik?*"

"*No.*"

"*Picture him with an envelope of Irakli's money. Eka's money.*"

"*No. Can't be him.*"

But Nino might be right. I can hear her giggling as she warps an old song to her needs.

"*Look behind you, watch where you go. Don't talk to folks
      you don't know.
Honest man, you've done wrong. Maybe not today, but it
      won't be long.
Your days have numbers, you're a disgrace. One day, you'll
      feel my cold embrace.
You've thought of me over and over again. Only one way to
      make this end . . .*"

I try to reason a gap into the racket she's making.

"*Just like that? Poof—coincidence? Here?*"

"*No coincidence, Bublik. Things you need the most always hide in places you wouldn't dare to look. Makes sense, if you think about it.*"

Nino chuckles.

"*Things you need the most? I don't need him!*"

Her laughter cuts short.

"*But I do,*" she whispers.

I stare across the room at the honest man who stole our money in London. He ate our food and drank our drink. He took the pounds and pennies meant for Eka and left, smiling and shaking hands. But Eka never got the money and we never saw the honest man again. We never saw Eka again either. The pipes clang at my sudden movement.

"Easy, friend," Davit says. "Don't make a fuss. Trust me."

Nino snorts.

"Trust me, he says! Let me at him and I'll spoon those eyes right out of his skull."

My eyes meet Davit's and I search for a sign of recognition on his face. I want him to know me. I want him to *see* me. Nodar interrupts.

"Listen, brother. Davit. Let us have a smoke."

Davit shakes his head.

"Come on, even the Nazis gave our lot cigarettes."

"Before they shot them."

Nodar laughs, but the laugh's a forgery. He doesn't sound like himself and there's a new look on his face I don't recognize. He's still not the Nodar I know, but the lunatics in that asylum have organized. They've picked a leader.

"My mouth will get me shot anyway. Cigarette or no cigarette."

A hint of a smile from Davit, but he refuses nonetheless. Nodar doesn't quit. He wheedles, cajoles, and jokes with Davit until, at last, he gives us lit cigarettes to smoke hands-free. Nodar and Davit talk into the night while I try to contain Nino's furious hullabaloo within my skull. As I tire, she does too and only whispers blood and murder from time to time.

Turns out Davit used to live in Tbilisi. He had family there and he had family in Ossetia too. When the family in Tbilisi died out, he doubled down on the family in Ossetia. Hard to do, though, when a war breaks out. And now his family in Ossetia doesn't want anything to do with him because he joined the wrong army.

"I'm Georgian," Davit says. "What other army was I supposed to join? The Ossetian army?"

They both chuckle.

"I really thought we could win. Keep Georgia in one piece."

"Ah, brother, we couldn't win at falling over."

Davit gives us more cigarettes, carefully lighting them with his over-size sandpaper hands. He slumps into his chair and sighs.

"And now we babysit this forest—'secure the border.' But all we do is keep desperate people from their homes."

"Are there many?"

Davit nods. "Our orders are shoot to kill. We try to miss." He gestures in our direction.

"Didn't miss Dimitri, did you? Burned a hole right through his chest." Nino cuts in and I see Nodar's jaw clench at a similar thought.

A fragrant darkness has crept into the room from the forest. As their chatter quiets, my exhaustion wins out and Nino lets me nod off.

I'M WOKEN IN the dead of night by the static hiss of rain and the ugly gurning sounds of someone being strangled to death. A kerosene lamp knocked on its side casts a grotesque shadow-puppet show of two men trying to kill each other with their bare hands. Nodar and Davit are locked in a death grip on the floor.

Nodar's got Davit in a chokehold. The thin plastic tying his wrists together is lost deep in the flesh at Davit's throat. Davit's arm is out-stretched toward the rifle he left against the wall. He's nowhere near it. The gesture's more despair than hope.

With every muscle clenched bloodless, Nodar looks like he's trying to wrench Davit's head clean off. Only Davit's feet move. The heels of his boots clop on the floor. He's almost spent.

"Nodar! What are you doing?"

"Shhhh! Watch the door."

Davit's feet slow. His eyes are shot through with blood. Thick veins bulge at his temples. Gurgling somewhere deep in his throat, he makes one last attempt to free himself. His back arches off the floor.

For a second it looks as though he might succeed. But Nodar pulls tighter, throwing all his weight into the movement. Davit's entire body relaxes as one. His army boots produce a final, ineffectual clop-clop on the floor. He shudders and goes limp.

Breathing hard, Nodar heaves Davit's body off himself. His wrists are bleeding where the cable tie bit them to the bone. He hisses in pain as he pulls the sharp plastic out of the wounds. He turns to Davit and rolls him onto his side. Davit takes a faint, wheezing breath.

"He's out. But not for long."

Nodar gets to his feet with a groan. He stands in the middle of the room, looking like his own monument, listening for any sound from the soldiers downstairs. The only thing to be heard is the rain outside and the patter of blood dripping from his mangled wrists.

He cuts himself free on the jagged edge of the radiator. Then, using the exposed flame from the kerosene lamp, he burns through my plastic ties.

"Get up."

"What have you done?"

"He'll live. Get up."

"The fuck do we do now?"

"We have to get out."

Nodar starts pulling bricks out of the damaged corner wall, where years of rain have melted the mortar. The bricks come away like rotten teeth. He places each brick carefully, soundlessly, in a neat pile by the radiator. Within a few minutes he's made a hole big enough to crouch through. He sticks his head out into the rain and looks down.

"Fuck," he mutters.

"What's the matter?"

"Can't see a thing. You look."

I stick my head through the hole. I see nothing but a shifting mass of soggy darkness two floors down.

"It's too high."

"What's down there?"

"Nodar, it's too high."

"Tell me." His voice hardens.

"Nothing. Bushes, I think."

"I'm going."

"Nodar, you'll break your neck."

"Maybe. But I can't stay here." He points at Davit. "He'll wake up soon."

Nodar steps up to the hole he's made in the wall.

"I'll go first. Then you. Watch you don't land on me and paralyze us both."

Just before he jumps, he looks back at me.

"Fuck the human village, Mowgli."

He vanishes into the darkness like an out-of-shape, balding Batman. I hear a crunching thud and a string of swear words spoken low and angry. Behind me Davit coughs weakly and his crushed-windpipe breathing resumes.

"Poor fella, poor brave soldier. How will his fairy tale end? Nobody knows." Nino's caustic singsong voice cuts in.

I turn to look at Davit. He's slumped on his side and his breath barely ruffles the sawdust on the floor.

"This is why you have to read a fairy tale to the end, no matter what. For the happy ending. Let's read his ending, Saba."

"Are you crazy?"

"It's his fault. All of this. Greedy little soldier."

I never could quiet Nino when she wanted to be heard, living or dead.

"He killed Eka. As sure as if he'd shot her."

I shake my head.

"He killed Irakli too."

"Irakli's alive."

"Irakli's dead. Dead but still stumbling about, looking for things that can't be found."

I hear a soft whistle from outside. Nodar's impatient. I ignore him.

"You owe it to them. To Eka, to Irakli."

"I can't."

"Just a nudge. Poor little soldier. Put him on his back and maybe he won't breathe so good. Maybe he'll go down the path to Baba Yaga."

Nino's voice turns childlike and that's when I know she's won. She always wins, even when she shouldn't. I owe a debt I can't repay. I have to follow her. Always and into any darkness.

My eyes are fixed on the honest man, his earnest eyes closed to the world. Who knows what could have been if not for him?

"Just a little nudge."

Nino steadies my hands. Together we kneel and push Davit onto his back. With his throat crushed the way it is, that's all it takes.

"There, there, little soldier. Just follow those sweets," Nino croons.

Davit's breathing catches on something and stops. He makes swallowing, gulping sounds but no air's getting in. Lack of oxygen spasms his limbs. His head turns side to side, but he doesn't wake. The place where Eka's voice speaks from stirs but she offers no objection. In my dreams, I've killed this man a thousand times. But never like this; it was never this easy.

Another whistle from the forest snaps me out of it. I'm about to jump into the wet darkness outside when Lena clears her throat. I freeze.

"You can't leave him like this, Saba."

"He deserves it."

"Yes, he does. What about his family? Do they deserve it?"

I can feel Nino squirming to speak, but her voice could never override Lena's.

"Break the cycle, Saba, someone has to."

I rush back to Davit and pull him onto his side. Recovery position. I thump his back until a thick slug of saliva escapes his mouth and he starts breathing again.

"Go now, he might wake."

I step up to the broken wall and feel the wet brick and plaster beneath my palms. I glance back at Davit one last time and jump.

I land in the drenched soil on my tiptoes. The momentum makes me fall forward and knocks the breath out of me. Leaves stick to my face like wet tissue paper. I catch my breath and roll over onto my back, blinking into the falling rain. Nodar's face enters my vision.

"Get those leaves off you. Now."

"What? Why?"

"Stinging nettles."

I slap the leaves off my face, neck, and arms.

"Jesus, Nodar, I'm covered in this shit!"

"Hush, brother. So am I. Let's go, before he wakes."

We wade through the stinging nettle thicket. The only way to not get our exposed arms stung to death is to lift them over our heads. As I do so, entire branches of nettle caress my sides under my T-shirt.

"Fuck!"

"Shhh . . . They'll hear us."

I glance at the weak lamplight coming from the room we just escaped. I picture Davit's face, turning side to side in search of air. Those damaged sounds that seemed to come straight from his chest and not his vocal cords. What did Nino almost make me do? What did I almost do? I gag, double up, and empty everything I had in my stomach onto my feet.

"What's the matter?"

I shrug off his hand.

"I'm fine."

We scuttle crablike out of the nasty thicket. Nodar studies his arms and his wrists, slick with blood. He lifts his shirt to inspect the welts of nettle burns on his torso.

"Won't be pretty tomorrow."

He fishes a wet clump of nettle leaves out of his collar and swears.

"Let's go," he says and moves off toward the forest.

The sight of the Baba Yaga forest makes us both stop. The sodden branches sway in the wind and the forest looms over us like a crashing wave. As we head deeper in, the forest takes the sharp edges off all sounds. Even our voices sound spoken through cotton wool. Nodar keeps glancing over his shoulder.

"He was breathing, wasn't he? I think I just knocked him cold, that's all. He'll be OK."

Soon, the forest snuffs out any ambient light. The foliage is so thick that the rain only reaches us in occasional, oversize droplets. It's so dark I can barely make out my own hand in front of my face.

Nodar rummages in his pockets. "I took his matches."

He strikes a match and an orange glow blooms in his hands.

"Let's go."

We inch deeper into the forest, feeling our way forward by the ghost image the last match illuminated.

"Nodar, do you know where we're going?"

"Brother, this is my backyard."

We keep going until the matches run out. I close my eyes and open them again. There's no difference in what I can see. All that's left is the smell of wet pine, moss, dead leaves, and moist earth.

"Now what?"

"Don't panic, Mowgli, sit down. We're golden."

"Golden?"

"Shut up and sit down." An arm reaches out and tugs me to the floor. "They'll never find us in here."

Nodar spits. "How did I get nettle in my *mouth*?"

I hear him lie back and exhale. My arms, face, neck, sides, and even the gaps between my fingers are covered in furious, pulsing, itching lumps. Every nerve ending is begging me to scratch them. I lie back to take my mind off the sensation.

"If you have a happy place to go to, brother, now's the time."

I close my eyes and try to conjure beaches, peach-colored sunsets, green parks, and those early-winter days when you can smell the coming snow. But each image fetches up against the sight of Davit's feet, walking on thin air, and the burst capillaries filling his eyes with blood. The sad gulping sounds he made. His head lolling side to side. Lena saved him, but what if it wasn't enough? What if he still dies?

But then I remember one night from my childhood. I was in a bed, all alone in an unfamiliar bedroom. We must have been visiting someone. Pools of darkness filled the corners of the room—perfect hiding places for some other family's monsters. I kept my eyes open owl-wide. There was no way I'd sleep.

Irakli appeared in the doorway, haloed by cigarette smoke and lamplight from the other room. He came and sat down, shifting the bed with his weight. He didn't say much, and what he did say I can't recall. Vague words of comfort. Faint smell of tobacco and wine on his breath.

He put a hand on my chest. And finally, I slept.

Laid out on the lumpy wet forest floor, I try to feel the weight of my father's hand on my chest.

I'M WOKEN BY a distant gunshot. The sound is throttled by the forest, but it makes my eyes snap open. There's a dim, gray light forcing its way through the forest canopy. No way to tell what time it is.

"Nodar, did you hear that?"

He groans next to me.

"Nodar?"

My pulse pounds in my temples. My back has soaked up the moisture from the dead leaves on the ground. My front is dried stiff, starched by my own sweat and evaporated rainwater. My hands are swollen and throbbing. I look at them in disbelief—two bags of mottled pink flesh, twice their normal size and itching like you wouldn't believe.

"Was that a gunshot?" I say.

"We should go."

"I feel sick."

"That's the nettle poison."

Groaning and scratching, we set off deeper into the forest. After a few hours, we reach a small river. We wash our faces and scrub our nettle rashes in the cold water.

"Halfway there," Nodar says.

"Halfway where?"

"Home, Mowgli. Halfway home."

We follow the river until it slows to a creeping sludge. Stagnant pools of water trapped between fallen branches and rotting logs give off a ripe, earthy smell. Past the river, we wade into a clearing so densely carpeted with mushrooms that I can barely see the forest floor. Nodar crouches and peers at the mushrooms.

"We can sit on my balcony and roast these."

Together we decimate the field. Holding a teetering mountain of mushrooms in the kangaroo pouch he's made with his T-shirt, Nodar smiles that wrinkled smile I haven't seen since we left Ushguli. Taking off his T-shirt, he fashions it into a sack and carries it over his shoulder.

For the rest of the day, Nodar leads me through the Baba Yaga forest topless. When the trees start thinning, we stop. The sun's already setting. We sit concealed among thick blackberry bushes for a long time,

itching and swatting at the mosquitoes. We watch for patrolling soldiers, but none come. This close to his home, Nodar can't keep still any
longer.

"Fuck it," he says. "Both my ass cheeks are numb the whole way
through. I can't wait anymore."

At first, we walk head-down, jaws clenched, flinching at every sound
and expecting to be shot any second. But minutes pass and nothing
happens. Somehow, we've walked into South Ossetia completely un-
challenged. Nodar points toward a steep hill in the distance.

"Just over that ridge, Mowgli."

He vibrates with excitement. He tells me again about his grapes, his
wine, his balcony, the basement where Ketino hid her jams and pickles.
At the hillcrest, Nodar's almost running. But something makes him
stop. I catch up to him and we stand very still, side by side, and digest
the awful scene.

Laid out in front of us are the charred remains of a large brick farm-
house. A violent explosion has scattered the house and everything it
contained into the adjacent field. The sad rainfall of bricks, broken cinder blocks, pots, pans, cushions, and lumps of furniture is overgrown
with weeds. Something in Nodar's throat unhitches audibly.

"The gas tank," he says softly. "They set fire to the gas tank."

"I'm so sorry, Nodar."

"It's OK," he says. But I can tell he's crying as he stumbles down the
hill, away from the hand I put on his shoulder.

For a long time, I watch Nodar walk among the carnage. Occasionally he stops and picks something up, looks at it closely, and carries it
with him until something new makes him drop it.

Eventually, he comes back holding a photo of a little girl. The picture has been rained on and sun-dried dozens of times. The image is
barely visible. Nodar wipes away a layer of dried mud. There's a little
girl in the picture, sitting astride a blue tricycle. She's wrapped up

warm, hat and scarf, looking grumpy at the inconvenience and affront of it all.

"I took this." Nodar sits down beside me. "Couldn't make her smile that day, bike or no bike."

He sighs and puts the picture in his pocket. We sit and take in the scene.

"What do we do now, Nodar?"

"I've never made it this far." He shrugs. "Well, I guess we go see the villages. One by one." He points in the direction of the mountains. "Ossetia's a small place. If Natia or Irakli are here, someone will know."

"How many villages?"

Nodar closes his eyes and counts on both hands. "Ten or so. They follow the river north from here, until they dead-end."

"Dead-end?"

"The mountains, brother. They're—"

He jumps to his feet.

"The wine!"

"What?"

"My wine! It might still be OK!"

He pulls me to my feet.

"In the barn . . . where the barn was."

Nodar bounds off toward a sad clump of charred planks and bricks. We scramble into the rubble and start clearing it. He hurls pillow-size chunks of plaster and brick over his shoulder like they weigh nothing. Eventually, sweating and out of breath, we uncover what looks like a small clay disk resting in the soil.

"There. See that?"

"What is it?"

"My dad's kvevri. The one he made me wax every year."

He kneels by the kvevri lid. Using a nail pried out of a plank of wood, Nodar gouges long curls of age-yellowed wax from the clay lid.

"The wax seals the air out," he explains. "Maybe the explosion didn't crack the kvevri."

When the wax seal's gone, Nodar stops and takes a deep breath. He reaches out toward the lid and touches it as though expecting it to burn him. He crosses himself.

"Please, God." He glances up at the sky. "Give me something, you asshat."

Carefully he wrenches the lid loose. It comes away with the soft sound of clay grating on clay. We both peer into the hole. A still, liquid darkness shimmers inside. Then the smell hits us.

"Jesus, Nodar, is that the wine?"

He's speechless. The sweat from his brow's mixed with the tears streaming down his face. He's crying, grinning, and nodding all at the same time. He looks around, searching the ground for something. Not finding it, he shrugs and dips his whole arm into the kvevri. His hand comes out with a palmful of amber liquid. He tastes it and gives a long groan of pleasure.

"Saba, come try my wine."

I go to dip my own hand in the kvevri.

"No, no, you have to drink from the first cup."

I take an awkward sip from Nodar's dripping palm.

"Good, isn't it, brother?"

The setting sun throws long shadows across the field as we search through the rubble under Nodar's supervision. We scavenge together a cooking station—firewood, a dented frying pan without a handle, and the gritty remainder of sunflower oil in a plastic bottle. We build a little campfire and Nodar sets me to the task of grilling the mushrooms while he continues rooting through his exploded home.

"Careful you don't burn the place down," he says.

He finds armfuls of coarse wool blankets, singed pillows, and a large plastic jug, which he fills to the brim with his wine. Soon enough, we have a little camp going.

When the mushrooms are ready, we climb into our blankets with the jug of wine sitting between us. With the fire crackling by our feet, we sit, eat, and drink until all the mushrooms are gone and only the wine remains.

"Good mushrooms."

"Hunger is the best sauce, Ketino always says." Nodar chuckles.

We drink his wine until we're warm and smiling. Nodar tells me about his grandparents and how they built the house with their own hands back in the Stalin days. He tells me how he and Ketino were married in the village church and the huge, chaotic reception they had in the garden, right where we're sat now. He tells me how Natia grew up, running around the garden like a muddy little savage. Suddenly he pauses.

"Listen, brother, I know I said I wasn't sorry. . . ." He hesitates.

"Sorry for what?"

"Feeding that detective information."

"Don't worry about it—"

"You don't understand—I'm still not sorry. I couldn't turn down a chance to find Natia. Then or now. But I've repaid some of that debt now. As is proper."

He's quiet a long time after that. Eventually, he speaks in a tired voice.

"When this is all over, I have to go see Zurab. He deserves to know about Dimitri."

The words run out. Next time I look over at Nodar I find him asleep. I lie back and watch the stars a long time before I can rest.

For once, I've finished Sandro's scavenger hunt and still, Irakli's not home safe. What now, brother? I don't know the next step. There's no more trail to follow. I have to finish what you couldn't, and I'm terrified.

14

SIREN CALL

We follow the Liakhvi. Always. Most Ossetian villages perch along this river. The idea is to hit them all, one by one, looking for Irakli and Natia. The river has a slight orange tinge to it. With each passing day it turns a more sinister shade, as though a sloppy abattoir somewhere upriver is dumping gallons of culled blood right in the river.

The moon wanders the sky to no pattern I can discern. The first night it hovers behind us, peering over our shoulders. The next night, we stare right into its bleak face as we climb an unending rise toward the mountains. The third night, it abandons us altogether and we inch our way forward by the ghostly glow of the snow on the mountainsides.

The going is a lot harder than Nodar thought. It rains almost every day. Sometimes we lose the faint country paths and wade through long stretches of boggy marsh and mud. We can only sleep in short, restless snatches, wherever and whenever we find a place out of the rain and the cold.

The farther we get, the less Nodar sleeps. I wake in the dripping darkness to see the outline of his frown lit by the tiny coal of his cigarette. His face grows haggard and he's stopped finding the funny that's baked into every hardship.

The first two villages—Satkisi and Migdebuli—are abandoned. We sleep in houses stripped of everything but the wallpaper, on creaking floors surrounded by blown-out windows. Occasionally, we feed ourselves on dented tinned food we find along the way.

"Where is everyone?" I ask, but Nodar only shakes his head.

The next village, Damtsvari, is the biggest so far, but it's still only a modest collection of timber and concrete buildings. We find no shelter here. The houses stand empty. They've all been used for toilets—the stench is eye-watering.

"The army does that. Twist the knife." No more irreverent cadence to Nodar's voice.

The crop fields are worse. We can't rest here either. They've been torched. The vineyards are burned to a crisp. The burned vines retain their shape, but the slightest touch sends them crumbling to the ground.

We walk surrounded by a dead silence. No birdsong, no distant groan of cattle, not even crickets. Freakish, oversize dragonflies hover out of charred shrubs like miniature helicopters, survey the devastation, and dart away at our approach. Something crunches under my feet with each step.

"What is this, ash?"

"Salt," Nodar said. "Nothing will grow here for a decade."

"But why?"

"These are Georgian villages. They don't want us back."

"Who? The Russians?"

"Can't blame the Russians for everything."

"Georgians?"

"Ossetians."

"What's the difference?"

"No difference but the name."

Nodar sighs and walks away. We're done talking for the day.

KOKETI IS THE FIRST INHABITED village we find. It sits in the crook of the elbow the Liakhvi river makes around a rocky outcrop. Half of the village houses have waded into the watered-down blood of the river. They stand on wooden stilts, with the river rushing by underneath them.

Koketi is the first taste of hope. We might sleep indoors for the first time in days, at Vato's house. Vato is an old friend of Nodar's—someone he worked with years ago. He is a man with dust in his wrinkles, withered before his time. We find him living, quite serenely, one bad day away from starvation, on a disused farm.

While we sit at Vato's meager offering of stale bread, cheese, and wine, we hear that first siren call of hope. By this point we need it. Ossetia's having the opposite effect on Nodar to what I'd imagined. The abandoned villages, salted fields, burned houses, the smell of wet charcoal that seems to nestle into every pore, everything ravaged and falling apart—seeing these things has beaten Nodar down until he's barely looking up as we walk.

But tonight, under a dusty light bulb orbited by moths, Vato tells us how he met Irakli. He met him much like he met us—exhausted, dirty, and looking for a place to sleep. The only thing is, Irakli introduced himself as Valiko.

"Strange man," Vato says. "Came asking to use my phone. To call that silly radio station. Anyway, only this place and Elene's has a phone. Elene doesn't like strangers. Barely leaves the house nowadays, poor woman."

Vato shakes his head.

"Anyway, the night he stayed, he didn't sleep a wink. Sat till dawn, hunched over that damn radio. I nodded off, y'see. When I woke he was gone."

"When?" I say.

"I don't know. A month ago, maybe."

A month ago. Nodar and I exchange a look. Only a month.

"Where was he going?"

Vato shrugs. "Didn't look like he cared."

"Vato, we need to use that phone of yours," Nodar says.

Vato shows us to his battered cream-colored rotary phone from the days when Stalin was still trying to get his hands on the big red reins. Nodar dials the number for me. The line rings a long time before a gruff male voice answers.

"Yes?"

"You want to leave a message," Nodar prompts.

"Uh, I want to leave a message, please."

"What's the message?"

"Valiko, I—" The word catches in my throat.

"Valiko, what . . . ?" the disinterested voice says.

There must be some combination of words, some magic sequence of syllables, that will fix this. Make Irakli stop running. But I've no time to divine what that combination is.

"Valiko—your sons love you. We need you. There's still a way out of this. We're looking for you, in this place you've crossed into. Please, don't hide. You're safe here. Stop running. Your boys."

I can hear papers shuffling. Nodar gives me a thumbs-up. Then the voice reads my message, slow and deadpan.

"Valiko. We love you. We need you. We're looking for you here. Don't hide, you're safe. Your boys. Close enough?"

"Yeah, but when is—"

The line clicks and I hear the dial tone. I look at Nodar.

"That's it, brother. Customer service isn't a thing they've perfected yet."

"How many times will that play? When?"

"Listen, Mowgli, they don't really work to a schedule."

We sit around the chattering radio and wait for my message to play. In the meantime, our threadbare host gives us more news. There's an orphanage where the kids orphaned or made homeless by the war have ended up.

"It's right by Imediani—all the folks around here know about it. Though they won't say so." Vato shakes his head. "I'll never scrub that place from my brain."

"You've seen it?"

"Only once, but it was enough."

Nodar's face lights up. "Is my Natia there?"

"I don't know, brother. There's so many kids. It's chaos. I didn't stick around."

Vato has no way of knowing. Late that night, we hear my message go out:

> "Valiko, if you're listening, your boys love you and need you. They're looking for you here. Don't run, they say, you're safe here."

Neither Nodar nor I can sleep. He's itching to get going to the orphanage. As for me, a thick lump of dread sits undigested in my gut all night.

Look at me, Sandro. I'm doing alright. I'm making my own trail now, without your clues, without your safety net. You'd be proud, Sandro. You might not say it in syllables and sentences, but you might in our motherless tongue.

I picture Irakli drifting through these chicken-scratch villages. I wonder if he heard my message. I wonder what he'll make of it. Will he stop running? I think about seeing him again. Will he turn back with me? What will we do about the police? About Surik? I should be thinking about where he could possibly be heading and why he's going by "Valiko." But those thoughts aren't comfortable.

The red river won't let me sleep, burbling the way it is just within earshot. Vato sleeps the night fully dressed, boots included, over the covers. He explains in the morning.

"They're just nightmares."

He averts his eyes.

"But I swear, the whole house shakes like mortar shell's about to whistle through that roof."

He looks down at his boots.

"Grown man, scared of nightmares." He shakes his head. "But I can't help it. That sound, that mortar *whine*, makes me take off running every time."

He tugs at the laces on his boots. He's been going to bed ready to run, ever since the time he woke up in the middle of the shelling of Ossetia.

"Sometimes I'd cut up my feet on the stones outside. Once, the blanket tangled my feet and I fell. Brained myself on that radiator there. Woke up in a pool of blood."

He shows us a thin jagged line of scar tissue peeking out of his hairline.

"Since then, I sleep ready to run. Boots and all. Like I'm in the army again." Vato gives us a wilting smile.

THERE ARE STILL three villages between us and the Imediani orphanage, where all of Nodar's thoughts are focused. I can see it on his face. The next village is Didi Sopeli. It's during this punishing, rainy half-day march to Didi Sopeli that our cheery motto crystallizes.

"You can't walk out of this world, Mowgli, come on," Nodar says anytime I slow my pace, and I do the same.

We arrive in Didi Sopeli in the indigo light of a mountain sunset. Didi Sopeli's a slightly bigger village than what we've seen so far. There's a couple of paved roads, a grocery shop, a dinky café, and even a post office. Nodar gives it a hostile glance.

"Bastards," he says.

"What?"

He points at the low building. "No mail in or out of Ossetia since the war. But it's still open. Fuck knows what for. . . . I guess in case you want to post your neighbor his shovel back instead of handing it to him."

We loiter by the grocery shop, forming a plan. That night, no one invites us into their home with open arms. We sleep in a field, surrounded on all sides by cricket chirps.

In the morning, we ask around the village for Irakli. We get nowhere until I change tack and start asking after Valiko. Everyone knows of Valiko—the Georgian-English novelty who moved into Didi Sopeli for a while. He did odd jobs around the place in exchange for food and a place to sleep.

"Then one day, he just up and vanished like a fart in a gust of wind. Not a word to anyone," the bored, drooping man in the post office tells us.

"When?"

"Maybe a week or two ago." The man shrugs.

We're catching Irakli. Or we're catching Valiko. It's my turn to walk a few steps ahead of Nodar, turning back when he dawdles and saying:

"You can't walk out of this world, Nodar. Come on."

We spend another night in the open, in a scratchy dell by the river. Neither of us sleeps. Nodar smokes sullenly as I sit and feed the red river small stones from the shore, until the mountains etch themselves out of the darkness at sunrise.

Look at me, Sandro, I'm doing alright. Days without proper food, days without a shower, I'm still going. I'm doing alright. But these people don't want us here. They don't really hide it. We bring nothing but trouble to their doorstep.

Exhausted and bone-creaking, we set off along the river toward the next village—Sasveni. With the carrot of Natia dangling just out of reach, Nodar's back to his normal self.

"Let's go, Mowgli. You can't walk out of this world."

Sasveni is worse than the rest. No one will talk to us. But in Sasveni, Nodar has an old friend.

"Mamuka won't turn us away," he says.

Mamuka did the polar opposite of Nodar when the war started. He ran north, farther into Ossetia. When the scruffy war ended, Mamuka found himself living in Sasveni.

He's a tall man, strong and broad-shouldered. He moves with care and dips his head in doorways, in a house that seems a touch too small and fragile for his size. He offers to have us for as long as we need.

"Once a month, the Russian trucks come. Bring in supplies, petrol, food—we can't grow enough to feed ourselves since the war. But I have plenty for us. A guest is a gift from God," Mamuka says.

But we're within touching distance of the orphanage where Natia might be. I'm surprised when Nodar agrees to stay one night, never mind any more than that.

We sit in Mamuka's garden, wrapped in thick woolen sweaters he loaned us, and watch the sun dip behind the razor-sharp contour of the mountains. While we wandered Ossetia, the mountains took notice. They've crowded in on us. The air's grown colder.

For a while Mamuka tries to talk to Nodar of old times and shared friends. But Nodar's restless. He barely listens.

"Where's this orphanage, then?" Nodar finally broaches the subject.

"Remember the little forest by Imediani?" Mamuka says.

"Yeah, there's nothing up there but snow and trees."

"And the old prison."

"God, the prison?"

"That's it, friend," Mamuka says. "The girls in Sasveni, the two nurses, remember them?"

"I think so."

"Well, they took in a bunch of kids up there, to keep them safe and all that. The old prison was the likeliest place. Close by. Plenty of room."

"Mamuka, that place was a ruin when *we* were kids."

"It still is."

Nodar and Mamuka share a knowing look.

"Once people heard about it, that was that. Any lost kids, orphans, accidents . . . well, they all end up at this *orphanage*."

"What do they eat?"

"Imediani folks help out. Food, supplies, medicine. Even we do, from way down here."

Mamuka sits up in his chair.

"Nodar, listen, they've got over a hundred kids up there. Ghosts, all of them."

Nodar takes a deep breath. "Is Natia there?"

Mamuka shifts in his seat. "Look, last time I saw her she was a baby. I wouldn't recognize her."

Nodar rummages through his pockets, producing the photo he found.

"Here's a picture."

"How old is this?"

"She just turned four there."

Mamuka looks away. "I don't know, Nodar."

"It's old, but it's the only picture I have, brother. Please. Look."

"I don't know, alright? I'm sorry."

Something makes Mamuka stand up and pace back and forth.

"Look, truth is, I don't go up there. Not unless I have to. The place scares me."

He crosses himself.

"I drop off the food when I can. But I can't go inside. You don't understand, it's no good in there, Nodar. Sometimes I can't even get out of the car. They take the food from the trunk and I leave."

After that, Nodar doesn't ask anymore. Mamuka falls silent. He doesn't try to talk of times gone by, and I don't feel like sticking my foot in the situation by asking more questions about more missing relatives. I wait, impatiently.

In the morning, when I finally manage to ask about Irakli, Mamuka drops a hand grenade on the breakfast table, right among the hard-boiled eggs, bread, and cheese we're eating. He describes this crazy foreign guy who'd been through the village a few days ago.

"He went by 'Valiko,' though," Mamuka finishes and looks at my face. "What? Something wrong?"

"Did you say a few *days* ago?"

"Yeah, why?"

"That's my dad."

When I get my heart to slow back down, I ask where he was heading.

"North. Elvari, I think."

Elvari, the dead end of Ossetia. I look at Nodar for a reaction, maybe some reassurance. But all I see in his eyes is the fairy-tale prospect of finding Natia at the orphanage.

15

IRAKLI

On the seventh day of our glorious invasion of Ossetia, we finally reach the orphanage. For the last few hours of the walk, Nodar hasn't said a word.

"You can't walk out of this world, Nodar," I try and he says nothing back. I guess he's bracing himself.

The low, wide prison building is submerged in a layer of creeper plant so dense that we don't see it until we're right on top of it. As we approach, the old prison reveals itself unwillingly. A darker green shape on a background of the surrounding trees. The perimeter fencing is clipped clean by scavengers, leaving the remaining barbed wire cutting the passing wind. As we approach the open-mouthed entrance, Nodar's steps slow. He hesitates. He knows he won't come out of there the same.

We're greeted by an overwhelmed-looking group of nurses and a doctor. They're dressed in a strange mixture of faded medical uniforms and hardy, mud-stained farm work-wear and boots. With numb expressions on their sleep-deprived faces, they scan us for what we've brought. It isn't much—a sack of rice and some vegetables Mamuka gave us.

"More rice," a haggard nurse says and walks away, muttering to herself. "I need rice like I need an arsehole in my armpit."

The welcoming party disperses, disappointed by our meager offering. Only the doctor stays behind. Nodar explains the situation to him and tells him about Natia. The doctor nods like an undertaker being given instructions.

"Not many of your kind around here."

"What do you mean?"

"You want to take one away." The doctor walks away, talking to us over his shoulder. "There's a new child dropped on our doorstep five, ten times a month. Usually at night, when we can't see them."

He looks like a man long past surrender.

"They're right to be ashamed."

"Who?" Nodar says.

The doctor shrugs. "Who knows? At first, they only brought kids from the city. Orphans, from the shelling. But now . . ." He trails off.

"Now what?"

"Now, they bring discards. Defectives. Unwanted pregnancies. Mostly disabled, or seriously ill, or both. Food's scarce. So's medicine. Most people can't handle the burden of a sick child."

"They just leave them here?"

"They know we'll take them in."

"How do you keep going?"

The doctor stops walking and turns to us. "The math adds up."

"What?"

"More die than they bring. Only just. And so it keeps going."

"Die?"

"Look around, friend. This is no place to get better. Next time bring medicine. Not rice."

The doctor walks away again.

"What about the government?" Nodar says after him.

"What government?"

"Well, whoever's in charge."

"No one's in charge."

The doctor pauses in front of a set of sturdy wooden doors with frosted steel-wire windows.

"Listen, I'm not a doctor. I'm a farm vet. I was. I retired."

"A vet?"

"Cows, pigs, horses—you get the picture. I know how to birth foals, calves, pig litters. I know nothing about doctoring."

For some reason, he holds up his coarse, dirty hands as though for evidence.

"Those nurses, they're not nurses, they're farmers."

Nodar frowns.

"Why are you here?"

"I'd leave this second if someone replaced me. Want to take my place, friend?"

Nodar stays silent.

"Always worth asking."

The doctor puts his hand on the wooden door.

"You people bring supplies, but it's not enough. We need a doctor, equipment, disinfectant, basic medicine, beds, pillows, sheets, bandages, syringes . . ."

He trails off, daunted by his own list.

"Anyway. This is where we keep the *unwell* ones. Pray yours isn't here."

The doctor shoulders through the doors and we follow. The cavernous room we enter is the prison dining hall. A mismatched collection of

HARD BY A GREAT FOREST

beds, military cots, and mattresses line the walls. One, sometimes two kids to a bed. Various ages. Various levels of disabled. All lumped into one room. A slow, shifting mass of quiet discomfort.

There are no voices to be heard here. Only troubled breathing and fever-dream half moans. The smell of urine, disinfected vomit, and undiagnosed, untreated sickness hits us as we step in. Immune, the doctor strides straight into the stench.

No heads turn as we walk through the hall. Nodar's eyes scan the room. There's real fear in them, the kind you can't hide. We walk past a row of cots sectioned off from the others by curtains. The kids in these beds have their arms tied down by their sides with towels. They lie unstruggling and follow us with their eyes.

"Why are they tied down?" I manage.

"If we don't, they hit themselves, scratch themselves."

The doctor moves on, unwilling to linger. Periodically he turns to search Nodar's face, asking the question he isn't saying aloud. Nodar scans the room and shakes his head. The doctor nods and we continue the tour.

Any second, any one of these kids could turn out to be Natia and I'll have to witness the end of Nodar. The doctor leads us through another creaking set of doors into the main prison courtyard.

"This is where we keep the *well* kids." A bitter smirk crimps his face.

We find ourselves in a large hall, lined on all sides by the rusting, peeling steel bars of holding cells. Some kind soul tried to cheer the place up by painting the steel bars in bright, alternating colors. But either the paint or the goodwill ran out partway.

Unlike in the first room, all heads turn at the noise of us walking in. The doctor pauses, waiting for Nodar. As I scan the faces, I catch a faint echo of the little girl in Nodar's photo. In the back corner of the hall, greasy-haired and grimy, wearing an ill-fitting dress, the girl looks in our direction. But it isn't me she's staring at. I turn and see Nodar lock eyes with her.

He frowns and cranes his neck to get a better look. My eyes snap back to the girl. As I see the first shock of recognition on her face, Nodar goes from standing by my side to sprinting up the hall. Roaring words rendered incomprehensible and scattering children before him, he heads straight for the little girl. He shimmies between beds, stumbles, recovers, and reaches her at a run. He whips the poor girl completely off her feet, swinging her side to side. Then he hugs her to his chest so hard that I worry he might break her ribs.

By the time I get to him, Nodar's put her back down. He's dropped to his knees and is gripping her by the shoulders. They're both crying.

"Natia," he says.

He keeps repeating her name, stuck on some ecstatic loop. Natia's quiet. She won't say anything back. Tears stream down her cheeks unchecked. She's smiling. She's happy. But she won't say a word. Instead, she burrows her head into Nodar's chest, where it's safe.

"Natia?" His voice sharpens a touch.

Small shake of her head—she still won't speak.

"OK, OK." Nodar strokes the back of her head.

Still clutching Natia to his chest, he stands up, lifting her clean off the floor as though she weighs nothing at all. He turns to the doctor, eyebrows raised.

"She always this shy? She never used to be."

The doctor shrugs. "Mute. Been here two years, never said a word."

"She's no mute! Nati, say something for Da."

Looking up from the tiny wet patch she's printed onto Nodar's shirt, Natia only stares back.

"It's OK, Nati, it's OK."

Realizing he's holding her aloft like a doll, he puts her down. Immediately, she clings to his side.

"It's OK. Come on, let's take you home. Let's take you to Keti."

Natia's eyes widen at the mention of Keti. A small intake of breath, as though she's about to say something. But no words come. I catch the look on Nodar's face. I know losing something precious hurts. But getting it back broken is a sharper pain.

On the long walk back to Imediani village, Nodar entertains us with fresh fairy tales from Tbilisi. He explains the way the animals had to leave the zoo for a few days because of the flood. He recounts, word for word, what Boris the Hippo and Misha the Bear said to us when they asked us for directions in Tbilisi. In fabulous detail, he tells Natia just how we rescued Kiki the Fox from the roundabout. I watch him pull the name Kiki out of his ass mid-sentence and can't help but smile.

"Nati, remember when we saw Artyom the Tiger that day in the zoo?"

Natia nods.

"Well, let me tell you something. Saba here scratched him right under his chin, after we freed him from the bear trap that caught the poor fella. He even purred a little, I think, right, Saba?"

"Only a little," I say.

I'm complicit now. Natia looks at me—I've gone up in her estimation. There's a hint of disbelief on her face. She's almost old enough to call bullshit on Nodar's tall tales. I wish she would, because I know he will double down, and the tales will only get more ridiculous.

Still barefoot, Natia walks oddly, only when Nodar deems the terrain safe. She walks with her heels never quite touching the ground. The rag they had her wearing at the orphanage barely qualifies as a dress.

"You need a good bath, don't you, Nati?" Nodar says, wiping a streak of dirt from Natia's cheek with his own grimy thumb. "We need to find you some shoes too."

She smiles at her feet and stays silent. She still clings to Nodar. Physical contact between them doesn't lapse unless it can't be helped, and even then, only for a second.

In these rare breaks from his performance, Nodar falls back a pace, pretends to look at something while wiping his eyes with the back of his wrist. Meanwhile, Natia instantly retreats to her safe place—silent, expressionless, eyes downcast.

Me, I find it hard watching them without thinking of Sandro. Back when Irakli was still promising us Eka, he and I would spend hours talking, planning, and plotting for her return. We had plans for every practicality. When she walked into our flat, she'd see Sandro first, on the sofa. I'd be hiding behind the door. Just when she'd say, "Where's Saba?" I'd jump out and, boo! Surprise! Maybe she'd be like Nodar is now, not crying but just wiping her eyes from time to time.

I wish I could tell Sandro what finding Natia means. Can I replicate this miracle without you, brother? Can it be done twice—can I find Irakli?

WHEN WE GET TO IMEDIANI, I decide to stay behind, while Nodar and Natia continue on to Mamuka's house back in Sasveni. I spend the day wandering the town, lit by a bright, heatless sun. I go house to house, asking after Irakli and Valiko.

No one knows a thing. The trail has vanished. Maybe Irakli didn't come through here. People eye me with distrust. They hear my accent and speak to me curtly, eager to get away. Some doors close on me without comment. The last house I try is a rickety wooden structure, leaning into an adjoining barn. It leans so alarmingly that it doesn't look habitable.

It's occupied, of course. I can see the flames of a lamp through the gaps in the woodwork. I knock on the door and wait. A disheveled man eventually answers. His limbs are slow with sleep and he keeps rubbing his eyes with the heel of his palm.

"Well? You just gonna stand there catching flies?" he says in a flat tone.

I ask the standard question about Irakli.

He frowns. "Today's Friday, right?"

"What?"

The man brings up his fist and, while staring at the sky, unrolls his index finger. Then his middle finger. Then he stops. I hold my breath.

"Two days ago," he says. "But only if today's Friday."

"What do you mean?"

"Did I stutter? I saw your Valiko two days ago. Heading for Elvari."

A rush of blood goes down my legs and arms. Two days.

"Stopped here for water." The man points to the well in his garden. "Everyone does. It's the only decent well in the village."

I almost run back to Sasveni to tell Nodar the news. He'll know the best way to get to Elvari. The sun has long set by the time I reach Mamuka's place. As soon as I see Nodar and Natia, my heart sinks. This isn't going to be easy. When I tell Nodar, he refuses to go to Elvari on foot with Natia in tow.

"We'd have to sleep in the open. I can't do it, brother. Not with Natia. It's almost dark anyway—let's think tomorrow."

I would leave Nodar and go on my own, but I've no idea how to get to Elvari. I'm not angry with him—I understand. Natia needs all his attention. Even I can't stand seeing the shadow that comes over her sometimes. She becomes entirely inert, more a doll than a living, breathing child. She flinches at loud noises, even at Nodar's voice.

The next morning is no different. She sits and stares glassily at the kitchen table, letting the rest of us guess at what horrors can mute a child like this. It's hard to watch. I can feel Irakli inching away from me. He's edging closer to some invisible border I can't follow him across. I should be chasing him down. But instead, I sit in Mamuka's living room and watch Nodar try to glue back a broken daughter.

Mamuka walks out shaking his head.

"I have an idea," he says.

He returns not long after, bearing hope. He's borrowed one of the only two working cars in Sasveni. It's an army-green Lada Niva—a Soviet off-roader. It's been dented and hammered out so many times that it looks like it was gnawed into shape. We have to jump-start it to get going.

"This thing hasn't started willingly since Gorbachev sat farting into Stalin's armchair in the Kremlin," Mamuka says. "If you stall or switch the engine off, we're walking."

Nodar the "Soviet Shit-bucket Whisperer," as he dubs himself, has no trouble with it. During the long, slow drive to Elvari, he tries to entertain us in the face of Natia's unrelenting silence.

"Natia, say something to your da," he begs. She just looks at him and looks down at the shoes Mamuka fashioned for her out of old slippers and army-green duct tape.

The route to Elvari zigzags up a steep mountain dirt track. It's so narrow in places that the wheels of the Niva don't always fit. Every now and then, we hear the sound of pebbles skittering down a near-vertical drop and feel the unmistakable sensation of one of the wheels driving on thin air.

When we finally clap eyes on it, Elvari is a meager collection of houses that look like they weren't built by human hands. They've grown out of the mountain soil of their own accord. They're clustered by the river against the monolithic background of the Caucasus. This close to its unknown source, the river is almost the same vivid arterial color I saw running down the hill in Vake after the tiger attack.

"Nodar, look."

"They say the mountains bleed into this river."

It's growing dark when we reach the village. Our headlights bring people out of their homes to watch. Nodar stops the car, and the villagers gather around us, muttering. We get out and ask around for Valiko.

"He's at Guram's place," a voice says from the small crowd. Several others make noises in agreement.

The villagers point to a house on the outer rim of the village. With my heart lurching in my chest, I lead the final charge. Guram's house is a small wooden structure past which there are no more villages, no more roads, and no more people. Nothing but a thousand miles of empty, glaring, cold mountainsides dressed in ragged patches of snow. The other side of those mountains is Russia.

We find Guram sitting on a small wooden stool out front, whittling a fence post. He's an old, leathery man with a disgruntled expression on his face. As I approach him, my belly feels like I've eaten fistfuls of snow. Trapped within the confines of his ordinary human frame is the power to end lives.

"Hello there, uncle."

The man looks up and squints, almost hiding the blue-green mismatch of his eyes.

"Who are you?"

"I'm Saba. I've come to—"

I stop because suddenly I don't know how to finish the sentence.

"We're looking for Irakli," Nodar intervenes. "Goes by Valiko sometimes."

The man shakes his head and goes back to sliding long curls of wood from the fence post with his knife.

"Crazy bastard," he mumbles.

The front door of Guram's house is ajar as though someone's just walked through it and is about to reappear.

"Irakli!" I call out.

I hold my breath, the way I used to in the gap between lightning and thunderclap when I was a kid. I can't look away from the door. But no thunderclap comes. No one appears.

"Where is he, uncle?"

The man shakes his head.

I try to keep the tremble out of my voice. "We've come a very long way for him. Where is he?"

Something in my voice gives the man pause. He looks at me. "God knows. Probably playing hide-and-seek with the wolves by now."

"What do you mean?"

The man sighs. "He came yesterday. For a place to stay the night. A guest is a gift from God, I said. But maybe not every guest."

He lets the fence post fall to one side and puts away his knife.

"He had a radio. Kept trying to tune it to that idiot station. I told him, I said, signal's bad here, son. Wind blows funny and it's gone. But he wouldn't stop. Kept me awake all night."

"Uncle, tell me where he is."

"He left. He's gone. Crack of dawn."

"Gone where?"

I already know the answer, but I watch the man point over his shoulder at the mountains.

"Crazy whoreson left his bag, left his radio, and left everything else. Just walked out into the mountains and didn't stop. I sent the boys to look earlier. No sign of him. If he's not back by now, he's never coming back. Bastard just walked out of this world."

The man stands up with a groan. He walks over and pulls a thin stack of folded pages from his pocket.

"Here. I want none of his blood on my hands."

Mutely, I take the *Kaleidoskupi* pages from him. This is it—Irakli's final crumb. These pages hide his parting message. I can't look. Not yet.

Instead, I glance around, hoping to see Sandro's graffiti smiling at me from some unlikely angle. Where are you, brother? I need you. But

Sandro's never set foot here. His careful touch is nowhere to be seen or felt. This is my trail now. Irakli's *my* responsibility.

Something heavier than penciled pages slides through my hands and falls to the ground. A small dense rectangle lies in the mud. Brash gold lettering announces: "British Passport." This is Irakli's passport. An artifact of a life given up. I pick it up, open it, and lock eyes with an Irakli from a time before he lost his grip on this world.

That's when my wiring glitches, like it did when they shot at us in the Volga. The laughter comes on slow—only a trickle at first. But soon it bubbles and overflows until I can't contain it.

Nino and I used to run headlong down the big grassy hill in the botanical garden. It was so steep that you could barely keep up with your feet. Poised on the thin edge between running and falling, the run would squeeze hysterical laughter out of us both. I start laughing just like that and I can't stop.

Maybe it was something about the way the old man said "walked out of this world" in the exact intonation Nodar and I had been using. We'd been saying it all this time—"You can't walk out of this world, Nodar," "You can't walk out of this world, Saba." And then Irakli went and proved us wrong.

Some of the villagers followed us up to Guram's house. I can feel them all staring at me like I've lost my mind. Maybe I have. Another spasm shudders through me. Tears stream down my face. I'm still laughing.

"Saba?" Nodar says.

This sets off another peal of laughter. I can't get any words out. I can barely breathe. Nodar comes over to hug me and stops my knees from folding up. I guess I stop paying attention after that. They usher me into the house and try to calm me. A couple of times they have to prevent me from going after Irakli.

"Suicide," they keep saying, holding me back. "It's too cold, nowhere to shelter. It's suicide, you won't last the night," they repeat, like they're casting a spell to keep me still.

When enough of them return to their own homes and we're left alone, I realize this is Guram's home—the last place Irakli stayed. This thought sets me off chuckling out tears again.

We're in no state to be traveling back tonight. Nodar gives Natia the cot to sleep on and posts up in an ancient high-backed armchair, on guard duty. I quiet myself and pretend to be calm, while inside I can feel a constant trickle of that laughter.

When Nodar drifts off to sleep, I make my escape. I sneak out into the cold moonlit night. The air's so sharp it stings my nostrils. I set off in the direction Irakli chose for me.

Melted and refrozen snow, dusted with unsightly man-made grit, crunches under my feet as I tiptoe past the last of the houses. The looping tracks of the villagers searching for Irakli fall away as I get farther from the village. Out here, the snow's pure white and unmolested, the way snow should be. Only one set of tracks mars this landscape. Soon, a fresh snowfall will erase them forever.

I stop and stare at Irakli's footprints. I try to divine from their contours what he's thinking. I want to know if finding him out there will change anything. Will he reconsider and come back with me? Or will he walk out of this world anyway and take me with him?

Somewhere miles out into the mountains, I see the faint twinkle of a light. I know it in my bones to be Irakli. He's alive, still heading in the direction he chose. I take a few steps in that same direction. There is an invisible border in these mountains. Pass that border and you're too far gone to swim back. Irakli's long past that border and I must be fast approaching it.

It's Eka's voice that saves me in the end.

"Fairy tales have to be read to the end, Saba," she says softly. *"This isn't the end."*

"Isn't it?"

"No. It's bad luck to leave them unfinished—fairy tales have happy endings."

"Maybe not all of them."

"Straighten your back, Saba. Let Irakli go. Think of Sandro."

Eka's right. Some things have a momentum of their own—they can't be stopped. Some things in this world can't be fixed. I turn my back on Irakli and his failing pilot light. I retrace my own steps back to the village.

My return wakes Nodar. He jolts awake in the armchair and glares at me, confused.

"No, Saba. Don't."

"It's OK, Nodar, I'm not going anywhere. Go back to sleep."

I still have the last pages of *Kaleidoskupi* in my pocket. They might hold a message from Irakli. That message may be his last. But then, with no help from the voices, I realize the truth.

By the time he set foot in Ossetia, Irakli had no way of following his own crumbs out of this forest. There's no message in these pages, no final meaning. They're just the only crumb he had left, to mark his passing here.

I can't bring myself to read them. Not yet. Instead, I pull out his passport and stare at his photo until the morning comes.

MAMUKA DRIVES US back to Nodar's exploded house in the unwilling Niva. I spend the car ride in a stupor. Everything's had the volume turned down. Natia and I become kindred spirits. We say nothing, feel nothing, accept any fate put before us, and smother any conversation Nodar and Mamuka try to start up.

It's a long, slow drive, tiptoeing down country roads and dirt tracks. Nodar spends it working on Natia. He's stopped asking her to "say something." Instead, he launches into an unending variety show of jokes, stories, fairy tales, and magic tricks. Natia smiles sometimes, but other than that she sits still, making herself as small and unnoticeable as possible.

Nodar manages to force a small squeak of almost-laughter out of her by producing a sudden, window-rattling fart after a particularly long silence. It's not much, but it's a glimmer of things to come.

"Nati! Was that you?" He rolls his window down. In that moment, I know with a dead certainty that Nodar will fix whatever silenced Natia.

We say our goodbyes to Mamuka by the collapsed gate to Nodar's house. Nodar smothers Mamuka's handshake in a bear hug.

"I won't forget this, brother."

Mamuka waves the thanks away, exactly the way I've seen Nodar do so often. His face grows serious.

"Cross the forest at night, like I told you. The soldiers are watching. Don't use that flashlight unless you've no choice. That thing will be like a lighthouse beacon in there."

"I know, I know," Nodar says.

Mamuka gets back in the car. "Just pray this tin can makes it back to Sasveni."

He thumps the side of the Niva and drives off. Just before he disappears over the hill, the car gives a final, wheezing beep. We wave and watch Mamuka crest the hill and vanish.

While we wait for the sun to set, Nodar waltzes Natia through the remains of their home. Soon, very soon, he tells her, they will build it anew.

"It'll be twice the size, with a huge balcony. And a hammock, a firepit . . . maybe even a tire swing. You want a tire swing, don't you, Natia?"

Nothing but silence from Natia.

"We'll build one together, I promise. Soon."

He sounds just like Irakli. Promises not yet lies.

The sun's nearly gone by the time we reach the Baba Yaga forest. The twilight has drained all color from the foliage.

Our world orbits a mysterious counterpart, they say. No one's privy to that world but the dead or dying. But sometimes our orbits intersect. On the edge of the Baba Yaga forest, once again we rub shoulders with that other, kinder world and its magic spills into this ugly place.

As we skirt the tree line, wading through blackberry thickets and swaths of stinging nettle, the fingertips of the forest begin to twinkle. Bright, Christmas colors—tinsel silver, green, and red. It's subtle at first, but then the dying sun catches them just right and there's no denying it. There are sweets hanging by their bright, sparkling wrappers from the branches of the monochrome trees. They form a coruscating trail that leads into the forest.

"How . . . Who left these?" I barely manage. "The nearest village is a ghost town."

Wide-eyed, Natia stares at the sweets. Nodar's eyes wrinkle up as he smiles.

"Maybe it's the ghosts, Mowgli. Don't you believe in ghosts?"

Nodar nudges a bright red sweet, to make sure it's real.

"Here we go now, this is how Baba Yaga lures you in. . . ."

He looks down at Natia and whispers to her in confidence. "Baba Yaga's not real, Natia. This is just kids playing tricks."

What kids, I want to say. But I don't. We find more sweets hanging among the branches like miniature Christmas baubles. As we follow the trail, Nino wakes.

"Good idea, Bublik. Follow the trail."

Her voice makes me shiver. I've been ignoring her lately. So she starts her own twisted version of an incantation I remember from bedtimes and campfires:

"Baba Yaga, give me health,
Baba Yaga, give me witchcraft and wealth."

Nodar's already among the first trees. I follow him while Nino continues her chant.

"Baba Yaga, visit my dreams,
Baba Yaga, teach me living and dying,
Baba Yaga, teach me catching and skinning,
Naughty boys that ignore Nino speaking."

I still don't answer her.

THE FOREST SNUFFS OUT all light before we even reach the river. We're lost again. We inch forward, holding hands, in a darkness we can feel on our skin. When the forest chokes out the last of the light, Natia breaks. She stops walking. Nothing Nodar or I can do will get her to stop whimpering and shaking.

"Da's here, Natia. Da's right here. It's only a bit of darkness."

I feel her tiny hand squeeze mine.

"I need that flashlight, Saba. I can't just . . ."

I hand him the flashlight. There's a click and a brilliant white beam slices into the darkness. It's bright and sudden—whatever creatures stalk us barely have time to scuttle out of the way.

"Who needs retinas anyway?" Nodar says, blinking.

"Point it down, Nodar!"

The effect of the light on Natia is immediate. Her breathing slows. Her grip on my hand loosens. We can move on, but it's still slow going. Every time Nodar cuts the light, Natia starts whimpering and shaking again.

"Any second now, mummy's boy. That broken girl will get you a belly-ful of bullets!" Nino shrills right in my ear.

Nodar tries carrying Natia, but that's worse.

"Saba, she's shaking like a leaf."

So, we light the flashlight again and move on. Nodar's careful to only point it at the forest floor.

"You're lit up like a Christmas tree, but you'll never see another Christmas." Nino's manic singsong voice cuts through like a knife.

By an unnerving coincidence we find ourselves in the patch of mushrooms Nodar and I decimated on the way into Ossetia. He points the flashlight at the mushrooms, which seem to shy away from the light.

"Look, Mowgli, they've already grown back."

Nodar swings the light around the forest floor. I hear a twig snap somewhere in the darkness, or maybe something louder but farther away.

"Here it comes!" Nino yelps.

That's when I see the first bullet. A tracer round streaks a singed-orange trail through the darkness above Nodar and thuds into a tree.

"Fuck was that?"

Nodar ducks and clicks off the light.

"Think someone saw us?"

He doesn't answer.

"Nati, where did you go? Say something."

There's no response. I can't hear much over Nino's cackling.

"Broken girl can't speak!"

Nodar clicks the flashlight back on and swings it around until he finds Natia. She's standing by an oak tree, wide-eyed and pale like a forest ghost. He runs over to her and picks her up.

"There you are. You OK?"

In picking her up with the flashlight still in his hand, Nodar swings the light beam through the trees like an unmanned searchlight.

"Nodar, the light!"

"Fuck if I don't get us killed."

He clicks the light off. Natia starts to whimper miserably.

"Shhh, Natia, it's OK. We can't light the flashlight for a while now. Be brave for Da."

It's too late. We all hear it—the volley of gunfire in the distance. The forest around us fills up with dirty-orange streaks of light.

"Pretty, pretty fireflies!"

All we can hear is the crack and whine of bullets flying past us and the arrhythmic sound of them hitting tree trunks, snapping off branches, and thumping into the soil. The trees overhead shower us in broken branches, twigs, and leaves.

"Nodar, they know we're here!"

"Run!" comes the response.

"Where?"

"The river! They won't see us there."

The flashlight clicks on again and I see Nodar and Natia running. I try to follow. The bullets follow his light. We run toward the river. We're almost safe. A few seconds and we'll be hidden by the riverbank. That's when I look up and see a sizzling orange bullet trail extinguish square in the middle of Nodar's chest.

"Nodar caught a firefly!" Nino screeches.

In the first days of spring, my grandma Lena would take our winter blankets and hang them on a line in the yard. She would take a sturdy wooden paddle and beat the dust out of them. That's the sound the bullet makes hitting Nodar. A loud, final thud.

The impact stops his upper body, but his legs swing out with the momentum. He loses hold of Natia's hand and the flashlight and lands on his back with a grunt. The flashlight spins a monochrome kaleidoscope of shadows through the birch trees and lands by Nodar's side. Natia vanishes in the darkness like she never even existed.

"Nodi, say something! Nodi, say something!" Nino's voice comes so clear that I'm sure she's possessed Natia to scream the words.

I run to Nodar and kneel by his side. His upper and lower body are at odds with each other. His chest rises and falls and his hands scrabble through the leaves, looking for the flashlight. His lower body lies still and misaligned, just how it landed.

"Nodar."

They say when death is near your mind does strange things. You slip into old memories of this world, or catch a glimpse of that other world. Not so for Nodar. He's right here in the mud with me. He's fighting. When his hands find the flashlight, he swings it side to side until he finds Natia. She's a few feet farther down the bank, staring back at the light, oblivious to the bullets streaking past all around her.

"Natia, get down," Nodar says.

I run over and tug her to the ground. I drag her back to Nodar. He puts one hand on her and smiles. His whole body relaxes at the touch.

"Da's here," he exhales.

"Nodar, look at me. I'm going to lift you."

I've no idea where to take him, or why, or what I'll do with him when we get there. But still, I slide my hands under him and try to lift. His back is slick with hot blood.

"No, don't," he says, tightening his grip on Natia.

Bullets are landing all around us, throwing up clumps of dirt and dry leaves.

"Nodar, we have to move."

I lift his torso, but his legs stay dead still. The movement makes him cough up blood. One or both lungs punctured. I lower him to the ground as softly as I can.

"Nodar, can you move your legs?"

His breathing is slow and labored. Each breath is a daunting weight he heaves off the ground. Each weight heavier than the last. Every exhale comes with a sick pulmonary rattle. Air pumped through inert vocal cords produces senseless groans. But Nodar keeps working. He keeps lifting that weight, over and over.

In all the films I've seen and books I've read, when someone dies, they make some dramatic, meaningful gesture. I guess that shit doesn't translate into real life.

"Mowgli," he says so serenely that I hold my breath. "Mowgli, you're standing on my hand."

I look at my foot, which is crushing his fingers into the ground.

"Shit, sorry."

"It's OK." He smiles. "It doesn't hurt."

His eyes drift from me toward Natia.

"Nodar, say something!"

But Nodar doesn't. He lets out a long sigh and doesn't breathe in again.

I HAVE TO GET NATIA somewhere safe, somewhere the bullets can't reach us. But she won't let go of Nodar. Smeared in his blood, she leaves tiny red handprints all over his face and arms as she searches for some part of him that isn't yet gone.

She wipes the tears from her eyes with hands dipped in Nodar's blood. Her nose and cheeks are daubed crimson. For a second, I don't know why, I try to clean the blood from her face with my own hands. There's blood on those too, idiot. The bullets thump into the soil all around us. We have to go.

I rip Natia from Nodar with a heave. It kills my heart, the sound she makes. We leave Nodar where he fell, bloodied and skyward-eyed. I drag Natia down to the river, where the soldiers can't see us. She scratches, struggles, and fights me the whole way. I throw the damn flashlight in the water to free up both my hands; otherwise she'll get away.

With Natia clutched to my chest, I slosh downstream for a long time, until I can't see the bullets anymore. Sopping wet, we stop and sit on the forest floor. I hug her to my chest while she whimpers and struggles to escape. Eventually she either faints or falls asleep, I can't tell which. Her breathing slows. I sit there all night and listen to the forest until sunrise. Nobody bothers us. Nobody comes for us. Maybe they feel they've done enough. They probably have.

We don't go back to see Nodar. I convince myself I'm doing it for Natia's sake. But if I'm honest, I can't face the sight of him dead. That day we walk farther along the stream. We're slow. Natia keeps looking over her shoulder. Often I have to stop and drag her forward by force. I don't say anything. I don't know what to say, or how to say it. I just keep dragging her along.

"*Let her go. What good is she anyway?*" It's Nino again. "*Dead weight, faulty orphan girl. Leave her.*"

I don't dare respond. We follow the river until it ends in a bog, where we spend another night in the dark, much like the night before. I grip Natia to my chest through another panic attack. When she falls asleep, I sit up all night blinking at the darkness like a blinded owl.

The next morning Natia resigns to her fate and follows me unprompted. I'm not sure which is worse. I've resigned to my fate too. To be honest, I no longer care if we get caught or shot. I just want it over.

That day we walk out of the forest and back into Georgia. Hand in hand, Natia and I stride out into the sunshine like nothing happened. Someone must be watching over us. Maybe the Mother of Georgia, with her blue and green eyes, can see us here too. A sword for her foes and a cup of wine for friends. Maybe *she* arranged our safe return.

Or maybe you only get this lucky when you've shed all hope. Either way, Natia and I must have blithely walked through the smallest, most temporary gap in the patrolling soldiers.

. . .

SINCE THEN, the gap closed behind us and now we're hunted. We're hunted and they have our scent. By now, the soldiers have found what we left behind in the forest.

We can feel them combing the fields behind us. We hear the radio squawks and chatter the wind carries to us in snatches. Sometimes, when they're closer, we even hear their voices. At night their flashlights sweep the fields with cold discipline.

We need to find a main road, any road, back to Tbilisi. If we can do that, then maybe we can get home. And maybe there we could be safe. A lot of maybes.

We haven't slept in days. We haven't washed. We're exhausted. But hunger's a funny thing. Eventually it overrides all concerns. We've found someone's orchard: grapevines bearing dusty, sour green grapes, apple trees, and a vegetable patch. We should keep going, keep running, but we're starving. So we wait in the bushes like thieves for the darkness to descend on this little farm.

When the sun sets, we creep into the orchard and eat our fill of unripe grapes, sour apples, and carrots pulled right from the soil, still tasting a little like mud. Then we take our churning acid bellies to the barn and fall asleep side by side in the stale hay.

The morning catches us unprepared. We have to sneak out of the barn in full, burning daylight. The farmer spots us from across his field and runs into the house. He reappears holding a shotgun.

"Hey, you, stop!"

We take off running. He aims and fires a parting shot at us, but he's not close enough to hit anything but thin air and our nerves. The soldiers would have heard the shot. They'll converge here. Today we can't rest. Today we don't feast uninvited. We need to run.

We go field to field, sometimes holding hands. It's surprisingly easy to get lost in a cornfield. We can't call out to each other. Even if we could, the soldiers might hear.

That afternoon, with the sun at its peak, we hit a patch of vineyards. Vineyards are the worst. Long featureless corridors of vines and their sparse dusty leaves. We've no choice but to walk right along these corridors. We're so exposed here. Any second, we could hear a rustle, a heavy footstep, and see a soldier step into our corridor. I try to picture this, plan what I'd do. But it's no good—every scenario ends with someone shot and bleeding to death in the dust.

The real problem is we don't speak when we should. We must communicate, spot things for each other. But no, we do our sweaty, terrified escaping in total silence. Today we didn't hear any radios or any voices. That's a good sign. Maybe we've lost them. Maybe there's no wind to carry the sound. Hard to say. Or maybe they're so close they're keeping quiet until they're right on top of us.

"Say something," I ask with a dry croak in my voice.

I get no response from Natia. The only voices that will talk to me now are those of the dead. They've grown louder and they've grown in number.

"It doesn't matter if they lost you, if they're behind you, or if they're right on top of you. Doesn't change a thing. Keep going. Find a road," Anzor keeps telling me.

What if we're heading in the wrong direction? What if you zoomed out and saw us on a map—tiny, hopeless ants—and saw us inching farther into the wild countryside? What then? I want to ask Anzor this, but I've stopped answering the voices since our return trip through the Baba Yaga forest.

"Just keep going, child. You'll hit a road eventually, any direction you go," Eka lies to reassure me. It's hard not to talk to her.

Whenever we hear something suspect, we freeze and watch mute panic reflect in each other's eyes. But we still don't speak. No, that's when Nino speaks.

"Sing us a song, Bublik."

I grit my teeth.

"Aren't you curious what it's like? To get shot right in your warm tum-tum?"

She's shrill, unevenly cheerful, and sinister. A sewing needle in your candy apple.

"I promise it only hurts for a second," she confides.

I ignore her and go on, bowed by the racket she makes. Whenever we rest, I do scrambled, slipshod math in my head:

Back when Nodar drove us through the fields in the Volga, it took about four hours to get to the forest from the main road. But what speed were we going? We kept stopping to clear the path. So, let's average it out to ten miles an hour. OK, what's walking speed—four, five miles an hour? Therefore, it should take no longer than eight hours to find the road, give or take a few hours. It's been three days since we came out of Baba Yaga's forest and we still haven't found a road.

We spend this night like we spent the night with Baba Yaga. We sit huddled among the exposed roots of an oak tree, eyes wide open, listening. Not a wink of sleep.

On the fourth day, we hear a truck rumble by in the distance. Eka was right. Eka's always right. We've finally hit a road. We sidle onto it cautiously, checking for soldiers. There are none in sight. In fact, there are no soldiers, no people, and no cars. Nothing but empty road in sight. There will be a car or a truck along here soon. There must be. Maybe we'll be OK.

We hold hands and start in what I think is the direction of Tbilisi, casual, like it's the most natural thing to be doing. This is the dusty half motorway, half dirt track that brought Dimitri, Nodar, and me here in the first place.

"Here we are," I say more to myself than to Natia.

She doesn't say anything back. Hard to say if she ever will. She looks up at me. There's no expression on her face. No relief, no fear. Blank. We look like a couple of Disney film orphans—and that's close enough to the truth. I look up and down the road and see no movement.

"Let's go home," I say and squeeze her limp hand. "Let's go see Ketino."

Natia stops. Her eyes widen at the word *Ketino*. Her hand gives me a tiny squeeze and pulls me along the road. I barely follow. Somehow, she senses I'm inches from my limit and takes charge. Glancing back at me, she tugs harder and sets me in motion almost against my will. Just like Nodar did that first day at the airport. Her father's daughter; she's just like him.

We walk along the road most of that day. No one stops for us. At one point we scuttle into the adjacent field to let a BTR go by. It rumbles past slow, with soldiers clinging to its armor-plated back like cockroaches to a loaf of bread left overnight. They don't look like they're searching for anyone or anything in particular. Just ambling by. I feel Natia's hand grip mine a little tighter.

This is how we communicate now. I hold her hand like I'm holding an injured sparrow. She won't let go of mine. She grips it tighter when she can't help it, or tugs it to direct my attention. It isn't much, but at least we're talking to each other now, best we can.

The sun's almost set when someone finally takes pity on us. An open-back Kamaz truck rumbles to a halt, throwing gravel at our ankles. Natia's hand clenches tight. The truck cab and bed seem disarticulated from each other, creaking and moving at odds. A fat-faced man hangs his head out of the window. He takes a soggy toothpick out of his mouth.

"You two look like you need help. Where you headed?"

Natia's hand tugs me away from the truck. I don't trust the man, she says. Something off about him, she says. I look down at her—what other choice do we have? Her hand relaxes. I guess you're right, she says.

We edge closer to the truck. The passenger seat is a haphazard assortment of cardboard boxes, sacks, and stuffed garbage bags. The man follows my gaze.

"Real, genuine Ossetian souvenirs. For the city idiots."

He shows me his teeth.

"Listen, you want a ride or not?"

He revs the engine and puts the truck in gear.

"Where you going?" I ask.

"Tbilisi."

No more objections from Natia, so I nod.

"Got no room up here. Get in the back if you like."

"Thanks."

I scramble into the empty truck bed and pull Natia up after me as the Kamaz takes off. It's a long journey. We wedge ourselves into the front corner of the truck bed. There's a faint smell of dung. It doesn't bother Natia. She must be exhausted. She leans her meager weight into my side and falls asleep in minutes.

I sit in this dung truck and sway with the rhythm of the road, jostled by potholes and buffeted by the wind. I sit and keep the voices at bay, old and new.

I try to find the golden silk thread of meaning that led me here from that day I landed in Tbilisi. I thought Irakli was that thread. I was wrong. Then I thought Nodar might be the thread. But Nodar's gone. Maybe it's Natia. Maybe Sandro. A lot of maybes again.

"God only ever gives you what you can handle." It's Irakli's inept voice, trying to reassure me. He's been in my head too.

Fuck you and your god, I want to say. I almost killed a man getting into Ossetia. That wasn't Nino, that was me. There will be a price to pay for that.

Dimitri's dead. They burned him and left him in the car. Nodar's dead. Natia's probably past fixing and that will kill Ketino.

For his efforts—the reason we even came close—Sandro was arrested, beaten, tortured, and punted back to London in handcuffs.

Me, I'm completely adrift.

Only the willingly ignorant can sit around and summarize such terrible things into pert little sentences about some god. Gods only exists because sometimes reason is too stark and too true. There is no golden silk thread of meaning that brought me here. Meaning and reason are not the same thing. Sometimes there's no meaning to why things happen. But reason cuts the bullshit like a knife.

"This is your fault. You brought me here. Their deaths are on you. You're the reason, Irakli. You're the reason without the meaning. So, please, stay frozen. Stay dead."

I want to scream at him, tear him down to the ground. But what's the point, speaking to a dead man?

Sometimes you make a decision and spend your time reinforcing it, patching it up, struggling to make it hold. Other times a decision shapes itself in your mind, perfectly formed, crystalline and unbreakable. I know with unshakable certainty that the voices have to go.

I let them have their farewell. I owe them that much.

Anzor, my superhero uncle, who taught me everything useful I know. Stern, frugal with his approval. The best you could hope for was a wry smile, a pat on the back, no words. Translated, that gesture said, "Well done, and do better next time." All his praise, always, cut with magic that made you try harder.

"At last, Mohammed made it to the mountain," he says. I can see that wry smile.

"Bye, Anzor."

"Keep your eyes open on the way back, Mohammed," he says, and he's gone.

Lena, my spartan grandma. Spine turned to steel to equip her for the life she was given. Lena, my army. No one says my name like she does.

"Lena." I pray for a response.

I hear a soft cough that signals her presence, but she speaks no more words. Just like that, promptly, she's gone. That's just how she was. No dawdle to that woman. She's gone but I know I'll always feel her stern touch steer me from danger.

Eka, she stayed so we could escape. It broke both our hearts when we spoke. What's the use of more words? Eka's more part of me than anyone else. She knows. She goes willingly.

Nino. She won't go quietly, or gently, into any good night. She'll fight. Nino, my sister in all the ways that matter but blood. The keeper of my secret. I brace myself for her razor-blade voice.

"What if I promised to stop trying to get you killed?"

"You don't keep promises."

Nino scoffs.

"'Nino always wins, even when she shouldn't. I owe a debt I can't repay. I have to follow her. Always and into any darkness.' Those are your words, mummy's boy. Remember?"

Nino's is the voice of a life cut short—furious at all the wonderful things the real Nino left unsaid and undone. Because of me. I've nothing left to mollify her with. Nothing left to say.

Again, I try to picture her face. For the first time in years, it works. It's only a moment, but it's enough. Sharp, haughty nose, brown eyes with faint freckles beneath. Always a cheeky expression on her face that says she knows something you don't. The real Nino.

I offer her an unfair trade. I ended her life, but I saved Natia's. That's not good enough, I know, but it's all I've got. I'll live my whole life and never do better. Nino might have smiled at that—yes, she does know something I don't. She always will.

"Goodbye, Nino." The final words of a complicated spell.

The person I really want to hear from has no voice. He doesn't need one—I know what he wants. He's focused on his Natia. I promise you, Nodar: on a day not so far from now, the whole world will hear her voice, whether it likes it or not. Natia deserves a say. She deserves to fill her life with amazing things. I promise to witness as many of them as she'll let me, so that somehow, maybe you will see them too.

Only two voices left in my shrinking family. Mine and Sandro's. But we're real, living voices, bound by more than mere family ties. Soon, I'll find a way to tell him what happened past the end of his trail, after the great forest. I'll tell him this fairy tale, to the end. Only two of us left now, brother. But it's enough.

The sun has set. It'll be dark soon. I take out the last roll of *Kaleidoskupi* pages that Irakli left in Elvari. I clench them in my fist and try to focus on practicalities.

How much do the police know now? If I give the detective Irakli's passport—a trophy for his hunt—will that be enough to sate him?

How will I tell Ketino about Nodar? I know she and Natia won't survive without the L&M-scented miracle of Nodar and his Volga. Without Nodar they'll be homeless in weeks. They need me.

I think about my life back in London. I worry about my house phone ringing out, unanswered. I worry about the letters, bills, and final demands for rent piling up on the doormat. I worry about my half-hearted life there crumbling back into the sea, like a sandcastle against a rising tide.

They say you can never go home again. But what if you can? What if you *should*? What if no matter what you do with your life, you'll somehow always end up in that place you didn't want to leave?

With a warning rumble, the Kamaz comes off the gravel road and onto the smooth motorway into Tbilisi. This is the last stretch. We accelerate and the wind picks up. Natia shifts in her sleep but doesn't wake. Lapsed for a moment, her hand finds mine again.

I look from her to the *Kaleidoskupi* pages Irakli left behind. The wind's already tugging at their edges. I loosen my grip and let my fingers uncurl. It's not just the pages I'm setting free. I'm about to jettison the past and all its dubious heroes. For good. Page by page, the wind takes everything.

I put my arms around Natia to shield her from the worst of the chill. I turn my face toward Tbilisi. Whatever lies in wait for me there, I'll be OK. I can handle it. For now, there's nothing to do but close my eyes and feel the wind wash me clean. In this new silence, the driver hits the gas. The engine roars and hurls us forward into the night, ever faster, toward Tbilisi.

Acknowledgments

I would like to thank the following people:

Sara O'Keeffe, for taking a gamble on me, that sliver of the smallest blue macaron, and for giving me a hat to hold on to. Tell Vanessa and Tom thank you for juggling so many spinning plates.

Sarah McGrath and Alexis Kirschbaum, my ever-vigilant editors, for constantly pushing me to improve, and for patiently hammering this novel into shape.

The Riverhead and Bloomsbury teams, for the incredible amount of work you put into bringing this novel out. But especially for so many dream-come-true moments that I will remember forever.

The tragic victims of the early drafts of this novel, in the order they suffered—Alecia H. Richards, Mark Dowling, Sami Miah, Carles Miralles Chacon, Gleb Chernov, Malkhaz Vardiashvili, Luka Vardiashvili, Ketino Japaridze, Lewis Massey, Emily Heritage, Irakli Kandelaki, and Sarah Ives (!?). Thank you for your support and encouragement.

My fiancé, Hannah Wright—a decorated veteran for suffering through too many drafts, harebrained ideas, and for giving me the best breadcrumb in the trail.

Khaled Hawwash, for unwavering support, hard truths, and for inventing The Plan. It worked, I wrote a book. Freedom 45, mate.

All my family and friends in Georgia. I miss you all the time, even when we're together.

Alik Kandelaki, my uncle, for teaching me everything useful I know.

Tina Kandelaki, none of this would have happened without you.

And especially Nina, for standing watch . . .